BOOK THREE

THE COBRA KING
OF KATHMANDU

Children of the Lamp

BOOK THREE

THE COBRA KING OF KATHMANDU

P. B. KERR

ORCHARD BOOKS/NEW YORK
AN IMPRINT OF SCHOLASTIC INC.

All rights reserved. Published by Orchard Books, an imprint of
Scholastic Inc. ORCHARD BOOKS and design are registered trademarks of
Watts Publishing Group, Ltd., used under license. SCHOLASTIC
and associated logos are trademarks and/or registered
trademarks of Scholastic Inc.

Grateful acknowledgment is made for permission to reprint lyrics
from the following songs:
"Come Together" © 1969 Sony/ATV Tunes LLC. All rights administered by Sony/
ATV Music Publishing, 8 Music Square West, Nashville, TN 37203.
All rights reserved. Used by permission.
"All You Need Is Love" © 1967 (Renewed 1995) Sony/ATV Tunes LLC. All rights
administered by Sony/ATV Music Publishing, 8 Music Square West, Nashville, TN
37203. All rights reserved. Used by permission.

Art on pages 109 and 142 by Leyah Jensen.

The haiku on p. 359 has been reprinted by kind permission of Miss Naomi Kerr.

Library of Congress Cataloging-in-Publication Data
Kerr, Philip.
The Cobra King of Kathmandu / by P. B. Kerr. — 1st ed.
p.   cm. — (Children of the lamp; bk.3)
Summary: Twelve-year-old djinn twins Philippa and John and their friend Dybbuk
have further adventures as they travel the world in search of a priceless talisman.
ISBN 13:978-0-439-67023-4
ISBN 10:0-439-67023-3 (reinforced lib. bdg.)
[1. Genies—Fiction.   2. Magic—Fiction.   3. Twins—Fiction.   4. Brothers and sis-
ters—Fiction.   5. Kathmandu (Nepal)—Fiction]   I. Title.   II. Series: Kerr, Philip.
Children of the lamp; bk. 3.
PZ7.K46843Cob 2006
[Fic]—dc22   2006009854
10 9 8 7 6 5 4 3 2   07 08 09 10 11 12

Printed in the U.S.A.
Reinforced Binding for Library Use
First edition, January 2007

This book is for Brian Bookman

AUTHOR'S NOTE

(for those readers who might have forgotten what happened
in the first two books)

John and Philippa Gaunt are New York children who discovered they were djinn after having their wisdom teeth
extracted. Wisdom teeth, like wisdom itself, come precociously early with djinn kids.

Their uncle Nimrod, a powerful English djinn living in
London, took charge of their early training, in Egypt, which,
being a hot country, is well suited for the development of
djinn power. Djinn are made of fire. They do not care much
for the cold. Young immature djinn find it especially hard,
sometimes impossible, to focus djinn power in cold
climates.

John and Philippa have a great deal to learn about being
djinn, and their powers are still maturing. They are, however,
easily underestimated since, being twins — not identical twins;
the similarities between these two cannot be seen — they can
be as powerful when acting together as any mature djinn.

All of which helps to explain how it was that they were
able to aid Nimrod in foiling an attempt by Iblis, the most
evil djinn of all, to capture the seventy lost djinn of Akhenaten, and use them to affect the balance of power that exists between the three tribes of good djinn and the three tribes of
evil djinn — the Homeostasis.

While all this was going on, their djinn mother, Layla, stayed home and tried to remain outside the world of djinn. As she was married to Edward Gaunt, a human being and investment banker (although not necessarily in that order), this had been easy enough, at least while the twins' extraordinary powers remained undiscovered.

But when Philippa was kidnapped by Ayesha, the supreme djinn, who had apparently intended the girl to succeed her as the Blue Djinn of Babylon, Layla discovered she could hardly turn a blind eye to her own daughter's future. In order to command the respect of all djinn — good and evil alike — the role of the Blue Djinn demands great independence of mind. It is also a position that requires considerable personal sacrifice since the Blue Djinn is obliged to give up family and home and live alone, beyond good and evil.

And so Layla had intervened to assist John's impossibly brave and heroic rescue mission to Iravotum — which is the Blue Djinn's secret underground kingdom in Babylon — while it was being attempted.

In the process, Layla discovered that the Blue Djinn's real purpose had been to make her, not Philippa, the next Blue Djinn. And, in order to ensure that Philippa might enjoy what remained of her childhood, Layla had complied with Ayesha's wish that when Ayesha died, she, and not Philippa, should be the next Blue Djinn.

Philippa and John were understandably shocked to discover that Ayesha was their own grandmother. But as yet, they remain quite unaware of the secret pact made between

Ayesha and Layla and that very soon, their beloved mother will be leaving home forever.

If Iblis remains the twins' greatest enemy, they have the consolation of some good friends. Mr. Rakshasas is a very aged djinn and close colleague of Nimrod, whose own powers are waning. Although born in India he learned his English with an Irish accent. Nimrod's faithful butler is Mr. Groanin, from Manchester, who has just one arm, having lost the other to a hungry tiger in the British Museum. Dybbuk is a djinn boy who lives in Palm Springs, California, with his mother, a djinn doctor, Jenny Sachertorte. Mr. and Mrs. Gaunt have a faithful housekeeper, Mrs. Trump, who continued to work for the Gaunts even after Philippa had secretly granted her wish that she should win the New York State lottery.

P. B. Kerr, February 2006

PROLOGUE

BEING SOMETHING THAT HAPPENED JUST A FEW WEEKS AFTER THE TWINS, JOHN AND PHILIPPA GAUNT, WERE BORN IN NEW YORK CITY

The beginning of the horror occurred, as horror often does, in the dead of night, when most people were asleep. The house where this terrifying event took place was a government building in London. A deceptively large, brick Palladian house in Whitehall, with the oldest and most celebrated address in the world. Outside the famous black front door stood a policeman, and on the opposite side of the street were more government buildings all the way up to Westminster and the Houses of Parliament and, beyond, the muddy River Thames.

Long after midnight on a cold April morning in the last years of the last millennium, number 10 Downing Street was quiet. An eleven-year-old girl was alone in her room, but she was not sleeping; she was lying under the quilt with a flashlight, reading a book. Her father, the Prime Minister of Great Britain and Northern Ireland, and mother were fast asleep down the hall, and on duty downstairs in an office behind the Cabinet Room were the Prime Minister's detective, and his press secretary. At approximately 12:40 A.M., the girl glanced up from her novel with a frown of puzzlement. She thought she heard the sound of laughter. Odd, female laughter. The giggling of someone mischievous and juvenile.

Funny.

She poked her head out from under the tent of her quilt and listened carefully for a moment, then dismissed it.

I'm hearing things.

But as the girlish laughter returned, she sat up and, no longer able to concentrate, tossed her paperback aside.

That giggling. It gives me the creeps.

She got up to investigate. Pulling on a dressing gown, she opened her door and looked down the hallway. The giggling seemed to be coming from her parents' bedroom.

What's going on? That's not my mother who's laughing. She doesn't laugh like that. Since moving into Downing Street, she doesn't laugh at all.

The girl padded down the hall and the giggling suddenly grew louder, more mischievous, even a little bit nasty, but as she pushed open the Prime Minister's bedroom door and stepped into the room, the giggling abruptly ceased — if only for a moment.

What the heck is going on?

Her mother was huddled in the corner of the room looking round-eyed and plainly terrified. Her father was sitting bolt upright in bed but with both eyes closed and breathing heavily through his flared nostrils as if he had been running. He didn't look like himself at all. His face was pale, his pajamas were soaked with sweat, and his hair lay matted on his head like damp straw. Then his eyes flickered open, rolled up into the top of his head like a couple of marbles, and closed again.

Then she noticed the heat. The room. It felt like an oven. She padded over to the window. Opened it. She touched the radiator. Cold.

That's very odd.

"What's wrong with you, Mum?" she said softly.

"There's nothing wrong with *me*," her mother whispered nervously. "It's your father."

The girl went over to her father's bedside and leaned closer to him, brushing aside his teddy bear, Archibald, with the back of her hand. "Dad? Are you okay?"

More heavy breathing through the nostrils. He grinned wolfishly, and then his green eyes opened and focused on her in a peculiar way that caused a shiver to run down her spine.

"Stop it, Dad. This isn't funny. You're scaring Mum."

This was when he started to laugh. Except that it wasn't him laughing at all. It was the laugh of a young girl that came out of his mouth, almost as if there were someone else inside him, someone alien and unwelcome and possibly unwholesome, too. Someone or some*thing.*

If this is you that's doing this, Dad, if this is supposed to be some kind of a joke, then it's not very funny because you're doing a pretty good job of scaring the pants off me, do you know that?

3

Cold, expressionless eyes that were quite at odds with the giggling held her inquisitive stare for several more seconds before the voice of a girl — who sounded not much older than she was herself — spoke at last.

"Get me the Home Secretary," said the voice. "And the Metropolitan Police Commissioner. And the Director of Public Prosecutions. And the Attorney General. I want someone arrested and thrown into the Tower. Immediately. Tonight. There's no time to lose."

"You can't throw someone into the Tower," the girl said. "Not anymore. Not just like that. There are proper procedures to be observed. Laws."

"Then get me the Queen on the telephone," said the voice. "I want to make a new law. Right now. A law that will permit me to arrest and execute someone. Tonight."

She felt her jaw drop onto her chest.

"Well, what are you waiting for, you stupid girl? Get on with it. Don't you know who I am? I'm the Prime Minister. And while you're at it, close your mouth. You look like a goldfish. Not a very intelligent goldfish, either. I've seen cleverer faces than yours on a broken clock."

Badly scared, the Prime Minister's daughter backed away from him, trying to flatten down the hair on her head that was now standing on end.

"And fishface? Make sure everyone knows I'm serious about this. Otherwise a vulgar display of power will be forthcoming. Got that, fishface?"

The Prime Minister giggled girlishly, which was the cue for his young daughter to start screaming.

"Babies are peculiar-looking creatures," observed Nimrod. "I mean, they're quite, quite beastly, aren't they?" Visiting New York to see his newborn niece and nephew, John and Philippa Gaunt, he viewed the twins in their hospital cribs with something close to horror. He disliked babies intensely, not least because he could remember only too well the whole grubby, incontinent horror of being a baby himself. This is often the case with mature djinn, many of whom develop a perfect memory of everything that has ever happened to them, and are quite unable to forget anything. "And it's odd, isn't it? How nearly all of them manage to resemble Winston Churchill. Or Benito Mussolini. The way they're so leaky and pugnacious. Not to mention their disquieting predilection always to be the center of attention."

Nimrod's sister, Layla, who was also a djinn, sat stiffly in her hospital bed, listening to her brother's tactless comments with growing irritation. The twins themselves, sensing their uncle's fastidious distaste, began to mew loudly in chorus, like a pair of hungry cats.

"And twins!" added Nimrod, raising his voice above the din. "Such a handful for you, my dear. Looking at these two little brutes, I quite begin to believe the legend of how Rome was founded. The way the twins Romulus and Remus were placed in a trough and thrown in the River Tiber, only to be rescued by a she-wolf and a woodpecker. Yes indeed, they do box the ears, rather. Extraordinary, the way they wave their arms about, like a couple of undercooked lobsters."

"Was there something else?" Layla asked, smiling patiently. "Or did you just come all the way from London to be rude about my babies?"

"Rude? Me? I should say not," protested Nimrod, and collected a shoe box off the floor. "As their only uncle I've brought them the traditional djinn gift of a proper oil lamp. One each. None of that pewter rubbish from Malaysia, mind. These are solid silver. The real thing. From the Ottoman Empire. With interiors lavishly designed by yours truly."

"Well, you can take them away again," said Layla. "My children are not going to be brought up as djinn, but as human beings."

"Light my lamp, Layla," he said. "Whatever do you mean?"

"Exactly what I say," said Layla. "Their father is a human. Why not?"

"And a very agreeable human at that," said Nimrod. "But these children are not and never could be mundane. You know that."

"I'll thank you not to use that word," said Layla.

"Mundane?" exclaimed Nimrod. "Why not? That's exactly what a human being is, my dear. There can be no getting away from the fact that djinn power only ever passes through the mother. At some stage in the future — most likely in ten or twelve years' time, when their wisdom teeth come through — you and your husband, Edward, will have to

6

face up to the reality of who and what the twins are. They are children of the lamp, Layla."

"I'll thank you to forget that," said Layla, "and to leave us alone. Permanently. I want no contact with djinnkind. And that includes you, brother."

"Very well," said Nimrod, feeling more than a little hurt. "But while you might remove the child from having contact with other djinn, you cannot remove the djinn from the child."

Nimrod flew back to London that same day.

He had not long returned from New York and was in the basement vault, wrapping newspaper around the two Ottoman Empire silver oil lamps he had intended to give to John and Philippa, when his one-armed butler, Groanin, appeared in the doorway.

"There is a person in the hall, sir," he said, uttering the word "person" in the way another butler might have said "pig" or "hyena." "He wishes to speak with you urgently."

"Does this person have a name?"

"It's a little hard for me to say, sir."

"Why? Cat got your tongue, Groanin?"

"That's not what I mean, sir. I mean his name is a little hard for me to pronounce."

"Have a stab at it."

"Very well, sir." Groanin gathered his thoughts, his lips, and his tongue, and then said, "Dr. Ruchira P. Warnakulasuriya."

"Yes, I see what you mean, Groanin. That's quite a mouthful. Any idea what he wants?"

"He wouldn't say precisely what he wanted, sir. Only that it was a matter of the gravest national security. Oh, yes. He also said that you knew his father, the Fakir Murugan."

"You'd better show him into the library, Groanin."

"Yes, sir," said Groanin, and shimmered away, muttering quietly.

Nimrod locked the two oil lamps in the vault, and then went to find his visitor. The doctor's late father had been a famous Indian holy man and an acquaintance of Nimrod's. As a sign of his religious devotion and great holiness, Fakir Murugan had spent ten years of his life sitting on a tall pole with eight daggers embedded in his chest and back. It was the sort of thing holy men did in places like India. Nimrod had never understood why, only that it seemed to keep them happy in some wretched way, and Nimrod had never been one to interfere with another man's idea of happiness.

In the library, Nimrod found a small, tubby man, wearing a blue pin-striped suit, tinted glasses, and a handsome-looking gold watch. Seeing Nimrod, the doctor bowed and then kissed Nimrod's hand respectfully. The Fakir Murugan had known Nimrod was a djinn, and Nimrod guessed that so did his son.

The doctor came straight to the point: "Forgive me for the intrusion, most esteemed sir," he said. "However, a situation of grave national importance has arisen."

"Yes," said Nimrod, lighting a cigar. "So Groanin was telling me."

"I have a medical practice, a very successful one, in Harley

8

Street. One of my patients is the Prime Minister's wife, Mrs. Widmerpool. And over a period of time I have become her friend and confidant." Dr. Warnakulasuriya fiddled with his tie as if he were a little embarrassed about having to drop the name of such a famous and influential person.

"That must be nice for you," said Nimrod, who wasn't in the least bit impressed.

"Yes," said Dr. Warnakulasuriya. "And this is how it is that I, rather than Mr. Widmerpool's own doctor, came to be involved in a situation that now requires great delicacy and discretion."

"You intrigue me," said Nimrod, puffing out a smoke ring that turned into several large, human-shaped ears.

"Oh, very good," said Dr. Warnakulasuriya, noticing the smoke ears. "Very good." And then remembering the urgency of his mission, he continued, "Sir, the fact of the matter is, I believe Mr. Widmerpool to be possessed by a djinn, and I'm here to ask you if you would be good enough to carry out an exorcism."

"An exorcism?" said Nimrod. "What makes you think that this is a djinn possession and not something else? A demon, perhaps."

"I'm not my father, sir," said Dr. Warnakulasuriya. "However, within the limits of what I know about the djinn, I've made a prudent judgment, and I am convinced that this is djinn possession, yes. For example, Mr. Widmerpool's bedroom, where he is currently under restraint, is hot rather than cold. Also I struck a match near his mouth and he didn't

9

blow it out. Instead he sucked at the flame, like a man trying to drink tea from a saucer."

"Yes, that's a very good description." Nimrod nodded. "Anything else? A particular smell, for example."

"I noticed there was a strong smell of sulfur," said Dr. Warnakulasuriya.

"Describe the voice that spoke to you when you conversed with the Prime Minister."

"It was the voice of a girl," said the doctor. "I should say that it was a young girl of about twelve years old. Educated. American. Mischievous and insulting. She gives orders to all who come near her as if she expects to be obeyed because the orders come from the Prime Minister's mouth. In the beginning the orders were all the same: to arrest a man, have him taken to the Tower of London, and there executed by having his head cut off."

"Oh? What was his name? This man she mentioned."

"An unusual name. Foreign-sounding. I mean, not English. Here, I wrote it down." Dr. Warnakulasuriya searched in his vest pocket and then handed Nimrod a business card with a name written on the back. "Although I'm not sure if I have spelled it correctly."

Nimrod looked at the name in silence and then put the card in his trouser pocket. "Go on," he said. "You said, in the beginning all the orders were the same. What were her later orders?"

"When it became clear that nobody was going to order this man arrested, the orders changed. They seemed designed merely to embarrass Mr. Widmerpool, making him seem as if he'd gone mad. For example: She ordered his press secretary to have a warrant issued for the arrest of the American president on a charge of high treason if he refused to tear up the Declaration of Independence and then fly here immediately to take an oath of allegiance to Her Majesty the Queen."

Nimrod smiled. "Interesting idea," he said. "I wonder if that might work." He thought for a moment. "Tell me, Dr. Warnakulasuriya, is there a cat living at number 10 Downing Street?"

"A cat? Yes, I think so. Why do you ask?"

"Because we shall have need of a cat to carry out this exorcism."

"So you *will* help."

Nimrod looked out of the window and smiled. "Why not? It's an excellent day for an exorcism."

The Downing Street cat was called Boothby. He was an adopted stray, a long-haired black and white with a fondness for cookies. Despite his reputation as a killer of baby birds, Boothby was held in high regard at number 10 and, until Nimrod arrived that April morning, the only real discomfort he had suffered since coming to Downing Street had been on the day when he was nearly run over by the U.S. president's two-ton bulletproof Cadillac.

Upon his arrival at number 10, Nimrod asked not to see Mr. Widmerpool but to see Boothby. Nimrod was shown into the Pillared Room where Dr. Warnakulasuriya came to him bearing the cat in his arms. The doctor disliked cats; he disliked having cat hair all over his tailor-made suit, but more especially he disliked the scratch he received as the animal struggled to escape his reluctant embrace.

"Ow," said the doctor, sucking blood off the back of his hand. "Beastly little parasite! How dare you? Beastly little swine."

For a moment he looked as if he was going to kick the cat. But Nimrod, sensing the real reason for the cat's distress, picked him up. "This room is haunted, doctor," he explained. "By the ghost of Mrs. Gladstone. We had better find an alternative room, otherwise the cat will never settle down long enough for me to do . . . er . . . what needs to be done."

The doctor, who clearly knew his way around number 10, led them into the Terracotta Room, where Nimrod, still holding Boothby, sat down on a sofa and started to stroke his new feline friend.

"I wonder if you would pass me that ashtray," he said to the doctor.

The doctor handed over the ashtray.

"Tell me, did you give the Prime Minister anything to drink? A glass of water, perhaps?"

"No. I took his pulse — it was very fast — a sample of his blood for analysis, examined his pupils, his tongue, and pressed the lymph glands in his neck to see if they were swollen. And indeed they were. And yes, now I come to think of it, the sulfurous smell I mentioned earlier seemed only noticeable after I had pressed Mr. Widmerpool's lymph glands."

"That's because the lymph glands are the center of possession," said Nimrod. "Where the djinn chooses to reside, so
to speak. Your massaging those glands would cause a pure
essence of sulfur to come forth from the Prime Minister's
body. Djinn have much higher levels of sulfur than mundanes — I mean humans. For your information, the average
human body contains only enough sulfur to kill all the fleas
on a large dog. But the average djinn body contains enough
sulfur to kill all the fleas on a woolly mammoth. For this reason, humans have a much keener sense of smell than djinn.
It's one of the few advantages you humans enjoy over us."

Nimrod was telling all this to Dr. Warnakulasuriya not
because he wanted to improve the doctor's knowledge of
the djinn — if anything, Nimrod was secretive about such
arcane matters as those he had described — but because he
was aware that the sound of his voice, which was deep and
sonorous, had a soothing effect on the cat. Nimrod wanted
Boothby to feel relaxed enough so that he might allow his
whiskers to be touched.

A cat has twenty-four movable whiskers, twelve on each
side of its nose, and Nimrod needed seven of them to perform
the ritual of djinn exorcism, which is also known as Katto,
although for reasons that have nothing at all to do with cats.
He was not a cruel man, and he thought it was unfortunate
that the ritual forbade the use of djinn power in obtaining a
cat's whiskers, since it seemed certain that Boothby would
object to giving up almost a third of his own complement of
whiskers. And even while he talked to the doctor, Nimrod

13

was trying to think how he might make it up to Boothby after the theft of his whiskers had been carried out.

"You'll forgive me for reminding you, sir," said Dr. Warnakulasuriya, glancing anxiously at the ceiling, "but this situation is not without some urgency. The Prime Minister is entertaining the German chancellor for lunch. So, perhaps you could see him now and judge for yourself what needs to be done."

Dr. Warnakulasuriya smiled nervously. He had no idea why Nimrod thought this cat was so important, especially when in a room upstairs the Prime Minister was chattering away like a mischievous schoolgirl. At the same time, however, he was aware that some djinn had the reputation of being quick-tempered and, according to his late father, often needed to be soothed and generally flattered before they would do anything for a human being. So he bowed obsequiously and added, "That is, when you are finished playing with the cat, sir."

Nimrod said nothing and carried on scratching Boothby underneath his chin. The cat purred contentedly and, for a moment, the doctor found himself closing his own eyes. But the next second, the doctor almost jumped out of his skin as Boothby let out a banshee's scream and scrambled up the curtains as if in fear for his life. Nimrod dropped something in an ashtray, got to his feet, and then walked briskly over to the window.

"QWERTYUIOP!"

The doctor gasped as a large plate of raw fish appeared

magically in the djinn's outstretched hand. He had no idea why the cat had behaved as he had done but that hardly seemed important beside this exercise of supernatural power. This was the first time he'd ever seen djinn power in action and it impressed Dr. Warnakulasuriya very deeply indeed. Meanwhile, Nimrod held the plate of fish up to the curtain rod where Boothby had taken sanctuary, and was now apologizing to him.

"The fish," breathed the doctor. "You made it appear. Out of thin air. Just like that. Is it not so?"

"I think it's the very least I can do in return for Boothby's assistance in this ritual," said Nimrod. "Don't you?" He let the cat catch the smell of fish in his nostrils before placing the dish on the floor.

"Yes, I'm not entirely clear about that. How exactly is he going to help us, sir?"

"He already has," said Nimrod, and collecting the ashtray, showed the doctor the seven whiskers he had plucked from poor Boothby's face. "Whiskers." Mistaking the doctor's puzzled expression for one of shock and disapproval, Nimrod added, "Don't worry. They'll grow back." He nodded at the door. "Right then. Let's get cracking, shall we?"

Nimrod entered the Prime Minister's bedroom slowly. Mr. Widmerpool was lying on his back, head propped against a pillow. Standing over him was a tall, blond-haired woman Nimrod recognized immediately as the Prime Minister's wife, Sheila. Her arms folded, she looked tense and tired. In a corner of the room, a girl about eleven or twelve years old sat in a chair; he guessed this must be the Prime Minister's youngest daughter, Lucinda. Behind her stood the Prime Minister's press secretary, who regarded the arrival of Dr. Warnakulasuriya and Nimrod with a mixture of relief and irritation.

"Well, it's about time," he said, glancing at his watch. And then, looking at Nimrod's red suit with disbelief, he added, "And who are you? Santa Claus?"

But the Prime Minister's wife was more grateful and welcoming. Tearfully, she grasped Nimrod's hand and squeezed it. "Bless you for coming," she said. "Bless you."

"Calm yourself, dear lady," said Nimrod, sniffing the air. "The Prime Minister's predicament will soon be remedied, I can assure you." He moved her away from the bed.

"Oh? And who might you be?" It was the Prime Minister who spoke — or rather the young female djinn that currently inhabited his body. Nimrod had no doubts on that score; the smell of sulfur as the Prime Minister opened and closed his mouth was quite unmistakable.

"I might ask you the same question," said Nimrod. He sat down on the side of the bed. "That is, if I wasn't more interested in *why* you're doing this. Bottle me, if it doesn't make me cross to see you treating the Prime Minister in this disrespectful way."

"That's just it, isn't it? You can't see me. Not if I don't choose to let you see me."

"I'm asking you nicely to leave. Now."

"Suppose I don't want to," said the girl inside the Prime Minister, giggling.

"Then I'll make you leave."

"Oh? And how will you do that?"

"That's my business."

The girl giggled and made the Prime Minister sit up. "I'm having too much fun to leave now," she said.

Nimrod waved his hand and quietly uttered the word he used to focus his power. "QWERTYUIOP!"

Immediately, the other djinn guessed that something was wrong. "What happened? What did you do? I can't move."

"Nothing to be alarmed about," said Nimrod. "I've just put you under a kind of restraint, that's all."

"Why? What are you going to do? Call the police," yelled the voice inside the Prime Minister, "and have this man arrested immediately."

"You've given your last order," said Nimrod, removing one of the cat whiskers from the ashtray. "Bottle me, if you haven't."

The Prime Minister looked warily at the whisker. "What is that?"

Nimrod produced a cigarette lighter from the pocket of his red jacket. "I imagine you've heard of the proverb that a singed cat is always better than he looks. Well, there is no smell a djinn hates more than the smell of a singed cat." Nimrod chuckled. "In ancient times, the Katto ritual of djinn exorcism required a whole cat. These days, we're not quite so cruel and, thank goodness, no more than seven cat whiskers are needed."

Nimrod waggled his empty fingers and then produced a swimmer's nose clip out of thin air, to the increased astonishment of Dr. Warnakulasuriya, who was standing right beside him. Nimrod squeezed it over his nostrils so that he would avoid inhaling the burning cat's whisker. "My suspicion," he said, "is that you hoped to create a political stink by what you've done."

"That's not how it was at all," said the djinn inside the Prime Minister. "At least not in the beginning. I wanted Iblis arrested, that's why I did this. Arrested and executed and tortured. Not necessarily in that order. I imagine you've heard of Iblis? Thanks to him my family is ruined."

Nimrod nodded as the djinn explained her reasons. The name of Iblis was indeed known to him. As the head of the Ifrit, one of three tribes of evil djinn, Iblis was generally held to be the wickedest djinn in the world.

"What on earth made you think the Prime Minister could help?" asked Nimrod.

"No other djinn, including my own father, seems to have the guts to do anything about his evil," said the voice. "So I decided to seek a mundane source of help. The Prime Minister. But he's not the man I thought he was. My mother's going to be really disappointed when I tell her. She's always going on about what a great guy he is. Well, he's not. He's got no power at all."

"This is your last chance to leave," said Nimrod.

"Light my lamp," sneered the djinn, "a man's got no business being leader of a country if he can't lock people up when he wants. So I intend to make him pay for being so ineffectual. With the political stink that's going to come to him." She laughed.

"You're about to get more of a stink than you ever bargained for," said Nimrod.

"You're bluffing."

"We'll see."

With the Prime Minister's head and body held quite immobile by Nimrod's powerful binding, there was no way that the djunior djinn could avoid the burning cat's whisker that Nimrod held just inside one of the Prime Minister's nostrils.

"Ahh! Stop it! That smells horrible. Take it away!"

"You asked for this." Nimrod dropped the ash of the cat's whisker and lit another, and another. The stink of Boothby's burning whiskers was now so strong that Lucinda Widmerpool felt obliged to cover her nose and mouth with her hand. But this was only for a second, as the urge to point at what was happening to the bed overcame her sense of smell.

The bed is rising up off the floor!

She stared at it, transfixed. One foot. Two feet. Three feet. The weight of her father and the man in the red suit who was holding another burning cat's whisker seemed to count for nothing. The bed drifted up another foot and hovered in the air like a magician's trick in a magic show.

"Good gracious me," exclaimed Mrs. Widmerpool, while the Press Secretary swore loudly several times.

"No cause for alarm, dear lady," said Nimrod, lighting the sixth of the cat's whiskers. "This is what we call the magic carpet stage of the exorcism when the djinn's wish to fly away becomes almost overwhelming. Almost. One more whisker ought to do it."

"Good gracious me," repeated the Prime Minister's wife, who was less alarmed about the levitation of her bed than what was now revealed underneath it: half-eaten pizzas, old newspapers, toenail clippings, several documents marked TOP SECRET, some odd socks, a parking ticket, a signed photograph of Her Majesty the Queen, some chewing gum (chewed), some foreign coins (mostly French francs), and a broken tennis racket.

"Stand clear, ma'am," yelled Nimrod, as Mrs. Widmerpool bent down to retrieve the picture of the queen.

A moment later the bed suddenly dropped onto the floor, and the bedroom window flew open as the mischievous djinn made her invisible exit.

"The winner," said Nimrod. "And by a nose, I think." Waving his hand and muttering his focus word, he removed the restraint he had placed on the body of the Prime Minister, who was already looking and, more important, sounding like himself again.

"What's going on?" he asked nervously.

Nimrod stood up and moved away from the bed as Dr.

Warnakulasuriya stepped in to take Mr. Widmerpool's pulse, and to listen to his heartbeat through a stethoscope.

"Honestly, I feel fine." The Prime Minister smiled as his daughter handed him his teddy bear.

"Prime Minister," said Nimrod, "can you remember anything of what happened to you?"

Mr. Widmerpool looked sheepish. "A bad dream, I thought," he said. "I couldn't control my own words or actions. It was like there was someone inside my head deciding what I said and did." He glanced at his Press Secretary for a moment as if wanting to check that he was saying the right thing. "A girl, I think. Quite a young girl. No older than my own daughter, I'd say."

"Is it possible that this girl had a name?" asked Nimrod.

"I dunno." Mr. Widmerpool thought for a moment and then shrugged. "Tina?" He looked at Nimrod. "Mean anything to you?"

Nimrod shook his head. "Well, I must be going, sir," he said and waved away the several expressions of enormous gratitude that now came his way. Even the Prime Minister's irascible press secretary was full of effusive thanks. "Tish, tosh," said Nimrod. "No need to thank me. Light my lamp, no need at all. It was only my duty as a patriotic Englishman. We can't have the British Prime Minister making an exhibition of himself in front of the German chancellor. No, we leave that kind of thing to the French president."

Dr. Warnakulasuriya escorted Nimrod back to the

entrance hall where, very respectfully, he kissed his hand once again. "My father, the fakir, told me about the djinn and their great power," he said, "but, sir, to my enormous shame and embarrassment I believed very little of what he said. I am a man of science, you understand. Not superstition."

"And yet it was you who brought me here."

"In truth, Nimrod, I only half believed you could help. Until you made that bed rise up. To say nothing of the way you made that nose clip appear out of thin air. Not to mention that fish for Boothby."

"Bottle me, it was only a fish, not a gold bar," Nimrod said modestly.

"But it could just as easily have been a gold bar, could it not? And the djinn you drove out of Mr. Widmerpool. To have the power to do such a thing, to take over his body like that. She could have done almost anything."

"It was everyone's good luck that she had little or no experience of handling such a possession. If she — Tina, or whatever her name is — had managed to take over the Prime Minister's speech centers, well, yes, there's no telling what she might have achieved." Nimrod looked at his watch. "I'm going out to look for her now. After several hours being in someone else's body she might wish to have my assistance in recovering her own. Bodies that are left lying around have a habit of being taken away. Even in London." Nimrod smiled brightly and clapped the doctor on the shoulder.

"Tell me," said Dr. Warnakulasuriya, removing his

glasses, "is it true? You really have the power to grant three wishes?"

Nimrod could see where the conversation was headed. "Your father, the fakir, who was a very wise man, once told me that it is better for a man to have a will than to have a wish."

The doctor nodded gravely but Nimrod could see that he was hardly convinced by his own father's words. Indeed, Nimrod perceived an indefinable change come about in the man's eyes, but more than ten years would pass before he understood exactly where this change would lead the impressionable young doctor from India.

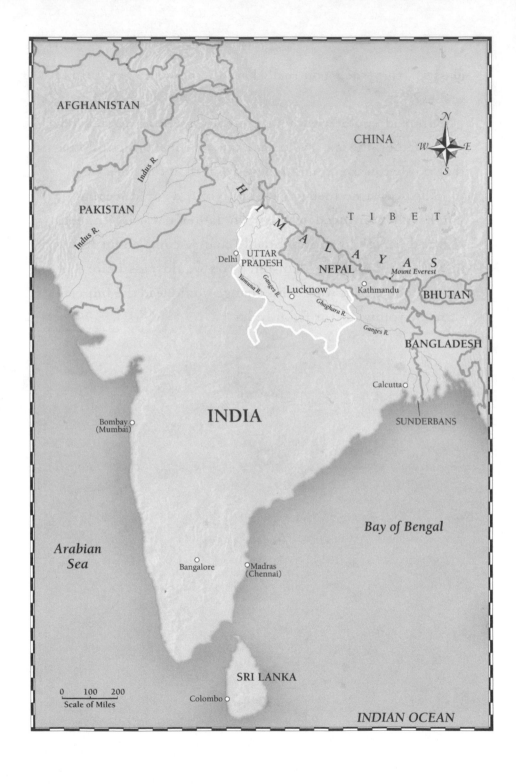

CHAPTER 1

CARTOON NETWORK

It was seven A.M. in the principal's office at the Sonny Bono Preparatory School in Palm Springs, California. As usual, the janitor, Mr. Astor, washed and polished the floor and then removed a plastic bag containing Miss Sarkisian's garbage from the wastepaper receptacle beside her desk. Near the top of the bag, inside an empty soda can, Dybbuk Sachertorte felt the motion of Astor lifting the bag and quickly strapped himself into the jet-aircraft seat he had installed in the can especially for this purpose. Then he pulled on a helmet and a neck brace to prevent any possible whiplash injury from the impact the twelve-year-old djinn knew was imminent.

Djinn are rarely hurt inside a bottle or a lamp or, for that matter, a soda can, but injuries were not unknown: Dybbuk's grandmother had once suffered a concussion when a glass whisky bottle she had been traveling in had shattered unexpectedly. And Dybbuk did not act a moment too soon. The next second, the janitor opened the window and dropped the garbage bag into a bin in the schoolyard below.

In any event, Dybbuk's precautions were enough to ensure that he enjoyed a comfortable landing. Inside the can he remained in his seat for a minute, until he was certain that Astor was gone, before finally beginning his transubstantiation. Steering the smoke that carried his atoms and molecules out of the can, through the loosely tied neck of the bag, and then the bin and onto the ground, he reassembled himself in his mundane human shape. Chuckling with pleasure at the success of his mission, he went straight to his friend Brad's house and knocked on the other boy's bedroom window.

"Open up. It's me, Buck." Dybbuk loathed his own name and much preferred to be called Buck, who was a courageous dog in a great book by Jack London, and Dybbuk's favorite character in literature.

A few seconds passed and then the window opened, and Dybbuk climbed inside to be met by a boy of approximately the same age. The human boy was tall, although not as tall as Dybbuk, and skinny as a whip, whereas the djinn boy was bigger in the shoulders.

"You didn't," said Brad.

"I did," said Dybbuk and unfolded several sheets of paper for his friend to look at.

"No kidding? These are the real test questions?"

"Not just the questions," Dybbuk said proudly. "I got the answers, too."

"No way," said Brad, now sounding close to incredulity. "But how? I mean there's CCTV outside Miss Sarkisian's office, and an alarm. And the papers were in a safe. What are you, Buck? Some kind of cat burglar?"

Dybbuk hadn't ever told Brad that he was a djinn, just in case his friend begged him for three wishes. Even Dybbuk knew that it isn't always a good thing for a human to have their dearest wishes granted. Wishes are affected by the Chaos Effect, which means that sometimes they have a habit of turning out in ways nobody could have foreseen. So he just looked evasive and said, "A cat burglar? Yeah, something like that, sure."

"Really?" Brad's admiration of his friend now knew no limit. "Like in a movie?"

"Never mind that now," said Dybbuk, brandishing the test questions and answers. "We've got a couple of hours' studying to do if we're ever going to pass that test."

The day after the test — which both boys passed with the highest grades in the class — Brad Blennerhassit's father, Harry, invited them both for a celebratory lunch to a downtown restaurant near his antiquarian bookstore. Brad's mother was dead, and he and his father were very close. Close enough it seemed for the boy to have informed his father of how it was that he had achieved such remarkable results on the test. But instead of delivering a stern lecture about cheating — which was what Dybbuk expected and certainly deserved — Mr. Blennerhassit smiled and offered Dybbuk his thanks.

"Come again?" asked Dybbuk, almost choking on his hamburger.

"I mean, what you did showed tremendous ingenuity and resourcefulness," said Harry Blennerhassit. "There are not many boys who could sneak around a CCTV, bypass an alarm system, and crack a combination safe. That was quite the little heist you pulled off there, my young friend. Yes indeed, quite the little caper."

Dybbuk shrugged, hardly daring to admit to the crime in case this was some kind of trick designed to trap him into a confession.

Mr. Blennerhassit sipped his coffee and was silent for a moment. With his anxious-looking forehead, wide nervous smile, and cherry-sized nose, Harry Blennerhassit's face was like a clown's, without the makeup. "Do you think you could do something like that again? I mean, pull a heist?"

Dybbuk glanced uncertainly at Brad. "Is your dad joking or what?" he said angrily. "Because if he is, I don't like your having told him in the first place. And in the second, I refuse to say anything about it on the grounds that it might incriminate me. If my mother finds out about this, I'm history. Relations between me and her are bad enough as it is."

"Buck, it's okay," insisted Brad. "Honest. Just hear my dad out, will you? He's got a business proposition for you."

"All right," said Dybbuk, "I'm listening."

"A while ago," said Mr. Blennerhassit, "I was in Munich, in Germany. In connection with my business as a dealer in rare books and engravings. And in an old shop I found a portfolio of technical drawings by Paul Futterneid, a jewelry designer who had worked with the famous Carl Fabergé. I bought the drawings and discovered that one of them was a design for a German Field Marshal's baton, about a foot and a half long, and made of ivory inlaid with diamond studs and golden eagles.

"But what was really interesting was that the baton was hollow and contained a secret chamber that could be opened by pressing the correct combination of studs and eagles. It became clear that the secret chamber must have been designed to hide something very valuable when I discovered that the baton had been owned by Hermann Goering."

"Who's Hermann Goering?" said Dybbuk with a shrug, since it was obvious from the way Harry Blennerhassit had pronounced the name that it was someone he was supposed to have heard of.

"He was Hitler's deputy as well as head of the Nazi armed forces," explained Brad.

"So what happened to it?" asked Dybbuk. "To the actual baton itself."

"I'll tell you," said Mr. Blennerhassit. "In 1945, a month after the Allied victory in Europe, when the U.S. Army was in Germany gathering the spoils of war, General Patch, commander of the American 7th Army, captured Goering and gave the baton to President Harry Truman, as his own war trophy."

"Since then," said Brad, "it has been displayed in the military museum at Fort Benning, Georgia. I mean, it's just sitting there, Buck. Lots of people have handled it but, so far, none of them seems to have discovered the secret mechanism and, more important, whatever it was that Goering might have hidden inside it before his capture. Such as diamonds, perhaps. Dad says that Goering was very fond of diamonds."

Dybbuk was fascinated. He loved stories about World War II and he loved stories about lost treasure, and this story was about both. "Wow," he said. "I wonder how many diamonds you could fit inside a thing like a German Field Marshal's baton?"

"Let's find out, shall we?" Mr. Blennerhassit placed a bubble-wrapped object on the table. "You see, Buck, using the original design drawing, I've had a copy made. This particular baton is made of resin and the diamonds are imitation but it looks and feels exactly like the real thing." He tossed aside the bubble wrap to reveal the fake baton. And picking it up, he began to press the studs and then the eagles. "The mechanism is fully working, of course."

Even as he spoke, one of the diamond-studded end caps opened and, turning the baton upside down, Harry Blennerhassit emptied several handfuls of Brazil nuts onto the table. "There are thirty-five nuts there," he said. "If each of those nuts was a diamond, Buck, well, you can imagine how much they'd be worth."

"Millions," said Buck, grinning.

"A third of whatever we find is yours, Buck," said Brad. "All you have to do, buddy, using your very special skills as a burglar, is to swap this baton for the real one in the military museum at Fort Benning."

Dybbuk thought for a moment. Money was of little interest to him: Being a djinn meant that he could have money whenever he wished for it. But excitement and fun were a lot harder to come by in a place like Palm Springs, which is full of old people, and the caper being proposed by Brad's dad sounded as if it would be a lot of fun. It wouldn't even be a crime, Dybbuk decided — certainly not if, at some later stage, he swapped the real baton back again. As for whatever was inside it, that could hardly be described as stealing. Dybbuk really didn't see how you could steal something that the museum didn't even know it had. But could he do the job without letting the Blennerhassits in on his little secret — that he was a djinn? Because that would spoil everything: They'd be more interested in being granted three wishes than in what was hidden inside Goering's baton. Concealing his being a djinn from them might actually be trickier than swapping the batons.

Tricky, but not impossible. Dybbuk started to nod.

"You mean you're in?" Brad asked excitedly. "You'll do it?"

"Sure, I'll do it," said Dybbuk, and grinned. *This*, he thought, *is going to be fun.*

The three flew to Atlanta, Georgia, where they hired a car, and then drove sixty miles south to Fort Benning and checked into a guesthouse on the base. From there they walked a few blocks east to the Infantry Museum where a large variety of weapons, uniforms, helmets, vehicles, and objects were on show. Among these was Air Marshal Hermann Goering's baton.

"It's hard to believe, isn't it?" observed Mr. Blennerhassit. "All these years it's been lying here and no one guessed that it was hollow. Eh, boys?"

But Dybbuk was only half listening. He was already trying to figure out a plan. Seeing a portable drinks cabinet once owned by General Ulysses S. Grant gave him an idea. He could transubstantiate and then hide away in one of the amber glass bottles until after the museum had closed. That would be easy enough. But making a second transubstantiation with the real baton in his hand would not be possible for the simple reason that djinn power does not work on diamonds. It was clear that the baton would have to be hidden somewhere and that he would have to take it out in some other way. But how? Dybbuk found the answer inside the museum shop. And it was so obvious that he started to laugh out loud at his own ingenuity. He would hide the real baton inside a poster tube and then simply buy the poster it contained when the museum opened the following morning.

"You think you can do it?" asked Brad, hearing Dybbuk's laughter.

"Sure. I can do it."

Dybbuk looked at his watch. The museum would be closing in a few minutes and, aware that Mr. Blennerhassit's backpack contained the fake baton, Dybbuk told Harry to take it off and give it to him. "No time like the present," he said. "I'll do it tonight. But don't expect to see me until tomorrow morning. After the museum has opened. Okay?"

Harry Blennerhassit shrugged off his backpack and handed it over, but it was clear to Dybbuk that he was worried about something.

"What's the matter?" groaned Dybbuk, rolling his eyes upward. "Cold feet?"

"Maybe. Look, you're just a kid," said Mr. Blennerhassit. "If this goes wrong, it's me who'll go to jail, not you."

"Relax," insisted Dybbuk. "I'll be all right. Trust me. I've got a genie that looks out for me."

This was true of course. Dybbuk's mother was also a djinn, although she would hardly have approved of what her son had gotten himself into. Dr. Sachertorte thought Dybbuk was touring battlefields of the American Civil War with Brad and Mr. Blennerhassit. Which was what Dybbuk had told her. Not that he had really given a great deal of thought to what *she* would have thought. Right now, having fun was all that he cared about.

"Harry, I know what I'm doing," he said. "Believe me, you'd be surprised what I'm capable of."

For once, Dybbuk was as good as his word, and the very next morning at ten thirty, about half an hour after the military museum had opened for the day, he was back at the Fort Benning guesthouse with a big smile on his face and a large poster tube in his hand.

"Thank goodness," said Brad's father, "you're all right."

"Of course I'm all right," said Buck.

"You've got it?" said Brad. "The baton?"

"This isn't a map of the fort," said Dybbuk. "Sure, I've got it." He flipped the lid off the poster tube and allowed the baton to slide onto Brad's bed.

"He's got it," said Mr. Blennerhassit, and danced around the room with Brad for a moment. When at last he stopped, he breathed a loud sigh of relief and locked the room door. "I was getting really worried something might have happened to you, Buck. You were gone such a long time."

"These things take patience," said Dybbuk. "Patience takes time. That's why they name burglars after cats instead of mutts, I guess." He threw himself down on the bed next to the baton and swept a length of hair out of his eyes. In his jeans, T-shirt, and motorcycle boots, he looked more like a young rock star than a cat burglar.

"You must be starved," said Brad, who was now thoroughly in awe of his classmate.

Dybbuk was about to say that he wasn't hungry at all since he'd already fixed himself some breakfast while inside one of Grant's bottles, but checked himself just in time. "I'm too excited to be hungry," he said. "Man, this is fun." He lofted his hand in front of Brad, who slapped it amicably.

Mr. Blennerhassit picked up the baton and held it reverently. "I can't believe I'm actually holding this," he said. "It's like history in my hands."

Dybbuk, whose interest in history was limited to old war movies, smiled patiently. "I guess so," he said and waited for the man to get to the interesting part.

"I'm almost afraid to open it," said Mr. Blennerhassit, who was now twitching with nerves. Sweat started on his forehead. He bit his lip and grimaced. "Suppose there's nothing inside it, after all."

"Only one way to find out," said Dybbuk. "Come on, Mr. Blennerhassit, open it up. The suspense is killing us."

Harry Blennerhassit pressed the baton's diamond studs and golden eagles in the sequence described by Futterneid in the original design. As soon as this was completed, there was a small *click* and one of the end caps depicting a diamond eagle carrying a Nazi swastika sprang open smoothly.

"Awesome," said Dybbuk, jumping off the bed in anticipation of it being covered with diamonds as Mr. Blennerhassit upended the baton on top of the bedspread.

Their smiles froze as, from inside the eighteen-inch-long baton, slid — nothing at all. No diamonds, not even a single gold coin. Mr. Blennerhassit held the baton up to his eye, like a telescope, and peered anxiously inside.

"Wait a minute," he said, suspending their collective disappointment. "There is something in here. It looks like some rolled-up papers." He tugged the papers from the tube and unrolled them carefully. Then he let out a gasp.

"Just tell me that I didn't steal Goering's poster tube," said Dybbuk.

"As a matter of fact, Buck, I think that's exactly what you stole." Harry Blennerhassit started to laugh. "Except that these aren't posters. They're cartoons."

"Cartoons?" Brad frowned. "They don't look like any cartoons I've ever seen."

This was true. These were drawings on a thick, ancient paper — drawings that looked like scenes from the Holy Bible.

"You misunderstand," said his father, grinning from ear to ear. "For you a cartoon is just some junk on the TV."

"That makes two of us," admitted Dybbuk.

"But a cartoon is the proper name for a drawing made as a design for a painting. Hermann Goering was quite an art collector. I'm no expert, but these look like they were drawn by the old masters. This one looks like it was drawn by Leonardo da Vinci. And this one by Michelangelo. So's this one. And this one could be by Raphael. This one might be another da Vinci. My guess is that these were intended to keep old Goering in some style after the war. Just one of these would probably fetch at least ten or fifteen million dollars. And there are six of them. No, wait. Five. This sixth one isn't like the others at all. I'm not sure what this one is. It looks much more recent. Not that it really matters. As a collection, I'd say the other five drawings would probably fetch at least seventy-five million dollars."

"All right!" said Dybbuk and slapped Brad's outstretched hand. "I always did like cartoons."

"Me, too," agreed the other boy. "So what do we do now, Dad?"

"We go home to Palm Springs. Soon as I get back home I'll call one of those big museums, with plenty of money, and see if they're interested in buying. And if they don't want to buy, we'll try the auction houses." He nodded firmly. "You can take my word for it, boys. There will be no shortage of buyers. All over the world there are people who would kill to get one of these drawings."

CHAPTER 2

THE BIRTHDAY PARTY

John and Philippa Gaunt were getting ready to celebrate their first birthday as djinn among whom it is the custom that all previous birthdays count for nothing, and that a djinn's true first birthday only occurs on the next calendar birthday that follows the extraction of wisdom teeth, and the resulting endowment of djinn power.

"You mean I'm only one year old?" John asked his djinn mother.

"That's right, dear," said Mrs. Gaunt.

John looked appalled. "You're kidding."

"Does this mean that there's only going to be one candle on our cake?" asked Philippa.

"Exactly so. Incidentally, that's a custom — having fire on a cake — that humans have borrowed from us."

But John was not about to be diverted from his outrage. "But it's so unfair," he said, "and a bit embarrassing. I mean, if anyone coming to our birthday party finds out, they'll laugh."

"I don't see why, dear," said Mrs. Gaunt. "Especially as only djinn will be coming. I'm afraid that's another tradition you're obliged to observe."

While the twins had wanted their mundane friends to come to their party, it was quite clear that Mrs. Gaunt had already decided differently. And they could see there was no point in arguing about this with her. Since their return from Babylon, Mrs. Gaunt seemed more distant somehow and less likely to brook any dissent from her children, both of whom remained happily unaware that she would soon be leaving them to become the next Blue Djinn of Babylon.

"Not that there will be many djinn there, either," she added. "This year your birthday coincides with Samum, which is a djinn holiday, so most of New York's djinn will be out of town." She shrugged. "Still, that can't be helped. It would be quite unthinkable to have a first birthday party on any other day than your proper birthday."

"Samum?" repeated Philippa. "What's that?"

"Literally, it means 'smoke without fire,'" explained Mrs. Gaunt. "Which is what happens in a transubstantiation. Samum is the day when we djinn celebrate what it is to be a djinn."

"But we don't know any djinn kids," said John. "Apart from Dybbuk."

"And the awful Lilith de Ghulle," said Philippa. "And I'm certainly not inviting her."

"I've already invited some other children of the lamp," said Mrs. Gaunt. "Most will be out of town with their parents, of course. But there are a few who've said they can come."

"A few?" said John. "How many?"

"Four," said Mrs. Gaunt.

"It sounds more like a card game than a party," observed John.

"It won't be anything unless we go and do some shopping," said Mrs. Gaunt.

They walked a few blocks to a small supermarket on Third Avenue, where Mrs. Gaunt bought her groceries and a newspaper. The headline on the front page declared that another dentist's office in Manhattan — the tenth that month — had been broken into. John and Philippa hurried inside the store, trying to ignore the homeless man who was sitting by the entrance holding out an empty paper cup in his very dirty hand, and asking for spare change. To the surprise of her children — not to mention the even greater surprise of the homeless man himself — Mrs. Gaunt opened her purse, took out a fifty-dollar bill, and folded it into his paper cup. Delighted, the man stood up, doffed his grubby baseball cap, and thanked her profusely. Inside the supermarket, the two children regarded their mother with disbelief. They had never paid much attention to their mother giving money to homeless people before, but they could hardly not pay attention to it now. Fifty dollars was fifty dollars.

"Fifty bucks," said John, shaking his head. "You gave that guy fifty bucks. You only meant to give him five, surely."

"No, dear. I gave him exactly what I intended to give him."

"But fifty bucks," said John. "What's he going to do with fifty bucks? I mean, he could spend it on anything."

"That's rather the point, dear," said Mrs. Gaunt.

"You know what I mean. Do you always give homeless people fifty dollars?"

"Perhaps," she said. "I was homeless once myself. I know what it's like to live on the streets."

Looking at Layla Gaunt, with her fur coat, her ostrich-skin handbag, and her Manitas Del Plata shoes, it would have been hard for anyone — let alone her own children — to believe this. Mrs. Gaunt oozed glamour the way a delicious truffle oozed chocolate. But Philippa remembered something their uncle Nimrod had told the twins about her mother.

"Nimrod told us you were homeless when you met Dad. Is that really true?"

"That's right." And upon leaving the supermarket, Mrs. Gaunt told her children the full story.

"Have you ever questioned why all djinn are rich?" she asked them.

Philippa shrugged. "It's a little hard to imagine how djinn could be poor," she said. "If you have the power to grant three wishes and stuff like that, I kind of doubt you'd be living on welfare."

"Unless you're an outlaw djinn," said John, "who's forced to live in the House of Kafur in Cairo, where the use of djinn power is strictly forbidden."

"There are some djinn," said Mrs. Gaunt, "who have questioned having any wealth at all. I'm referring to a djinn cult called the Eremites who seek to imitate the lives of angels and saints and go without any possessions whatsoever. For a while I was an Eremite myself. And you're right, Philippa: That's how I met your father. He thought I was just another homeless person in New York, but he still tried to help me and because of that I fell in love with him and married him. Your father may be small of stature, but he has a great soul."

"So there are some homeless people here in New York who are actually djinn?" said John.

"Not just in New York. London. Calcutta. Cairo. Anywhere. And it's not just djinn who live this way. Some are angels. 'Let brotherly love continue,' it's said, 'and be not forgetful to entertain strangers, for thereby some have entertained angels unawares.' That's the philosophy by which all Eremites live their lives. All they seek is to bring good luck to a really deserving mundane. To a human who does them a good turn, unaware of the true nature of the being they're helping."

"And that's why you gave that man fifty bucks," said Philippa. "In case he was another djinn."

"In case he was an *angel*, Philippa. I flatter myself that I know when I'm standing next to another djinn. But angels being more powerful than we are, are also better at disguising themselves. In fact they can do pretty much anything they have a mind to."

"It sounds very noble, being an Eremite," observed John.

"Yes, I suppose it is," said his mother. "But it's not without its dangers. Which is why I want you to promise me that you'll never become Eremites. At least not until you're older. I won't always be around to protect the two of you."

To the twins, this seemed a very curious thing to say. Life

42

without their mother seemed almost unthinkable. But they promised not to become Eremites all the same, and then they returned home. After they had carried their groceries down to the kitchen, Layla announced that she had something important to show them.

"Earlier on, when I mentioned your father's soul," she said, "it reminded me that your first djinn birthday is the perfect occasion for you to take a look at your soul mirrors."

"What *is* a soul mirror?" asked Philippa.

"The synopados. You mean Nimrod never told you —?"

"No."

"Come with me," said Mrs. Gaunt. "It will be easier if you see it for yourselves." And she led them up to the attic, which was somewhere they had never before been allowed to go.

"You always said there were bats in here," said Philippa, as her mother pulled down a ladder that led up to the attic. "I hate bats."

"That's why I said it," said Mrs. Gaunt. "To dissuade you from ever coming up here."

They went up the steps. Mrs. Gaunt lifted the hatch, felt for the light switch, found it, and flicked on a very dim lightbulb, stooping as she entered. The twins followed, nervous, aware that they were about to see something strange that was outside their previous experience.

In the attic they glanced around. Anonymous cartons on the hardwood floor. But no dust. No cobwebs. And certainly no bats. Just a strong smell of mothballs that John remarked upon.

"Bats hate mothballs," said Mrs. Gaunt.

The roof looked to be in an excellent state of repair. There was a skylight but it was a dull, cloudy day and the attic remained gloomy and full of shadows. Despite this, John noticed a crack in the wall. Recognized it, even.

"That's the same crack that's behind the headboard on my bed," he said. "The one that appeared just before we had our wisdom teeth extracted. It comes all the way up here."

"I suggest you follow it, John," advised his mother.

The crack led them to the back of the attic and behind a cold-water tank where a pair of old artist's easels stood, covered in dustcovers.

"You'll find what you're looking for under those old dustcovers," she said.

John took hold of one, and Philippa the other.

"Well, go on then," said Mrs. Gaunt, seeing them hesitate. "What are you waiting for?"

"I'm afraid to," said John.

"Me, too," said Philippa.

Mrs. Gaunt looked around the attic. "All right," she said. "It is rather gloomy in here."

She uttered the word she used to focus her djinn power, which was NEPHELOKOKKYGIA. This lit up the attic like a summer's day and the dustcovers fell away from the easels to reveal two mirrors.

These were peculiar-looking mirrors, being made of metal, with a convex glass surface and a back adorned with an elaborate design. Most peculiar of all was the fact that light coming in through the window and reflected from the front of the mirror displayed an almost luminous image of the mirror's elaborate design on the back, but nothing of what appeared in front of it. John placed himself squarely before the mirror and then shrugged. "I don't get it," he said. "Either I'm a vampire and I don't have a reflection, or this is some kind of trick."

"Don't look at the front, you idiot," his mother said, laughing. "That won't tell you anything." She waved her hand in a circular motion. "Go around to the back. That's the business end of a synopados."

Full of trepidation, the twins stepped around the back of the ornate, metal, exotic-looking mirrors from which a luminous image seemed to emanate, like something reflected from somewhere other than an attic in an old brownstone house in New York. And as the twins stared at these images with fascination — for these were their souls — Mrs. Gaunt talked to them using words and ideas they did not completely understand:

"Spirit and matter, body and soul, flesh and psyche — it is given only to the djinn to comprehend the mystery of where one ends and the other begins, and to recognize the absurdities that are spoken by those parlor priests and pop-injays, the psychologists. To see the very spring of life revealed to you, children! Just think how many mundanes have dreamed of seeing into themselves and truly understanding who and what they are. On one side of the mirror the world without you in it, for all flesh is passing. And on the other, the soul that hides in the shadows. But only you should see it. No one else but you should gaze upon it, for only you can affect what it looks like. Which is why it's up here, hidden away. A synopados is a secret thing, very personal to a djinn."

She was silent for a moment, to allow the children to be quiet with their own thoughts.

"Fascinating," whispered Philippa, who only half recognized what she perceived as herself, for it seemed there was a constantly changing aspect to the brightly colored image she saw, which rendered it mysterious and indescribable. One moment it was one thing and the next moment it was another. And yet it was pleasing to look upon and rather like something she had once seen on a computer, something called a fractal, which is a kind of shape-shifting, mathematically generated pattern within a pattern.

John was thinking much the same thoughts as his sister. But for just a moment, he now recalled the fifty dollars his mother had given to the homeless person and, in the depths of himself, he realized that her generosity bothered him a little. The very idea that she should have given fifty bucks to someone less worthy of her generosity than himself rankled him. Immediately when this thought occurred in his head, something dark and unpleasant appeared on the synopados. It was very small, but quite distinct. As if this mean-spirited thought had immediately appeared on his otherwise immaculate soul, like a tiny spot of black paint. And it frightened him a little, for what might his soul look like if he did something really bad? "Amazing," he breathed.

"Whatever happens to you," said Mrs. Gaunt, "whatever you do, you'll find it appearing here, in the image of your soul. Be mindful of that, for in everything you do, even the best of us has heaven and hell inside. And it is here that you will always learn that lesson."

Instead of there being four other children at the twins' birthday party, there were only three. Dybbuk didn't turn up, which seemed especially rude given that his mother, Dr. Jenny Sachertorte, had said that he would come. Not that Philippa was at all surprised. On both of the two previous occasions she had met Dybbuk, she had thought him quite ill-mannered.

Any disappointment John felt at not seeing him again was swiftly overcome by the presence of Agatha Daenion, who struck him as three wishes rolled into one. The other two djinn kids who came to the birthday party were Jonathan Munnay and Uma Karuna Ayer — both of them older, more powerful, and less affected by cold than were John and Philippa. Over the traditional birthday djinn flambé dinner of prawns sambuca, steak au poivre, crêpes suzette, and birthday cake, the twins' three young guests spoke about themselves and revealed how each was set on helping mundanekind in some specific way.

"I'm going to be a wish consultant," said Agatha. "I want to advise mundanes on how to avoid wasting three wishes. According to the *Baghdad Rules*, it's forbidden for a djinn who grants wishes to give advice on how to use them. So my idea is that a good djinn will give my business card to any human who has been lucky enough to be granted three wishes. It's also very much to the advantage of the djinn's individual conscience that the mundane manages to wish for something worthwhile. Because it's perfectly awful when you have to grant someone a wish knowing that it's for something really bad."

For John, the thought of disagreeing with Agatha about anything seemed quite unthinkable. Even so he had to admit she had a very good point. His own experience of granting wishes was limited. Nevertheless he still hadn't forgotten how horrible he had felt the time he'd been obliged to turn Finlay Macreeby into a falcon.

Philippa observed her brother and smiled, approving of his liking Agatha, although wishing for his sake that it might have looked a little less obvious. She herself was of the opinion that there would have been no need for a wish consultant if grammar had been taught properly in schools, so that mundanes could be trained to mean exactly what they said. Not wishing to be rude to her guest, however, she kept this opinion to herself.

Jonathan Munnay said he shared Agatha's principles and that these were what were inspiring him to become a psychiatrist. "I figure I could listen to people's problems," he said, "and then use djinn power to try to figure them out. Anonymously. So if someone came to me feeling depressed, I'd try to do something behind the scenes to cheer them up."

"Such as?" Philippa inquired skeptically.

"I dunno. All I know is that there's not much that doesn't look better with the addition of a little good luck."

"Oh, I agree, absolutely," said Uma Ayer. She lowered her voice. "That's why I've decided to renounce my tribe, wealth, and position and become an Eremite. Starting tomorrow, I'm going to become one of New York's home-less, and I'm going to help people who truly deserve to get three wishes. Doing good anonymously just like you said, Jonathan. My mother doesn't know about it. Which is why I want you all to promise to keep it a secret."

All this high-minded talk left the twins feeling a little guilty about celebrating their birthday at all. They had wanted to show off their new laptop computers, which were a gift from their father, but somehow, this seemed inappro-priate. Neither of the twins wanted to appear shallow and selfish in the serious eyes of these other young djinn. And they were quite glad when at last the party ended and their guests went home.

"I wouldn't want too many birthday parties like that one," said John. "The whole point of having a birthday party is so that people can make a big fuss over you. It's the one day of the year when it's all right to be a little selfish. Instead, I feel like this wasn't about me at all, but something else."

"I feel exactly the same way," admitted Philippa. But after a while, she added, "All the same, it has made me think that it might be nice to help someone. Someone who really needed help."

"While the weather is colder, there's no point in even

thinking about it," said John. "Until you're a grown-up, djinn power only works when it's hot, you know that."

"Oh, sure. It's just that talking to those djinn made me think I need a sense of purpose, that's all. I need *a mission*."

Little did Philippa know but she and John were about to get one.

Always a light sleeper, John awoke with the certainty that there was an intruder in the house. And intruders were on his mind because the previous day he'd heard his mother telling his father that the family dentist, Dr. "Mo" Larr, had been the victim of a recent break-in himself, at his office on Third Avenue. Nothing had actually been stolen, but all of Dr. Larr's patient records had been left strewn all over his office.

John crept out of his room and, peering over the banister, glimpsed a light moving around behind the library door. On a hot summer's evening and armed with full djinn power, John would have tackled the burglar himself. But the night was a cold one and, entirely powerless, he had no alternative but to alert his mother and father.

His father, Edward, was a small man but what he lacked in height he made up for in guts and courage, and no sooner had John told his parents about the intruder than Mr. Gaunt had leaped up and collected a Native American war club from under his bed, ready to give battle. Mrs. Gaunt eyed the war club with some skepticism.

"And what are you planning to do with that?" she asked her husband.

"Defend my family, of course," said Mr. Gaunt.

"Ed, you'd better let me handle this," she said, pulling on her silk dressing gown and stepping into a pair of matching slippers. "It may be that this is no ordinary intruder. This might just be one of the Ifrit, or even Iblis himself, here to be avenged on our children for what they and my brother did to him last summer in Cairo." There was no fear in Mrs. Gaunt: She carried herself down the stairs like a warrior queen.

Reluctantly, Mr. Gaunt put down the war club. He could see Layla was right, although he hardly liked that she was right. "Where's Phil?" he asked, glancing around anxiously.

"Still asleep," said John. "Let Mom handle it, Dad. If it is a djinn, it will take more than a Mohican war club to stop him."

He and his father crept after Mrs. Gaunt and were just in time to see her fling open the library door and switch on the light.

John stifled a cry of fright as he caught sight of not one but two intruders. They were wearing orange shirts and trousers and their heavily bearded faces were smeared with yellow paint, like savages. One of them was holding Mrs. Gaunt's ostrich-skin purse, and the other an ancient Tibetan cash box that had sat on the library mantelpiece for as long as John could remember. Then he heard his mother shout her focus word. This was followed by a loud bang because, when delivered in anger, djinn power always makes a noise. At the same moment, John and his father found themselves blinded momentarily by a bright flash and a cloud of smoke and when they looked into the library, the two men wearing orange clothes had disappeared. On the floor in the places where they had been standing were two bottles of red wine.

Mrs. Gaunt dusted her hands, picked up the two bottles, and handed them to her husband. "Here," she said. "A little something to compensate for your injured male pride."

"It makes a change from turning people into dogs, I suppose," said Mr. Gaunt. He looked at the labels on the bottles. "What have we here? A Chateau Lafite Rothschild 1966. And the 1970. Excellent choice. But why the different years, Layla?"

"Those are the years in which those two burglars were born," she said coolly.

"What were they after, Mom?" asked John, advancing into the library.

"I'm sort of wondering that myself," said Mr. Gaunt as he pulled the cork out of one of the bottles and poured himself a glass. "That box was a gift to my father from the thirteenth Dalai Lama."

Meanwhile, Mrs. Gaunt produced a small key on a gold chain around her neck and turned it in the lock of the Tibetan cash box. She lifted the lid and took out a small blue velvet pouch and emptied the contents onto the palm of her hand. For a second, John expected to see diamonds or perhaps several gold coins. Instead he found himself staring at eight teeth.

"They're our wisdom teeth," he said. "What would anyone want with them? And who were those guys? Were they djinn? Were they Ifrit?"

"They were mundane," said Mrs. Gaunt. Seeing her husband grin patiently, she added quickly, "I'm sorry, I mean human."

"That's all right," said Mr. Gaunt. "Don't worry about me, Layla. I know what I am and I'm not ashamed of it." He tasted the wine, swooshing it around his cheeks and gums like mouthwash. Swallowing it at last, he shook his head in wonder and said, "Oh, good. Very good." He drank some more and made an appreciative groan. "The wine just breaks in and overpowers you, ransacks your palate, hijacks your whole mouth, and steals away your taste buds. There's just a hint of lead pipe here, and I'm getting some gelignite, some old sneakers, and jammy cassis. Or do I mean jemmy cassis?"

"It's all my fault," said Mrs. Gaunt, returning the teeth to their blue velvet pouch. "I should have put these in the safe months ago. As soon as you and Philippa had them extracted. There's no telling what might have happened if these had fallen into the wrong hands."

"Like what?" said John. "What might have happened?"

"We'll talk about it in the morning, dear," said Mrs. Gaunt. She removed a book from the library — a copy of *Safe Strategies for Financial Freedom* — and opened it to reveal a hollowed-out section containing a large key with which she then unlocked the family safe. The safe itself was an extremely handsome object, about the size of a large TV set, painted green and black, inlaid with gold, and had once belonged to the French emperor Napoléon III. Mrs. Gaunt put the blue velvet pouch inside the safe, slammed the door shut, and locked it.

"They'll be secure enough in there," declared Mr. Gaunt, finishing a second glass of wine. "An army couldn't get into that thing."

"Nevertheless," said Mrs. Gaunt, "I think it's high time I installed some extra security in this house. Special security. Deadly security. The djinn type of security."

Early the next morning, Philippa inspected the scene of the crime while John explained in detail what had happened.

"She turned them into *what*?"

"Two bottles of red wine." John pointed out the two bottles of wine that were standing on the library table.

"But one of them is half empty," protested Philippa.

"Dad drank two glassfuls of that one."

"I don't believe it." She sniffed at the neck of the open bottle.

John shrugged. "You know how fond he is of expensive wine."

"Yes, but it's not every bottle of wine that's been walking around five minutes before you drink it," objected Philippa. "Talk about young." She shook her head. "You know it's a shame Mom is so hot-tempered. It would have been useful to have found out more about these two men. You say they were wearing orange clothes?"

"Yeah. They were kind of weird. Their foreheads and cheekbones were painted yellow." He pointed at the floor. "And they were standing just about where you are now when she zapped them."

Philippa dropped down onto her hands and knees and peered closely at the rug.

"What are you doing?" asked John.

"I've seen cops doing this on TV, whenever there's a crime. It's called a fingertip search. For evidence."

"What kind of evidence?"

"This kind." Philippa stood up, holding something in the palm of her hand. It was a small, round flat piece of slate, with a broken hole near the edge, as if it had once hung on some kind of necklace. Painted on the stone was an orange snake, and next to it what looked like a question mark, with the dot missing underneath. "Have you ever seen this before?" she asked.

"No."

"Then it's sure that one of those two guys must have dropped it. Come on. Let's go show it to Mom."

They went up to their mother's dressing room and found her staring at a glass tank full of the ugliest tropical fish they had ever seen. "Oh, good," she said. "There you are. Take a look at this. It's part of some new security measures I'm putting in place. Piranha fish. They'll eat just about anything. A school of these will strip the flesh off a living cow in just a few minutes."

John gazed into the tank, awestruck at the sight of the curiously bug-eyed fish.

"The tank is bulletproof, of course," she said. "And there's a powerful binding on it, so that it's djinn-proof. At least to all djinn except you two and me."

"Er, how exactly are these fish going to protect us?" asked Philippa. "I mean they're in there, and we're out here."

"Take a closer look," said Mrs. Gaunt.

Philippa pressed her nose up against the glass and saw that there was a second, smaller tank inside the larger one, only this one appeared to be full of air. "There's a key in there," she observed. "It's inside the smaller tank."

"It's the key to the safe," said Mrs. Gaunt. "There's a little air-lock door to get the key in and out of the second tank without letting any water in."

"I don't get it," confessed John. "What's the point of the smaller tank? No one would be crazy enough to put their arm in the larger one."

"No?" Mrs. Gaunt rolled up her sleeve and plunged her arm into the tank of piranha fish. "It's all right," she said, noticing her children's very obvious alarm. "They won't attack me. Nor you for that matter. But the animals in the second tank are a very different story. You'll have to be more careful with them."

"I'm looking," said John, "but I can't see a thing."

Reaching down into the water, Mrs. Gaunt tapped on the top of the second tank. Immediately two large spiders tried to attack her hand, and Philippa screamed with horror. "*Phoneutria fera*," said Mrs. Gaunt. "Brazilian Wandering Spiders. Their fangs are sharp enough to pierce a fingernail. Just half a milligram of their venom is enough to kill a man, or a djinn, so whenever you want this key you'll have to make sure that these two have been well-fed first."

"But what's it all about?" asked John. "Why is it so important to protect some old teeth?"

"Have you never heard of the tooth fairy, John?" His mother smiled kindly. "This mundane practice has its origin in an ancient superstition that was influenced by the law and practice of contagious djinn binding. Anything from a djinn's body — hair, blood, fingernails — will remain in contact with that djinn. But most especially the djinn's wisdom teeth. Those must be carefully guarded for they maintain a contact with the djinn that continues for the duration of his or her life. Using them, a person who knew what they were doing could make an amulet to protect themselves against the power of that djinn. Or worse, they could make a talisman to give them enough power over that djinn to enslave them.

"And that's exactly why I'm taking these extra precautions. To protect you both. I had thought the CCTV and the burglar alarms would be sufficient protection. But after what happened last night, I realize how wrong I was. We can't afford to take any chances. Especially after what has happened to Dybbuk."

"What *has* happened to Dybbuk?" asked John.

"He's disappeared," said Mrs. Gaunt. "He had just returned from a trip to the Civil War battlefields with a friend from school and his father, when he went missing. That's why he never showed up at your birthday party."

"He'll turn up," said John. "You know what Dybbuk's like."

"I'm afraid it may be worse than that," said Mrs. Gaunt. "The two mundanes with whom he went on the trip, a Mr. Blennerhassit and his son, Brad, have been found dead at their home in Palm Springs. And under suspicious circumstances. It seems that the police are anxious to speak to Dybbuk."

"You mean they think he might have murdered them?" asked John.

Mrs. Gaunt shrugged.

"No way!" said John. "Dybbuk may be rude, unreliable, devious, untrustworthy, mischievous, and dishonest, but he's not a murderer."

"He turned one of the boys in his class into a cockroach, didn't he?" said Philippa.

"That was just for a day," said John, shaking his head.

"Look," said Mrs. Gaunt. "Right now, the police just want to talk to him. I expect they want to make sure he's safe and to eliminate him from their inquiries, that's all." She shook her head and sighed. "Of all people, this had to happen to Jenny Sachertorte. After what happened to her daughter."

"Dybbuk has a sister?" said Philippa.

"*Had* a sister," said Mrs. Gaunt. "She was older than Dybbuk. But she disappeared, too. Of course, this was years ago. But a mother never gets over the disappearance of a child. Her marriage to Mr. Sachertorte certainly never recovered from it."

"What happened to her?" asked Philippa, horrified.

"No one really knows for sure," she said. "Trapped inside a bottle or a lamp. Enslaved by another djinn. Who can say? But don't ever ask Dybbuk or his mother about it, okay?"

The twins nodded.

"It's a bit of a coincidence, though, don't you think?" said Philippa after a moment or two. "His disappearing and some people breaking in here to try to steal our wisdom teeth. Maybe these two events are connected."

"Connected?" said Mrs. Gaunt. "How?"

"To answer that," said Philippa, "I'd have to know more about what happened in Palm Springs. And," she added pointedly, "more of a clue to go on than one and a half bottles of red wine."

Mrs. Gaunt looked sheepish. "You're right of course, Philippa. It was impetuous of me. I was angry at the two men. Angry at them because they'd broken in here, and angry at myself because of the way I'd treated your father. Any man should have the right to defend his home without the interference of his wife. It made him feel small. I thought that a couple bottles of his favorite wine might make up for me dealing with those two characters myself."

"I think it worked," said John. "He was in a pretty good mood after two glasses of the stuff."

"All the same," said Mrs. Gaunt, "Philippa's right. It would have been nice to have known more about who they were."

"Perhaps this will help," said Philippa, handing over the stone medallion. "I found it on the floor of the library. One of the burglars must have dropped it when you were turning wrongdoers into wine."

Mrs. Gaunt examined the medallion carefully. "It looks like a snake," she said. "A cobra. More than that, I really don't know. But I know a man who does. Mr. Rakshasas. There's no one who knows more about these things than him."

"Maybe we should send it to him," said Philippa. "By courier."

"No need for that," said Mrs. Gaunt. "I'll just send it to Nimrod, by djinnternal mail."

"What's that?" asked John.

"Watch." Mrs. Gaunt put the little stone medallion in her mouth and, not without some difficulty, swallowed the object whole.

For a moment, John and Philippa were too astonished to say anything.

"Nimrod will cough that up in less than an hour," said Mrs. Gaunt. "Of course it's something that only works between djinn who are closely related. And mature djinn at that. But it certainly saves on time and postage. Not to mention the very useful effect it has on curbing the appetite. In New York even a djinn can never be too thin."

CHAPTER 3

TOOTH AND NAIL

It had been so long since djinnternal mail had passed between Mrs. Gaunt and her brother, Nimrod, that she forgot to observe the normal etiquette, which was that she ought to have telephoned him first and warned him what was about to happen. If this had happened, Nimrod would have made sure he was somewhere private when the item arrived, and thereby avoided any embarrassment. Instead he was at his dentist's office in London's Wimpole Street, having his teeth cleaned and polished, and the arrival of some djinnternal mail could not have come at a more inconvenient time.

Mandy Mandibular, the hygienist, was just finishing with the ultrasonic descaler when suddenly she stood back from her patient and pulled off her mask to reveal a pretty face that was pale with shock.

Nimrod, who had been terrified of dentists ever since the extraction of his own wisdom teeth many decades before — the roots of those teeth were so deep that his dentist, Dr.

Jorrid, had been obliged to enlist the services of another patient in her waiting room, a circus strongman named Belzoni, to pull on the pliers — eyed Mandy Mandibular anxiously. "What is it?" he asked. "An abscess? A cavity? Something awful? What?"

Mandy swallowed and pointed at Nimrod's mouth. "There appears to be something advancing up your windpipe," she said. "Some sort of object."

"An object?" Nimrod sat up in the chair, snatched off the bib he was wearing, and then coughed in a horrible, choking sort of way. "Bottle me, but you're right," he said between more gurgling, choking noises. But by now he had guessed what was happening and how an object — whatever it was — came to be occupying his windpipe. For a brief moment he cursed Layla for using djinnternal mail without telling him beforehand. At the same time, however, he was glad that relations between the two of them were now so restored and back to normal that his sister felt able to send him something in this way.

Another moment passed and then Nimrod put his hand up to his mouth, spat the object onto his hand, and examined it carefully.

"What on earth is it?" asked Mandy Mandibular, who, for a terrified moment, had thought it might be some kind of alien, parasitical creature that had been living inside Nimrod's body, like something unspeakable in a sci-fi movie.

"It would appear to be some kind of stone medallion."

"Really? But how on earth did it get there?"

62

Nimrod smiled, trying to think of an explanation that might border on what was just about humanly possible. "It's something I swallowed by accident," he said, "when I was a child. It must have been in there all this time."

Mandy Mandibular was looking skeptical.

"What?" said Nimrod. "Did you never swallow some foreign object when you were a child, Miss Mandibular? A coin? A button, perhaps. No? I myself swallowed a watch once. Not to mention several dice and even a roll of film. Indeed, I have always been something of a pelican in that respect. But light my lamp if I hadn't quite forgotten this little medallion."

Nimrod did not bother to make any further excuses. He could see that he was only making the situation worse and, exiting the office onto Wimpole Street, he smiled as he tried to imagine what Miss Mandibular's face might have looked like if he had told her about some of the more spectacular things he had sent or received in his djinnternal mail. A favorite fountain pen. A pair of spectacles. A jar of honey. A set of keys. A TV remote control. Not to mention several paperbacks. And once, a small statuette.

Aware that Layla would hardly have bothered sending the stone medallion unless it was a matter of urgency, Nimrod went straight home and, having telephoned her and learned the circumstances of its discovery, he got an ancient-looking brass lamp from the drawing room and a clean dust cloth and brought them into the library. The lamp was made of brass and slightly tarnished, as if it could have used a good polish. The handle was large and curved like a cow's ear, and the lid looked like the onion-dome roof on some ancient Persian palace. Nimrod summoned Mr. Rakshasas from his lamp with a vigorous polishing.

A thin, ancient-smelling smoke filled the library in Nimrod's London home, gathered in a very local cloud, and took on a very human shape before clearing to reveal a man wearing a white suit and a white turban. He shook his head wearily. "It's taking me longer and longer to transubstantiate these days," he complained. "I used to manage it in just a few seconds. Now it seems to take several minutes." He stretched painfully. "Getting old, I suppose."

Nimrod did not contradict Mr. Rakshasas. The fact that he was old, very old, was quite incontrovertible.

"But what's your urgency, man?" said Mr. Rakshasas, who, despite looking like an Indian, sounded much more like an Irishman. "To be sure, you were polishing that lamp like a butler with a new dust cloth."

Nimrod told him about the break-in at his sister's home in New York, and the attempt to steal the wisdom teeth of his niece and nephew. "They found this on the floor," he said, handing over the medallion. "I think it's Indian. Layla sent it to me in our djinnternal mail. About an hour ago. I think it's relatively undamaged."

"You can't spoil a rotten egg, I'm thinking," murmured the old djinn, turning over the medallion in his bony fingers. "I had hoped never to see this symbol again."

"So you recognize it?"

Mr. Rakshasas sighed and nodded. "'Tis a Naga stone. It

64

serves a dual purpose: protecting humans from snakes — or so it is believed — and propitiating the snake god. The snake is a king cobra. That and the symbol next to it are not a sight for these old sore eyes, to be sure."

"Symbol?" Nimrod looked more closely at the medallion on Mr. Rakshasas's outstretched palm and the curious squiggle next to the snake. "You mean that sort of question mark, without the little dot underneath?"

"That's no question mark. That's the Brahmin numeral 'nine.' This means 'Nine Cobras,' Nimrod."

Nimrod frowned. "Nine Cobras. What's that?"

"There was an ancient cult called the Aasth Naag, or the Eight Cobras. I had hoped that it was extinct. But lately I've had the strangest feeling, Nimrod, which I was unable to put into words. Now, seeing this symbol again, subtly changed, improved perhaps, leads me to understand that feeling. To give it a name and a shape. The shape of a snake." He smiled wryly. "A scabby old head fears the comb, I suppose." The old djinn sat down in an armchair and let out a very weary sigh. "You say that they were after stealing the children's wisdom teeth?"

"Yes."

"That's bad. That's very bad. They'll be after making a new talisman, to be sure. Layla must be warned to take some precautions. Improve the security in her home."

"I believe she already has," said Nimrod.

"That's good. Of course if it's making a new talisman they're after, the Naag cult obviously doesn't have the old one. That's good, too." He stroked his long white beard thoughtfully. "I must find out more."

"Will you go to New York?" asked Nimrod.

"You don't bother with the monk when you can look for the whole monastery. No, my friend, I need to go to India. To seek out the Green Dervish himself."

"The Green Dervish," said Nimrod. "Yes, of course. He's an angel, isn't he? On that Indian island. He knows pretty much everything that's happening on the Indian subcontinent."

"Aye, that he does." Mr. Rakshasas nodded. "If the Cobras are active again, that's where they'll be based. And the Dervish will know how and when and precisely where."

"Then I'm coming with you, Mr. Rakshasas," said Nimrod. "Besides, you'll need someone to carry this lamp."

"I'll be glad of your company, Nimrod, and no mistake. But it's not by lamp I'll be traveling. Until this business is finished, I'll keep to my mundane shape. Being inside my lamp would just make it easier for those heathen devils to steal me. No, we'll leave the lamp here. Locked away in your vault. Safe. With the inside of the lamp looking after itself, as usual. I'd like to see the djinn foolish enough to go in there uninvited." He thought for another moment and then added, "Another thing. We'd best travel inconspicuously, like three men called Murphy on a bus to Cork. And we must keep ourselves and our whereabouts a secret from all the world and his dog. No, not even Mr. Groanin should know where we're going. He can remain here, just in case. Besides, India's no place for a man with a stomach like Groanin's."

"Whatever you wish, Mr. Rakshasas," agreed Nimrod. "I say, you don't think it's possible that Iblis might have something to do with this, do you? After all, it's only a few months since he threatened John and Philippa. He's generally a man of his word when something nasty is involved."

"Iblis? He's a snake, to be sure. But only by temperament and inclination. No, my guess is that he'd be as wary of the Aasth Naag as any djinn who has wisdom teeth to protect. No, he wouldn't get involved with them, I'm certain of it."

"All the same, for the sake of the twins I'd feel better if I knew where he was. And what he was planning."

"A shady lane breeds mud, and no mistake. If we were looking for him we'd only have to get our hands dirty to find him. But to put your mind at rest for now, Nimrod, I doubt he'll try anything while Layla is still living in New York. He wouldn't want to risk having his revenge while she's around. Not with the power she'll wield when she's the Blue Djinn."

Iblis had a score to settle. Six months before, in Cairo, he had been defeated by Nimrod and his infuriating young nephew and niece, John and Philippa Gaunt, in an attempt to recruit the seventy lost djinn of the ancient Egyptian king, Akhenaten, for evil. But for these three, the Homeostasis — the balance of luck that exists in the world — might forever have been affected, and bad luck would have held sway. In defeating him, the three Marid had imprisoned him in an antique perfume bottle. And there he might have remained but for a greedy American and a gullible French Guianan boy, who, in return for three wishes, was persuaded to let him out. Not that Iblis had given the boy three wishes, of course. Rewarding humans who did him a service was hardly his style and, instead, he had inflicted a diminuendo binding on the boy, and turned him into a living doll. Iblis had no involvement with any kind of cobra cult, that much was indeed true, but it was not true that he would have no involvement in the events that were about to transpire. Driven by hatred of the twins, Nimrod, and Mr. Rakshasas, he was about to become involved, albeit in a way that neither he, nor anyone else, could ever have foreseen.

Hidden away in his luxurious suite of rooms on the penthouse floor of the Croesus Hotel in Las Vegas, Iblis the Ifrit spent all day in bed monitoring several computer screens that showed how much human beings were losing in Ifrit-owned casinos all over the world. Outside his tinted window was a helicopter and, next to it, a swimming pool, a bowling alley, and a library. Not that Iblis read books or bowled or swam or flew in his helicopter. The truth was that, preoccupied with the idea of revenge, Iblis had let himself go a bit. His fingernails were as long as pencils and his beard was down to his chest, and if he ever wanted anything he only had to clap his hands and his mundane American slave, Oleaginus, would fetch it for him. His only true friends were the dozen black rats he kept as pets, which he allowed to crawl over his bed and person like so many small dogs; indeed, some of them were almost as big as dogs.

There were only two things that persisted in spoiling Iblis's life of uninterrupted, squalid luxury. One was the view of the hotel casino across the street. Iblis regarded the Aladdin, with its fake Arabian Nights decor, as almost a personal insult and he had often considered destroying the place with an earthquake. The only thing that stopped his carrying this out was the thought that one day he might buy this casino himself and change the name and decor to something that was more pleasing to him.

The other thing that spoiled his life of luxury was his continuing lack of vengeance upon John and Philippa Gaunt. There were good reasons for this, however: One was because he hadn't yet been able to think of something sufficiently horrible to do to the twins, and the other was because he had learned that Layla Gaunt was to be the next Blue Djinn of Babylon — this had made him decide to delay any vengeance, at least until Layla was out of the way or they were away from her, for fear that he incur her powerful wrath. All the same, he considered he had to plan some sort of revenge and with this in mind, he summoned Oleaginus into his cold-eyed presence.

Oleaginus bowed in the doorway of the vast bedroom, and advanced to the foot of his master's enormous bed. He placed a paper bag, which contained a treat for the rats, on the floor, and flinched as one of the rats that were as black and shiny as Iblis's silk pajamas crawled up his leg and jumped inside the bag. As always, Iblis was looking extremely angry about something, and sensing that he was about to be given some important orders, Oleaginus wiped his clammy hands on his shirt and took out a notebook and a pencil.

"Nothing is to happen to those Gaunt twins while they remain on the island of Manhattan, in New York," said Iblis, without removing his eyes from the computer screens.

"Yes, master."

"However, I want them put under surveillance. Them, and that ridiculous uncle of theirs, Nimrod. Him and his preposterous friend, Mr. Rakshasas. The minute the twins leave Manhattan, I want them bottled and caught and brought back here. Bottled and caught, but not harmed. The same goes for Nimrod and Rakshasas. Is that clear?"

"Yes, master."

"Djinn-binding kits and miniature thermal cameras for their detection will be issued from Ifrit stores."

"Yes, master."

"Of course, the mission is not without its hazards. Layla Gaunt is especially powerful, as is her brother, Nimrod. So whoever is successful in carrying out my orders will be rewarded. Handsomely rewarded. In the usual way." Iblis snapped his fingers impatiently at Oleaginus. "It's been so long since I did something nice for a mundane, I can't remember what the usual way is. Remind me, Oleaginus."

"Three wishes, sir?"

"Three wishes. Yes, precisely. Three wishes beyond the scope of normal human avarice."

Oleaginus licked his lips and swallowed.

"Yes, I know what you're thinking, Oleaginus. It's written all over your stupid face like the headline on my morning newspaper. You're thinking that you'd rather like the chance to win such a reward yourself. I must admit it's almost an intriguing thought to consider what a wretch like you might do with three wishes. For a start, you could wish for hands that didn't feel like two pieces of wet fish. And perhaps you could wish to have a face that wasn't uglier than the winner of the World's Ugliest Camel Contest. That would be nice, wouldn't it? Third — let's see now — yes, I know. You could wish for a personality. Nothing too charismatic. Just a few qualities to complement your toadlike obsequiousness. A little conversation, perhaps, or an original thought or two. Maybe even a teaspoonful of charm. Oh, let's be generous — a tablespoonful. Yes, I can see how three wishes might suit you very well. So, since it's your birthday, I'm going to give you a three-week holiday to see if you can do the job. Without pay, of course."

Oleaginus felt his heart leap inside his pigeon-chest. "You're too kind, master."

"Yes, I know. One more thing. The djinn binding. Do it properly. When I have all four of them bottled up, the twins, Nimrod, and Rakshasas, I want to be able to get them out from time to time, and gloat over them without hazard to my person. You understand?"

"Yes, master."

"Now give me the bag."

Oleaginus handed his master the bag from which Iblis removed a goat's head and, amid a loud chorus of squeaking rats, the most evil djinn in the world tossed this dainty morsel onto the floor. As the rats fell noisily onto the head and started their revolting feast, Iblis smiled with pleasure.

"Listen to them," he said. "These little children of the sewers. How beautifully they sing."

Oleaginus smiled thinly. "Quite lovely," he said.

"Don't let me down, Oleaginus. I'm sure you would taste every bit as good as a goat's head. Better if you should happen to be alive when the feast begins. Do I make myself clear?"

"Yes, master."

CHAPTER 4

TWINS

It took the twins several hours to configure their new Bungle laptops. The Bungle helpline, located thousands of miles away in India, was no help at all. The person on the other end of the line, a cool-sounding American who said his name was Joey and that he was originally from Cleveland, Ohio, seemed to know very little about computers. Indeed, to John's ears, it sounded much like Joey was giving the very opposite advice of what was really needed to get the laptops working properly. After almost an hour of useless and contrary suggestions, John hung up on Joey, deciding that the best thing to do might be simply for him to read the computer manual. And in this way, finally, he succeeded in getting their laptops working. No sooner had this happened than John received an e-mail from Dybbuk:

urgent u meet me at Bannerman's Island on Hudson River not far from u. Matter of life and death, so plz don't tell anyone. Espec not your mom as she will tell mine. My mom will try to help me and put her own life in danger. Come alone. And plz be careful you're not followed. Two people have been murdered by the men who are after me. They won't hesitate to kill again. Yours in fear for his life, Buck S.

John showed the e-mail to Philippa and asked her what she thought. "Send an e-mail back asking what it's all about," said Philippa. "I mean, that message could be from anyone."

"No, that's his e-mail address, all right," said John. "And the spelling looks familiar, too. Besides, I already sent him an answer. It got bounced back. And I was thinking, if he really is in danger he might not be able to pick up his e-mails anymore. The message he sent us was dated the day of our birthday party. And anything might have happened since then."

Philippa got a local guidebook to establish where Bannerman's Island was. "It's seventy miles up the Hudson River from New York City," she announced. "A two-hour train ride to Newburgh. And listen to this. The island is closed to the public. Once you arrive in Newburgh, the only way to get to the island itself is by canoe. He could hardly have chosen a more difficult place to get to."

"Maybe that's the whole point," said John. "If it's difficult to get to that might mean it's a safer place for him to be."

"But the difficulty of getting there is only half of my objection to going," said Philippa. "It's cold upstate. Even

74

colder than in the city. We'll be going there without djinn power, with no chance of having any when we get there."

"That would certainly explain why Dybbuk's in fear for his life," said John. "And all the more reason to go, I think."

Philippa shook her head, exasperated with her brother. There were times when she thought he had more courage than was good for him. "If the situations were reversed and we sent him an e-mail like that one," she said, "I bet Dybbuk wouldn't come and help us." She paused before adding, "I have no idea how long a canoe trip from Newburgh to this island might take. But somehow I can't see Mom letting us just take off for the day. Possibly longer. Have you noticed how watchful of us she's become? She's even taken to locking up my hairbrush in case someone tries to steal it to make a talisman."

"Really?" said John. "I haven't noticed her taking my brush."

"What would be the point?" said Philippa, smiling. "You never brush your hair, anyway. All I'm saying is that if we take off to this Bannerman's Island like Dybbuk wants us to, then she'll probably think we've disappeared as well."

"Those are all very good reasons for staying at home and doing nothing," said John. "But the fact is I'm still going. Just because Dybbuk hasn't been much of a friend to us doesn't mean we shouldn't behave like friends to him." He shrugged. "Look, there must be some way we can do this without setting Mom's alarm bells ringing."

"Sure there is," said Philippa. "It's called djinn power.

But unfortunately we don't have any. Not right now. Not until the weather warms up a bit."

"Then let's find someone who does have some power."

"Nimrod?"

"Exactly. Maybe when we explain, he'll come and help us. Dybbuk didn't say anything about not telling him."

Philippa telephoned Nimrod's home in London and spoke to Mr. Groanin.

"I'm afraid sir's gone away, Miss Philippa," Groanin said stiffly. "Him and Mr. Rakshasas."

"Did he say where they were going? A forwarding address? Contact telephone number? Cell phone?"

"He chose not to confide in me," said Groanin. "I say, he chose not to confide in me. His own butler. Of course, it is Samum. The djinn holiday."

"Yes, of course," said Philippa. "I'd forgotten about that. Did he say when they'd be back?"

"No, miss. But I can't imagine it could be for very long. Nimrod didn't even ask me to pack a suitcase for him. And Mr. Rakshasas has left his lamp here in the vault."

"That's not like him at all," said Philippa.

"No indeed, miss. Will that be all?"

"Yes, Mr. Groanin. And thank you."

Next, John telephoned Mr. Vodyannoy, his djinn friend at the Dakota, a building on the other side of Central Park, and Mr. Gwyllion, who owned The Sealed Book on West 57th Street, but they were away, too. He even tried Agatha

Daenion and Jonathan Munnay, their young friends from the birthday party, but without success.

"We must be the only djinn family in New York not to observe this holiday," complained John, and shook his head grimly. "It's all Dad's fault, of course. He doesn't even take all the mundane holidays he's entitled to, let alone the djinn ones."

"Then there's nobody around who could help us," said Philippa. "It looks like we'll have to forget the whole idea."

But John still wasn't quite ready to give up the idea of helping Dybbuk. He thought hard for a while and then said, "There is someone in the city who might know what to do: Uma Karuna Ayer."

"The one who said she was going to become an Eremite?"

"Exactly. Which means she's highly unlikely to have done something as selfish as taking a holiday."

"Yes, but how are we going to find her if she's living on the streets, like a homeless person?" said Philippa. "Besides, she isn't much older than us, and is probably just as power-less right now."

"That's true," admitted John. "But she might know a djinn who can help. And as for finding her, where better to look for a leaf than in a forest?"

"You're beginning to sound like Mr. Rakshasas."

"As a matter of fact it *was* something he said," explained John. "But what I meant was this: We'll look for Uma where there are lots of other homeless people. Washington

Square Park. Grand Central Station. The Lower East Side. According to what I was reading in the newspaper the other day, the A or the C subway tunnel that leads off the Chambers Street Station might be a good place to start. There are plenty of homeless people living down there. And another thing: We'd better go at night. That's when you notice homeless people the most. If they have a home, they'd probably be there instead of on the streets, right?"

They waited until after dark, when they were supposed to be in bed, and then slipped out of the house, unnoticed by their parents, who were busy hosting a dinner party for some of Mr. Gaunt's banking friends. They caught the A train downtown to Chambers Street and quickly discovered first, that it was not true that there were homeless people living in the New York City subway tunnels, and second, that going among the city's fifty thousand homeless people was not without danger, especially at night. One man, whom they met outside a coffee shop on Washington Square, followed them for a while and although they soon lost him, they were still walking very quickly and looking nervously over their shoulders by the time they reached Union Square, several blocks farther north.

"This was a stupid idea," said John, when eventually he recovered his breath. "Why didn't you talk me out of this, Phil? The way you normally do when I have a stupid idea."

"Because you were right," said Philippa, pointing through the window of a bank. There, sitting on the floor of the ATM lobby, was the filthiest-looking hobo she'd ever seen, and next to him, wrapped in a dirty sleeping bag, was a tall, thin, blond girl wearing clothes that were only fashionably thread-bare, and who was only half as grubby-looking as her male companion. It was Uma Karuna Ayer. Seeing the twins, Uma jumped up, stepped out of her sleeping bag, and opened the door.

"What on earth are you guys doing here?" she asked.

"Looking for you," said John, with one eye on the old hobo standing behind her.

"Did my mother put you up to this?" demanded Uma.

"No, not at all," said Philippa. "We were hoping you could help us. A friend of ours is in trouble and needs help. But he's a couple of hours away by train and we can't go there without our mother finding out that we're not at home."

"Hey, I know what that's like," said Uma. "That's one of the reasons I'm here. To do something on my own." She let out a sigh and looked sad. "Look, I'd like to help you. Only it's cold and I'm kind of low on power. Until it gets a little warmer outside, it's as much as I can do to zap myself a cup of coffee."

"Then if you don't mind my asking," said John, "what's the point of being an Eremite if you can't help yourself? What you're doing is dangerous, Uma."

"Oh, I'll be all right. The weather is supposed to improve in a few days." She looked around at her unkempt companion. "Until then, my friend Afriel will look after me."

Philippa pulled a face. "And who's going to look after

Afriel? The two of you look like you could use a square meal."
And so saying she handed them each ten dollars from her
purse. "Here."

Afriel pocketed his money and then tugged a forelock of
the matted yellow hair on his forehead with a filthy finger
and thumb. He smelled like a moldy cheese sandwich. A large
big toe that was the shape and color of a pickled walnut was
poking out of one of his sneakers. Every time Philippa looked
at him she wanted to find a handkerchief and cover her
nose and mouth. "I'm much obliged to you," he said in a voice
that sounded as if it had been scraped out of a tar barrel.

"Don't mention it," said Philippa, meaning this quite
literally because when Afriel spoke, his pungent breath made
her want to throw up.

"Tell me," said Afriel. "Is that all the money you have?"

Philippa felt Afriel was just a little ungrateful. "Er . . .
yes," she said. "It seems like it. Why? Isn't it enough?"

"I have some cash," said John. "You're welcome to it."

Afriel took John's money and pocketed that, too. Then
he smiled. "Since you've been kind enough to help me and
Uma, I'm going to help you."

"What can *you* do for us?" Philippa smiled.

"Normally I don't help djinn," said Afriel, ignoring her.
"I'm only supposed to help humankind. But since you're
both half human, I suppose it's all right."

"How do you know we're djinn?" asked Philippa. "Are
you an Eremite, too?"

"No." Afriel smiled. "Not an Eremite."

"Afriel is an angel," said Uma. "He's the angel of youth."

John looked somewhat skeptically at the filthy-looking figure standing next to Uma. He looked greasier than a pizza box and older than his own father. "You're kidding," he said. "And what? You help mundanes that have been kind to you, is that it?"

Afriel nodded and smiled a big smile that seemed to urgently require several hours' worth of tooth brushing.

"'Be not forgetful to entertain strangers,'" said Philippa, remembering what her mother had told her, "'for thereby some have entertained angels unawares.'" Even as she said it, she thought that it would have been a brave person who would have entertained someone as smelly as Afriel. But she had to admit that there was something about his piercing blue eyes that made him seem a little extraordinary.

"Yes," said Afriel. "Except that that's not really my thing. There's too much self-belief around these days. Self-belief, and the belief that science has all the answers. My job is to bring about the kind of odd accidents and strange happenings that astonish people, in order to show that scientists don't have the answers to everything. The sort of amazing things that help people to believe in something other than themselves."

"You mean like miracles," said John.

"Miracles are just one of the things I do," said Afriel. "I also perform wonders, portents, signs, omens, eye-openers, marvels, phenomena, and enigmas. Except on Sundays, of course. I never work on Sundays."

"Angels are much more powerful than djinn," Uma added helpfully. "There's not much Afriel can't do, if he puts his mind to it."

"I'm moved by your kindness to me and Uma, and your friend Dybbuk," said Afriel. "It is Dybbuk you intend to help, isn't it?"

"Er . . . yes," said John, who guessed that angels probably knew lots of stuff without anyone having to tell them.

"He's going to need your help in more ways than one," said Afriel. "I can't say anything else. That would be interfering with Fate. But I can fix things at home for you. Give you both an alibi. Or more precisely an Elsewhere. Two Elsewheres, since there are two of you. As far as your own djinn power is concerned, I'm afraid you'll have to wait for some warmer weather. Miracles I can do. But I'm afraid the impossible remains impossible."

Philippa nodded. "What's an Elsewhere?" she asked Afriel.

"An Elsewhere is someone to provide you with an excuse," said Afriel. "And who better to do that than your good selves?" With a filthy-looking finger, Afriel directed the attention of John and Philippa to two figures who were suddenly standing right behind them. "John. Philippa. I'd like you to meet John and Philippa."

John felt his jaw drop as he found himself face-to-face with . . . himself. "It's me," he said, astonished. "How on earth did you do that, Afriel?"

"Not on earth," said Afriel, "that's for sure." He shrugged and then started scratching himself. "Like I said, this is what

I do. Incidentally, just to be a little pedantic here? What you're looking at doesn't count as a miracle. That's a marvel."

"It's a marvel, all right," said Philippa, who was no less astonished than her brother to be facing her exact twin. She walked around the back of Philippa 2, which was a view of herself she had never seen before. "Is this really what I look like?"

"John is merely your biological twin," Afriel told Philippa. "But this is your identical twin. She will think, speak, and behave exactly like you. Nobody could tell you apart, except you. Not your mother. Not even John."

"She hasn't said anything," observed John. "If she was really like Philippa, she'd have interrupted by now and asked an awkward question."

"Thanks, John," said Philippa. "But he's right, Afriel. She doesn't say much."

"They won't begin to behave like you until you send them home to take your place," said Afriel. "You see, each of them is a true extension of yourself. It's simple quantum mechanics, really. Despite what Einstein believed, it really is possible for the same thing to exist in two places at once. It's what's called a Superposition. There's no logical explanation for it. Nothing a scientist could explain. Not for another hundred years, anyway. And that's precisely why this is marvelous."

"So as soon as we send them home," said Philippa, "these two will start being us."

"In all but two important respects," said Afriel. "First, they don't have souls. That's something even *I* can't make. So don't let them anywhere near your soul mirrors or your mother will guess and the game will be up. The second thing is these two cannot take your places indefinitely. It's something to do with subatomic decay, which would take too long to explain. Just remember this: Your Elsewheres will only last for an aeon, which is a proper unit of time in the ethereal universe, and not the immeasurable period of time that is sometimes written about down here."

"Exactly how long is an aeon?" asked John. "In Earth terms."

"Exactly one million seconds. Or to put that in numerical units you might find it easier to grasp, 11.57407407407407 407407407407407 days." Afriel chuckled. "Now you know why it's easier just to say an aeon."

"That's not nearly as long as I thought it was," observed Philippa. "An aeon, I mean. I thought it would be longer. Like thousands of years or something."

"All time is relative," said Afriel, "and an aeon down here means something very different from what an aeon means up there. That's what we call a time paradox, and another story altogether. But the bottom line is wherever it takes place, an aeon is the length of time it takes a thought to move through the mind of God, which is to say, not much time for Him, but quite a bit of time for you. That's another paradox."

John tousled John 2's hair playfully. "So what happens to this guy after an aeon?" he asked.

"He will disappear. They both will. It'll be 999,999 seconds and they'll still be there, and the next second . . ." Afriel clicked his fingers. "Gone. In the blink of an eye. Just like Cinderella's coach and horses. And talking about time, don't you think you'd better get going? If you're quick you can still catch the last train up the Hudson River from Penn Station." He shrugged. "Take my word for it, okay?"

Philippa shook her head. "We ought to go home first," she said. "We need some money to buy train tickets."

Afriel shook his head. "No, you don't. You've got money. You've got tickets."

John searched his pockets and found that Afriel was right: He did have a train ticket, and there was certainly more money in his wallet now than there had been when he left the house. "Hey, what do you know?" he said. "He's right."

"There's even a canoe waiting for you at the Newburgh Boating Club. So as you can see, there's no reason for delay."

"Thank you, Afriel," said Philippa, and momentarily forgetting how badly the angel smelled, kissed him on his stubbly cheek. "Thanks for everything."

"You too, Uma," said John, and kissed her, which she didn't seem to mind at all.

They flagged down a cab and told their Elsewheres to get in.

"Remember," said Afriel. "One aeon from now, they won't be there to cover for you."

"We won't need them that long," said Philippa.

"In which case, just come back and tell them to disappear." Afriel clicked his fingers. "Just like that."

John and Philippa ordered the taxi driver, a handsome Indian man wearing a large orange turban, to first take them to East 77th Street and on to Penn Station. But when, a few minutes later, they got out and John produced some money to pay the man, the driver shook his head. "Your money is no good," he said.

"Why?" asked John.

"One pair of twins is good luck," said the driver, waving John's money away, "but to have two sets of twins is very, very fortunate."

CHAPTER 5

BANNERMAN'S ISLAND

It was well after midnight by the time John and Philippa arrived at the Newburgh Boating Club but, as Afriel had promised, there was a canoe waiting for them, fully equipped for a nighttime journey, with flashlights and camping gear. The elderly boatman at the club didn't seem at all surprised to see two children turning up at that late hour. Nor did he lecture them about the foolishness of taking a canoe out on the Hudson River in the dark, as most adults would have done. The twins quickly formed the impression that this was just another aspect of Afriel's earthly mission to astonish people and make them believe in something other than themselves.

"Your being so nice to us, it's not an enigma, exactly," Philippa told the boatman as he held the canoe steady for her, and she tiptoed aboard. "Nor even a marvel. It's more of an eye-opener, really. And not what we're used to at all."

"We aim to please," said the boatman. "Where are you two kids headed, anyway? If you don't mind me asking."

"Bannerman's Island," said John, sitting down in the stern of the canoe.

"Back in about 1920, there was a fire and explosion on the island," said the boatman. "And there are some ruins just under the waterline. When you reach the old harbor, make sure you paddle slowly and carefully, so you don't rip the bottom off the canoe. It's made out of birch bark, in a traditional Iroquois design, so it wouldn't take much to damage it."

"Thanks for the advice," said John and, settling himself in, picked up his paddle. Philippa, sitting down in the bow, switched on the big flashlight that was going to illuminate their trip along the river.

"Since you're willing to take it, then here's some more," said the boatman. "Bannerman's Island is haunted. Me, I wouldn't go there in the middle of the day, let alone the middle of the night. But I can see you kids are set on going there, so I figure you must've got a good reason. Anyway, if you *do* decide to come back here tonight — and heck, I wouldn't blame you one little bit if you did — then just knock on the door of the boathouse. Since my cat, Magnus, died, I get kind of lonely, and I welcome any company. No matter what the time of day or night."

"We'll certainly keep all of that in mind," said John. He pushed away from the little jetty with the paddle and then dipped it silently into the black depths under his elbow. Minutes later, the boathouse had all but vanished in the darkness behind them, and the Indian canoe was gliding smoothly through the cold, calm midnight waters of the broad and powerful Hudson River.

They kept the western bank of the river in sight, and through the moonlit trees came eerie bird calls that echoed across the still water like hostile savages, so that it was all too easy for John to imagine himself to be a character in the pages of a novel by James Fenimore Cooper, such as *The Last of the Mohicans.* Not that he'd actually read this book, but he had seen the movie. It was a pretty good movie. Philippa, who was better read and more of a city girl than her outdoor-loving brother, twitched nervously in the bow of the boat and thought of goblins, Ichabod Crane, and the horrible headless horseman.

"This is about the creepiest thing I've ever done," she remarked as something large moved in the branches of a tree overhanging the river, and she glanced up fearfully, half expecting Rip van Winkle to drop into their canoe.

"Cool it," said John.

"Cool it?" Philippa yielded to the shiver that was creeping across her shoulders. "I'm freezing as it is."

John paddled faster. She was right. It was cold and he was glad of the physical exertion, knowing that it would help to keep him warm.

Finally, after almost an hour of paddling, the flashlight picked out a thickly shrubbed hill almost a hundred feet tall, rising straight out of the water in front of them. John let the canoe drift through a sort of fortified gate and then steered them into the shore. Jumping into the shallow water, they dragged the canoe carefully up onto the bank between some bushes. An owl *hoo-hoo*-hooted as if in welcome and gradually, high above them in the gloom, they made out the silhouette of what looked like a real Scottish castle. In the window of the highest corner turret, a light burned dimly.

John grabbed the second flashlight and led the way through the bushes and up a steep pathway. Philippa followed. At least she did until they came to a drawbridge. There she stopped and let out a soft moan of disquiet. "I refuse to go on without a clove of garlic and a silver crucifix," she hissed at her brother's back. "Not to mention a mallet and a couple of sharp stakes. The boatman was right. This place has got 'haunted' written all over it, in neon signs three feet high. What's a creepy Scottish castle doing here, anyway? In the middle of the Hudson River. It doesn't seem right."

"Where else would you suggest we look?" he said, somewhat exasperated. "If Dybbuk is on this island, it stands to reason he'd be here. I mean this castle is all there is."

"And if he's not here? Then what? I'm not sure I want to meet anyone who's prepared to stay in a place like this. I've seen more welcoming graveyards than Bannerman's Island."

"Take it easy," said John, who was really no less scared than his sister, just better at hiding it. "Tell you what: You stay here, and I'll have a look around, see if Dybbuk's here, and then we'll go home. Okay?"

"And leave me here on my own?" Philippa shone the flashlight up the wall of the castle in front of her. "No way. I'm coming with you."

"Good," said John, who wasn't very enthusiastic about going into the castle by himself.

They crossed the drawbridge and passed beneath a portcullis and a coat of arms. Outside a wooden door as big as the mouth of a subway tunnel, John raised his fist to knock and then seemed to think better of it.

"What's the matter?" asked Philippa.

"It's open, that's what's the matter," said John, pushing at the door, which opened with a creak as loud as a machine-gun blast.

Inside a large hall stood a suit of armor bearing an enormous ax. Behind this was an old church organ that, most unnervingly, was playing one continuous high note by itself. John gulped. "Is there anyone there?" he asked, addressing the bench in front of the organ.

Philippa walked toward the organ and immediately grasped what was happening. "It's the wind in one of the pipes," she said, "that's all." She turned to find that John was no longer behind her. He was standing at the threshold of a great sitting room and staring at something with such a look of horror on his face that Philippa felt her blood turn cold.

"Look at this," he whispered.

She hardly wanted to look but curiosity dragged her feet forward until she could see what he saw. Lying on a sort of daybed in front of a huge, empty fireplace was what looked like a very old man. The old man was wearing a tailcoat, striped pants, a vest, spats, and a shirt and tie, and appeared to be sleeping — or dead. But it was the hairiness of the man that was most alarming to the twins and it was several seconds before Philippa guessed that this was not a man's body at all, but that of a large ape.

"Is he dead?" she whispered.

"I sincerely hope so," said John. "I would hate to have to explain to a gorilla what we're doing in his house, uninvited, at this time of night." He glanced at her questioningly. "It is a gorilla, isn't it?"

"I don't know. I've never seen a gorilla up close before. Certainly not one wearing a tailcoat."

Both of them let out a yell of fright as something banged loudly behind them and, running back to the front door, they found it shut. "Do you think it was the wind?" John asked breathlessly, and pointed at the organ, which was still sounding the one high, tremulous note, like a kettle that had been left to whistle. "Like in the pipe?"

"I sincerely hope so." Philippa shivered; she also had the distinctly unnerving sensation of feeling something brush past her, like a trailing cobweb, and hearing the voice of an invisible girl whisper something in her ear.

That was when the organ started to play a real piece of music, and both of the twins realized that while the wind might have closed a door or even played one solitary note, it could hardly have managed a whole Bach Toccata and Fugue in D Minor.

"Come on," said Philippa, grabbing the door handle. "Let's get out of here. Before that weird monkey wakes up."

But the door was firmly locked.

Now thoroughly terrified, the twins pulled at the handle of the door with all their strength until, just as suddenly as it had begun, the gothic organ music stopped and they heard a boy's mocking laughter. A moment later the curtain behind the organ was hauled aside and out stepped Dybbuk, still chuckling cruelly and shaking his head at the effect his prank had had on John and Philippa.

"Your faces," he said, cackling. "I wish I had a camera. I swear, you both look like you just met the Wolfman. That was so hilarious."

"I'm glad you find it so amusing," Philippa said stiffly. Her fists were clenched and if Dybbuk had been standing any closer she probably would have punched him. "We certainly wouldn't have bothered coming all this way, and at great personal risk, if we'd thought that this was how you planned to greet us."

"I'm sorry, but I couldn't resist it. I mean this place is just made for practical jokes like that. Isn't it great?"

"And we thought you were actually afraid for your life," said John. "That's what your e-mail said, anyway."

"I am. That was true. Every word of it. Honest."

"Yeah, sure," John said bitterly. "I can see it was true from the big grin on your stupid face."

"No, really," insisted Dybbuk. "I'm very grateful you're here."

"Come on, John," said Philippa, "let's go home."

"No, wait," said Dybbuk. "Hear me out, please."

"All right," said John, "but this had better be good."

They went back into the enormous sitting room.

"Who's your friend?" John asked, staring uncomfortably at the ape.

"That's Max. He was my great-aunt Felicia's butler for more than thirty years."

"Is that her?" asked Philippa, staring at a large portrait of a beautiful and striking young girl, aged about ten, which hung above the fireplace. "Your aunt? I mean, when she was a kid?"

"No. That's my sister, Faustina."

"I'd forgotten that you have a sister," said Philippa.

"Had," said Dybbuk. "She's not around anymore. Okay?"

An awkward silence followed.

"How come your aunt had an ape for a butler?" asked John, changing the subject.

"She never liked mundanes very much," said Dybbuk, "which is one of the reasons why she bought Bannerman's Island. Human beings tend to avoid the place. For obvious reasons. Anyway, she got Max from a zoo when he was still young, and endowed him with some human qualities such as speech and other higher brain functions. He was a pretty good organist, apparently. Anyway, I guess they got along okay. At least they did until yesterday when poor Max keeled over and died. He was sixty-one, which is considered to be very old for a gorilla. But even so, it was a bit of a surprise to me, I can tell you." He shook his head sadly. "Poor Aunt Felicia is going to be really upset about it when she comes home."

"Where is she now?"

"With my mother. Looking for me."

"Looking for *you*?" said Philippa.

"Max was pretty good about that. He got it, you know? He understood that if I went home with my mother I'd be putting her life at risk."

"Why don't you tell us exactly what this is all about?" said Philippa. "From the beginning."

"After the three of us got back to Palm Springs from Fort Benning," said Dybbuk, continuing his explanation, "Mr. Blennerhassit showed the drawings we'd found inside Goering's baton to a guy from some museum in Malibu. He said two were by Leonardo da Vinci, one by Raphael, one by Michelangelo, and one by Botticelli. But the sixth picture, a watercolor, was from a much later period, and much less valuable. He said it wasn't his period but he thought it was something called a 'Company picture,' whatever that is. Anyway, I liked it better than all the others and since it wasn't worth more than fifteen hundred bucks, Mr. Blennerhassit agreed that I should keep it as a souvenir."

They were still in the big sitting room by the truck-sized fireplace. The couch they were all huddled on looked as though it had come from the bedroom of a Chinese emperor. Above their three heads hung a brass chandelier, which was as big as a child's jungle gym, along with the picture of Dybbuk's sister, Faustina. Now that he had mentioned it, Philippa could see the similarity: the same dark hair and dark eyes, the same pale complexion, the same thin, piano-player fingers, the same high cheekbones. The same willful, mischievous look.

Was Faustina dead? Philippa wanted to know but guessed she would have to wait until she could ask her mother about this. Faustina was a subject Dybbuk had seemed sensitive about.

"So, to go back to the guy from the museum," said Dybbuk. "He was a little bit evasive about an actual price for the good stuff. I mean, all he did was talk about historical significance and how priceless it was. And priceless doesn't mean anything to me. So when he left I went on this Internet auction site to try to find out, which was how I came to find out that there was a copy of Hermann Goering's Field Marshal's baton up for sale. I mean, the exact copy of the one I had left in the military museum in Fort Benning. When I told Mr. Blennerhassit, he was really mad about it. Furious. And he phoned the jeweler who'd made it, a guy called Hyman Strasberg in New York, because it was obvious that Strasberg must have made not just one copy but two. And that he had kept one for himself to sell later on.

"But instead of speaking to Strasberg, Harry Blennerhassit found himself talking to some New York cop, who told him that Hyman Strasberg was dead. And, get this, that he'd been bitten by a poisonous snake. Harry told him that he was real sorry to hear that, but that he didn't think he knew anything that could help them. Which he didn't. I mean, it just looked like an unfortunate accident. It's not like there aren't any poisonous snakes in New York. There are timber rattlesnakes, the massasaugas, and copperheads. Okay, I admit they're not exactly common, but they're around. Since being here,

I've actually seen a copperhead on this island. At least I think it was a copperhead."

Philippa glanced around nervously. She disliked snakes almost as much as she disliked bats and spiders. "You seem to know a lot about snakes," she told Dybbuk.

"Snakes? Sure. I've got a little gopher snake named George at home. I used to have a rattler named Ryan, only he escaped down the toilet."

"That's a comforting thought," said Philippa.

"I've always liked snakes," continued Dybbuk. "It's one of the reasons I wanted that Company picture. Because there was a snake in it. But I didn't remember that until after I was home again. And it occurred to me that maybe there was a connection between the picture and the snake that had killed Mr. Strasberg. So later on, after supper, I went back to Brad's house — I mean Mr. Blennerhassit's house. And soon as I got there I knew something was wrong."

Dybbuk let out a long sigh and looked grim for a moment, and when he took up the story again, there were tears in his eyes. "Their stuff was all over the place, like someone had robbed them. The baton was gone but, weirdly, they left the pictures that had been inside it. And then I found the two of them." Dybbuk swallowed hard and tried to control his feelings. "Brad and his dad, Harry. They were dead, both of them. Their faces were all blue and their eyes were red. Which, given what had happened to Hyman Strasberg, made me think snakebite." Dybbuk's voice was growing unsteadier by the second. "So I took a closer look at the two of them and I found fang puncture marks on their hands and legs. Lots of them. As if they'd both been bitten several times." He shook his head and wiped a tear from his eye. "So I just grabbed all of the drawings and hightailed it out of there. Went home. Sent you guys the message and then lit out by whirlwind for Bannerman's Island. My aunt had been staying with my mother, which was one of the reasons I figured no one would ever think to look for me here." He shrugged. "And that's it, until you guys showed up just now."

"I wonder if that can be true," said Philippa.

"Every word of it, I swear."

"No, no," said Philippa. "I mean what you said, that no one would ever think of looking for you here."

"The cops are looking for you," said John. "They want to ask you some questions."

"I can't help that," said Dybbuk. "Do you think they'd believe any of this? Me, a kid, breaking into that military museum? They'd arrest me for sure."

"Where were you when Max died?" asked Philippa.

"Asleep."

"Upstairs?"

"No, there's a secret room behind the organ, where you can switch it on to play by itself and operate the front door automatically. There's a bed in there as well and I always stay there when I come here. Ever since I was a kid I liked the idea of staying in a secret room."

"How long were you asleep?" asked Philippa.

Dybbuk shrugged. "Ten, twelve hours. I was exhausted after the flight here."

"Doesn't the noise of the wind in the organ disturb you?" asked John.

"No. The room is soundproof. Once you're in there you can't hear a thing."

"Is that so?" said Philippa and, getting up from the couch, she went over to the dead gorilla and started to examine his hands and feet.

"You don't think . . ." said Dybbuk, following her over to Max's body.

"I've certainly never seen a dead gorilla before," said Philippa. "And it's a little hard to see his skin color underneath all this silver-black fur, but —" She opened the gorilla's enormous, leathery hand and, spreading the thick fingers open, felt her breath catch as she perceived two black puncture marks on the fleshy part of Max's palm. "Tell me, Buck," she said. "Does this look like a snakebite to you?"

"Yes," whispered Dybbuk, "it does."

"Then," said Philippa, "whoever or whatever killed the Blennerhassits and Mr. Strasberg was also here. Looking for you. And instead, they killed Max." Philippa took off her glasses and looked squarely at Dybbuk. "Which makes you very lucky, Buck. Very, very lucky."

"Poor old Max," said Dybbuk. He swallowed a huge lump of emotion and then another tear rolled down his face.

Furiously, as if angry with himself, Dybbuk brushed it away. "He was always a real stand-up kind of guy, you know?" he added. "Someone I could rely on."

The twins jumped with fright as a large black cat leaped off the bookcase and onto Max's enormous, still chest.

"Don't worry," said Dybbuk, collecting the cat in his arms and nuzzling him affectionately, it seemed to Philippa, for comfort. "This is just Hendrix. He belonged to the Blennerhassits."

"You took their cat?" said John.

"Rescued him, more like. I could hardly leave the poor thing behind, could I? Chances are the police would have put him in the local animal pound. And who knows what might have happened to him in a place like that?"

"Yes," said Philippa. And then, "Of course!" she said with the force of revelation. "Hendrix must know *exactly* what happened! He probably saw the whole thing! Here, and in Palm Springs! All you have to do is ask him."

"You mean one of us should give him the power of speech? Like Max?"

"Well, not us, obviously," said Philippa. "It's still too cold for us, Buck. But you could probably do it." Dybbuk was shaking his head. "Couldn't you?"

"Since I arrived on the island, I've had no power at all," he said. "You know I almost didn't make it here at all. My whirlwind gave out on me before I landed. It's a lot colder here on the East Coast than on the West Coast. I forgot about that." Dybbuk stroked the cat fondly for a moment. "But even if I did have djinn power, I doubt I could make this cat talk. I haven't got the experience. It takes a fully grown djinn like Aunt Felicia to endow an animal with the power of speech."

"All right, then," said Philippa. "What about taking possession of the cat? We've all done animal possession. It's about the first thing you learn when you find out you're a djinn. If I was inside this cat perhaps I could read his mind. Look inside his memory. That way we'd find out exactly what happened."

"Why didn't I think of that?" said Dybbuk.

"Because you're not as clever as she is," said John.

"Is there a sauna in this house?" asked Philippa. "Or some other ways of getting hot enough to use djinn power?"

"A sauna? In this old place?" Dybbuk laughed bitterly. "There's not even a shower. There are plenty of baths, but no hot water. Max wasn't much of a plumber. Plumbing's not something gorillas have the patience for. And Felicia doesn't like soap and water very much. She prefers using djinn power to keep herself clean. She says it keeps her skin looking younger. So she irradiates herself: She allows a large amount of heat to escape from her body to destroy all the dirt and bacteria on her skin. That's something else you can only do when you're fully grown. I watched her do it once. You sort of catch fire for a second. It's amazing to see."

"I've got an idea," said John, yawning, for by now it was very late. "First thing in the morning we'll build a sweat lodge in the garden. That's how Native Americans used to keep themselves clean. We can get hot that way. Hot enough to get our power back."

"Why didn't I think of that?" said Dybbuk.

"Because," said Philippa, "you're not as clever as he is."

In the morning, they made a fire in the huge fireplace and then placed several large stones among the hot coals. Then they buried poor Max in the garden.

It was a simple funeral, with no casket and no religious ceremony, just the shallow grave dug by John and Dybbuk, and some flowers picked by Philippa. Dybbuk spoke a few tremulous words over the dead gorilla's grave.

"Gorillas can bluff, like they do in the wild, but they never lie," he said. "Even the ones that can talk. They just don't know *how* to lie. Which makes them better than a lot of humans I know. Not to mention djinn. If a gorilla likes you, he likes you forever, and without strings. Which makes them pretty loyal. If my aunt was here she'd probably say that Max was the best friend anyone could ever have had. I pretty much feel the same way. He let me stay here without asking any questions, and he never tried to give me any advice. Which is typical of a silverback gorilla. And what makes them such good butlers. Unlike humans, who are kind of gabby by nature, gorillas are close-mouthed, and know how to respect someone's privacy."

To her surprise Philippa realized that he was looking at her as he said this, which made her wonder if Dybbuk hadn't guessed how badly she wanted to ask him a question about his sister, Faustina.

"I'm sorry for what happened, Max," he added in conclusion. "Really I am. I'm gonna miss you, buddy. You were a real gentleman."

Then, to Philippa's surprise, Dybbuk wiped his eyes with a clean handkerchief. She was not surprised to see him cry again. But she was surprised to discover that he owned a clean handkerchief.

After the funeral was over they cut down some small trees and erected a sort of igloo structure on the lawn that they then covered with rugs and old blankets until the lodge was well-insulated against the outside air. Last of all they dug a shallow pit inside the lodge where they placed the hot stones, and then sprinkled cold water on them, which turned immediately to steam. In this way, the temperature inside their improvised sweat lodge quickly climbed until it was hotter than a tropical jungle. The three young djinn stripped down to their underwear and crawled inside.

Gradually the intense heat warmed their flesh, penetrated their bones, and then the marrow in their bones, and the subtle fire that burns within all djinn at no hazard to their person was kindled and invigorated until they all felt their power restored.

"That's better," said John, pouring more water onto the stones and increasing the temperature inside the sweat lodge even further. "The way I'm feeling now I think I could probably grant three wishes to the greediest man in the world."

"So who's going to do it?" asked Dybbuk. "Who's going to take possession of Hendrix?"

"He's your cat now," Philippa told Dybbuk. "Maybe you should do it."

"Yes, but it was your idea," said Dybbuk. "Besides, if you don't mind, I don't really want to see what happened to Brad and his dad. Not to mention Max. They were my friends."

Philippa nodded. "I understand." She shrugged. "Okay, I'll do it."

"I'll go and get the cat carrier," said Dybbuk, crawling to the doorway in the sweat lodge. "Give me a few minutes before you do anything. Okay?"

"Okay."

As soon as djinn have lost their wisdom teeth and had their Tammuz — the initiation ceremony that heralds their entry into the world of the djinn — animal and human possession is one of the first things they are taught. Philippa already had some experience in this area having previously taken possession of a camel, a squirrel, and an Egyptian policeman. She waited until she heard Dybbuk outside the sweat lodge again, and then closed her eyes, gathering her concentration into one hard spot in the center of her forehead, so that when she uttered her focus word, the whole of her being was like the rays of the sun gathered together by a convex lens: "FABULONGOSHOOMARVELISHLYWON-DERPIPICAL!"

It was dark inside the sweat lodge and, as soon as he had heard his sister utter her focus word, John crawled outside to watch.

A moment or two later, he and Dybbuk heard a loud meow from inside the cat carrier as Philippa signaled she was now inside Hendrix.

She was there for several minutes for, although a cat's memory is quite selective, it is almost two hundred times as retentive as a dog's memory, and lasts as long as two weeks, exceeding even that of an orangutan. When eventually Philippa crawled out of the lodge, having recovered the possession of her own body, she faced the two boys with wide eyes and a surprised whistle on her lips.

"I had no idea that cats lead such interesting lives," she said. "All that stuff about nine lives is true. Only the lives don't run one after the other, but consecutively. All at the same time."

"Never mind that now," said Dybbuk. "What did you find out about Max?"

"That we were right. That Max was murdered by the same people who murdered Brad and his father. They arrived in secret, with a basket full of snakes, and let them loose on the floor of the house. As soon as Brad and his father had been bitten, they revealed themselves and offered them antivenom in return for what they were looking for. The same thing happened to Max."

"And what *were* they looking for?" asked Dybbuk.

"Not the baton," explained Philippa. "And not the Leonardo cartoons. They were looking for the Company picture. The one you took as a souvenir."

"I knew it," said Dybbuk. "But did you find out why?"

"No. Only that they're prepared to kill for it. Mr. Blennerhassit told them you had it, Buck, and they still let him and Brad die. Max, however, told them nothing."

"Good old Max," whispered Dybbuk.

"But who *are* these people?" asked John. "Did you find *that* out?"

"I think you may be the only person, John, who has actually seen them. They looked like the same men you described after the attempted burglary back home. Orange clothes. Yellow paint on their faces. And one of the men I saw in Hendrix's memory was wearing the same kind of medallion that we found on the floor of the library, the day after. The one Mom sent to Nimrod by djinnternal mail."

"Whatever happened with that?" said John. "We never did find out what that was." He thought for a moment. "But they weren't after a picture. Those two were after our wisdom teeth." He shrugged. "At least, that's what Mom thought."

"Is someone going to tell me what you're talking about?" Dybbuk asked.

The twins told Dybbuk about the break-in at their home on East 77th Street, and the medallion they'd found with the cobra on it.

"A cobra?" said Dybbuk. "The snake in the Company picture is a cobra. A king cobra, to be precise."

"Buck? That snake you saw. Here, on Bannerman's Island," said Philippa. "I don't think that was a copperhead at all. I think that was a cobra, too. When I was inside the body and mind of Hendrix I noticed that one of the snakes got away when the killers left, and they were obliged to leave it behind. That's why Hendrix climbed on top of the bookcase."

"I think it's time we take a look at this Company picture," said John. "Don't you?"

Back in the living room, they sat in front of the roaring fire, with the picture spread out on the floor in front of them.

It was a watercolor, depicting a scene in what looked like the India of the British Raj. In the background, spectacularly located on top of a cliff, was a large pink fort, and in the foreground, several rather fierce-looking Indian tribesmen who were dancing around a large, hooded cobra, which, reared up on its tail, seemed to be almost as tall as they were. For a long time the three young djinn stared at it, batting one theory around and then another.

"On the face of it," observed John, "it's hard to see how Hermann Goering and these snake people could have been interested in the same thing."

"Except to say that we already know what Goering was interested in," said Philippa. "Expensive pictures. Diamonds. Gold. Anything worth a lot of money."

"Which this picture isn't, of course," said Dybbuk. "Fifteen hundred bucks. That's what the expert from the museum said it might be worth."

"*Might be,*" repeated John. "Even the experts get things wrong."

"But I don't think it's likely that, as a picture, it would be worth more than a da Vinci drawing," said Philippa. "Do you?"

"No." John picked up the picture like a newspaper and scrutinized it carefully. "Doesn't make sense," he said.

"Be careful, John," said his sister after a moment or two. "You're too near the fire."

But John wasn't listening. He was trying to see if he could make out the design on the medallions the Indian tribesmen were wearing around their necks. He hardly noticed how near the fire he was or the rising temperature of the paper on which the old watercolor was painted.

"John! Look out! You're going to burn it!" Just in time, Philippa snatched the picture from her brother's careless grasp before it could be scorched. She started to scold him for his negligence and then checked herself. "Wait a minute," she said. "There's something happening to the picture."

They all looked closely and saw that Philippa was right. There was indeed something happening to the picture or, more precisely, to the paper it was painted on. A series of symbols had started to appear, just above the pink fort — a sort of invisible message that the heat from the fire had made apparent again.

"Wow!" exclaimed John. "Secret writing."

Philippa held the picture near the fire once more and, very carefully, let the heat permeate the length and width of the paper, so that none of the message would remain invisible anymore. Finally, with all of the writing revealed, they laid the picture on the floor again and studied the message closely.

"It's not writing at all," Dybbuk said finally. "It's a series of dancing snakes. Each with a number attached to its tail."

"It looks like a series of doodles," said John.

"Except that no one would have gone to the trouble of drawing a series of doodles in invisible ink," said Dybbuk.

"And nobody would commit murder for a few doodles," said Philippa. "No, it's clear that these dancing snakes mean something."

"A sort of code, maybe," said John.

"Exactly," said Philippa. "Which we'll have to solve if we're ever going to find out what this is all about." She sighed. "If only Mr. Rakshasas hadn't gone away for the holiday. I bet he could shed some light on what this means and who these people are."

"Well, he can't have gone away for long," said John. "Didn't Groanin say that he'd left his lamp in London?"

"That's right, he did, didn't he?"

"In which case," said John, "he and Nimrod might be back home by the time we got there. London."

"London?" exclaimed Dybbuk. "Who said anything about going to London?"

"Do you want to stay here?" said John. "Those people who killed Max might come back."

"But how will we get there? It's cold over the Atlantic. And I'm not about to risk my neck flying a whirlwind again."

"There are *other* ways of flying, Buck," said Philippa. "Even for djinn."

"In which case we'll need money, passports, tickets, and clean clothes. And what's going to happen to Hendrix? We can't leave him here on an island any more than we can take him with us on a plane," Dybbuk reasoned.

"I've got an idea," said John. "Remember that boatman?" he asked his sister.

"Of course," she said. "His cat died. And he said he was lonely, didn't he?"

John nodded. "Exactly. He seemed like a kind man. And I'm sure he'd like a cat."

Dybbuk nodded. "Okay," he said. "Sounds good."

"That only leaves the small matter of the tickets and the money and the clothes." John picked up a stone and dropped it into the hot coals. "It looks as though we're going to have to spend some more time in the sweat lodge."

CHAPTER 6

THE GREEN DERVISH

Arriving in Calcutta from London, on the trail of the Nine Cobras cult, Nimrod and Mr. Rakshasas stepped out of an air-conditioned airport and grinned with pleasure as the furnace heat of India, with its pungent dry wind, warmed their faces. It was not yet midday but already the temperature was 116 degrees Fahrenheit — ideal if you happened to be a djinn, but almost intolerable for most mundane beings. Even the flies didn't bother them for the simple reason that insects dislike the intensely sulfurous taste of djinn blood. Calcutta's many beggars were a different story, however, and every time the car taking Nimrod and Mr. Rakshasas to their hotel stopped at a traffic light, children would tap at the windows for a few coins, or the devotee of some Hindu cult or ashram would try to hand over a leaflet explaining the benefits of meditation, yoga, or Ayurvedic.

The two djinn spent the night in the largest suite at the

Grand Hotel and left by whirlwind early the following morning while everyone was asleep. (Whirlwind is a djinn's natural mode of travel, not a magic carpet. Any self-respecting djinn wouldn't be caught dead riding something as clichéd as a magic carpet.) They were headed for nearby Sagar Island, which lies at the mouth of the holy River Ganges, and the Temple of Ninety-five Domes.

"I've always wondered why it's called that," said Nimrod as he steered the whirlwind to the edge of a large lake situated at the back of the temple. "I've counted the domes on several occasions and there are in fact one hundred and eleven."

"They're modest men, the mundanes who built this temple," replied Mr. Rakshasas. "Sure they wouldn't want it to be thought that they were showing off or anything. Saying you've got ninety-five domes when you've got one hundred and eleven is just them being humble. It's that and the fact that counting has never been seen as all that important in this part of the world. One rupee fairly got is worth a thousand that are not."

As soon as they had landed by the shore of the lake, Nimrod and Mr. Rakshasas collected several large lily pads, and on these placed some lit candles as well as several handfuls of jelly beans that Mr. Rakshasas had brought especially from a candy shop in London. Then they pushed the little flotilla out onto the beautifully serene lake and waited.

While they waited, Nimrod ate some of the jelly beans. "I'd forgotten how good these are," he told Mr. Rakshasas.

"It's a sweet tooth you're having, Nimrod, right enough. But don't eat any more or I'll have none to offer Himself if he's eaten all of the jelly beans we already sent him."

"Is the Green Dervish so very fond of jelly beans?"

"Oh, yes. Especially the green ones. 'Tis their simplicity he likes the best, I'm thinking."

At last a figure appeared on the horizon. Seated cross-legged on a dolphin — which is not an easy way to ride a dolphin — he came toward them, steering the creature with a long black walking stick. Wearing only a tiny orange loin-cloth and a garland of matching orange flowers, the Green Dervish was well-named, for his skin was a greenish shade of dark brown. Powerfully built, clean shaven, handsome, and with his spectacularly long black hair gathered in his lap, the Green Dervish, who in reality was an angel, looked more like a wrestler. He came to the shore where the two djinn were standing but did not dismount from the dolphin.

Mr. Rakshasas put his hands together in front of his heart and bowed. *"Namaste,"* he said, using a popular Hindu salutation. Nimrod did the same.

"Namaste," said the Green Dervish. With his little finger he touched a small green emerald that was attached to his forehead and turned the finger toward the two djinn. A warm green light enveloped them for a few moments, nourishing the marrow in their bones and the secret fires in their souls.

"Thank you," said Mr. Rakshasas. "That was a most agreeable sensation."

"And thank you for the jelly beans. Do you have any more?"

Mr. Rakshasas handed over the last bag and bowed again. "This is my good friend, Nimrod," he said.

Nimrod bowed again.

"You are welcome," said the Green Dervish, and popped another jelly bean into his mouth.

"We seek information," said Mr. Rakshasas.

"About the Naga cult of the Nine Cobras?" asked the Dervish, for, unlike djinn, angels can read minds. "Yes, I can see that. And it is as you had already guessed. The Nine Cobras is the successor of the Eight Cobras that existed many years ago."

"As always you understand everything," said Mr. Rakshasas, smiling kindly at the Green Dervish. But it wasn't merely the Green Dervish's opinion that was being sought here. There was also a sort of supernatural diplomacy that needed to be attended to. India is an ancient country, full of traditions and local customs that even the djinn must pay attention to. As well as the Green Dervish's advice, Mr. Rakshasas and Nimrod were subtly seeking his permission for them to use djinn power on the Indian subcontinent.

"I dislike these wicked cults as much as you do, Rakshasas, old friend," said the Green Dervish. "But destroying them is something else. Even a djinn as old and experienced as you will have to be very careful. Among the people of this country, snakes are held to be holy, for it is believed that they bring the rains and that those who die of snakebite will be resurrected. Such cults attract the weak-minded and the credulous, of whom there are a great many in this wonderful country."

Mr. Rakshasas nodded. "A weapon which you don't have in your hand won't kill a snake, I'm thinking," he said. "Besides, it's not the snakes I'm after, it's the devils who handle them."

"I will help you as much as I can," said the Green Dervish. "But first I must ask you a service, djinn, for while many have asked this of me, my vows do not permit my leaving this place. There are two *bagho bhuths*, which I would ask you to get rid of, for they have killed many people in these parts. Several hundred it is said. Too many, to be sure. What is certain is that they are particularly aggressive and seem to enjoy killing people more than they enjoy eating them."

"*Bagho?*" said Nimrod. "That's the Bengali word for tiger, isn't it? Surely you need a tiger hunter, sir."

"These are no ordinary tigers," insisted the Green Dervish. "They hunt as a pair. I have spoken to Bonobibi, the forest angel, and she tells me that these are in fact djinn, like yourselves, who choose to live inside the skins of these two man-eaters. Which is probably why local people call them *bhuths*. Ghosts." He shrugged and ate another jelly bean.

"A pair of tigers, you say," said Mr. Rakshasas. "Sure I once heard of a pair of crocodiles who were possessed by evil djinn who liked the taste of human flesh. In a village not so very far from here." He stroked his beard thoughtfully. "Those two crocs were never caught. Not as far as I know. It may be that those two djinn were looking for a change of skin. Which is as good as a rest, right enough."

"Already I perceive that you are more than equal to this

task," said the Green Dervish. "Set a djinn to catch a djinn, I always say."

"We'll see what we can do," agreed Mr. Rakshasas.

"Come back when the tigers are gone and we'll talk again. But try to remember that tigers are no less important to these people than snakes." The Green Dervish clapped his hands, summoning three priests from the Temple of Ninety-five Domes. "These priests will tell you where to look." The Dervish tapped the dolphin on the head with his stick and, still eating his jelly beans, floated away again.

Nimrod raised his eyebrows. "Am I to take it that we must hunt tigers without killing them and without being killed ourselves?"

"There's more than one way to skin a cat," said Mr. Rakshasas and, sitting down on the grass, started to think of other ways of skinning a cat than killing it.

The three priests of the Temple of Ninety-five Domes were called Mr. Chatterjee, Mr. Mukherjee, and Mr. Bannerjee, and each wore the white robes of a *sadhu*, which is an Indian holy man. Patiently they sat around Mr. Rakshasas and waited for him to finish thinking.

"These ghost tigers, the *bagho bhuths*," he said eventually, addressing his question to the three priests, "where and when was the last attack?"

"This very morning," said Mr. Chatterjee.

"At seven o'clock," said Mr. Mukherjee.

"A villager collecting honey about three miles from here," said Mr. Bannerjee.

"Then we will not have far to go," said Mr. Rakshasas. "It's a good omen, for no man except a fool travels a long way to meet a hungry tiger. What kind of place is it — where the honey collector was killed?"

"It is a fishing village," said Mr. Chatterjee.

"In a mangrove swamp," said Mr. Mukherjee, who never spoke until Mr. Chatterjee had spoken first.

"It is a bad place for men," said Mr. Bannerjee, who always spoke last. "But a very good place for tigers."

"We will need a boat," said Mr. Rakshasas.

"We have a boat."

"Fifty feet long."

"With a twenty-horsepower engine."

"Excellent," said Mr. Rakshasas, rising stiffly to his feet. "We will also need two large metal tubs, two gallons of goat's milk, six bottles of dark rum, six bottles of brandy, and several pounds of sugar."

The three priests looked at one another and then at Mr. Rakshasas, whereupon each of them shrugged, in turn.

"If you remember," said Nimrod, "we brought some supplies with us, from our hotel in QWERTYUIOP! Everything that's needed, I should say. Or had you forgotten, Mr. Rakshasas?"

"I had forgotten that, yes," said Mr. Rakshasas, smiling at Nimrod. "We did bring some supplies, didn't we? Remind me where you left these supplies we brought."

"I took the liberty of putting them in the temple's boat." Nimrod smiled at the three priests. "I hope that's all right."

The three priests bowed to Nimrod as if to indicate that this was perfectly all right with them.

"Then we'd best be hurrying along," said Mr. Rakshasas. "Before the milk spoils in this heat."

Mr. Chatterjee took charge of the boat's steering; Mr. Mukherjee kept an eye on the map of the Sunderbans, which was the name of the huge mangrove swamp where they were going; Mr. Bannerjee squatted in the stern of the boat, keeping a watch out for tigers, who have been known to swim after boats and grab unwary fishermen.

The Sunderbans is the largest area of mangrove forest on earth and is home to more than a thousand tigers, which sounds like a lot until it is remembered that once there were perhaps twenty times as many. Lots of the Sunderbans tigers are man-eaters by choice rather than of necessity. A man or woman — or more often a child — in the mangrove forests is an easy and delicious meal for a hungry tiger, and among the local people it is not considered at all remarkable when this happens. What is perhaps remarkable is that it doesn't happen more often.

The spot where earlier that same day a honey collector had been killed by the two tigers — there were paw prints to prove this — was marked on the muddy bank by a honey pot placed upside down on a long pole. Seeing this, Mr.

Chatterjee switched off the engine and steered the long, narrow boat onto the bank where the man had met his death. By now it was growing dark and it was plain to the two djinn that the three priests were getting very nervous — for dusk is a dangerous time in the mangrove forest: It is when the tiger goes hunting. So, as soon as all the supplies were unloaded, Nimrod told them to push off.

"Come back at dawn," he told them.

"We cannot leave you here," said Mr. Chatterjee.

"It is very dangerous here," said Mr. Mukherjee.

"You will both be killed and eaten," said Mr. Bannerjee.

"Don't worry about us," insisted Nimrod.

"But you have no gun."

"You have no weapon of any kind."

"How will you kill the ghost tigers with a tub full of milk?"

"I was wondering that myself," admitted Nimrod, catching Mr. Rakshasas's twinkling eye.

The old djinn chuckled. "Sure there's many a good hen came out of a tattered bag," he said. "Now the three of you be off before we change our minds and ask you to spend the night here with us."

At this, the three priests were swiftly on their way, clearly terrified at the very idea of spending the night in the swamps.

"We'll need some sort of watchtower," Mr. Rakshasas told Nimrod when the sound of the boat had finally gone away. "To keep an ear and an eye out for those tigers. It ought to be at least fifty feet tall, and ideally it should be camouflaged. With a spotlight, probably. And a couple of comfortable armchairs. There should be some facilities for making tea, and some night-vision goggles or binoculars."

Nimrod set about creating the kind of facility envisioned by Mr. Rakshasas — for the other djinn used his own power only very rarely on account of his great age. "QWERTYUIOP!" said Nimrod when at last he was satisfied that he was visualizing the safest, most secret, and most comfortable watchtower imaginable. Suddenly, where before there had only been trees and bushes and mud and water, there was now a djinn-made structure that soared above their heads like a small rocket gantry. Their overnight accommodation completed, Nimrod turned his attention to watching Mr. Rakshasas pouring the milk, the brandy, and then rum into the two metal tubs.

"Tiger's milk," said Mr. Rakshasas, adding almost a pound of sugar to his mixture. He stirred the cocktail carefully, scooped some into a cup, and invited Nimrod to taste it.

"Actually, it's rather good," said Nimrod. "A little like a Brandy Alexander."

"I hope the tigers agree with you. I couldn't think of a better way to persuade them to stay still long enough for us to deal genially with them. In the proper djinn sense of the word. They are djinn after all. I was rather thinking that if this works, as I think it will, you might work a transmutation on them." He showed Nimrod a steel thermos he had brought from the boat. "And put them both inside this."

Darkness had taken hold of the mangrove forest like a great black sticky glove, squeezing a variety of nocturnal noises from the trees and the creeks and the bushy undergrowth. High in their watchtower, with only the fruit bats and each other for company, Mr. Rakshasas and Nimrod sat in two veranda chairs, watching the stars and the moon, and enjoying the sweltering heat. Neither of them spoke more than the occasional whisper and when the forest around them grew silent, Nimrod guessed that something was up. Peering through the darkness at Mr. Rakshasas, he saw the older djinn nodding back at him, with a finger pressed to his lips.

Nimrod tried to remain completely still but could do nothing about the curious prickling sensation of his skin and his hair standing on end. A strong smell of death, meat, and blood came drifting up from the ground immediately below their vantage point. Then something big was moving around in the undergrowth that surrounded the bottom of the watchtower. Minutes passed before a low growl rumbled through the sticky gloom like the engine of a small motorcycle. It was a tiger all right. But was it one of the djinn tigers? In the darkness it was impossible to tell.

There followed a second growl from somewhere else, and Mr. Rakshasas held up two fingers. There were two tigers. Tigers are solitary creatures and it is rare for them to hunt in pairs. It had to be the djinn tigers.

Several more minutes elapsed and then they heard the sound of a large tongue lapping something liquid. Then another. There could be no doubt about it. The tigers were drinking the tiger's milk! Mr. Rakshasas grinned. His plan was working. "It won't be long now," he whispered into Nimrod's ear.

The lapping sounds and the two tigers' breathing and contented rumbling, amplified by the twin tubs their heads were in, grew louder, until the mangrove forest echoed with the noises of two drunken tigers. And still they kept on lapping at the tiger's milk, for these two tigers were very greedy indeed and did not stop until they had licked up every drop. Then, being very drunk, they became argumentative with each other and sparred fiercely for several minutes until they were overtaken by tiredness and, yawning loudly, they lay down to sleep.

Hearing the sound of snoring, Mr. Rakshasas switched on the spotlight and aimed it down at the foot of the watchtower. Lying on the ground were two enormous tigers, each nine or ten feet long and weighing five or six hundred pounds. And what was most remarkable about these tigers was not their size but their color, for these were melanistic tigers in that their coats were not striped, but almost completely black.

"Well," said Nimrod, climbing down the watchtower. "Black tigers, eh? That would certainly explain why these are thought to be ghost tigers. At night they must be almost invisible."

On the ground the two human-shaped djinn inspected the stupefied djinn tigers more closely.

"They're out cold," said Nimrod. "And they're going to

have the most dreadful headaches when they awake. I wouldn't like to be around when that happens."

"No, indeed," agreed Mr. Rakshasas, who was kneeling beside one of the passed-out tigers and examining its teeth. He nodded and then took a longer look at the other tiger. "It's my considered opinion that these two are twins," he said at last.

"Then they must also be djinn twins."

Mr. Rakshasas nodded. "Those two crocodiles I mentioned to the Green Dervish," he said. "I seem to recollect that it was djinn twins of the Ghul tribe that possessed them. Which leads me to suppose that these are the same two, and that they stopped being crocodiles and became tigers, most likely in search of a different kind of thrill." He shook his head. "Sure it was a long time ago, almost fifty years, so I can't remember their names."

"No matter," said Nimrod and when he had finished transmutating the two djinn tigers safely inside the steel thermos, he affixed a sticker to the outside that simply read TWIN DJINN. HANDLE WITH CARE.

"Let's hope we can keep a lid on this," said Mr. Rakshasas. "And I don't mean that thermos you're holding, Nimrod. Sure there'll be dancing in the swamps when news gets out that the *bagho bhuths* have vanished from the Sunderbans. So let's hope those priests don't guess who and what we are and blather it to their friends. It wouldn't do at all if the Nine Cobras cult found out that we were in its own backyard."

CHAPTER 7

SOME LIKE IT HOT

It was snowing when John, Philippa, and Dybbuk arrived in London from New York on their mission to find Mr. Rakshasas. A black cab took them from Heathrow Airport to Nimrod's well-appointed house near Kensington Gardens. Philippa rang the doorbell while John paid the driver, and Dybbuk hauled their small quantity of luggage up the front step. When no one came to the door, John took hold of the fist-shaped knocker, rapped it loudly several times, and then, crouching down, peered through Nimrod's mail slot. Another minute passed with still no answer, whereupon Dybbuk sat down on his suitcase and started to complain.

"That's just great," he said. "Now what are we going to do?"

Philippa buttoned the front of her coat and pulled her hat down around her ears. "We'll wait," she said firmly. "Groanin's probably gone to buy a newspaper or something.

He's like a bear with a sore head if he doesn't get his daily paper. I expect he'll be along soon."

"Suppose he's gone on vacation himself," offered Dybbuk. "It might be days before he comes back — or anyone else for that matter. They'll find our frozen bodies here on the doorstep."

"It could be worse," said John.

"How could it be worse?" demanded Dybbuk, who, for all his tough talk, wasn't nearly as resilient a character as either John or Philippa. "We don't have any money left. It's too cold to use djinn power, and we've got nowhere to sleep tonight. So how could it be worse?"

"You could be in the same position as your friend Brad and his father," said John. "Not to mention Max the butler, and Mr. Strasberg, the jeweler in New York. They're all dead, aren't they?"

Dybbuk thought about that for a moment, recognizing that what John had said made a lot of sense, and then nodded.

"Besides," added John, "I'm sure Phil's right. Any minute now Groanin will come along the street, find us all sitting here, and say —"

"What on earth are you doing here? I say, what the heck are you kids doing here?"

Dybbuk looked up and saw a tall, stout man with a bald head and one arm. He was wearing a bowler hat, pin-striped trousers, a long black coat, and carrying a copy of *The Daily Telegraph*. It was Groanin.

The twins jumped up and hugged him fondly.

"But what are you doing here?" repeated Groanin. "I thought I told you his nibs and Mr. Rakshasas had gone away."

"We were kind of hoping that by the time we got here, he would have come back," said Philippa.

"Well, he hasn't," Groanin said flatly. "Nor has Nimrod. I haven't heard a squeak out of either of them. Not since they left." He nodded at Dybbuk. "Who's he?"

"This is Dybbuk," said John.

Dybbuk rolled his eyes in his head and made a noise like a bassoon. He hated his name. "Buck. Just Buck, okay?"

"He's in trouble," continued Philippa. "He broke into a U.S. military base, stole a Leonardo da Vinci, and there are some people with poisonous snakes who want to kill him, probably."

"Is that all?" remarked Groanin. "Then you'd better come into the house. Before you catch your death of cold. Which, on an April day as cruel as this, seems a much more likely proposition than dying from snakebite." He handed Philippa his newspaper. "Here, hold this a minute." He put his door key in the lock, turned it, and pushed the door open in front of him. "Not that I know much about snakes, mind. Tigers! Now that's a different story." Groanin hurried them all indoors and into the kitchen and, while he made them a hot drink, he told them how he had lost his arm to a tiger inside the British Museum. The twins had heard the story before, but it seemed no less gruesomely fascinating the second time.

"Speaking of libraries," said Philippa. "I've had an idea. Since Mr. Rakshasas hasn't come back yet, maybe we could use his library. The one inside his lamp. I believe you said he'd left his lamp here when he went away with Nimrod."

"That's right, he did," said Groanin. "And it was most unlike him to do so. That library is his pride and joy. Not that I've seen it myself, mind you. But Nimrod said it contains more than ten thousand books."

"Aren't we forgetting something?" said Dybbuk. "Without djinn power we have no means of doing a transubstantiation and getting inside his lamp. England is no warmer than New York." He shivered. "Nor is this house."

"That's the way I like it," said Groanin.

"I can't see how we can transubstantiate here unless this house has a sauna or a steam bath."

"What do you think this is, sonny?" demanded Groanin. "The YMCA?"

"Then we'll have to make another sweat lodge," said John. "In the backyard. Of course we'll have to cut down the smaller trees, and then cover the structure with some of these old rugs. . . ."

"You'll do nothing of the sort," said Groanin. "I say, you'll do nothing of the sort. Damage the master's trees? And use his priceless Persian rugs for a — what did you call it? A sweat lodge? I should say not. As Nimrod's butler it's my job to look after his house and his yard, not to preside over its wanton destruction."

"Did Nimrod give you any idea of when he would come

home?" asked Philippa, thinking it best to change the subject. She waited for a moment and when Groanin didn't reply she said, "Have you even heard from him?"

The butler's expression grew darker and more troubled and he rubbed the stump of his arm, which always gave him pain when he was worried about something. "Not a word, miss." He shook his head. "And no, he didn't say when he and Mr. Rakshasas would return home. It's most unlike them, make no mistake."

"And you've got no idea where they've gone?" said John.

"All I know is that Nimrod came back from the dentist looking quite exercised about something and, a short while later, announced that he and Mr. Rakshasas were off on their travels, and that he was sorry he couldn't tell me where they were going, but that it was for the protection of me and some others who might be stupid enough to follow them. By which I assumed he meant you and John, miss."

"Thanks a lot," muttered John.

"Don't mention it."

"Anything else you can remember?" persisted Philippa. "Try and picture him telling you all this." Seeing a look of reluctance come upon Groanin's heavily jowled face, she added, "Mr. Groanin, they might be in trouble, so it could be important."

"Very well, miss." Groanin closed his eyes for a moment. "If you think it will help."

"Can you see him yet?" she asked. "In your mind's eye."

"I confess my mind's eye has become a little shortsighted,"

said Groanin. "Wait, there is something. He was holding something in his fingers when he told me they were going away. A stone of some kind. With some sort of picture or design on it."

"Did it look like this?" John picked up a pencil and, on a sheet of paper, hurriedly drew the design of the stone medallion his mother had swallowed. Groanin opened his eyes, put on his glasses, and stared at the drawing.

"That's it," he said. "The very same. What's this all about?"

John explained about the break-in, and how Mrs. Gaunt had sent Nimrod the medallion using djinnternal mail. "I think it's safe to assume," he said, "that wherever Nimrod and Mr. Rakshasas have gone must have something to do with that medallion."

"Which makes it all the more imperative," added Philippa, "that we get inside Mr. Rakshasas's lamp and use his library. If we can find out something about that medallion, then we'll have a better idea of their destination. And then go after them ourselves."

Groanin frowned. "I'm not so sure about the wisdom of that," he said. "After all, the master did say that not telling me where they were going was for my own protection. And yours, by implication."

"Yes, but he doesn't know about the attempt on Dybbuk's life," said John. "Or the full details of the break-in at our house. We've got no choice but to follow him now. Until we catch up with Nimrod and Mr. Rakshasas, Dybbuk's life is in danger. Perhaps ours as well."

Dybbuk shivered, not with cold but with horror. He had become almost used to the idea of his life being in danger, but when someone else mentioned it, he started to feel afraid again. And to relive some of the terrible things he had seen back in California. The idea of ending up like Max or Brad was not appealing. He'd had several bad dreams about Brad and Mr. Blennerhassit already.

By now Groanin could see the logic of what John and Philippa were saying. They simply had to get into Mr. Rakshasas's lamp. But how was he to help them do that? "Let me see," he said. "Somewhere hot enough for you three to recover your djinn powers and effect a transubstantiation, is that it?" He nodded. "Come to think of it, I might know the very place."

Driving Nimrod's Rolls-Royce, Groanin took the three djinn children to Kew Gardens, which, while not necessarily the largest, is certainly the oldest botanical garden in the world, and a very popular attraction for visitors to London, especially during the summer months. Near the center of the Gardens is the Palm House, a Victorian-built greenhouse that is as big as three aircraft carriers and in which are created conditions similar to those existing in a tropical rain forest. With the temperature inside always in the high eighties and the atmosphere made artificially humid by hidden steam jets, the Palm House is home to a jungle of giant bamboos, coffee bushes, rubber trees, banana plants, and mango trees, and the air is always sweet with the scent of frangipani and white spider lilies. Of course, it's not as hot as a sauna or a Native American sweat lodge or, for that matter, a desert, and Groanin and the children were inside the Palm House for almost an hour before the three young djinn felt the power returning to the marrow in their bones.

"I think we're ready for our entrance, Mr. Groanin," Dybbuk told the butler.

Groanin nodded and placed the djinn lamp of Mr. Rakshasas between an African oil palm and a betel nut palm and then mounted a white spiral staircase to keep a lookout. Fortunately, it being a cold, wintry sort of day outside, there were very few tourists in the Palm House, and the three djinn were transubstantiated and inside the lamp in less time than it took to say: "FABULONGOSHOOMARVELISHLY-WONDERPIPICAL!" (Philippa), "ABECEDARIAN!" (John), and "ZYGOBRANCHIATE!" (Dybbuk).

Now, because the inside of a djinn's lamp or bottle exists outside time and space, normal three-dimensional space does not apply. Some djinn who choose to spend a lot of time inside a lamp — such as Mr. Rakshasas — create a living space for themselves that is as large as a house so that, except for the absence of windows, it would be impossible to imagine oneself inside any kind of an object at all. And this was certainly the first impression John, Philippa, and Dybbuk had of the inside of Mr. Rakshasas's lamp. The interior was huge.

"I don't know why," said John, "but I always felt rather sorry for old Rakshasas, having to spend so much time in his lamp. I thought it would just be some stuffy old room he had in here. But look at this place. It's enormous."

Dybbuk grunted and shook his head. "It's not what I'd call comfortable," he said. "It's just a library."

"Yes, a library," said Philippa, who was slightly awestruck at the size of the place. She looked up, she looked down, she looked from side to side, and in every direction she looked there were shelves of books. A wrought-iron staircase led to the stacks of shelves above and below. "But what a library. There must be thousands of books in here."

"What sort of book are we looking for, anyway?" asked Dybbuk, swallowing a charcoal pill to ward off the feeling of claustrophobia he was already experiencing — a common sensation among the djinn. The sight of so many books made him feel almost as uncomfortable for, not unreasonably, he connected books with schoolwork, which was not something he cared for at all.

"Anything on snakes, I guess," said Philippa. "And snake cults." Remembering the picture Dybbuk had found inside Goering's baton, she added, "And Indian companies, and codes, too, probably."

"That's not going to be easy," said John, examining the first two or three books that came to hand. "None of these books seems to be in any kind of order."

"That's impossible," said Philippa, turning to look at the nearest shelf and finding a book on astronomy next to one on gardening that was next to a book about Salt Lake City. Running up the stairs onto the floor above she looked at another shelf that seemed to be home to everything from a novel by Charles Dickens to a book about the sculptures of Rodin.

"This is ridiculous," she complained, as she came back downstairs. "How can anyone stand a library with no kind of order? How does he ever find anything?"

Dybbuk laughed. "So how *are* we going to find what we're looking for?"

"Maybe there's a kind of order that we just haven't understood yet," said Philippa. "Either way, we'll have to split up and search in different sections. John, you go downstairs. Buck, you go upstairs, and I'll stay on this level."

Dybbuk rolled his eyes and groaned loudly. "I hate libraries," he said, moving sulkily toward the stairs. "Oh, by the way. Something you might like to remember when looking for a book on snakes: The proper word for the study of reptiles — it's 'herpetology.'"

"I'll keep it in mind," said John and went downstairs.

Philippa walked slowly along a dim, narrow corridor that was lined with shelves and shelves of books, glancing from side to side at the various, unrelated titles and trying to pretend that there was nothing creepy about the library, but knowing in her bones that there was. For one thing, the light switches worked automatically so that whichever section of the corridor she was standing in was lit while the section in front of or behind her was completely in darkness. This made her feel isolated and alone, even though she could easily hear John chatting away to himself, and Dybbuk whistling loudly.

For another thing, there was the sound of a large pendulum clock ticking, although there was no obvious sign of a clock. And everything creaked like the inside of an old ship.

Creepiest of all, however, was the strong sensation she had that she was being watched by someone — this despite the knowledge she had that Mr. Rakshasas lived in the lamp by himself. The sensation that she was being observed became a certainty when, removing a book from a shelf, she saw something or someone move quickly away in the darkness on the other side of the shelf.

"Who's there?" she called. When there was no answer, she added angrily, "If this is you fooling around again, Buck, you're going to be so sorry."

Then she felt a chill run up and down her spine as, somewhere far away in the library, Buck started to whistle again — the same flat, almost tuneless melody he was always whistling. Normally she might have been irritated to hear anyone whistling in a library, but on this particular occasion she was grateful for it. The idea of being alone with — well, whatever it was, would have been too horrible.

Something in the darkness moved once more. "John?" she said, almost whispering now. "Is that you?" But even as she spoke she knew it wouldn't be her brother. Perhaps because he was her twin, John wasn't the kind of brother who went in for trying to scare his sister. That would have been like scaring himself and certainly he would have felt any fear that Philippa experienced.

Another sound. This time, pages turning in pitch-darkness

somewhere behind her now, so that there was no way back to John and Dybbuk without confronting it, whatever it was. Almost simultaneously it occurred to Philippa that it might actually be Mr. Rakshasas himself and that, perhaps, he had never even gone on a trip with Nimrod. She called his name, but there was no reply. The fear in her started to give way to anger.

"Look here," she said. "I don't know who you are but I'm a friend of Mr. Rakshasas. A very good friend, too. And he wouldn't appreciate your scaring me like this. Not at all. Do you hear?"

"Little fool," hissed a reptilian voice. "Don't you know never to enter another djinn's living lamp or bottle without his permission? You could have been killed. All of you."

The light in the next section of the corridor came on, and Philippa found herself face-to-face with a hideous but vaguely human-looking lizard. Except for the fact that the creature had already spoken and was wearing a neat gray suit, she would hardly have dared speak to him.

"What — I mean, who are you?" she stammered.

"I am the bottle imp," hissed the creature. He pulled a book off the shelf, opened it, and quickly turned the pages with a long sharp claw before thrusting the open volume into Philippa's hands. "Here," he said. "Read."

Philippa took a deep breath, glanced at the title of the book, which was called the *Oxford Book of Imps*, and then at the page that was open.

"This part," said the imp, tapping impatiently at one

particular paragraph with his long claw. "There. Read aloud. Please."

" 'There are several kinds of imps,'" said Philippa, reading loudly in the hope that John and Dybbuk might hear her and come to her assistance. " 'There are the children of hell. There are creatures of Beelzebub. There are mocking imps and there are petty fiends. There are flibbertigibbets, about whom the less said the better. There are frolicsome imps and there are imps that once were children. There are little demons and evil spirits. And there are bottle imps that the djinn employ to guard the lamps and bottles wherein they sometimes live.'" Philippa paused for a moment and looked up.

"Read on," insisted the bottle imp.

"'Imps, some of whom were sorcerers or their apprentices in a previous life, are often regarded as being venomous but strictly speaking, this is not true. Because of the imp's unpleasant taste for rotting animal flesh, the bacteria in its mouth are extremely dangerous and have often caused death to humans and even djinn who were unlucky or foolish enough to be injured by the teeth or claws of one of these ancient creatures. Even a small bite or scratch inflicted by an imp can be fatal if not medically attended to.'"

"My name was Liskeard Karswell du Crowleigh," said the bottle imp. "And I was once a great sorcerer, and you're very lucky I didn't attack you as I'm supposed to."

"I'm very sorry," said Philippa. "But Mr. Rakshasas never told me that there was a bottle imp in his lamp."

"Of course he wouldn't tell you," sneered the imp. "It's

not the sort of thing you go around telling other people about. Does your father go blabbing that you've got a burglar alarm?"

"No," said Philippa. "But what I said's true. My friends and I really wouldn't have come in here if we'd thought Mr. Rakshasas would have minded. Not for a minute. Only he's disappeared, you see. Or at least nobody knows where he is. And we were looking for some clues as to where he might have gone and what might have happened to him."

"What sort of clues?"

"I dunno." Philippa shrugged. "A book, maybe."

"Any particular book? You see, I'm also the librarian."

She resisted the very obvious temptation to tell Liskeard Karswell du Crowleigh that he wasn't doing a very good job and that the library was more disorganized than the epicenter of an earthquake. "I'm not exactly sure," she said.

By now the sound of Philippa's conversation with the bottle imp had summoned John and Dybbuk, who, on seeing the imp, had armed themselves with a metal paper spike and a pair of scissors, neither of which would have been a match for the imp's sharp teeth and claws. Catching sight of his sister's skeptical eye, John shrugged and said, "These were the only weapons we could find. Our djinn power doesn't seem to work in here."

"That is because Mr. Rakshasas prefers it that way," said the imp. "In case your power should cause anything to be lost or mislaid."

Dybbuk laughed scornfully. "I can't see how that would

be possible," he said. "I've seen trash cans that were better organized than this library."

"That is because you do not understand the system," said the bottle imp. "Mr. Rakshasas himself often used to complain of not being able to find things in here. That was until Nimrod organized the wish catalog, as a birthday gift for him. You only have to wish to find your book and it will be brought to the reading room."

"And where's that?"

"Next to the bedroom."

The imp led the way along another long corridor and then up a flight of wrought-iron stairs that clanged like a bell underneath their feet.

The reading room was the size of a tennis court and furnished with a desk, a map table, a newspaper rack, more shelves, and several handsome red leather library chairs.

"Cool," said Dybbuk. "It's like a gentlemen's club."

"Take a seat," the imp told them. "And make a wish. Your books will be brought to you. But try to be specific. If you don't know the author, wish for the general subject and then a one-sentence description of what it is you'd like to read about."

"Subject, herpetology," said Dybbuk.

"Snake cults of the Indian subcontinent," added Philippa. "Handling and worship."

"And art," said John. "Paintings. Company paintings. Also from the Indian subcontinent."

"Codes and ciphers," said Philippa, which was about as specific as she could manage regarding this subject.

"And don't forget Hermann Goering," said Dybbuk. "Art collector and Nazi."

The three children paused as they tried to think of another subject that was relevant to their inquiry and, when nothing came to mind, they sat back in their library chairs and drummed their fingers impatiently on the armrests.

A minute or so passed before the first book floated into the library and deposited itself on the table. Philippa picked it up, looked at the title, which seemed quite promising, and started to read. Other books swiftly followed and soon all three children were absorbed in their chosen books.

Written by a Colonel Mountstuart Wavell Killiecrankie, M.C., the book Philippa had wished to read described the origin and history of the Aasth Naag, a snake cult founded in 1855 in Kathmandu, the capital of modern Nepal. To her considerable astonishment, Colonel Killiecrankie described how the leader of the cult, a man called Aasth Naga, had come into possession of four wisdom teeth stolen from the mouth of a young boy djinn named Rakshasas. Aasth Naga had used these teeth to fashion a talisman — a snake made of gold and a huge emerald called the Koh-E-Qaf, famously shaped like the head of a king cobra.

Using this talisman, Aasth Naga had made the boy Rakshasas his slave, choosing to demonstrate this same power to his fanatical followers through a wish that had made him immune to the bite of any poisonous snake. The colonel described how people would bring cobras and kraits from all over Nepal and Nagapur, a northern province of India, to bite Aasth Naga. On one famous occasion, Aasth Naga had allowed himself to be bitten by no less than eight king cobras without any ill effects, and it was this feat that became celebrated in the name of the cult that then grew up around him.

Two years after the cult was founded, Indians fought a war of liberation against their colonial masters, the British. Naturally, Colonel Killiecrankie's book made much of Indian cruelties while making light of the barbarities inflicted by his own side in suppressing the so-called "mutiny." A treaty was signed between the British and the king of Nepal — the Rana — by which Nepal agreed to help the British. Aasth Naga opposed the treaty, however, and, learning that he intended to lead his many and fanatical followers in a second mutiny against the British, Colonel Killiecrankie, commanding a regiment of Nepalese Gurkhas, had acted decisively, killing Aasth Naga and stealing the cult's famous talisman, the golden Cobra King.

And there, the colonel's self-serving account of the cobra cult of Kathmandu ended — rather abruptly it seemed to Philippa, as if he had not had time to complete it.

"Do you think that it's the same Rakshasas?" Dybbuk asked Philippa when she had finished describing the contents of the colonel's mercifully short book. "I know we djinn live a long time, but he would have to be more than a hundred and sixty years old, wouldn't he?"

Philippa shrugged. "How old is your great-aunt?"

"A hundred and thirty."

"Well, our grandmother is almost two hundred," said John. "So it just has to be Rakshasas whom the colonel was writing about. Why else would Rakshasas and Nimrod get so spooked by that cobra medallion?" He smacked his fist into his palm as his thinking unfolded some more. "Of course! They must be worried that the cult has been resurrected. Because whoever has possession of that Cobra King talisman gets power over Mr. Rakshasas."

"I agree," said Philippa. "It just has to be the same Rakshasas. Besides, look at the picture in this book. It's more or less the same design as on the medallion. Except that the squiggle beside the snake looks different."

"What I was just saying fits in with what's in this book," John said excitedly. "About paintings. A Company picture is a painting that was commissioned by the British East India Company, which was part of the Raj that ruled India until the mutiny of 1857. In the same way that a modern tourist uses a camera to take a picture of an interesting site, a Company employee would pay a local artist to paint some local scene to send back to England."

"I'll bet that picture is something to do with the Cobra

King," said Dybbuk. "If the talisman's made of gold and has a huge emerald head then that must be the reason why Hermann Goering thought the picture was as valuable as a drawing by Leonardo da Vinci. Because the fat old so-and-so must have known that the picture is a clue to getting your hands on a really priceless object." He shook his head and brandished the book he had been reading. "Not that there's anything about it in this book about Goering. Matter of fact it's the most boring book I've ever read." Dybbuk tossed the book aside, which earned him a reproachful look from Liskeard Karswell du Crowleigh and a yell from John when the book flew across the library table and struck him on the head.

"Hey, watch it, will you?!" yelled John. Rubbing his head, he picked up the book about Goering and replaced it on the table. "Now look what you've done," he said, noticing that one of the pages had come out of the binding. "You've damaged the book."

John opened the book on Goering with the intention of pushing the loose page neatly back into place and discovered that it wasn't a loose page at all, but a sheet of neatly folded notepaper, covered in tiny blue handwriting that looked like something an elf might have written. John recognized the hand immediately and felt his heart give a leap.

"This is Mr. Rakshasas's handwriting," he said, quickly scanning the first paragraph. "It's a note to himself . . . about the possible fate of Colonel Mountstuart Wavell Killiecrankie's East India Company picture!"

*   *   *

After the three children had transubstantiated themselves into Mr. Rakshasas's djinn lamp in the Palm House at Kew, there was little reason for Groanin to hang around. Keeping the lamp warm enough for them to get out of the lamp again was more easily achieved than keeping the children warm. So he retrieved the lamp from its position underneath the betel nut palm, dropped it into a small backpack he was carrying, and made his way outside.

Heading east toward the main gate and Kew Green where he had left the Rolls, the one-armed butler quickly realized that he was being followed by two men, with two others approaching from the sides, and it was obvious that they meant to intercept him, most probably with the intention of stealing the lamp containing the children. Groanin quickened his pace, but it was clear he was going to have to defend himself if the children in the lamp were not to be lost.

Everyone has heard of unarmed combat. But few people have ever heard of one-armed combat, and it so happened that Groanin was a black glove in Sharawaggi, which is a Japanese martial art based on lopsidedness and abnormality, and uses any physical defects and shortcomings as a trap for the unwary.

He dealt with the first two attackers expertly, leaving them sprawling and winded on the grass. The third attacker caught hold of Groanin's wrist only to find his own arm twisted like a key in a windup toy, which left the rest of him no choice but to somersault through the air or suffer serious injury. The man landed heavily in a bed of tulips with an impact that was enough to jerk a large king cobra out of his trouser leg. And, seeing Groanin, the cobra reared up on its tail and hissed aggressively at him, spitting venom that narrowly missed the butler's ear.

"Blimey!" yelled Groanin and, closely pursued by the snake and yet more thugs who appeared from behind some trees, he ran through the main gate toward the safety and sanctuary of Nimrod's Rolls-Royce. But even as he reached the Rolls another large king cobra appeared from underneath the car, preventing Groanin from taking hold of the door handle. And realizing that now he really was on the spot, Groanin pressed a black button on his remote-control key chain, initiating the discrimen — an emergency wish that Nimrod had thoughtfully attached to the Rolls for the benefit and protection of its one-armed chauffeur. As soon as it received the signal from the key chain, the driver's window slid down, the stereo system turned on, and one loud word boomed from the car's loudspeakers — the discrimen word that Nimrod had recorded on a compact disk: "THEOMORPHOLOGY!"

The radiators of nearly all Rolls-Royce cars are adorned with a silver mascot known as the Spirit of Ecstasy, or sometimes the Flying Lady. But the silver lady on Nimrod's Rolls-Royce was no fashionable bauble, having been modeled on Medusa, the Gorgon, whose very glance was enough to petrify anyone who looked upon her face, turning them to stone. As soon as the discrimen word was heard on the car's loudspeaker system, the mascot jumped off the radiator and, growing rapidly until it was the size of a real woman, faced down Groanin's several attackers, turning first the cobra nearest the car to stone, and then one of its human handlers.

Shielding his eyes from Medusa's terrible stare, Groanin opened the door of the car, leaped into the driver's seat, and drove off, breathing a loud sigh of relief. "Thank goodness for theomorphology," he said. "Whatever that is."

His mind was not entirely at rest, however, for a Rolls-Royce without its mascot is like New York without its Empire State Building, or an F.A. Cup Final without an F.A. Cup; and Groanin was already asking himself how he would be able to replace the Flying Lady on a car built in 1955. He need not have worried. Somewhere between Kensington and Kew, the mascot, now returned to its normal size, caught up with the car and climbed back on its rightful place atop the radiator, so that Groanin was able to complete his journey with all the proper style, to which, of course, he had long become accustomed, for it is a universal truth that many butlers are bigger snobs than their masters.

Quite unaware of the drama that was unfolding outside the djinn lamp — for Mr. Rakshasas had wisely thought to include a set of passenger ship's stabilizers in his library's construction — Philippa and Dybbuk listened carefully as John read out loud the short note Mr. Rakshasas had written to himself and which they had found inside the book about Hermann Goering.

"'The British behaved abominably in India before and

after the mutiny.'" John read slowly because Mr. Rakshasas's handwriting was very small and the light in the reading room wasn't very good, which struck him as odd, given that the reading room itself was located inside a lamp. "'And, to be sure, none behaved more abominably than Colonel Mountstuart Wavell Killiecrankie, M.C. Following his theft of the Cobra King from Kathmandu, Killiecrankie set about exterminating the cult that had brought it into existence, and of which I was the principal victim. He himself remained quite unaware of anything but the Cobra King's cash value — the flawless emerald "head" weighed more than 1,300 carats and is worth a pretty penny. But I say again no one British officer behaved more abominably than Colonel Killiecrankie, for although I owed him my own liberation from slavery and servitude to the Aasth Naag cult, I cannot bring myself to excuse all the cruel things he did to the poor native Indians and Nepalese who were its members. And it is hardly a matter of surprise that before he could even think about selling the Cobra King, he found himself in fear for his life and was forced to go into hiding. To no avail. For in 1859, the year after his book was published, the colonel was bitten and killed by a king cobra in circumstances that remain shrouded in mystery.

"'What is clear, however, is that the Cobra King was never found and that Colonel Killiecrankie, realizing his enemies were closing in, managed to hide the talisman. It is also clear that before his death he also managed to communicate with his family and to send them some instructions on how to find the Cobra King. No one knew what these instructions looked like but, over the years that followed the colonel's death, it became clear to me that the family had not directly profited by this knowledge, and I concluded that the talisman had been lost forever.

"'But in 1895, the colonel's daughter, Millicent, married a rich German banker named Otto Kringelein. They had a very beautiful daughter, Fania, who inherited her father's extensive art collection upon his death. This collection was confiscated by the Nazis in 1936. Among the pictures, which found their way into the possession of the Third Reich's Field Marshal Hermann Goering, was a simple East India Company picture of a scene from the British Raj. Goering treasured this picture above almost all others, and it seems likely that he discovered that somehow the picture concealed the key to a great fortune. The picture disappeared in 1945, and I think that it must have been destroyed during the last days of the war. But all my life I have dreaded that one day it, or the Cobra King itself, will be found and once again I will find myself enslaved by the thanatophidian cult of the Aasth Naag.'"

Dybbuk made a noise like a bassoon and rolled his eyes. "Thanatophidian," he said. "What the heck does that mean?" So he wished for a dictionary and when one from the library floated into his hands, he looked up the word and discovered that it meant "the study of venomous snakes."

"There's something I don't understand," said Philippa. "Let's say the cult *is* looking for the Cobra King." She shrugged. "What's the point? Anyone knows that Mr. Rakshasas is now so old he's almost run out of djinn power. I'm very fond of him, but what's the point of enslaving a djinn who's too old to do stuff like grant you three wishes?" She paused for a moment as a thought occurred to her. "Unless . . ."

"Unless what?" said Dybbuk, prompting Philippa when she remained silent.

"Unless," she said carefully, "the cult isn't just looking for the Cobra King of Kathmandu, but is also looking for some wisdom teeth to make a new talisman. In order to enslave some younger, more powerful djinn." She met John's eye. "Like us."

John nodded. Being Philippa's twin, he had been thinking much the same thing himself. "That would certainly explain the break-in," he said.

"So now what are we going to do?" asked Dybbuk. "If we stick around here in London, without djinn power we're liable to find ourselves kidnapped or worse. We ought to go somewhere warm. Where we can protect ourselves."

"Dybbuk's right," said John. "But where?"

"Until we work out a way of decoding the dancing snakes on the East India Company picture," said Philippa, "I think there's only one place we *can* go. To Kathmandu. In Nepal."

"I'll bet that's where Nimrod and Mr. Rakshasas have gone," said Dybbuk.

"Then we'll follow them," said John. He smiled and added, "Only Groanin's not going to like it there."

"What makes you think he'll want to come?" asked Dybbuk.

"He won't *want* to come," said Philippa. "But he'll think he *ought* to come. So he can look after us."

"A guy with one arm?" Dybbuk laughed, still quite unaware of the dramatic events that were taking place outside the lamp and of Groanin's heroic part in these. "As if."

CHAPTER 8

ICE-COLD IN CALCUTTA

The Maidan, a huge square of parched-looking grass in front of the Victoria Memorial Gardens, is one of the most popular public places in Calcutta, India, especially in the evening when thousands of Indians come to walk around, take carriage rides, eat roadside snacks, enjoy the breeze, or watch the nearby musical fountains. Cows graze, people argue, and fakirs demonstrate their extraordinary powers of endurance or physical flexibility. It is the loudly beating heart of modern Calcutta.

Nimrod and Mr. Rakshasas were wandering around the Maidan looking for some sign of the Aasth Naag cobra cult, for it was here that the Green Dervish, in gratitude for ridding the Sunderbans of the two djinn tigers, had advised them to begin their search. "You need not travel very far to find members of this terrible cult," he had said. "You will find its followers as near as Calcutta. In the Maidan. There you will encounter the enlightenment you seek, my friends.

Right under your very noses. But if you do travel only a little farther west, and you are in luck, now it may even find you. But a word of warning to you both, esteemed djinn. Be very careful of the cold while you remain in Calcutta. Wrap up warmly, especially at night. I am thinking you must even keep your windows closed and your door locked or you will catch a dreadful chill."

Since the evening temperature was ninety-nine degrees Fahrenheit, the possibility that the night would turn cold seemed a very remote one, and Nimrod said as much to Mr. Rakshasas. "That's the trouble with angels," he said, feeling rather exasperated with the Green Dervish. "Sometimes it's almost impossible to understand their prophecies."

Mr. Rakshasas shook his old, turbaned head. "Sure they wouldn't sound like angels," he observed, "if they told you the winner of the three-thirty race at Leopardstown. Angels are more subtle. They are indeed a riddle wrapped in a mystery inside an enigma. If it's plain speaking you want, then it's a weighing machine you need, not an angel."

"Perhaps," said Nimrod. "But sometimes it's a little puzzling, that's all I'm saying. The very idea that we could be in for a cold night. That, and what we're doing here now."

"'Tis not their way to be obvious," insisted Mr. Rakshasas. "We will understand what he says when the time is right and not before."

But Nimrod was hardly persuaded by the older djinn. "Light my lamp but I'm beginning to think we're on a wild-goose chase," he said. "We've been here for an hour and we've discovered nothing."

"You tread a little heavily," said Mr. Rakshasas. "But I can't fault your way around the facts. It's not that I don't think it's here, what we're looking for, you and I. Just that we're not able to see it. Not tonight, anyway. Perhaps if we came back tomorrow night. Besides, ever since we got here I've had this itch on the back of my neck that says we're being watched. And, to be sure, there's no point in laying a snare for a fox if the fox is watching you doing it over the top of his newspaper."

"Hold on a moment," said Nimrod. "Look there." He pointed at a young man sitting on the ground a few yards away who was entertaining the crowds with a display of snake charming. A huge king cobra, the biggest Nimrod had ever seen, was rising slowly from a basket and swaying in time with the snake charmer's flute. More remarkable was that from time to time, the charmer would reach out and touch the snake on the head. And as they watched, eventually the snake was encouraged to slither up the man's arm and to coil itself about his neck from where it continued to hiss aggressively at the crowd.

"I wonder," said Nimrod. "Could he be what we're looking for? Surely, only a true member of the Aasth Naag would dare risk a bite from such a big snake." He paused. "Or he could be a djinn, of course."

"To know that," said Mr. Rakshasas, "we'd have to examine

the snake and see if its fangs have been removed. And sure it's difficult to see how even we could do that in front of all these people."

"No indeed," said Nimrod. "I think we've already drawn enough attention to ourselves since we got here." He was referring to the fact that Messrs. Chatterjee, Mukherjee, and Bannerjee — the three priests from the Temple of Ninety-five Domes — had guessed the true identity of the Green Dervish's two visitors, and news about the djinn who had defeated the ghost tigers was now all over West Bengal. "We shall have to be more careful in the future. I completely forgot I'd made that watchtower. I should have remembered to get rid of it again before those three priests returned in the boat."

"Aye, it's always difficult to work a miracle and not expect people to give you a funny look." Mr. Rakshasas watched the snake charmer for a few more minutes and then shook his head. "No. I don't think he can belong to the cult. Look closely. He's not wearing a Naga stone — the medallion your sister sent you. I doubt he'd risk touching the snake without one of those around his neck."

"Yes, I take your point," said Nimrod and dropped a few rupees into the snake charmer's basket. "Come on," he said. "Let's go and have some dinner. I'm ravenously hungry."

The two djinn walked away from the Maidan in the direction of their hotel. Along the way several local people tried to sell them things: a carpet, a pair of carved wooden elephants, some flowers, a bag of pani puri. A little farther on, the disciple of a guru called Masamjhasara, from the Jayaar Sho

Ashram in Lucknow, offered them a CD of the guru describing his means of attaining spiritual enlightenment, while another man offered them his services as a tour guide. A third man took their photograph. India was nothing if not bustling and on the move and with so many people trying to sell them something, the two djinn didn't notice that their picture had been taken with a thermal camera. For most people this would hardly have mattered, but for djinn, who are made of fire and whose bodies emit a very distinctive dark red heat signature, it mattered a great deal. As Nimrod and Mr. Rakshasas were about to discover, and with a big price to pay. And in a way that the Green Dervish had already foretold. But, as Mr. Rakshasas might have said, that is the problem with prophecy: Sometimes it has to come true in order for it to be properly understood.

India is the home of curry and the hottest curry is called a *phal*. Curries are hot because of the number of chilies used in the recipe. The more chilies that are used, the hotter the curry. Djinn, being made of fire, enjoy very hot curries — especially *phal* — and are able to tolerate more chilies in a *phal* than any mundane could ever bear.

For many years, Mr. Rakshasas had been going to a family restaurant next to Calcutta's General Post Office called the Siraj-ud-Daula Curry House. The proprietor, a Mr. Hinduja, knew Mr. Rakshasas very well and, aware of his fondness for very hot *phal*, usually served him a very special twenty-one-chili *phal* that he called the *vasuki*. The *vasuki* was considered to be so hot that only one mundane, the restaurant's head-waiter, Mr. Mittal, could eat more than one mouthful. This had always served a very useful purpose for a djinn like Mr. Rakshasas since, in this way, Mr. Mittal was able to check that the *vasuki* was hot enough. On this occasion, however, the two djinn discovered that Mr. Mittal was at home, sick, and unable to come to taste test any *vasuki* prepared in the Siraj-ud-Daula's kitchen.

"Mr. Mittal was taken ill this afternoon," explained Mr. Hinduja. "Quite suddenly. Yes, I'm afraid to say that he is now indisposed. Not wholly sick nor in full measure ill, you understand, but very substantially unwell."

"Nothing he ate, I hope," said Nimrod.

"Most honored guest, no," insisted Mr. Hinduja. "Not here, anyway."

"Perhaps we ought to come back another time," Nimrod said to Mr. Rakshasas. "When we're able to rely on Mr. Mittal's services as a food taster. I should hate to take the risk of eating a curry that wasn't hot enough. I couldn't bear the disappointment."

But as he spoke, Nimrod sniffed the air hungrily, like a dog in a butcher's shop, and was noticeably hesitant about leaving the restaurant.

"Yes, perhaps you're right," said Mr. Rakshasas. "But sure, sometimes to eat without any risk at all is to go hungry."

Nimrod grinned. "Well said, Mr. Rakshasas."

And so saying, the two djinn sat down at the table offered them by Mr. Hinduja, which was the best in the restaurant, and then ate the hottest *vasuki* there had ever been in the history of curry, with not twenty-one but twenty-five whole chilies. In fact, it was so hot that the cook and the rest of the staff came out of the kitchen to watch the two djinn eat it — although only Mr. Hinduja was aware that they *were* djinn — and to marvel that anyone could eat such a hot curry.

Very hot curry has one great disadvantage, however: The strong flavor of a curry can easily hide the bitter taste of a sleeping potion. This was all the opportunity needed by the Aasth Naag, whose spies had been watching Nimrod and Mr. Rakshasas ever since they had left the mangrove swamps of the Sunderbans. And it was a relatively simple matter for one of the cult members to come in the open back door of the restaurant's kitchen and add a powerful but slow-acting sleeping potion to the hot *vasuki*, so that when Nimrod and Mr. Rakshasas asked for second helpings, as they always did, the two djinn consumed rather more than they had been expecting.

"That was a *phal, phal* better *phal* than I have ever had before," Nimrod told Mr. Hinduja when he had finished eating. Acknowledging the applause of the restaurant's admiring staff with a modest wave, he placed several large banknotes on the table and stood up. "It was positively Vesuvian in its incandescence, Mr. Hinduja. A veritable taste conflagration and quite deliciously fiery."

"Dessert?" asked Mr. Hinduja, offering the two djinn a menu.

Mr. Rakshasas shook his head. "I couldn't swallow another

thing," he said. "Not if my life depended on it. Besides, it's been a long day and I'm tired. In the morning, you'd better look for me in the fireplace, Nimrod, because tonight I expect to sleep like a log."

They were both yawning before they got back to the hotel, and they were asleep before they could put on their pajamas. They didn't even stay awake long enough to lock the door to their suite nor to close the French windows on their balcony, as the Green Dervish had recommended they should. Which made it quite easy for the thugs employed by the Aasth Naag to come into the suite and load the two unconscious djinn into a laundry basket.

From the suite Nimrod and Mr. Rakshasas were taken downstairs and, under cover of darkness, loaded into the freezer box of a refrigerated ice-truck, which was a sensible enough precaution in case either of the djinn woke up during the long journey by road that now lay ahead of them. For deep-frozen djinn are quite powerless.

Once they were on the road, the head thug telephoned the cult leader and told him the good news. After more than 150 years, the Aasth Naag had not just one djinn in its power again, but two.

It wasn't only the cult of the Aasth Naag who, in the wake of the affair of the ghost tigers of the Sunderbans, had started to spy on Nimrod and Mr. Rakshasas. Iblis the Ifrit also had a spy in Calcutta. His name was Upendra Downmidhary and, as soon as he heard that two djinn were in the area, he made several inquiries about Nimrod and Mr. Rakshasas at the hotel where they were staying. Then he telephoned Oleaginus, who arrived in Calcutta on the next plane from Las Vegas.

Neither man was particularly good at spying, however, and between them they managed to keep the Grand Hotel under twenty-four-hour surveillance without even noticing the two djinn being abducted. The following day, when the two djinn did not appear for breakfast, lunch, or dinner, Oleaginus began to suspect that something had gone wrong. "We saw them go into the hotel last night," he said, thinking aloud. "So either they're still in their suite, or they've transubstantiated and gone somewhere else without us noticing."

"They are djinn." Upendra shrugged. "That is what djinn do, is it not? Disappear, appear, in a puff of smoke."

"Not if they don't have to," said Oleaginus. "The fact is they prefer not to use djinn power unless it's absolutely necessary. Something to do with conserving their energy. Either way, we must have missed them somehow."

"If they have gone out for the day," said Upendra, "then perhaps we could search their room. I have a passkey I stole from one of the hotel maids."

Oleaginus disliked the idea of doing something so obviously criminal. Being entirely ignorant of India and its laws, he wrongly thought that he was in a country where thieves were punished by having a hand cut off. At the same time, however, searching their room seemed like a very good idea. That way he might obtain some hair from a brush or perhaps even a fingernail that would enable him to put a binding on

159

the two adult djinn and bottle them up, according to his master's instructions. Iblis would be so pleased with him. It wasn't as good as capturing the twins, but surely it was the next-best thing.

He called the room on the hotel lobby phone in a last attempt to check if anyone was in there and while he waited for an answer, he let his greedy mind gambol through the streets of Monte Carlo, which was where he planned to live on the proceeds of his three wishes, like a modern Count of Monte Cristo. "No reply," he said after a while. Hanging up, he rubbed his hands. "Come on. Let's go and do some evil."

Using the stolen passkey, the two men let themselves into the huge suite with its two king-size four-poster beds, gold faucets, and three balconies. As they had expected, it was empty. But the closets were full of clothes, mostly Nimrod's, and it was plain that the two djinn had not checked out. "These djinn really know how to live, don't they?" observed Upendra.

"Of course they do, you idiot. Have you ever heard of a djinn that was poor? No? Of course you haven't. Only a moron would expect a djinn to live anywhere but in the lap of luxury."

"Yes, sir," said Upendra, and went into one of the enormous bathrooms.

"Why are you going in there?"

"To look for a hairbrush or a toenail, like you said."

"Idiot. I can see you don't know very much about the djinn. One thing they never do is leave a hairbrush lying

around. They always put them in the safe. Same with toenails."
As if to prove his point, Oleaginus pointed to a large wad of
rupees that had been left on one of the bedside tables.
"Money? That's a different story. They've really no respect
for money at all and wouldn't dream of keeping that safe.
Money's just something they can make whenever they need
some. But a hairbrush? Now that's something really valuable."

Oleaginus opened the closet and, using a heavy screw-
driver that he took from the attaché case he had brought with
him, forced open the door of the room safe in only a few
minutes. Inside, as expected, he found two hairbrushes, a
used handkerchief — no less useful to someone like him for
obvious, if nauseating, reasons — a small change purse containing a couple of fingernail clippings, and even —because
Nimrod and Mr. Rakshasas were unusually careful with such
matters — a pair of toothbrushes. All of these things would
have been exciting enough to the servant of Iblis. But there
was another object in the safe that he picked up and regarded
as if it had been the Holy Grail itself: the thermos that Mr.
Rakshasas had brought out of the Sunderbans.

"I don't believe it," Oleaginus said, breathlessly pointing
to the label on the thermos. "Look. It says 'TWINS.'" He
laughed out loud. "Oh, that would be too much to hope for,
surely. I mean, the last I heard, those two Gaunt kids, John
and Philippa, were in New York. Our people have them
under constant surveillance." He shook his head as if trying
to dislodge a few extra thoughts from his already overworked
brain cells. "But if that *was* the case, then why would Nimrod

keep this thermos in the safe? How many twins does he know, for Pete's sake? Here, where's that thermal imager I brought from the States?"

Upendra handed over his American colleague's attaché case. Oleaginus opened it up, folded out the imaging device, switched it on, and carefully placed the thermos under the lens. Inside the thermos, two dark red shapes paced up and down their glass cage, like little masses of hot protoplasm observed underneath an electron microscope. There could be no mistake about it. The thermos contained two djinn, all right.

"Bingo!" said Oleaginus.

"But if these *are* the twins, John and Philippa," said Upendra, who was more intelligent than the American, "then who is it that is being kept under surveillance in New York? Either your people are not doing their job properly, or . . ."

"Or what?" Oleaginus demanded irritably.

Upendra shrugged. "No, I can't think of an 'or,'" he admitted.

"No, but I can. They must be watching a couple of Elsewheres in New York. You know? Doubles intended to provide an alibi or a diversion. Of course you'd need an angel to make an Elsewhere. But from what I've heard those kids can be quite persuasive." He nodded, liking his theory. "Yes. That would make a lot of sense. It would certainly explain how they might come to be in two places at the same time. There, in New York, and here, in this thermos."

Oleaginus folded up the thermal imaging device, then

put it and the thermos in the attaché case and closed it. "Come on," he said. "Let's get out of here."

"But what about the hairbrushes? And the toenails?"

"Oh, forget them. A bird in the hand, so to speak. Besides, Iblis was quite clear that it's the twins he's really after." By now the grin on the face of Oleaginus was enormous. His three wishes were in the bag! Had to be! He shook his head, as if in awe of what he had achieved for himself. "Iblis is going to be so surprised when I hand them over," he said. "I can't wait to see his face."

CHAPTER 9

NUNC FORTUNATUS SUM

Arriving in Kathmandu after a ten-and-a-half-hour flight aboard a Gulf Air plane from London to look for the pink fort in the Company picture, Groanin and the three children found themselves in a seething Asian metropolis that was a world away from the kind of place they had imagined. Instead of steely eyed mountaineers, granite-jawed explorers, and inscrutable priests, they found themselves surrounded by hippies, carpet sellers, coach-loads of tourists, riot police, and saffron-robed student priests from places like Buffalo, New York, and Detroit, Michigan, selling the enlightenment they had found at one ashram or another.

"What's an ashram?" asked Dybbuk, glancing over the leaflet he had been handed only seconds after leaving the airport, and climbing into a battered taxi that was now taking them all to their hotel.

"It's a sort of religious retreat," explained Groanin. "For

those in search of quiet and meditation, and whatnot. A load of rubbish, if you ask me." He waved one of the student priests away from the open window of the taxi. "If it's enlightenment they're after, they should read an encyclopedia or a decent newspaper. They won't find it with their eyes closed, humming some daft mantra."

The twins looked at each other and smiled. It was always fun traveling abroad with Mr. Groanin. "What's a mantra?" asked John.

"A word they repeat over and over again to help them empty their heads of what little was in there in the first place."

"Why?" Dybbuk asked simply.

"Good question," said Groanin. "So that they might discover the meaning of life, I suppose. Or some such claptrap."

They checked into their hotel and then wandered around the city where a different kind of discovery awaited them. As well as the numerous snake charmers that were to be seen in Durbar Square, the exteriors of most of the city's many temples seemed to include some kind of cobra carving. In the Deotalli Durbar palace, the golden statue of a former king of Nepal sat on his throne sheltering under the hood of a giant cobra. They were certainly in the right part of the world as far as cobras were concerned.

Despite this, Philippa soon suspected that they had come to the wrong place, because none of the buildings in Kathmandu looked anything like the pink fort in the East India Company picture they had brought with them from London.

It was an opinion shared by a young man called Padma Trungpa who worked behind the front desk in the hotel where they were staying.

"I can tell you that this is not a Nepalese building in your picture," said Padma, looking at their picture. "To me it looks more like a fort in the northern Indian state of Uttar Pradesh, which is just south of Nepal. But even if you were to go there and search in such a way for such a fort as you are doing is to be looking for a needle in a haystack. India has more forts and palaces than it is possible even to imagine. I am afraid to say it, but you have set yourselves a most impossible task."

The little quartet went up to their rooms with only the return of the children's djinn power to stop them feeling wholly discouraged, for it was stiflingly hot in Kathmandu. Too hot for Groanin, who was soon complaining bitterly to the very children he had insisted on accompanying. "I don't know why I let myself be persuaded to come here," he said. "I don't think I've ever been as hot as this. Really I don't."

So, using djinn power, John made Groanin a big electric fan, which seemed to make him feel a little more comfortable — enough to stop complaining, anyway. Then John turned his attention to the Company picture that Philippa had spread on the table in his room, and more particularly, the baffling jumble of writhing snakes that ran along the bottom of the paper.

"Any idea what it means yet?" he asked her.

Philippa looked at it and shook her head. She had

understood very little of the book on codes and ciphers she had borrowed from Mr. Rakshasas's library. If anything, it had left her feeling more puzzled than ever. "Not so far," she murmured thoughtfully. "Only that it can't be a very difficult code. Or else why would Killiecrankie have written his message in invisible ink?"

"Good point," admitted Groanin.

"It reminds me of something," said John, staring hard at the line of dancing snakes. "But what?" And suddenly he remembered. "What am I talking about? Of course I know what it reminds me of. Why didn't I think of it before when we were in the library? And me a fan of Sherlock Holmes, too! This is just like 'The Adventure of the Dancing Men.' Which is one of the most famous stories Conan Doyle ever wrote. Except that instead of dancing men, these are dancing snakes."

Dybbuk groaned like a bassoon and rolled his eyes. "Are you going to tell us what you're blabbing on and on about?" he said, brandishing a Tibetan prayer wheel he had picked up off the coffee table. "Or am I going to have to beat it out of you with this thing?"

"Nay, give over and learn something for once," Groanin told Dybbuk. "John's right. I say, you're right, our John. Them snakes is just like the dancing men and that Sherlock Holmes story." He glared impatiently at Dybbuk. "Now if only we had thought to bring a copy from London, we could all remind ourselves how his nibs sorted out the code in his head, like."

"ABECEDARIAN!" said John, and four copies of *The Return of Sherlock Holmes*, the collection of stories featuring "The Adventure of the Dancing Men," appeared on the table in front of them. It was the same paperback edition as the one John had on his bookshelf back home in New York.

"That's the ticket," said Groanin.

"Elementary, my dear Groanin," said John.

"Now then, I suggest we all read the story. I say, read the story and then apply our minds to the solution of the mystery that lies in front of us. Just as Mr. Holmes would have done."

Dybbuk groaned again. "What? More reading? Seems like all I've done since I hooked up with you guys is read a lot of stupid books." He shook his head in exasperation. "ZYGOBRANCHIATE! I wish I know what this code meant and how it worked."

"Wishing doesn't work like that." John laughed. "You'd better check your *Baghdad Rules*," he told Dybbuk. "Section four, subsection three, paragraph one. 'You can't wish for what you don't know. You can only wish *for what you know*.'" It was a subtle distinction that few people could have grasped.

Dybbuk knew this of course, since he wasn't nearly as ignorant or contemptuous of books (including the *Baghdad Rules*) as sometimes he pretended to be. "I was just saying it," he said. "I wasn't trying to make it happen."

"Then why did you utter your focus word?" demanded Philippa. "If you weren't trying to make your wish come true?"

"Habit," said Dybbuk. "That's all. Just habit."

"Now then, children," said Groanin. He picked up one

of the copies of the Sherlock Holmes stories and opened it, bending the cover back against the spine in a way that made Philippa wince. "We've got a story to read. That is, if we are ever going to stand a chance of making Dybbuk's wish come true."

Dybbuk bit his lip. "Buck," he said. "It's just Buck, okay?"

Philippa had drawn a grid on a sheet of paper so that there were twenty-four squares. In each square she had drawn a snake from the code, or left it blank.

"According to Sherlock Holmes," she said, "*e* is the most common letter in the alphabet and even in a short sentence, it's likely to be found more often than any other letter. Looking at our code, the snake that points to the left and that has a five attached to its body occurs twenty-eight times. More than any other. Which, given what Holmes says, makes it likely that it's an *e*." She wrote the letter *e* next to this snake in her grid.

"Here's another thing," said Groanin. "Have you noticed how, with some of the snakes, the tongue is visible and with others, not? Again, given what Holmes says about the dancing men, it seems fair to conclude that the presence of a forked tongue is used to break the line of snakes up into words." He drew a line on the message after each snake with a tongue. "From which deduction, it's now clear that some of these words have only three letters.

"Now then, the most common words of three letters in English are 'the,' 'and,' 'for,' 'but,' 'not,' 'all,' and 'too.' If you add that to what Philippa has just said about the letter *e*, then we're able to make a guess at six whole words almost immediately. And doing that also gives us the letters *t* and *h*." He wrote a *t* and *h* in two of the boxes on her grid and then underneath the snakes on the message, and smiled. "This is just like doing the crossword," he said.

"Or Scrabble," said Philippa.

"I hate Scrabble," said Dybbuk.

John decided it was his turn and pointed to all the words that could be made of only two letters. "These must be two-letter words," he said and started to write down all the two-letter words he could think of. "Words like 'of,' 'to,' 'in,' 'is,' 'be,' 'he,' 'by,' 'or,' 'at,' 'it,' 'if,' 'on,' er . . ."

"'Er' is not a word," said Dybbuk.

"I know, I just couldn't think of any more two-letter words," said John.

"'As,' 'an,' and 'so,'" said Dybbuk, quickly filling in the list, which left John feeling that Dybbuk was probably better at Scrabble than perhaps he was letting on.

"All right, then," said Philippa, reviewing their progress. "Given what we know about *t* and *h*, that means we can identify which two-letter words are which. And, in turn, this gives us the letters *o*, *i*, *f*, *a*, and *n*." She added these letters to her grid and smiled. "We're getting there," she said. "We're really getting there."

She was right. Gradually, with the help of Sherlock Holmes and a process of simple elimination, they were able to see how the code was not really complicated at all. Snakes that had heads pointing to the top left hand corner of an imaginary square indicated the first six letters of the alphabet; and snakes that had heads pointing to the bottom left indicated the next six letters, if *i* and *j* counted as one letter. Snakes with heads pointing to the top right indicated the letters *n*, *o*, *p*, *q*, *r*, and *s/z*; while snakes with heads pointing to the bottom right counted for the letters *t* through *z*. Very soon Philippa and Groanin had written out Colonel Mountstuart Wavell Killiecrankie's message in full.

I scotched the snake not killed it. And fled to this terrible place of misery where I shall probably die at the hand of my enemies. But I am in luck now. And you, too, would do well to come down here and discover a king's ransom in the green eyes of the cobra king of Kathmandu. Look for the third snake. But beware the eighth. M.W.K.

But while the actual words were now plain to Groanin and the children, their true meaning still eluded them. Dybbuk groaned. "All that and we still don't know what the colonel's message means." He shook his head. "He wasn't taking any chances, was he? No wonder his family didn't find anything."

"What does 'scotched' mean?" John asked Groanin.

"'To hurt something dangerous,'" said Groanin. "But don't ask me to explain why that is. I've no idea. I know nothing about Scotland."

Dybbuk shook his head. "We must have made a mistake somewhere."

"There's no mistake here," insisted Groanin. "Take it from someone who does a lot of crossword puzzles."

"But it doesn't make sense," said John. "How can you say that you're about to die at the hand of your enemies? And then say that you're in luck?"

"S'right," agreed Dybbuk. "Rakshasas said Colonel Killiecrankie was killed by a king cobra. There's nothing lucky about that." Feeling frustrated, he slapped the Company picture with the flat of his hand and got up to wander around the room, stopping by a framed map of Nepal and northern India that hung on the wall.

"M.W.K.," said John. "Those are the colonel's initials all right. And there's nothing wrong with 'the green eyes of the cobra king of Kathmandu,' either. That all makes perfect sense. Maybe we *are* in the right city after all."

"Not according to the guy behind the hotel reception desk," said Dybbuk. He put his finger on the map and moved it from Kathmandu into Uttar Pradesh. "According to him, we should be concentrating our search down here somewhere."

"I'm afraid the lad's right," Groanin told the twins. "Architecturally speaking, we're way off the mark here." He opened a jar of baby food — which was the only kind of food he ever ate when he was away from England — and started to eat.

Dybbuk made a face. "I don't know how you can eat that stuff," he said.

"Nothing to it," answered Groanin. "You just open your cakehole and stick the spoon in."

Dybbuk laughed. "But it's gunk."

"Young man, I eat this gunk, as you call it, because my stomach can't abide any of that foreign muck. Curries and whatnot. This is sterilized. Food you could give to a baby with a clear conscience. And you can't get safer food than that."

"Baby?" Dybbuk was still laughing. "I wouldn't give that stuff to a dog."

Groanin frowned. "Maybe if you had a bad stomach, you might not find it so funny, young man. In fact, I wish you did have one, if only to wipe that stupid grin off your face." The days were long gone when Groanin, still possessed of a wish himself, had been more careful about using the word in djinn company. "Then, with any luck, you'd understand what it might be like to be me."

"Say that again," said Dybbuk.

"With any luck . . ."

"*Luck.*" Dybbuk grabbed the translation of Killiecrankie's message. "Yes — luck." He placed his finger under the words and started to read aloud: "'. . . And fled to this terrible place of misery where I shall probably die at the hand of my enemies. But I am in luck now.'"

He went back to the map on the wall and then let out a loud whoop, punching the air in triumph. Suddenly he felt so much better about himself. He'd figured out something important, on his own! Which made a very pleasant change from Philippa doing the brain work. Or, less often, John. At last he could look himself in the eye again.

"That's it!" he yelled. "That is it! It's so simple. I'm amazed you haven't figured it out yet, for yourselves."

John stared at the map blankly for a moment and shook his head, then he picked up the Tibetan prayer wheel and brandished it menacingly. "Are you going to tell us what you're talking about?" he demanded. "Or am I going to have to beat it out of you with this thing?"

Groanin groaned loudly. "Oh, let him enjoy his little moment of triumph," he said. "It's been long enough coming. And perhaps we shouldn't begrudge him it. His wish came true after all."

"Here's the answer," said Dybbuk, stabbing at the map on the wall with his finger. "Colonel Killiecrankie was making a play on words. A pun. He didn't mean that he was in luck, now. He meant that he was in Lucknow. Here. In Uttar Pradesh. In northern India. And only three hundred miles southwest of where we are now."

John, Philippa, and Groanin went to look at the map while Dybbuk continued dancing around the room with glee.

"I hate it when he's right," admitted Philippa and reached for her guidebook.

"'The state capital of the northern Indian state of Uttar Pradesh,'" said Philippa, reading from her guidebook, "'Lucknow is, perhaps, best remembered for the five-month siege of its British residents in 1857, during the First War of Independence or, as it is sometimes called, the Great Mutiny.'"

"It all fits in with the dates that we already know," said John.

"Of course it does," said Dybbuk, who wasn't about to tolerate any kind of challenge to his solution of where they should now concentrate their search for the pink fort and the lost Cobra King.

Philippa was flicking through the guidebook. "There's no mention in here of a pink fort in Lucknow, I'm afraid," she said.

"We'll find it when we get there," insisted Dybbuk.

"Awkward place to get to by plane," said Groanin, surveying the map. "I expect we'll have to fly there via Calcutta."

"No way," said Dybbuk. "Calcutta's in completely the opposite direction. Besides, who said anything about going there on a plane?"

"I hope you're not proposing that we go there by whirlwind," said Groanin.

"We've got full power back," Dybbuk said and then shrugged. "Why not?"

"I've never made a whirlwind before," admitted Philippa.

"Me, neither," said John.

"Well, I have," said Dybbuk. "From Palm Springs, California, to my great-aunt Felicia's house, on the Hudson River."

"You almost didn't make it," said Philippa. "That's what you said."

"Only because I went too far north. I should have stayed farther south, where it's warmer. Gone to Florida and then come up the Eastern Seaboard. Besides, we're in India now and, in case you hadn't noticed, it's hot. There's no way my djinn power is going to give out in this country."

But the next day — the day they had elected to fly to Lucknow — it wasn't Dybbuk's djinn power that was acting up, it was his stomach. He awoke feeling quite ill. "It's like someone is squeezing my insides with his fist," he said uncomfortably.

"You shouldn't have eaten all that curry last night," said Groanin, who was quite beside himself with satisfaction at having been proved right in the matter of "foreign food." "I told you not to eat any of that Indian grub. I daresay you don't think it's quite so funny now, young man. Me eating jars of sterilized baby food instead of all that muck you were wolfing down last night."

"It can't have been the curry that's making him feel ill," said Philippa. "All three of us ate it. Me, John, *and* Dybbuk. And I feel fine."

John stayed silent, feeling guilty, and hoping no one would remember Groanin's wish the previous day, that Dybbuk might have an upset stomach. John really hadn't meant to grant this wish at all but what with finding himself in possession of full djinn power for the first time in ages, and being still a little tired after the long flight from London, somehow he had just made the wish happen. "Subliminal wish fulfillment," Nimrod called it, when an inexperienced djinn granted a wish without being fully aware of it. He now realized with a shock that Groanin's wish must have been completely genuine.

"Can't you just wish it better?" he asked Dybbuk. "With djinn power?"

"Don't you think I've already tried that?"

John nodded. The fact was that using djinn power, he'd tried to cure Dybbuk's stomach upset himself but, uncertain of what he'd been doing, he thought he'd probably just made it worse. It was hard to say for sure.

"You guys will have to make this whirlwind by yourselves," whispered Dybbuk. "I'm much too sick to do it." Catching the look of uncertainty that passed between the twins, he added, "Relax. You'll be fine. There's nothing to it. Besides, you've got to start somewhere, and this is as good a place as any."

Groanin was shaking his head. "If you don't mind," he said, "I think I'll take a plane, after all."

"Don't worry, Mr. Groanin," whispered Dybbuk, clutching at his stomach. "I'll tell them what to do." He smiled weakly. "Think about it. If you crash in a plane, you're surrounded by a lot of jagged metal. But you crash in a whirlwind you're cushioned with air. Nothing's safer than a cushion of air, believe me."

Groanin closed his eyes and nodded. "I just know I'm going to regret this," he said. "I say, I know I'm going to regret this."

*　　*　　*

They went to a steep hill in the western side of the city. The hill commanded a sweeping view of the Kathmandu Valley, which, according to Philippa's guidebook, had once been a snake-infested lake. At the top of the hill stood the Temple of Swayambhu Ganapati, which was overrun with monkeys, pilgrims, and tourists. Away from the temple, near the parking lot, they found a quiet space where John set about whipping up a whirlwind. His first attempt flipped a car on its roof and his second spun away and out of control, chasing some of the monkeys all the way to the Natural History Museum at the southern base of the hill.

"Bloomin' heck!" complained Groanin. "You're going to get us all arrested, John. For Pete's sake, get it right before someone sees us."

"Someone has seen us," said Philippa and pointed across the parking lot to where an old monk in red robes was now bowing vigorously to them, his hands clasped reverently in front of him, and muttering a prayer. "Keep going, John," she added. "It's too late now to worry what he'll think."

"Looks like you've made his day," said Groanin as, at the third attempt, John managed to lift them all off the ground with a good-sized whirlwind. "I expect you've restored his faith in whatever it is he believes in."

"Well, I'm all for doing that," said Philippa and waved cheerily at the monk, who, to her delight, waved back.

"Talk about chariots of the gods," said Groanin, trying to hold on to something, but finding thin air wasn't much of a handhold. "Bloomin' heck!"

Dybbuk groaned loudly as the whirlwind lurched underneath them and then accelerated away, as if pulled by a team of invisible horses. A second or two later, he leaned over to one side and threw up onto the heads of some tourists, much to Philippa's disgust.

"Feeling better?" she asked crisply.

Dybbuk smiled weakly. "Better?" he said quietly. "Yes. A bit."

"Those poor tourists," she said.

But the mayhem caused by John's whirlwinds and Dybbuk's stomach wasn't yet over. As the body of air moved rapidly up and away from the hill, John tried to turn it on its axis, which caused the whirlwind to incline slightly, and then dramatically, so that they were almost tipped out of the top of it.

"Steady on!" yelled Groanin. "You'll dump us all out on the ground!"

"Sorry," said John, as once again Dybbuk threw up, this time onto the same troop of monkeys John's first whirlwind had chased down the hill.

"Straighten up," said Dybbuk, wiping his mouth on the back of his sleeve. "Push your heels against the wind. It will help your mind to focus on what you're trying to do."

John did as he was told and dug his heels hard into the eddying air. Immediately the whirlwind corrected its angle.

"Not too much," said Dybbuk.

"I think I'm getting the hang of it," shouted John, for

by now the noise of the wind in their ears had become rather loud.

"Blimey, I hope so," groaned Groanin. "I'll be leaving me own breakfast behind if this keeps on."

The whirlwind spiraled down the valley, passing directly over a hiker's hostel so that the wind's tail tore the corrugated-metal roofs off the bathrooms and toilets, and the annoyance and embarrassment of all those seated below was quite obvious to the few who were seated above. Despite his bad stomach, Dybbuk still managed to laugh.

"I should let you fly a whirlwind more often, John," he said.

"We're too low," said Philippa. "Everyone can see us."

It was true. Everyone on the ground could see the three children and the one-armed man sitting quite comfortably inside the moving vortex. A traffic policeman tried in vain to direct them away from the busy Durbar Square, and then ducked as a satellite dish the whirlwind had torn off the side of the Bonnington Burger Bar flew through the air toward him. Builders stacking bricks and shoveling sand at the not-yet-finished Hilary and Tenzing Base Camp Hotel scattered out of the wind's errant path. And in any city but Kathmandu, chaos would surely have reigned. But the capital city of Nepal is renowned for its tolerance and easy, laid-back ways; in truth, there were only a few people who reacted in a negative way to the sight of four Westerners flying, cross-legged, through the air. For many who watched, this was why they had come to Kathmandu in the first place, and they were of

the opinion that here were four masters of the secret art of
yogic flying, which is an aspect of transcendental meditation.
To these people, what they were witnessing looked like the
very proof of the enlightenment for which they were searching in the ashrams and temples. And so priests bowed, holy
men raised their hands to the sky, gurus applauded, yogis
adopted the lotus position and began to hop across lawns as
if they also might achieve takeoff, women threw flowers, and
hippies made peace signs and grinned vacantly.

"Cool," Dybbuk said and made a peace sign back to them.

"Which way is Lucknow?" asked John.

"That way," said Dybbuk.

John looked at Dybbuk, who was still horribly pale, as he
pointed vaguely toward the west. "Are you sure?" asked John.

"Sure, I'm sure," said Dybbuk, swallowing biliously.
"West a bit, south, and then straight on until noon."

Nepal is home to the highest mountains in the world,
among them Everest, K2 Lhotse, Makalu, and, perhaps the
most difficult actually to climb, Annapurna. John's flight
path took them over the southern edge of the Annapurna
Conservation Area, and it was here that they ran into an early
monsoon wind, which, despite John's very best endeavors,
began to push them north into the foothills of the Himalayas.

"We're drifting off course!" yelled Philippa.

"I know," he said. "I can't do anything about it."

There was no way that Philippa or Dybbuk could come to
his aid because only the djinn who created a whirlwind could
pilot it.

"We have to get out of this tailwind," said Dybbuk.

"I don't dare to go any higher," said John. "Haven't you noticed? It's starting to get cold." He glanced down. "Landing doesn't look like much of an option, either. There's snow down there." But the closer to Annapurna's snow-covered slopes they drifted, the colder John became until he found himself unable to maintain the whirlwind any longer, and they were forced to land in an ice field on the mountain's inhospitable north face, about ten thousand feet below the peak.

A bitter wind gusted down from the top, stinging their faces with light snow and chilling their bones to the all-important djinn marrow. And without any means of lighting a fire, there was no prospect of recovering sufficient body temperature to use djinn power. Nor indeed was there any sign of anyone in the huge snow valley below — hikers or climbers — who might have come to their assistance with something as ordinary as a hot drink. Within minutes it was quite clear to all four of them that they would die of cold unless someone quickly came to their rescue.

"Isn't it marvelous?" said Groanin. He sat down in the shadow of a large block of ice, tucked his hand underneath his armpit, and controlled his teeth from chattering long enough to add, in Dybbuk's direction, "Nothing safer, you said. And to think I was stupid enough to believe you."

"It's not my fault if he can't fly properly," said Dybbuk. "He should have gone south and then west. That way we would have avoided this weather system."

"I distinctly remember you said go west and *then* go south," John yelled above the wind.

"Don't blame me," said Dybbuk.

"No one's blaming anyone," said Philippa. "It's gone beyond that. Unless we think of something — and fast — we're going to die of cold here." She sat down beside Groanin and cuddled up close to him in a vain effort to keep warm.

Large fluffy clouds were already obscuring the sun so that the temperature was now dropping like a stone, and there was frost in everyone's hair.

When Groanin next spoke, his breath looked like a djinn transubstantiation as his body heat escaped into the cold Himalayan air. "If anyone's got one of those emergency wishes, this would be the time to use it," he said.

None of the three djinn children said anything.

"I might have known," Groanin muttered grimly. And then. *"Nunc Fortunatus Sum."*

"What's that?" asked Philippa.

"I was just thinking," said Groanin, putting his arm around her shoulders, "about what Colonel Killiecrankie wrote. I must say I wish I *was* in Lucknow."

"As a matter of fact, so do I." She gulped and then pointed down the mountain. "Look."

With long, powerful strides, an immensely tall figure was now advancing up the slope. The figure was vaguely apelike and covered in long, shaggy red fur. The head was large and pointed, while the face looked leathery and flat.

183

"Is that a bear?" Dybbuk said nervously.

"Bear nothing," said John. "That's a Yeti. That's the Abominable Snowman."

Groanin closed his eyes and prepared to pray. "Bloomin' heck," he said. "A monster. That's all we need."

CHAPTER 10

PLUPERFECT

Thousands of miles away in New York, the Elsewheres — the perfect doubles of John and Philippa that had been created by the angel Afriel — were behaving rather too perfectly. One of the things that makes an angel *angelic* is that angels have no capacity for the bad, the bungled, the inadequate, or the imperfect. This meant that John 2 and Philippa 2 had none of the ordinary failings that were possessed by the real twins — or any other children for that matter. It was not that John and Philippa were bad children. They weren't. But like all children — djinn or mundane — there were occasions when they were lazy, thoughtless, disobedient, or just plain mischievous. None of these naturally childish defects were present in John 2 and Philippa 2, and after a day or two of their being at number 7 East 77th Street, it began to be noticed that the twin twins were behaving like, well, angels, instead of normal young djinn. It was Mrs. Trump, the housekeeper, who noticed it first when she found Philippa 2 cleaning the bathrooms, and John 2 taking out the trash. This was on top of Mrs. Trump's earlier discovery that someone — it was now easy to see who — had done all her vacuuming and dusting.

"I don't know what you two are up to," remarked Mrs. Trump, nervously fingering her pearls, because she was a very wealthy woman and often wore expensive jewelry under her cleaning smock. "But whatever it is, I'm very glad for the help. This house is a lot of work. There are times when I think I'd have to have magical powers to keep it running smoothly."

"We're not up to anything, as you put it," said Philippa 2. "We're just trying to make your day a little easier, that's all."

"That's right," said John 2. "Now why don't you go and put your feet up for five minutes and let me make you a cup of herbal tea? You look like you need one."

"And what would your mother say?" demanded Mrs. Trump. "What would she think if she came in and found me being waited on hand and foot by you two? I would get fired, that's what would happen. She doesn't pay me to sit around and drink tea." But she sat down, anyway, and let herself be pampered for a while. How could she refuse? Philippa 2 had baked a cake for her. An *angel* food cake.

"Nobody ever baked a cake for me," said Mrs. Trump with a tear in her eye. "At least, not since I was a child." Not only that, but it was the best cake she had ever tasted. And the tea was very welcome, too. "I could get used to this." She chuckled, but after a while she shooed them out of the kitchen and set about preparing dinner, and she soon forgot all about the thoughtfulness of her employer's two children. At least she did until after dinner when, upon entering the dining room to clear away, she found that the twin twins had already done it. What was more, they had also rinsed the dishes and stacked them neatly in the dishwasher. "Well, I never," she said.

Mr. Gaunt noticed a change in the twins, too. How could he fail to notice a difference in their behavior when Philippa 2 got his morning newspaper and brought it to him in bed with a cup of coffee — the best coffee he had ever tasted — and John 2 ran his bath for him? The twin twins even managed to switch off all electric lights and appliances when they left a room, which was always one of their father's biggest pet peeves. Mr. Gaunt appreciated all that was done for him even if he soon formed the impression that the twins were buttering him up for some time in the future when they would try to call in a favor or indulgence. But until that moment arrived he decided to relax and enjoy it.

The twin twins were no less perfect in the eyes of Mrs. Gaunt but, unlike her husband, she concluded that her children had already committed some great indiscretion, and resolved to keep a close eye on them. But instead of discovering some secret misdemeanor, to her greater surprise she found John 2 playing fewer computer games, watching much less TV, and reading more. And, what was more, she found Philippa combing her hair regularly, brushing her teeth after a meal, keeping her room tidy, and eating properly. And both of them were taking a bath or a shower at least once a day. Without having to be told. All of which seemed like some kind of miracle.

Only Monty, the cat, knew the truth about the twin twins. Cats just know stuff that human beings and even djinn can never know. Especially cats who had once been female human beings, like Monty. Not that Monty didn't have a few clues: John 2 didn't throw things at her when she was sharpening her claws on the leg of John's favorite armchair, and Philippa — normally quite lax in these matters — stopped feeding her secretly from the dinner table. But it was mainly the smell she noticed that persuaded her that they were not the same twins. These two didn't smell at all, which was hardly surprising given their new fondness for keeping clean.

When Mrs. Gaunt found that John was taking two showers a day, she decided that something was wrong and summoned her djinn doctor, Jenny Sachertorte, who was Dybbuk's mother. "There's something wrong with the twins," she told Dr. Sachertorte. "I don't know what it is, but they're just not themselves."

"Be more specific, Layla."

"They're not normally so well-behaved. So obliging. So understanding. So thoughtful. So even-tempered. So obedient. So tidy. So diligent. And above all, so clean. I think they must be ill, or stressed, or something."

Dr. Sachertorte shook her head. "Layla, honey, if you don't mind me saying so, you're being a little neurotic about this. Most parents would be delighted to have children with faults like the ones you're describing. Besides, at least you know where your kids are. At least you know they're alive." Dr. Sachertorte swallowed uncomfortably as she tried to control her emotions.

"There's still no word from Dybbuk?" Mrs. Gaunt took her friend's hand and squeezed it affectionately.

"None. My aunt Felicia and I have looked everywhere for him." She sighed. "It's my fault. I've been too strict with him. I should have given him more leeway. But after what happened to his sister, Faustina . . ." Dr. Sachertorte wiped a tear from her eye.

"It's not your fault," insisted Mrs. Gaunt.

"No, Layla, it is. What was it Nimrod's godfather used to say? To lose one child is unfortunate. To lose two looks like downright carelessness." She blew her nose. "It's connected somehow with the death of his friend Brad and Brad's father. I'm sure of that. But I don't know how. The Palm Springs police don't seem to have a clue."

Mrs. Gaunt hugged Dr. Sachertorte. "You're right," she said. "Perhaps I am being a little neurotic."

"Any idea why that should be so?"

Mrs. Gaunt was silent for a moment.

"Shall I tell you why?" asked Dr. Sachertorte. "Well, isn't it obvious? It's because you're feeling guilty that you're going to leave them soon. To become the next Blue Djinn. Isn't that right?"

"You know about that?"

"Of course. Aunt Felicia told me. She had it from Edwiges the Wanderer. They're old friends."

"I see."

The Blue Djinn of Babylon — by convention, always a female and the most powerful of all the djinn — was obliged to exist in a state of moral indifference, in order to arbitrate fairly between good and evil. Secretly, Mrs. Gaunt had agreed to replace Ayesha, the old Blue Djinn, who happened to be her own mother, when Ayesha died, in order to prevent Ayesha from making Philippa the next Blue Djinn. For to be the Blue Djinn exacted a terrible price, requiring whoever held the position to live apart from her family and without Love, according to the cold rules of Logic.

"You're thinking it would be easier leaving the twins if they were being disobedient and thoughtless." Dr. Sachertorte shook her head. "But it's not them that's sick for something, Layla, honey, it's you. Because you know how much you're going to miss them when you leave home." She paused. "Am I right? Or am I right?"

"Yes. You're right." Mrs. Gaunt let out an enormous sigh. "But what can I do? I gave my word, Jenny. I had to. I gave my word to Ayesha that I would be the next Blue Djinn after she was gone. And it won't be long now. A matter of days, in fact." Mrs. Gaunt bit her lip. "What am I going to tell them, Jenny? What am I going to say to John and Philippa?"

"You want my advice?"

"Of course."

"Then tell them what Ayesha told you and Nimrod, when she became the Blue Djinn. You got over it, Layla. So will they. Tell them what she told you. And if they are half as thoughtful and understanding as you say they are, then they'll understand. I'm certain of it."

On the morning of Ayesha's death at her home in Berlin, Germany, Mrs. Gaunt found the two Elsewheres reading quietly in their rooms. This was more unusual for John than for Philippa and prompted Mrs. Gaunt to lay her hand on his forehead to see if he had a low temperature. His skin felt reassuringly warm, but John's behavior was sufficiently peculiar for Mrs. Gaunt to find a thermometer and place it under John 2's tongue. His temperature was exactly 101.6 degrees Fahrenheit; this, while being three degrees higher than human body temperature, is quite normal for djinn.[1]

"Is there something the matter?" John 2 asked Mrs. Gaunt.

"Apparently not," said Mrs. Gaunt. "Not with you, anyway."

"Me?" said John 2. "I feel fine."

"Do you, dear?" She shrugged. "You seem rather docile, that's all."

Philippa 2 drifted into John's room, the way Philippa

[1] A sick djinn's temperature goes down, not up.

sometimes did, in case Mrs. Gaunt had some instructions for her. She smiled pleasantly at Mrs. Gaunt and then sat down demurely: knees together, hands clasped in her lap, and with her back straight, the way her mother always counseled her to sit. She was even wearing one of the dresses Mrs. Gaunt liked instead of the jeans Philippa herself preferred.

"You both are," continued Mrs. Gaunt. "You're sort of tame really. I mean, look at the way you're sitting in that chair, Philippa. Normally you're all slouched. And you're wearing a dress. You never wear a dress except when I ask you. And John's reading a book, instead of watching TV. It's most unnatural."

"But Mother, you're always telling me not to slouch," said Philippa 2.

"And you're always telling me that I should read more and watch less TV," added John 2. "Which is what I've been doing."

"Yes, dear. You're right." Mrs. Gaunt sat down on the edge of John's bed and faced the two Elsewheres, still quite oblivious to the fact that these were only perfect copies of the real John and Philippa. "So I shouldn't complain when you do exactly what I tell you, should I? It's just that I'm used to a little bit more misbehavior from you both."

"Let me get this straight," said Philippa 2. "Are you saying you want us to misbehave?"

"No." Mrs. Gaunt smiled uncertainly. "That's not what I meant, at all. I just don't want you both to become too good to be true to yourselves. To lose your spirit."

Without realizing it, Mrs. Gaunt had put her finger on the exact problem with the two Elsewheres: An Elsewhere doesn't have a spirit for the simple reason that it doesn't have a soul. There was only one way Mrs. Gaunt could have discovered this was true of the twin twins, and that would have involved taking them up to the attic so that they might have looked upon their souls. But this did not occur to her. Besides, she had something else on her mind of course, and this was the small matter of telling the twins not only that their grandmother was dead, but also that she herself had agreed to replace her as the next Blue Djinn of Babylon and, therefore, that she would have to leave home immediately. And, realizing that Jenny Sachertorte was right, and that there was no point in pussyfooting around the issue any longer, Mrs. Gaunt came straight out with it and told them the news, the way her own mother had done, years before.

"I'm afraid it means I shall have to leave home forever," she said. "I shall have to leave you and your father, and go and live in Berlin. And Babylon, of course. Immediately."

"I think I understand," said Philippa 2, and wiped a perfect tear from her eye. "You did it for me, didn't you?"

"No, Philippa," said Mrs. Gaunt. "It was always me Ayesha wanted to succeed her. Not you. There's really no reason on Earth for you to feel responsible for what's happened."

"I thought it was a bit strange at the time," John 2 added calmly, for of course he could remember everything that the real John remembered. "The way everything was just settled, behind the scenes. In Iravotum." He shrugged. "It all makes sense, now."

Most of the time the Blue Djinn lived in Berlin. But Iravotum was the strange place in Babylon where, once a year, the Blue Djinn went to live in order to harden her heart.

The twin twins were quiet for a while as each considered how best to react and quickly formed the impression that Mrs. Gaunt would hardly have been helped by a great show of emotion. And they decided that the nicest, kindest, least selfish thing they could do was to think of Mrs. Gaunt's feelings and not their own, and to make it easier for her to do what clearly she had to do.

"Have you told Dad?" John 2 asked her.

"No, not yet." She shook her head. "I'm dreading it, of course. He's not as strong as you."

In fact, of course, they were much stronger than she had supposed. It was, she reflected, most probably the result of them being twins. Together, twins have an inner strength that nobody who is not a twin can ever possess or even understand. Mrs. Gaunt saw that she need hardly have worried about telling her children. But Edward Gaunt would be a very different story. Why hadn't she realized that until now? It was her husband she needed to worry about, not her children. What would become of him? How would he manage? How would he be able to go on without her?

Still under the delusion that these were her own dear children, Mrs. Gaunt hugged the two Elsewheres in her arms, kissed their heads, which smelled strongly and

uncharacteristically of shampoo, and perhaps a little disappointed by their reaction — for although she admired
their strength, she would have appreciated just a few more
tears — tried to put a brave face on her leaving home.

And then she guessed what was happening. *Wrongly.*

"Of course," she said, weeping openly now. "Of course.
That's why you've been so perfectly behaved. That's why
you've been so good, isn't it? That's why you're like this now.
Trying to make it easier for me to go. You guessed. You
guessed I was leaving. You guessed and you tried to make it
easier for me, didn't you?" She kissed the twin twins some
more. "Such wonderful, wonderful children, I have. Angels.
That's what you are. Little angels."

Which, of course, was very nearly right.

It was now that John 2 saw how he and Philippa 2 had
miscalculated a little, that Mrs. Gaunt had been hoping that
the real children might have at least *tried* to talk her out of
leaving home. And finally he said what he thought the real
John would probably have said, "Please don't go, Mother. We
won't let you go. If you leave, we'll come and bring you back."

"That's right," said Philippa 2, also understanding what
was now required to be said to make Mrs. Gaunt feel better
about herself. "We won't let you go."

"I'm afraid I have to leave," said Mrs. Gaunt. "Because I
gave my word. Just as you will, now. I want you both to promise me that you'll stay here and look after your father. That
you'll protect and keep him safe no matter what."

When the twin twins remained silent, in a way that they

thought was proper under the circumstances, Mrs. Gaunt thought for a moment and then, smiling bravely, said, "Well, I can't say I blame you. I don't suppose you would be the children I know and love if you promised such a thing. So, listen carefully. Here's what will happen if you do decide to leave here and come after me. Not to you. But to your father. Now listen carefully. Both of you. Have you ever heard of a man called Methuselah?"

CHAPTER 11

CARELESS WHISPERS

Standing in front of the four of them, seemingly indifferent to the blizzard of snow, the Yeti looked like a great wall of fur. John estimated the creature must have been almost nine feet in height. Yet the snowman did not seem to be particularly abominable. Not even slightly obnoxious. And instead of baring fangs, beating his chest, and roaring loudly, which was what everyone huddled on the Annapurna ice field expected him to do, the Yeti sighed and indicated that they should follow him back down the slope. Nobody moved. And seeing their fear, the Yeti spoke.

"*Komm,*" he said. "*Komm, komm wir müssen uns beeilen!*"

"He wants us to come with him," explained John, who spoke perfect German, as a result of a wish he had once made. "And says that we should hurry."

"Typical German," moaned Groanin, climbing, stiff with cold, to his half-frozen feet. "Always in a hurry."

"He certainly doesn't look like a typical German," said Philippa, with considerable irony.

"I don't care where he's from," said Dybbuk, who was already striding after the Yeti, "just as long as he takes us somewhere warm."

They followed the Yeti down the slope of Annapurna until they came to a doorway about ten feet tall, neatly cut into a large block of ice. The door was concealed with a larger block of ice that the Yeti readied himself to move back after they were safely inside. He pointed them urgently through the doorway. "Inside, quickly," he said, speaking English now. "Quick. Before you all freeze to death."

Inside the doorway they found themselves in a long corridor made of ice that seemed to lead inside the mountain itself. The corridor was well-lit with electric lights however and, after two or three minutes of walking, it brought them to a door made of thick, smoked glass that looked as if it belonged more in a New York bank than in a Himalayan mountain slope. Sensing their presence, the door slid open with a whisper, and a wave of warm air hit their grateful bones.

"Please," said the Yeti. "Go inside."

The interior of the Yeti's home was as minimally modern as its front door. The walls were made of glass and plain white plaster and a polished black floor seemed to flow like water throughout. In a long, low fireplace, a well-behaved fire made the otherwise clinical living space seem more welcoming.

"Welcome to my Himalayan home," said the Yeti as the

door closed silently behind him. "Please. Make yourselves comfortable."

This was easier said than done as there was hardly any furniture in this underground apartment. So they sat on the floor, huddled around the fire, waiting for their shaggy host to become more hospitable.

"You would like something hot to drink, yes?" asked the Yeti.

"If it's no trouble," said Groanin.

"No trouble," said the Yeti. The next word he spoke was "TOHUWABOHU," which seemed to be a focus word, for it was no sooner out of his large and prominent mouth than a large tray of hot coffee, chocolate, tea, sandwiches, scones, and doughnuts appeared beside the little quartet.

"You're a djinn then," observed Philippa. "Like us. Well, three of us, anyway. Mr. Groanin here is a human being."

"Pleased to meet you, I'm sure," said Groanin, helping himself to a cup of tea. "We thought you were the Abominable Snowman."

The Yeti smiled. "I *am* the Abominable Snowman," he said. "You see for many decades now, I've been coming to the Himalayas for a vacation, to get away from it all. A sort of retreat from the modern world, you understand. I like to walk and climb in the mountains, and to enjoy the fresh air. Not to mention the solitude. Solitude is very important to me when I am on my vacation." He chuckled. "I am afraid I am what you English call, a hermit, *ja*?"

"I'm not surprised," said Dybbuk, his mouth stuffed with

a sandwich. "Looking like that, I can't imagine you have many visitors."

Philippa shot the other djinn a look of strong disapproval. "Dybbuk. Don't be so rude."

"No, no," said the Yeti. "He is quite right, your friend. One of the reasons I am adopting this look is to scare people away. Although that is not the only reason I look like this. There are other, more practical reasons, also. This creature is my own design, you see." He showed them his bare, leathery-skinned foot, which was huge. "The foot is especially good for climbing. As are the legs, of course. And the fur coat keeps me very warm in any weather. Of course, it is only for outdoors. When I am indoors I take on a more conventional appearance."

And so saying, the Yeti changed into a man who clicked his heels and bowed to them sharply. "Permit me to introduce myself. I am the Baron Reinhold von Reinnerassig. Of the Jann tribe of djinn."

The baron was tall and blond with a wide, almost mischievous sort of face. His bright blue eyes seemed to twinkle even more than the small diamond stud he wore in one of his earlobes.

"So all those myths and legends about the Abominable Snowman," said John, when they had finished introducing themselves. "They're really about you?"

"I'm afraid so, yes." He shrugged. "In the beginning it was quite successful. The local people stayed away and left me alone. But then there began to be outsiders who mounted expeditions to try to capture me. Well, of course, I'm only here for a few weeks in winter, so it's not so easy to even find me. The rest of the year I am at my family home in Hohenschwangau, Bavaria."

"But why come here?" asked Groanin. "I should have thought you'd want to go somewhere warm, you being a djinn and all. And having hot blood and such like."

"The trouble with most hot countries and the nicest places," said the baron, "is that they're full of tourists. Fifty years ago, I used to go to Mallorca, the Maldives, Hawaii, Jamaica, the Virgin Islands." He shook his head and made a face. "But not now. They're so commercial, these places. Quite spoiled. So I come here instead. There are hikers, of course. And the odd group of mountaineers. But Annapurna is not so easy to climb. Especially at this time of year." He smiled warmly. "That's my story. What's yours? I saw your whirlwind and guessed what must have happened."

"We were flying from Kathmandu down to Lucknow," said Philippa. "When a wind blew us way off course."

"The cold air took away my power," said John. "And I had to make a forced landing."

The baron nodded. "It's a common problem when you're first learning to fly," he said. "Running short of operating body heat is an occupational hazard for djinn, I'm afraid."

"So how come you don't?" asked Dybbuk. "It's freezing on this mountain."

"Well, for one thing, it's very warm in here," said the baron.

"That it is," said Groanin, taking off his jacket and loosening his tie. "It's like an oven."

"And for another, it's also very warm when I'm being the Yeti. My fat and my fur coat mean that my body temperature stays the same as it is in here." He took hold of John's T-shirt and rubbed the material between his fingers. "The next time you go flying, I suggest you wear something warmer. A sheepskin flying suit perhaps."

"I'm always telling him to wear a coat," said Philippa, "but he never does."

John shrugged. "I don't like coats, that's all."

"Me, neither," agreed Dybbuk.

"Nevertheless," said the baron, "when you're flying on djinn power, I do strongly advise it. Indeed, if you're ever going to reach Lucknow from here, it will be a necessity, I think." He shook his head. "Not that I should want to go there myself. There or anywhere else in India for that matter. You see, there's another reason I avoid hot countries. I simply cannot stand snakes. And India's full of them. Of course, Nepal has snakes. But not up here. Not in winter." He grinned sheepishly. "Oh, I know it's ridiculous for a djinn to be afraid of snakes when we djinn are immune to snake venom, and when you consider that I'm not at all afraid of arachnids — scorpions and spiders — although we *are* affected by *their* venom. Silly, but there it is."

"We're immune to snake venom but not to spiders and scorpions?" said Philippa. "I didn't know that."

"Well, I knew it," said Dybbuk. "I'm amazed you didn't."

"So why did you run away from those guys in Palm Springs?" asked John. "The ones who killed Brad and his father?"

"Because I figured they might have guns as well as snakes," said Dybbuk. "I don't know anyone who's immune to a bullet."

"Let me get this straight," insisted John. "All djinn are immune to snake venom?"

The baron nodded. "Oh, yes. Those old snake cults. They got the idea from us, you see. I mean, the idea of handling poisonous snakes as a sign of your holiness and your power over death. That kind of thing. It's all nonsense, of course. No mundane ever survived a bite from a large-size cobra, at least not without medical treatment. It's only djinn who can do that."

"But that can't be right," said John. "Last summer we went to Egypt with my uncle. And the Ifrit put a cobra in my luggage. And my uncle said that I could have been killed."

"Ah," said the baron. "If the Ifrit put the cobra there, that's a different story. The Ifrit are good with snakes. It's their chosen animal. Always turning themselves into snakes. Very likely it was an Ifrit *inside* a cobra. A djinn cobra is a very different story from a regular one. A djinn cobra would certainly have killed you."

"But how can you tell the difference?" asked John. "Between an ordinary snake and a djinn one."

"Er, you can't. Not until it bites you. But most snakes are perfectly ordinary. So really there's nothing to worry about. Most of the time."

"Herr Baron, you mentioned snake cults," said Philippa. "Have you ever heard of the Aasth Naag?"

"The Eight Cobras? Oh, yes. It was a local djinn-worshipping cult, from Kathmandu, I believe. But it died out after the Great Mutiny of 1857."

"We think it's active again," said Dybbuk. "In fact, we're certain of it."

"Then you should be very careful," said the baron. "We all should. Because there's no telling what might happen to the world if they managed to obtain power over a djinn again. Human beings are easily led, and they might be persuaded to do evil things by a man who could prove his immortality to them by surviving the bite of a cobra."

"That's what *I* thought," said Philippa.

"I shall help you," said the baron. "I shall help you to get airborne again, and I shall even grant Mr. Groanin here three wishes in order to keep you safe, when you can't help yourselves."

"That's very kind of you, sir, I'm sure," said Groanin. Under the circumstances, he hardly felt he could reject the baron's kind offer. And he had little doubt that these might be very useful on the journey that lay ahead. At the same time, however, he was mindful of the responsibility of having three wishes — and from a powerful djinn, too. He had been given three wishes before and he knew only too well how the choice and responsibility of having three wishes could leave a person paralyzed with responsibility and choice. He had been relieved beyond all imagining when, after almost ten years of indecision, his third wish had been used up. What was even worse was that quite often there was no way of knowing how a wish might turn out. As Mr. Rakshasas was fond of saying, "Having a wish is like lighting a fire. It's reasonable to assume that the smoke might make someone cough."

With the baron's help (which included some warmer clothes), they resumed their journey to Lucknow, and arrived safely just after dark, so that there was no chance of seeing the pink fort from the air.

Dybbuk — for by this time he felt well enough to fly — landed the whirlwind a little way out of the city, on the southern bank of the Gomti, a sluggish, weed-covered river. Their presence in Lucknow attracted no more attention than their arrival, for not only had Dybbuk chosen a quiet place to land but, on the baron's advice, they had all become Indians themselves. This was not just a matter of Philippa wearing a sari, which is the dress worn by Indian women, nor was it a matter of Groanin and the two boys wearing the kurta, which is a knee-length shirt worn by Indian men and boys. It was much more than a mere change of clothing. Using djinn power, they had made their hair black and their skin several shades darker, too. They also made it possible for themselves to speak and understand Hindi, which is the official language of India. Mr. Groanin became Mr. Gupta, John became Janesh, Philippa became Panchali, and Dybbuk became Deepak. Their characters remained essentially the same, although there were some subtle differences.

For a while, being Indian did feel a little strange, but they quickly got used to it and, by the time they reached their hotel, the Chuna Laga Diya, they felt as Indian as a chickpea curry. Indeed, they soon very much preferred being Indian, especially when they discovered, as the baron had promised, that the local people did not try to sell them things because they were rich tourists, and left them alone.

"I really like my hair this color," said Philippa, observing her new appearance in the bathroom mirror of the hotel room she was sharing with John. "And I could never get as tan. Not in a million years. I always turn as red as a beet whenever I go to the beach." She looked critically at her brother. "And you. A little color suits you, John. It makes you much better looking."

"You think so?" John joined her in the bathroom and regarded himself critically. "Maybe. I dunno. As long as people don't pay any attention to us, I don't care what we look like." This was not true, however. John was just as thrilled to be an Indian as his sister.

But neither djinn's delight could compete with Mr. Groanin who, for the first time in his life, found himself able to eat the local food, because it wasn't just his outside that became Indian, but also his insides and, in particular, his ample stomach. He even managed to eat and enjoy a street vendor's kebab that, cooked over a dung fire, was something he could never have done as a proper English butler.

"I don't know why I was so afraid of foreign food,"

confessed Groanin. "Not when it tastes as good as this. To think what I've been missing all these years."

"Are you sure I couldn't tempt you with another jar of baby food?" asked Dybbuk.

"Baby food?" exclaimed Groanin, ordering a second cob of corn. "I never want to see that kids' muck again as long as I live."

The man from whom they bought this, their roadside snack, performed another very useful function in that he was able to identify the location and current status of the pink fort in Dybbuk's East India Company picture.

"That is the famous Jayaar Sho Ashram," he said. "It was founded by the Sadhguru Masamjhasara. It is one of the most famous meditation shrines and yoga centers in all of India. You'll find it just outside the city, south of the Charbagh Railway Station, on the road to Kanpur. You can't miss it. And not just because it's pink. No, you just have to follow all the English and Americans who go there in search of answers." The man chuckled and set about cooking another cob of corn on his lump of burning dung. "And to be relieved of their money, of course. The guru is very rich."

"Answers?" said Dybbuk. "What sort of answers?"

The man shrugged. "That's a very good question," he said. "Perhaps, if you go there, you can ask them this question yourself."

The next morning, Groanin and the three young djinn climbed aboard a bus heading south toward the airport and beyond. Traveling in the same direction were several Westerners who, despite their saffron-colored monks' robes and holy-man sandals, were easily identified by their fair skin and vacant smiles. John spoke to one of the young monks. "Are you going to Jayaar Sho?" he asked the young monk.

"I live there. I'm a sannyasin. A disciple of Guru Masamjhasara."

"But you're from the United States, aren't you?"

"Right. From Cleveland, Ohio."

"So why come all this way?" John asked the sannyasin. "If you don't mind me asking." There was something about his voice that seemed familiar to John.

"I don't mind you asking. The yoga, the meditation, the enlightenment. The whole ashram is a reservoir of energies emanating from all the people who have gone into deep meditation there. Even those who are unaware of meditation experience a state of meditativeness when they're there." He smiled a happy, empty sort of smile. "Where are you from, kid? Your English is excellent."

John shrugged.

"We're from around here," said Dybbuk. "We learn English at school. And I watch a lot of American movies on TV. That's one of the reasons my dad, Mr. Gupta" — he nodded in Groanin's direction — "wants us to have a look at the ashram. He's thinking about us all living there. So that we might channel our energies in a more spiritual way."

This was the cover story they had all agreed on before leaving the hotel that morning, so that they might stand a better chance of having good luck at the ashram, and Dybbuk knew what to say better than anyone. There were always rich, Hollywood people going for the weekend to his mother's health spa in Palm Springs, and he was well-acquainted with the kinds of things they said about their gurus and their yoga teachers. "He wants us all to bask in some real spiritual warmth."

"I'd be glad to show you around," said the sannyasin. "My American name is Joey Ryder."

"Did you say Joey?" asked John.

"Yes, but my ashram name is Jagannatha," said Joey. "It means 'juggernaut.'"

"Tell me something . . . er . . . Jagannatha. Do you operate a computer support center at the ashram? Giving people advice over the telephone on how to configure their computers 'n' stuff like that?"

"That's right," said Jagannatha. "That computer support center is one of the ways in which the ashram raises money."

John nodded. Joey was the person who had given him such terrible advice on how to install the software on the laptop he had been given for his birthday. He smiled thinly. "Nice to meet you, Jagannatha," he said. "My name is Janesh. This is my brother, Deepak, and my sister, Panchali."

"Pleased to meet you, too."

"We'd love for you to show us around the ashram," said Dybbuk. "What did you do before you came here? When you lived in Cleveland?"

"I was a nurse in a hospital."

The bus pulled up close to a sheer-sided sandstone outcrop of rock about a hundred feet tall. Philippa climbed down from the bus and, shielding her eyes against the sun, looked up at the top from which arose the crenellated ramparts of a dramatic-looking fort. "This just has to be it," she said.

"No doubt about it," agreed John.

"Awesome," murmured Dybbuk. "Totally awesome."

Built at the end of the sixteenth century, the pink walls of the fort appeared as awe-inspiring as they were obviously impregnable. Vultures wheeled above the topmost tower, from which now descended an ancient-looking rope elevator. With the exception of Jagannatha, it collected the other sannyasins that got off the bus, and began its slow and precipitous ascent up the side of the rock. Jagannatha came back and said that he would go up in the next hoist with the children and their father, Mr. Gupta.

Groanin watched the hoist, which was a simple basket of the kind to be found underneath any hot-air balloon, as it ascended to the top of the rock, with concern. To the one-armed butler's eyes, the trip up the sheer rock face looked an alarming one. Even dangerous. Nervously he flicked his eyes at the young sannyasin whom Dybbuk had befriended. "Who's the hippie?" he asked Dybbuk, speaking Hindi.

"He says his ashram name is Jagannatha," said Dybbuk. "But his real name is Joey Ryder and he's going to show us around the ashram. Me and John told him that we were thinking of joining. Like we all agreed." He looked at Jagannatha and then shook his head. "Don't worry about him. He doesn't speak Hindi."

When the hoist returned down the rock face, Jagannatha climbed into the basket and gestured to Groanin and the three children to join him.

"Is this the only way to get up there?" Groanin asked him, speaking English again.

"I'm afraid so," said Jagannatha. "It's safe enough, I think. You get used to it, anyway. Just try to be cool. And don't look down."

When they were all inside the basket, Jagannatha rang a bell that was attached to the rope and they began their slow ascent up the sheer face of the precipice. Groanin listened to the creaking of the basket and watched the straining ropes and pulleys anxiously. Deciding that he would never again complain about riding on a whirlwind, he glanced down at the hard ground below and then closed his eyes as a sudden feeling of vertigo took hold of him. "The things I do for you kids," he muttered. "I wish —"

"No!" exclaimed Philippa. "Don't!" But it was too late. Groanin's wish was out.

"— I was already at the top."

Of course, Groanin had quite forgotten that Baron von Reinnerassig had given him three wishes for emergencies. No sooner were the words out of his mouth than he disappeared. And it was fortunate that Jagannatha's attention was focused on the distant horizon rather than on the faces of his four fellow passengers who now numbered only three. But it wasn't long before even he woke up to this fact.

"Hey, what happened to your dad?" he asked Dybbuk with as much urgency as he was capable of, which wasn't saying very much. Horrified, he looked quickly over the side of the basket expecting to see a body lying smashed on the ground below.

For a very long moment, none of the three young djinn said anything. It was easy for them to see what had happened, but explaining it to a mundane, even one as credulous as Jagannatha, would have stretched the ingenuity and invention of a master storyteller.

"Where did he go?" wailed the sannyasin. "Mr. Gupta. He just disappeared."

"That's exactly what he did," Dybbuk said inventively. Storytelling, which can be a polite word for lying, was his forte. "Whenever he sees a rope above his head, he can't resist it, I guess. Our dad's a magician, see? A fakir. And his speciality is the Indian rope trick. He's only got to see a rope going up into the sky, and then he starts to climb up it and disappears." Dybbuk snapped his fingers. "Just like that."

John and Philippa winced with embarrassment. As explanations went, Dybbuk's did not sound like a very plausible one. Not that there were many explanations that would have been equal to the task of accounting for Groanin's disappearance from the basket.

Jagannatha peered up the rope toward the pulley that was

hauling them steadily up the rock face. "That's quite a climb for a man with one arm, Deepak," he said doubtfully.

"Of course it is," said Dybbuk. "That's precisely why he does it. To prove to himself and, more important, to us that he's still up to it. To doing the rope trick. He had an accident, you see." Dybbuk was warming to his fantastic story. "Before, when he used to get to the top of the rope, he would chop himself up with an ax and throw his various body parts down into a basket at the base of the rope. Which is the traditional way of doing the Indian rope trick, right? Then, one of us kids would throw a cloth over the basket and he'd miraculously reappear with all his parts in the right places. Only the last time he did it a dog ran off with his arm, so now he just sticks to climbing the rope and disappearing."

John looked at the expression of wonder on Jagannatha's openmouthed face and managed to stifle an overwhelming desire to laugh out loud, but only just.

"Of course, I've heard of the Indian rope trick," said Jagannatha. "I think I saw it performed at a show in Las Vegas when I was a kid. And I used to do a bit of voice-throwing myself. You know, ventriloquism. Only I never once did it without some sort of announcement." He glanced over the edge of the basket as if he still half expected to see Groanin's body lying on the ground almost a hundred feet below.

"Ask him all about it, when you see him at the top," said Dybbuk. "Unless, that is, you think he jumped. Or we pushed him out."

"No, no, no, of course not." Jagannatha spoke hurriedly, just in case they really had pushed Groanin out of the basket and were now thinking of getting rid of any witnesses. "Nothing could be further from my mind, Deepak. Honestly."

"When you think about it," said John, coming to Dybbuk's aid, with an argument he'd deployed before, in similar circumstances, "it's just like Sherlock Holmes says: 'When you have eliminated the impossible, whatever remains, however improbable, must be the truth.' You remember him getting in the basket, right?"

"Right," said Jagannatha.

John nodded toward the ground. "He's not in here. And he's not down there. Therefore, he must be up there. Right?"

"I guess so."

At last, the elevator reached the top of the precipice where another sannyasin secured the basket to a rickety-looking wooden platform and opened the little door to permit the four passengers to step onto the floor of the tower.

This was Groanin's cue to emerge from behind several empty cylinders of liquid nitrogen, which was where he had hidden himself on finding that his wish "to be at the top already" had come true. Fortunately the old monk who manned the elevator station, which was powered by an equally old donkey that turned a capstan, had not been looking at the platform when Groanin had made his sudden appearance in the tower, and he continued to remain quite oblivious to the fact that of the five new arrivals to the tower, only four had traveled there in the normal way. But not Jagannatha, who regarded Groanin with awe.

"That's amazing, Mr. Gupta," he said. "The way you got up that rope. Amazing."

Groanin smiled, uncertain as to what story could have been told to cover his disappearance. "Yes," he said. "Isn't it?"

"It's all right, *Dad*," said Dybbuk. "I told him all about your famous Indian rope trick."

"Did you now?"

"You must show it to me again, sometime, Mr. Gupta," said Jagannatha. "Only make sure I'm paying attention first. I wouldn't want to miss anything."

"No, you wouldn't," said Groanin, amazed that the young American monk seemed satisfied with such an unlikely explanation and staring daggers at Dybbuk for providing such a preposterous story. "It is, er . . . something to see, yes, even if I do say so myself. Only, if I might ask you a favor. Please don't mention it to anyone. I wouldn't like people to think I was trying to draw attention to myself."

"Sure." Jagannatha grinned. "No problem. Well, hey, let me show you guys around the ashram."

"Yes, if you would," said Groanin, pleased to change the subject at last. "That would be very kind of you."

It was a hot day to be walking anywhere, but on top of the rock it was like being on the sun's anvil. It beat down on the pink fort with a heat that, even for the Indian Groanin, as opposed to the English one, was almost beyond endurance. Despite his kurta and his soft felt slippers, Groanin found himself gasping for breath as Jagannatha showed them around the dormitories where the other sannyasins slept, the library, and the huge dome where Guru Masamjhasara usually spoke to his assembled followers. By the time they came to the computer support center, where dozens of sannyasins worked answering telephone calls from people who had bought a Bungle computer in Britain and the United States, Groanin was panting uncomfortably.

"Are you all right, Mr. Groanin?" Philippa asked him quietly.

The butler fanned himself with a copy of the ashram's newspaper and let out a breath. "Me? Yes, I think so, miss. I just wish it wasn't quite so hot, that's all."

As soon as he said it, a solitary black cloud appeared from nowhere and floated over the pink fort so that it shielded the ashram from the ferocity of the sun like an enormous parasol. The temperature dropped immediately by several degrees. "That's kind of strange," said Jagannatha, looking up at the cloud. "I've never seen that before."

Groanin winced. "Oops," he said in Hindi. "I did it again, didn't I? Wished for something useless." He shook his head, irritated with himself. "What a dreadful waste of two wishes."

"Don't worry about it," said John. "It could have happened to anyone."

"Nay, but it happened to me," said Groanin. "And not the first time, neither. It were exactly the same when I first met Nimrod and he granted me three wishes for rescuing him from a bottle he was trapped in."

"John's right," said Philippa. "Don't beat yourself up about it."

"Is everything okay?" asked Jagannatha. He understood nothing of what was being said by the four Indians, but it was plain from Groanin's manner that something had irritated him. "Janesh? Panchali? Is your dad all right?"

"It was the heat," John explained in English. "But since that cloud appeared he's feeling much better."

"I wish that was true," murmured Groanin unhappily, although his unhappiness lasted for only a second longer as, suddenly, his third wish was granted, and he felt much, much better. Not that Groanin seemed to mind in the slightest. He took a deep euphoric breath, flexed his chest and shoulder muscles, and nodded. "By heck, you know, you're right, our John. I do feel much better. Like I took a pill or something." He blinked happily and grinned a big, comfortable smile. "I haven't felt this good since Manchester City thrashed United five to one, back in 1989. And I thought I'd never feel as good as that as long as I lived."

"Enjoy it while you can," said Dybbuk. "But I've a horrible feeling we're going to regret the waste of those three wishes, mark my words. What just happened here was nothing short of a disaster."

"Sorry," said Groanin, not feeling in the least bit sorry and smiling happily all the while.

"Well, why don't *we* give him an emergency wish?" suggested Philippa. "A discrimen. Just in case something unexpected should happen."

"We can't," said John. "Not according to the *Baghdad Rules*. Not for a year and a day. A fourth wish would only undo the previous three. A fifth wish does something even worse. It comes with a sort of curse — it's called Enantodromia — so that whatever you wish for, you end up with the opposite." John shook his head. "You don't want to know what happens if you get as far as a sixth wish."

"No, I don't think I do," said Groanin. "Either way I'm not having another wish. Or even another three. I'm not going to risk anything happening to the way I'm feeling right now. Not for anything."

CHAPTER 12

HOLY ROLLERS

As the tour of the ashram at the pink fort progressed, it became apparent to Groanin and the children that, despite the certainty that they were now in the right place, they still had no idea of where exactly to look for the Cobra King of Kathmandu. The fort was huge. And it was quickly obvious that they were going to have to join the ashram if they were ever to stand a chance of finding the lost talisman.

"It's the only way to avoid suspicion as to what we're up to," said Philippa. "Besides, we can't keep going up and down in that rope elevator."

"Amen to that," said Groanin.

"Once we're members of the ashram — *sadhaks*, they call them — we can be here and keep our eyes peeled, and no one will pay any attention to us. At the same time, we'll get a clearer idea of which places we might look in."

"I think I already suggested that plan," said Dybbuk.

"Actually," said Philippa, "it was your idea to pose as

people who were only *thinking* of joining. But either way, it's a good idea."

Groanin told Jagannatha that they had decided to join the ashram; then, congratulating them all on having made a choice he was sure they would never regret, Jagannatha took them to see Guru Masamjhasara.

They found the guru, who was seated in a dentist's chair on top of the sacred shrine, surrounded by several dozen followers and hundreds of burning candles. The guru was a tubby man with a bushy Santa Claus–size gray beard. He wore white robes, a gold Rolex wristwatch, tinted glasses, and, wound around his head, a loose orange turban. Hanging in front of him was a gold bell that from time to time he would ring before speaking some choice words of wisdom to his followers, and mounted on an easel next to his chair was a picture of a living man wearing only a loincloth and sitting on top of a tall pole with not one, but eight daggers embedded in his chest and back.

"Ouch," said John, regarding the picture with horrified fascination. "That looks uncomfortable."

"That's the Fakir Murugan," said Jagannatha. "He was the guru's dad, and a very holy man. That's the kind of thing holy men did back in those days. Stuck knives in themselves. And sat on top of tall poles. To prove how holy they were."

"You wouldn't do that kind of thing now, I suppose," said Philippa, for whom the idea of anything sharp sticking in her body was horrible. "Things like sticking knives in yourselves, handling snakes, and lying on a bed of nails. Would you?"

"Me?" Jagannatha grinned. "Are you kidding? I hate knives. And I've never seen a snake up here on the rock. That's what we call it up here: 'the rock.'" Then, pressing his hands together reverently, Jagannatha approached the guru, bowed several times, and introduced the four new disciples, using their Indian names, Mr. Gupta, Janesh, Panchali, and Deepak.

The guru regarded them with amused indifference, as if his mind was elsewhere. Then he rang his bell, and everyone fell silent for a moment as he spoke. "Welcome, Mr. Gupta," he said. "And welcome to your children. I will teach you the process of conscious non-doing." His accent seemed to speak of an expensive education at an English boarding school. "And the art of effortless living."

"That suits me just fine," murmured Dybbuk.

"Me, too," confessed Groanin.

The guru leaned forward in his chair and scrutinized the four newcomers to his ashram. Then he rang his bell again. "I know you," he said and, for a moment, they held their breath, wondering if the guru really was enough of a holy man to recognize the three children for what they really were. But then, uttering a girlish little chuckle, he sat back on his chair, adding, "'You know me. One thing I can tell you is you've got to be free.' So, you will come together and do yoga for three hours a day. You will come together and do meditation. You will come together and purify your bodies and your minds. And you will come together and help to man our computer support center. You will give advice to lots of English people and Americans on how to set up and configure their personal computers and their laptops and their PDAs — whatever they are."

"But we don't know anything about how to set up PCs," said Philippa, glancing uncertainly at her brother, who knew a little bit about computers but certainly not enough to give professional advice to other people. To her relief John, Groanin, and Dybbuk all shook their heads in agreement. "Or PDAs. None of us do."

"That is so much the better," said the guru, giggling again. He lifted one of his dirty-looking feet, inspected it for a moment, and then rolled a large ball of toe jam out from between his toes with his fingers. Philippa was horrified. "Understand this, Janesh," he said.

"Actually, I'm Panchali," she said. Pointing to her brother, John, she added, "He's Janesh."

"My child. I teach the process of non-doing. Of simple living. To live simply it is necessary to free the world from the Western repression of computers and computing. So we give people who continue to live under this tyranny *bad advice. Terrible advice. Misleading advice.* But it is the *best advice.* We tell them that one and one and one is four, so to speak, in the hope that they will learn to hate their PCs and destroy them or throw them away and enter a world without computers. A limitless world of love and joy, of pencils and paper only." He giggled again. "Can you do this, my children? Can you tell a lot of stupid, rich Westerners the wrong way to install some software, for the sake of their immortal souls?"

"Nothing simpler," said Dybbuk. He grinned with relish at the very idea of giving people misleading advice.

"I call this process 'mental yoga,'" said the guru. "We twist their minds into knots so that by creating stress and hypertension, we lead them out the other side into a world of calm and relaxation. A world of effortless living. And of non-doing."

"I can buy that," said Dybbuk. "Sure."

Still giggling, the guru wiped his toe jam on his beard and then rang his bell three times. The audience was over.

"I think he liked you," said Jagannatha. "There was something about you all he seemed to think was out of the ordinary."

"I hope not," said Philippa, who thought the guru was revolting. Especially what he had done with his toe jam.

Jagannatha had escorted them from the shrine to their room in the dormitory, a triangular-shaped blockhouse with a thatched roof that was in a courtyard within the outer wall of the pink fort, next to an old, abandoned well. There were four beds, a washstand, a plain table, some prayer mats, and, on the wall, a large picture of a smiling Guru Masamjhasara sitting cross-legged and floating on thin air. *Almost like a djinn,* Philippa thought.

"Your yoga teacher will be along any minute," said Jagannatha. "She's kind of tough so maybe you should all take it easy for a minute." Bowing politely to them and then to the portrait of the floating guru, he left them alone.

"Hippie," snorted Dybbuk and threw himself down onto his bed, whereupon he winced: The mattress was much harder than the one he was used to back home in Palm Springs. "Thank goodness he's gone."

"I think he's rather sweet," said Philippa, and Groanin, who was still feeling on top of the world, agreed with her.

"I like it here," he said and, smiling happily, he lay down on his bed. "Everyone is so nice." By now, the cloud above the pink fort had disappeared and the heat had returned to the rock, but Groanin was still feeling better than ever.

John frowned, disliking this new Groanin and preferring the curmudgeonly moaner and groaner he had gotten used to. He almost hoped that something would happen to put a dent in the butler's newfound sense of optimism and well-being, which, of course, was only the result of the third of Baron von Reinnerassig's emergency wishes.

As it happened, John did not have long to wait, for there was a knock at the door and into their small dormitory room stepped a tall, thin woman with fair hair. She was wearing a leotard and under her arm was a rolled-up orange-colored rubber mat. She bowed to the picture of the guru and then to Groanin and the children.

"Hi," she said brightly. "My name is Prudence Crabbe, and I'm going to be teaching you yoga. It will be a private session. Just the five of us. To see what you can do. So, if you'd like to follow me to the yoga center, we'll get started."

"I have only one arm," said Groanin. "I don't think I can do yoga."

"Nonsense," said Miss Crabbe, who was Canadian. "Any-one can do yoga. Even you, sir." She added briskly, "Don't worry. Yoga's not about twisting yourself into impossible knots and contortions."

But that was exactly what it was about and, after less than an hour of doing yoga with Miss Crabbe, and with more than two hours of it still ahead of them, Groanin and the children were exhausted.

"The therapeutic effect and value of yoga," yelled Miss Crabbe as she helped them to hold a particularly painful position, "in all spheres of life is a well-known fact."

Groanin gasped for breath as he tried to stretch himself in the way Miss Crabbe had just demonstrated.

"It helps people to express and experience their divin-ity," she said.

"That's a laugh," said Groanin. "I couldn't feel less divine if I had a tail and a set of horns and a membership card from the Hellfire Club." And so saying, he collapsed heavily onto his mat and let out a loud and unhappy groan, which, to John's ears, sounded much more like the Groanin he knew and loved. "I can't go on. Really, I can't."

"Three hours of yoga a day is compulsory for all those wishing to stay on here at the ashram," declared Miss Crabbe without a trace of sympathy. "No exceptions. Those are Guru Masamjhasara's orders." She turned and bowed to another large portrait of the guru that hung on the wall of the yoga center. "Is that understood? No exceptions. Now then. This next position is called 'the crab.'"

And so, because he didn't want to leave the ashram without having had a chance to conduct a real search for the Cobra King, Groanin picked himself up and tried to keep going, but it was soon clear to the twins, if not to Miss Crabbe, that Groanin would have to stop or risk a complete collapse. At the same time, however — it also being obvious that Miss Crabbe was impervious to reason, pity, and humor — it became clear to John and Philippa that djinn power would have to be used against her, but in some subtle way.

They would have done something subtle, too, if Dybbuk had not done something first. And Dybbuk would not have been Dybbuk if he had used djinn power with subtlety.

"ZYGOBRANCHIATE!"

Given a few more minutes, the twins might have caused Miss Crabbe to lose her voice perhaps, or even to develop a crick in her neck that would have prevented her from doing any more yoga for the day; Dybbuk simply turned her into a crab. Considering that her name was Crabbe, this was not particularly imaginative on his part, but it was undeniably effective.

"Thank goodness for that," said Groanin, lying exhausted on the floor. He was too worn out to even move out of the way when the crab came crawling in his direction. "I really thought I was going to die."

"Couldn't you have turned her into something other than a crab?" Philippa spoke sternly to Dybbuk. "Miles away from the sea, a hundred and ten degrees in the shade, vultures in the air — crabs do not thrive in this part of the world, Buck. Unless you turn her back again and soon, Miss Crabbe will die. A cat. A mouse. Even a spider. I could understand that." She shook her head. "But a crab? Really, Buck, you are a clod."

"I dunno," said Dybbuk. "Crabbe by name and crab by nature. The yoga position we were doing was called 'the crab.' It seemed like the obvious thing to do." He laughed as the crab waved one of her claws at him, as if trying to attract his attention.

"Too obvious," said John.

"Well, I for one am grateful to you, Buck my boy," said Groanin. "If I live to be a hundred I don't think I will ever be more exhausted than I am right now. That woman. She's not human."

"Not anymore." Dybbuk laughed. "You got that right."

The crab, which was not a very big one, kept on waving her claws for a moment and then backed into a corner to await her fate.

"Turn her back quickly," insisted Philippa. "Before she dries out."

"All right," said Dybbuk. "But if she starts with the yoga again I won't be responsible for what happens to her." He paused for a moment to gather himself and then said, "ZYGOBRANCHIATE!"

Recovering her thin, almost double-jointed human shape, Prudence Crabbe remained huddled and silent in the corner of the yoga center for almost a minute.

"Are you feeling all right, love?" Groanin asked her, feigning innocence.

"What happened to me?"

"You've had a bit of a funny turn," said Groanin, "that's all."

"One minute I was demonstrating a yoga position and the next moment I had the strangest sensation that I was a crab." She sniffed at herself suspiciously. "What is more, I seem to smell of fish."

Dybbuk laughed cruelly.

"I daresay you've been doing too much yoga," insisted Groanin. "It's that or too much sun. If I were you I'd go back to your room and have a bit of a rest. See how you feel in the morning." He helped the bewildered Miss Crabbe to her feet and smiled kindly at her.

"Yes," she said quietly. "Perhaps you're right. I *have* been overdoing it. I must have been. The sun. Not drinking enough water. Dehydrated. There's no other explanation. It's not possible I could have actually been a . . ." She walked unsteadily to the door, in a sideways fashion — a little like a crab, it has to be said — and, to the obvious delight of Dybbuk and Groanin, left the yoga center without saying another word.

"Well," said Groanin. "That takes care of her."

Back in their dormitory room, Dybbuk unrolled the East India Company picture, spread it out on the table, and studied it carefully. "This is the pink fort, all right," he said. "There's no question about it. We're in the right place. The fort doesn't seem to have changed at all since this picture was painted. But where do we concentrate our search?"

He shrugged and glanced up at the portrait of the Guru Masamjhasara. "If there is any enlightenment to be had in this place, I wish he'd hurry up and give it."

"The answer's in that line of writhing snakes," said Philippa. "In Colonel Killiecrankie's message. I'm certain of it." She read the whole message aloud again:

"'I scotched the snake not killed it. And fled to this terrible place of misery where I shall probably die at the hand of my enemies. But I am in luck now. And you, too, would do well to come down here and discover a king's ransom in the green eyes of the cobra king of Kathmandu. Look for the third snake. But beware the eighth. M.W.K.'"

"It sounds like a clue in a crossword puzzle," said Groanin.

"You said that before," said Dybbuk.

"Maybe because it's true."

"Crossword puzzles are for kids," said Dybbuk.

"You wouldn't say that if you'd ever tried to solve the one in *The Daily Telegraph*," insisted Groanin. "Crosswords are not for kids at all. They're for people who like to test their own brainpower. It's *brainpower* not djinn power that's going to solve this little conundrum. You would do well to remember that, Dybbuk."

"Buck. Just Buck, okay? You would do well to remember *that*."

As Dybbuk and Groanin continued to argue for a moment or two, John walked to the door of the dormitory and stared out at the courtyard. This was overlooked by the higher, inner wall of the pink fort and deserted except for a few birds perched in the shade provided by the roof of the old well-house.

Suddenly John turned in the doorway and went back into the room where he smacked the table in front of Dybbuk, hard, with the flat of his hand, which made everyone jump. "I've got it," he said. "It's a pun. A play on words. The colonel doesn't mean 'well' to be an adverb describing the verb 'to do,' at all. He means 'well' to be a noun."

Dybbuk, who wasn't quite sure what an adverb was, stared at him blankly for a moment.

"Don't you see?" demanded John. He pointed urgently at the doorway. "The colonel was talking about the kind of well that's right outside our door. The kind of well from which you get water. And the kind of well you would do *well* to go down and 'discover a king's ransom.'"

They all got up and walked over to the doorway from where they contemplated the old well.

"Of course," said Philippa. "Where better to hide something than down an old well?"

"Saves digging a hole and burying it, I suppose," said Groanin.

"It just has to be that well," said John.

"Unless someone's noticed another old well in this fort," said Dybbuk. "Have they?"

But nobody had. They went outside to take a closer look.

The well itself was as old as the castle and shaded from the sun with an open well-house made of several stone pillars and an ornate domed roof. There was a large bucket and a thick rope. They peered over the edge into the cool, dark depths. A draft came up the shaft as if the earth itself was breathing through this same hole, which did nothing to reduce anyone's fear of actually going down the well.

"Someone will have to go down," said Dybbuk, stating the obvious. "To look for the Cobra King."

"Bags it's not me," said Groanin. "There's something about the idea of going down an old well I don't like. Especially at night."

"Who said anything about going down at night?" said Dybbuk who, in truth, was no more eager to go down the well than Groanin. Nor indeed were the twins. Djinn are, after all, given to claustrophobia, which is the result of the many occasions when mundanes have imprisoned them in so-called magic lamps. It's not that djinn dislike being inside oil lamps or bottles. Indeed some of them — Mr. Rakshasas, for example — enjoy this style of living. But djinn, like everyone else in life, much prefer to be the masters of their own fate so that they can come and go from a lamp as they choose.

"Nay, lad," said Groanin. "We can hardly go down there in the daytime. Someone would surely see us and wonder what we were up to. No, it will have to be tonight. After supper. Assuming that there is any supper in this place."

As if to support what Groanin had just said, Jagannatha came out of a door on the opposite side of the courtyard and walked toward them. "QED," said Groanin, which was something he always said when he'd been proved right, although none of the children knew what it meant.

"Hi, there," said Jagannatha. "How's it going?"

"I think we exhausted poor Miss Crabbe," said Groanin.

"So I heard." He grinned. "She's meditating now. Probably for the rest of the day. Which is why I came to get you guys for an early dinner. I figured you'd be hungry after all that exercise."

"Not so much hungry as thirsty," Philippa said inventively, and nodded down the shaft of the well. "We were just wondering if there was any water in this well."

"Down there?" Jagannatha glanced down the well with suspicion. "Yes, there is, but I wouldn't drink it. As a matter of fact I wouldn't drink anything around here that hasn't come out of a bottle or a sterilized container."

"Really?" said Groanin.

"However, after dinner," continued Jagannatha, "I'm afraid you're all on the night shift for the computer support center. Manning the Bungle Computers Helpline." He shrugged. "Sorry about that. But that's the way it is, you being new 'n' all." Noting their anxious-looking faces, he shook his head. "Don't worry. There's really nothing to it. Just read what's on the screen or make it up as you go along. It won't make much difference. Just make sure you sound like you know what you're talking about. Whenever I get stuck for something to say I ask the poor sap on the other end of the telephone if he has a UHT cable."

"What's a UHT cable?" asked John. "I've never heard of such a thing."

"That's the point," said Jagannatha. "There's no such thing. It drives them nuts when they find out that they don't have one. And you should hear them swear. Some smash their telephones. Some even smash their computers, which is the whole point of the exercise, of course."

"Isn't giving people wrong advice and knowing it to be wrong," Philippa asked him carefully, "a rather cruel thing to do to them?"

"We're just being cruel to be kind." Jagannatha smiled. "That's all. To free people from the tyranny of technology. To break the bonds of the modern dictatorship of silicon and microchips. Those are the guru's words, not mine. But he's right, you know. It's time people discovered more simplicity in life. And forgot about processor speed and their e-mail and Web sites and stuff. Have you ever asked yourself why people have personal computers when there are people in this world with not enough to eat?"

"I'm not sure it's that simple," said Philippa. "And I'm not sure I can or want to persuade anyone that I actually know what I'm talking about when it comes to computers."

"Hey, it's no sweat," said Jagannatha. "Honest. I'm your supervisor tonight, so if you run into any problems, like you accidentally make someone's computer work or something, let me know and I'll come and mess it up for you. Okay?"

Groanin, John, and Philippa continued to look skeptical, but Dybbuk was grinning broadly.

"This is going to be fun," he said.

In the dining hall they saw hundreds of other sannyasins. Some were Swedish, some were Canadian, some were Indian, and some were from Great Britain. But mostly the sannyasins were from the United States. They were all dressed in the same way and seemed to be very friendly. There was a lot of smiling at the ashram. Someone played a little harmonium. And quite a few of the sannyasins went dancing around the dining hall, garlanded with flowers and their faces painted, singing and banging drums and chiming little finger-cymbals rhythmically. Everyone else ate their meal underneath an enormous picture of Guru Masamjhasara, which Philippa found a little off-putting as she disliked being watched while she was eating. There was something about the guru's hairy face that made her feel uncomfortable. And in particular there was the fact that he seemed so dirty. If the guru was dirty, then what kind of example was that for those of his followers who worked in the kitchens preparing food?

After dinner, which was surprisingly good, they reported to the computer support center. It was a large room with dozens of telephones and TV monitors — but no computers — and the biggest picture yet of Guru Masamjhasara, as if it was his intention to remind everyone manning the computer support center that he was watching them.

Philippa's first caller was an old lady from Massachusetts

called Hester Cardigan who plainly knew how to switch a computer on and off, and not much else. She was having a problem connecting her printer. Philippa felt sorry for Miss Cardigan and wanted to tell her to go and find some kind neighbors who knew about computers and have them install the machine for her, but with Jagannatha and some of the other sannyasins eavesdropping on her conversation, she had no choice but to read the nonsense that was printed on her TV screen.

"No wonder your computer won't talk to your printer," Philippa told Miss Cardigan, without much enthusiasm. "You've got the old model of printer. You'll have to reboot the computer, and start it in safe mode so that we can reconfigure your printer preferences using your diagnostic tool kit. Then we'll download some updated software, reboot the machine again, troubleshoot your new drivers, check which ports you're using, run a new output protocol using ASCII, and then print a test page. But if your PC is the 76a instead of the 76b, you'll need to save all your settings and then download a separate set of drivers that are compatible with the port you're using. Nothing to it, really. Ready?"

There followed a long silence during which Jagannatha gave Philippa a thumbs-up sign to indicate that she was doing well, and then moved on to listen in on the advice that was being given out by Dybbuk. This was Philippa's chance and, lowering her voice, she now tried her best to address Miss Cardigan's problem in the best way she knew. "Miss Cardigan? Are you still there?"

"Yes," whispered Miss Cardigan tearfully.

"Forget everything I just told you to do. It's only supposed to confuse you. Don't ask me why, it would take too long to explain. Here's what I want you to do, and it's really simple. Click on the start menu. Now click on the control panel. Now click on printers and faxes. Now click on add a printer. Click on next. Wait for the computer to recognize your printer. And that's it."

There followed a longish pause, and then Philippa heard the sound of a printer whirring into action.

"It works," said Miss Cardigan, starting to cry.

"Good," said Philippa. "And by the way, here's some *really* helpful advice. Don't call this number again. Not ever." She flicked a switch to end the call and, turning around in her chair, smiled brightly at Jagannatha. "She's taking it back to the shop," said Philippa.

Jagannatha punched the air triumphantly. "Good job, Panchali," he said. "Bad advice is the best advice."

Unlike Philippa, however, Dybbuk had no scruples about what he was doing and laughed with glee as he took his fourth call of the evening. He was especially pleased to discover that his new caller taught mathematics at an elementary school in southern California. If there was one kind of living creature Dybbuk hated, it was a math teacher. The teacher, whose name was Norman Blackhead, was having a small problem with his modem.

"What speed is your modem?" Dybbuk asked carelessly.

"Speed?"

"Yeah, speed. 56. 128. 256. 512. What?"

"Er, 128."

"Kilobytes or megabytes?"

"Megabytes."

Dybbuk laughed. "It's kilobytes, Grandpa. The fastest modem in the world won't do more than about four megabytes a second. All right. Have you got a fireguard on your computer?"

"Er, yes, I think so."

Dybbuk laughed again. "It's a firewall, Grandpa, not a fireguard. Next you'll be telling me that you don't want to install your antibiotic program."

"Oh, but I do."

"You're sure about that?"

"Yes, quite sure."

"Well, you'd better speak to your doctor, Grandpa, 'cuz I can't help you." He paused for a moment. "What about an antivirus program? Are you planning on running one of those?"

Determined not to make a mistake again, the schoolteacher said, "No," which earned another guffaw from Dybbuk. "You'll have some big problems if you don't, Grandpa. Your system will pick up all sorts of nasty bugs when you're surfing the Internet. Okay, here's what I want you to do. Run your connection manager program and test your TCP/IP configuration using the ping command. That's 'ping' as in 'Pong,' Grandpa. Think you can spell that?"

Philippa listened to Dybbuk, more than a little horrified

at the relish with which he was handling the hapless helpline caller. There were times when she found it hard to believe that Dybbuk could belong to a tribe of good djinn, and she only managed to excuse his callous behavior by reminding herself that his parents were divorced, and that his best friend, Brad, had been murdered.

Meanwhile, it was now quite plain to John how, using the helpline number, his own attempts to configure the Bungle laptop he had been given for his birthday had come to nothing. And in spite of Guru Masamjhasara's declared desire to liberate people from the tyranny of technology, "for the sake of their souls," he agreed with his sister's opinion of the whole exercise — that this was not a nice thing to do — especially now that he had discovered what it was actually like, knowingly giving people misleading advice.

The twins thought it was just as well that their stay at the Jayaar Sho Ashram in Lucknow's pink fort was going to be a short one, otherwise they would have been strongly tempted to tell the guru exactly what they thought of someone who encouraged his followers to be so cruel to so many ordinary people.

CHAPTER 13

THE WELL-WISHERS

The night was well-suited to the secret and subterranean task that lay ahead of them. A full, almost violet-colored moon illuminated the unevenly paved courtyard where the ancient well was located. Bats flitted around the battlements on the inner rampart wall, but apart from their thin, almost inaudible squeaks, the night was a quiet one. The three children and Mr. Groanin would have to explore the well shaft with great stealth since any sound in the courtyard would echo and attract attention from one of several brightly lit windows on the inner wall. Behind these high windows, according to Jagannatha, in an apartment of great luxury, lived the guru himself.

Inspecting the well more closely, they dropped a stone down the shaft and counted up to fifteen before they heard a quiet splash in the darkened depths below.

"It must be a hundred feet deep," said John.

"More like a hundred and fifty," whispered Groanin. He

shook his head grimly. "By heck, I bet this well could tell a few tales."

"How do you mean?" Dybbuk asked nervously, for it was he who had volunteered to go down the well in the large metal bucket that was standing on the well's stone wall.

"I was reading about this here pink fort," said Groanin. "In the ashram's library. Apparently, after the mutiny the British forces threw dozens of poor Indians down this well." He paused for dramatic effect. *"Alive."*

Dybbuk gulped and in the echoing courtyard it sounded as loud as a turkey gobble.

"It seems that some even threw themselves down there, in order to escape a worse fate," continued Groanin, quite oblivious to the effect he was having on Dybbuk. "Mind you, I think this must have been long after Colonel Killiecrankie hid the talisman in the well. I doubt he'd have had the stomach to descend this well shaft if it had been bunged up with all those corpses."

"What happened to them?" asked Dybbuk, staring into the cold, dark depths, and finding it all too easy to imagine a man thrown to his death down there. He could hardly imagine a worse fate. "To all those corpses? Are they still down there?"

"They were taken away when the British decided to re-garrison this fort," said Groanin and dropped another stone down the shaft. This time the splash sounded more like a moan from one of the poor Indian sepoys who had met their deaths there. "Taken away and reburied so that the

British might have the use of the water. So the book said, anyway."

Groanin swung the water bucket over the side and put his foot on the brake that could lower it quickly or slowly or stop it altogether. "Right then," he said. "It *is* Dybbuk who's going down, isn't it?"

Even in the shadow of the little stone well-house under which they were standing, it was clear to John and Philippa that Dybbuk had lost his nerve for their endeavor. Not that the twins could blame him. Not after Groanin's thoughtless story. The well was as cold and damp and creepy as any crypt or tomb, and it was only too easy to imagine that some awful skeletal creature might yet remain in its hidden depths. Whoever went down in the bucket would need a great deal of nerve.

The bucket itself was as big as a trash can and fastened to a thick rope wound around a large spindle that ran across the well on an ancient-looking axle. There was a gear on the axle and, attached to this, a heavy wooden handle whereby the drum on the spindle could be turned, and the bucket raised. Try as they might, neither Philippa nor John nor Dybbuk could see how djinn power might be used to create a different means of descending the well shaft in a way that might afford someone a chance to be mindful of the last part of Colonel Killiecrankie's secret message: *"Look for the third snake. But beware the eighth."* Becoming a bird or even a bat might have made it easier to fly in and out of the well, but neither creature was equipped to shift a brick in the wall of the well shaft — as it seemed likely they would have to do — or indeed to carry the golden talisman. In providing them with a chisel, a decent-sized hammer, several powerful flashlights, and a walkie-talkie set, djinn power had already done as much as could practically be done.

As usual it was John who perceived a solution to the dilemma of which of them might be courageous enough to go down the well. "Do you think you could handle the weight of the three of us kids in that bucket?" he asked Groanin. "Instead of Dybbuk on his own."

"Nay, lad. Not even the weight of two kids," Groanin said sadly. "Not with just one arm. The lowering is no problem. It's all done with this foot brake, see? It's the lifting up that'd be the difficulty. A job like that calls for two arms, make no mistake. And as you can see, I've only the one."

"But what if you had two arms?" asked John. "And what if your new arm was really strong?"

Groanin frowned as he considered the idea. "Well, there's a thought," he said, sitting down on the stone wall that surrounded the well. "You'll forgive me if I think about it for a minute, John, on account of the fact that I've grown quite used to having just the one arm. So much so, that sometimes I wonder what I should do with two. Except when doing yoga, of course. I can see how an extra arm might come in handy for that." He sighed. "As you know, Nimrod has often offered to give me another arm and I've always said no. Not because I like having just the one arm, but because I should have to get used to having two again. But now that

I think about it again, I can find no good reason to say no. Except, perhaps, to wonder if you are up to the task. I'd hate to end up looking like Frankenstein's monster with something alien and horrible attached to me." But Groanin was nodding. "All right," he said, closing his eyes. "But to do it quickly would be best, before I change my mind."

Instinctively, John took hold of Philippa's hand and she took hold of Dybbuk's, so that they might concentrate their power for, with thirty-two bones in the human arm — two in the shoulder, three in the arm itself, eight in the wrist, and nineteen in the hand and fingers — to say nothing of all the blood vessels and muscle fibers, creating any part of a human body from scratch would have taxed the powers of any djinn, even one that was fully grown to adulthood.

"FABULONGOSHOO —"

"ABECEDARIAN!"

"MARVELISHLY —"

"ZYGOBRANCHIATE!"

"WONDERPIPICAL!"

The darkness around Groanin shimmered a little, like a heat wave, and a strong smell of sulfur filled the air — for the use of so much concentrated djinn power often leaves its own distinctively powerful scent.

The butler opened his eyes slowly. "Is it done?" he asked cautiously.

"Yes," said John. "It's done."

They crowded around to take a closer look at their handiwork as, for the first time in many years, Groanin extended

243

two arms in front of him, and then bit his lip as he tried to control his anger and irritation. "Nay, but you've given me two right hands, you young idiots! Look! The thumb's on the wrong side of my hand."

"Whoops," said John.

"Can't you just make do with it like that?" said Dybbuk. "I mean, no one will notice, will they?"

"Of course we can't leave it like that." Groanin threatened to smack Dybbuk with the back of his normal hand. "I'm not an experiment in the doll's hospital, you young pup."

So they did it again and this time they got it right — or rather left. They even managed to add a nice-looking watch on Groanin's left wrist, by way of compensation, and he seemed so delighted with it that it was hard to tell which he was pleased with more — the new wristwatch or the new arm to which it was fastened.

"Come on," said John, climbing into the water bucket. "Let's get going. We're wasting valuable darkness."

The air grew damp and chilly as the bucket sank down the well shaft carrying the three young djinn into the fearful depth of rock beneath the fort. For the most part the wall of the shaft had been cut through solid sandstone, but here and there were patches of brickwork, as if the rock had been shored up or, perhaps, something had been walled in.

In the bucket, John faced one way, Philippa a second, and Dybbuk a third so that they were able to examine all around the shaft as Groanin's foot lowered them gently down its enormous depth. Gradually, the moonlight grew fainter and then disappeared, and they had only their flashlights to illuminate their pendulous passage. Once or twice they glanced back up the shaft but after about fifty feet, the well mouth had all but vanished and there was only the rope creaking above them to connect them with the surface world of light and the living.

From time to time each djinn would touch the wall, hoping to uncover some concealed mark or loose brick that might reveal the Cobra King of Kathmandu. Despite the damp air, the walls were dry and clean, which was a surprise to them until they remembered the heat of India and the distance from the water below. This they hardly cared to look down upon for fear that they might see something horrible climbing up the walls to get them.

"Wait a minute," said Dybbuk, his voice echoing inside the well. "I think I've found something."

John lifted the walkie-talkie to his mouth. "Mr. Groanin, Stop lowering for a minute," he said.

The bucket stopped its descent although it continued to turn in a circle, like the bob on the end of a pendulum. John and Philippa followed Dybbuk's finger to a mark that was scored in the wall. And bringing a flashlight close up to the mark, they saw that it was the design of a cobra scratched neatly onto the brick.

"Since we're looking for the third cobra," said Dybbuk, "I should say that's the first one, wouldn't you?"

The twins agreed and John told Groanin to start lowering

again, but slower now, so that they might not miss the second cobra. Of course it goes without saying that they found it more unnerving to descend down the well shaft in a bucket than to go up the rock on the rope elevator, and it wasn't very long before each of them felt obliged to swallow a charcoal pill, which is the way the djinn settle their stomachs and overcome anxiety attacks.

Approximately sixty feet farther down, Philippa found the second cobra, roughly scratched on another brick. But they did not stop to examine it as, nearing the water at the bottom of the well, it was becoming colder now. Philippa felt herself shiver and was uncertain if this was due to the cold or because they had to pause and investigate a section of the wall that had collapsed in on itself, for it seemed that something could have been walled in behind these bricks. But none of the bricks were scratched with Killiecrankie's cobra sign, so they continued on down, and it wasn't long before the bottom of the bucket in which they were standing touched the surface of the water.

Quickly, John pressed the TALK button on the walkie-talkie. "Stop lowering," he told Groanin. "Stop, immediately."

The bucket went down another foot or two before they stopped, with the water a mere few inches below the lip of the bucket. Anxiously they shone their flashlights all around the well shaft, looking for the third cobra marking, but none was visible.

"We must have gone past it," said Philippa. "It must have

been back at that part where the wall had caved in on itself. Perhaps the brick with the third cobra fell into the water."

"Or someone got here before us," said Dybbuk.

"Nothing like being optimistic," said Philippa.

John placed his flashlight on a little ledge of brickwork and dipped his hand experimentally into the well water. "It's freezing," he said. "Absolutely freezing."

Philippa and Dybbuk followed suit, testing the water with their hands. John was right. The water in the well was like ice.

"It must be spring water," said Philippa. "Straight out of the mountain."

"We'd better go back up," said Dybbuk. "We must have missed it."

But before anyone could answer there was a loud splash as something hit the water beside them.

"What was that?" said John and, looking over the edge of the bucket, briefly caught sight of a walkie-talkie handset descending into the depths of the water below. For a split second he thought he'd dropped his own handset. Then he saw that he was still holding it. But even as he guessed it was Groanin's handset that had landed in the water, the bucket underneath his feet dropped suddenly, and before any of them could gather themselves to focus their djinn power, they all plunged over their heads into the freezing water.

"What happened?" yelled Dybbuk, when at last he managed to swim back up to the surface again.

"I don't know," John yelled back, and just had time to

grab the chisel from the bucket. He glanced at his now-useless walkie-talkie and threw it away, and then tucked the chisel under his belt so that he could use both hands to keep himself afloat. It was just as well that he had thought to place his flashlight on a ledge up on the wall because both Philippa and Dybbuk had now lost theirs in the water.

Gasping at the temperature of the water, each of them tried to find enough djinn power to convey them to the top of the well shaft but it was too late, for they were already chilled to the bone, rendering them all quite powerless.

"That idiot," said Dybbuk. "What does he think he's doing?" And he began to shout for help.

"Shut up," John told him. "Just shut up for a moment and let me think. Groanin wouldn't have done this on purpose. Something must have happened to him." And he told them about seeing Groanin's walkie-talkie hit the water a second or two before the bucket had dropped. "In which case it might not be such a good idea to shout for help. At least not right away."

"What are we going to do?" said Dybbuk. "None of us have djinn power. And there's no way we can climb all the way to the top on that rope. But if we stay here we'll probably drown."

"Nothing like being optimistic," said Philippa.

"Maybe there's something I missed here," said Dybbuk, slapping the water with frustration, "but I really don't see much to be optimistic about."

"It won't help if you lose your temper," said Philippa.

"Stop arguing, you two," said John.

"Who's arguing?" protested Philippa.

"Look, it could be worse," said John. "We could be in the pitch-dark. But the way I see it, with the light we still have a couple of options."

"Such as?" Dybbuk sounded unconvinced by John's reasoning.

"We'll have to climb to that spot back up the shaft where the bricks caved in," he said. "Then maybe we can push some more in and make a ledge and sit there until we're dry. Dry and warm enough to use djinn power again."

Philippa glanced up the shaft. The caved-in section of the wall was thirty feet above their heads. She wasn't at all sure she could manage what John had suggested and what Dybbuk was already attempting.

"Good idea," she said, and hoped for the best.

CHAPTER 14

JUJU EYEBALLS

Ever since the audience with his followers in the shrine
that morning, Guru Masamjhasara had been nagged by
the suspicion that he had met the man with one arm somewhere before. Of course it would have been at least ten
years ago and that man, who was Nimrod's butler, had been
English, and this man — the man he had seen that morning,
who called himself Mr. Gupta — was Indian. Nevertheless,
there was just something about this new recruit to the ashram
that strongly reminded him of Nimrod's butler. But what?
The guru had been a doctor then, with a thriving London
medical practice that counted the British prime minister's
wife among his patients. Which was how it was that he
had been summoned to Downing Street early one April morning in the last years of the twentieth century and asked to attend
the prime minister himself.

There were few doctors who would have recognized his
peculiar symptoms for, on the face of it, the prime minister

had seemed to be suffering from the delusion that he was a girl of about twelve years of age. The guru reflected that most doctors would have decided that the prime minister was a lunatic and ordered him committed to the local mental asylum. But Dr. Warnakulasuriya, as Guru Masamjhasara then called himself, had correctly recognized that the prime minister was possessed by a djinn. And, presuming to take advantage of his late father's acquaintance with Nimrod, Dr. Warnakulasuriya had gone straight to the djinn's house and asked for his urgent assistance. Which was when he had encountered Nimrod's one-armed butler. That was it, surely! This man — this Mr. Gupta — had only one arm!

At the time it had struck him as strange that a being such as Nimrod should have hired a one-armed servant. But this was not nearly as strange as anything that was to follow and which was to leave Dr. Warnakulasuriya convinced that he should abandon medicine altogether and become a holy man, like his father. And soon after the Downing Street exorcism he had come back to India and, using the proceeds from the sale of his London medical practice, purchased the pink fort at Lucknow, established the Jayaar Sho Ashram, and set himself up as a guru.

The ashram was now the matrix of a worldwide network of spiritual centers that numbered more than fifty, and the guru had several thousand followers. This made it a highly profitable operation, and now that the guru's plans were nearing completion, the last thing he wanted was any snoops spoiling things. Especially when they might be connected with Nimrod. So, just after midnight, the guru dispatched several of the larger *sadhaks* from the *Bahutbarhiya Jan Bachane* — his "wonderful bodyguard" — to bring this Mr. Gupta to him so that he might be questioned about who he was and what he and his children were doing at the ashram.

The *sadhaks* were on their way to the dormitory when they found Groanin loitering by the well in the pink fort's inner courtyard.

Finding himself approached and in some force, Groanin had panicked. First, he had tossed the walkie-talkie handset into the well hoping that it wouldn't hit one of the children. Then, reasoning that the children were djinn and could probably look after themselves, he had removed his foot from the brake that lowered the bucket and, tucking his new arm inside the body of his baggy Indian shirt, tried to look innocent.

Mr. Bhuttote, the largest of the *sadhaks*, pointed crossly at Groanin.

"What are you doing out here?" he asked, speaking Hindi. "Don't you know that it is forbidden to be out of your dormitory after midnight?"

"I've just finished work," said Groanin. "In the computer support center. I've been sitting down for several hours and I needed to stretch my legs and get some air."

"The guru wants to see you," said Mr. Bhuttote. "You'll have to come with us."

"Me? What about?"

"I've really no idea."

"But at this time of night?" Groanin pretended to stifle

a yawn. "Can't it wait until the morning? Yoga this after-noon and then the computer center. I'm exhausted."

"It can't wait," insisted Mr. Bhuttote. "We have our orders. If the guru says come now, then you must come now. Besides, Guru Masamjhasara never sleeps. As a matter of fact, he hasn't slept in twelve years."

"I'm sorry to hear that," said Groanin. "Insomnia, is it?"

"No," said another of the *sadhaks*. "There's too much going on inside his head for him to waste time sleeping."

"The poor chap," said Groanin and followed the *sadhaks* back to the shrine where he was told the guru was now waiting for him. "How awful for him."

"It's not awful at all," insisted Mr. Bhuttote. "His nights are devoted to the thinking of great thoughts. These great thoughts he shares with us and thanks to him we are all enlightened."

"Yes," said Groanin, hardly at all convinced. "I'm sure we would all miss hearing the guru's great thoughts."

John grabbed the rope and his sister's hand and pulled them toward each other. "You can do it, Phil," he said. Dybbuk was already thirty feet up the rope and near the caved-in sec-tion of the shaft wall.

Philippa was quite numb with cold. Her teeth were chat-tering together with a sound like the hooves of a tiny horse. She had never been much good in the physical education classes at school and, back in New York, if she'd been asked to climb thirty feet up a rope, she'd probably have said that she couldn't do it. Not without the subtle deployment of djinn power, anyway. But there are occasions when danger and desperation foster acts of great physical strength and endurance and this was certainly such an occasion. So she hardly needed any urging from John. Taking hold of the rope, she pulled herself high enough to stand on the tip of the submerged bucket and started to climb.

Meanwhile, awaiting his turn on the rope, John put his head under the water for a moment to take a look. Surfacing again, he shook his head and gasped. "I figure it's at least another hundred feet down to the bottom. The water's quite clear, though."

"Please," said Philippa, "I'd rather not know."

Something heavy hit the water again. She and John both looked up and saw Dybbuk holding on to the rope and kicking at the crumbled section of the well shaft. Another loose brick fell and hit the water. And then another.

"Careful," yelled John. "That one almost hit me."

"Sorry," said Dybbuk and swept some more bricks into the water before maneuvering himself into the large hole he had made. "Come on up," he yelled over his shoulder. "There's plenty of room, I think. See if you can bring the flashlight with you when you climb up."

It took Philippa all of fifteen minutes to reach the ledge. Her exhausting effort was not without its cost, however. Struggling to gain a foothold on the cavity Dybbuk had made in the wall, she accidentally kicked another brick over the edge, and instead of hitting the water harmlessly like all the others, this one hit the flashlight John had left balanced on a ledge, just as he was reaching for it, and knocked it into the water.

Dybbuk yelled with horror and John, who by now was almost halfway up the rope himself, had little choice but to jump back into the water in pursuit of what was their only source of light.

Somehow the flashlight, which was only water resistant, stayed lit, making it easy to pursue into the depths of the freezing mountain water. John kicked hard and wriggled toward the light with one arm and then the other as he struggled to catch hold of it. Twice his fingers touched it but failed to grab it, and only on the third occasion, with his lungs almost bursting, did he grasp it firmly, at last.

It was then that he saw it: a sinuous shape scratched on the brickwork. The third cobra! There was no time to go up for air. He didn't think he could make a dive like this again and still have enough strength left to climb up the rope. It was now or never. He swam toward the third cobra mark and, with just enough light to see what he was doing, poked the chisel into the mortar to loosen the brick that Colonel Killiecrankie had scratched more indelibly, it seemed, than upon either of the other two. He had even taken the precaution of scratching the number 3 next to it, just so that there could be no mistake. John felt the brick shift and pushed the chisel in some more, to lever the brick out.

Sitting on the ledge in the darkness, Philippa waited for her brother to return with a mixture of pride and concern for she was worried that he might succumb to the intense cold of the water. All that she and Dybbuk could see was the rippling shape of the flashlight beam underneath the surface of the water.

"Why doesn't he come back up?" muttered Dybbuk.

Philippa did not reply. And then, just as she was about to jump in again after him, the light surfaced, and to her considerable relief, so did John. He yelled something and held what appeared to be a small leather bag aloft.

"I've got it," he said breathlessly, waving the bag in triumph. "The talisman."

"Fantastic job, John," said Philippa, happy just to see that her brother was okay.

"Great!" yelled Dybbuk. "Good work, John."

"At least I think I have it. I saw the brick with the third cobra mark when I went down for the flashlight. I got that, too."

"Obviously," remarked Dybbuk.

"Well done," said Philippa. "Without that light we're sunk."

"It was about ten feet down. I had to put my whole arm inside the hole and it got stuck. For a moment, I thought I was going to drown."

The flashlight flickered and, for a second or two, went out altogether, giving the three of them a brief taste of a darkness that was so thick they could almost have chewed it.

"Let's hope this doesn't conk out," said John, and tucked the flashlight and the leather bag under his belt before swimming to the rope and starting to climb.

"What was the colonel thinking of?" complained Dybbuk, sweeping more bricks into the water. "Putting it there, below the surface of the water."

"You know, I'll bet the water wasn't this high when the colonel made that mark," said Philippa. "After the British Army repaired the well, the water level must have risen."

John was tired after his effort in the water — tired and very, very cold — so his progress up the rope was agonizingly slow. Once or twice he even slipped down a few feet, burning his hands on the rough rope, which at least served to take his mind off the pain in his exhausted shoulder muscles. Finally, he managed to get his feet onto the edge of the cavity. Dybbuk then took hold of John's shirt and with immense effort succeeded in hauling him safely up into the space on top of himself, bringing down yet more bricks and dust.

For a moment the flashlight flickered again. John rolled off Dybbuk, coughed a bit, retrieved the flashlight from under his belt, and inspected it, at which point it went out altogether, plunging them into darkness. He tapped the light gently against the palm of his rope-burned hand, hoping that it might come back to life, but this time, it didn't.

"Great," said Dybbuk. "That's just great. What are we going to do without that flashlight?"

"Maybe, if I take it apart," said John, "I can dry it. With time, there's no reason why it shouldn't work again."

Dybbuk was breathing rapidly and it was plain that the darkness was already beginning to aggravate his claustrophobia. Blindly he felt in his pockets and found another charcoal pill. It crumbled soggily in his fingers and he had to wipe it into his mouth.

"The important thing is not to panic," said John. "And not to make any sudden moves so that none of us slips off this ledge and falls." He started to unscrew the base of the flashlight. "Who knows? Maybe we'll dry out and warm up before the flashlight does, in which case our problems will be solved."

Dybbuk started to calm down again. (Charcoal pills act very quickly.) "All right," he said. "I'll buy that."

"In the meantime," said John, "why don't you see — I mean, why don't you try to make some more space for us?" He emptied the batteries into his hand and then turned the body of the flashlight upside down, to shake out any moisture.

"Can I do something?" asked Philippa.

"Sure," said Dybbuk. "I'll start digging behind us. I'll hand you a brick or a piece of rock and you chuck it into the water, since you're nearer the edge than me." He pushed himself as far back into the cavity as he could and, pulling away a handful of brick and rock, handed it carefully to Philippa. "Here," he said. "The wall's quite rotten so it ought to be easy enough. Now I know what a mole feels like."

Philippa launched the chunk of masonry Dybbuk had handed her into the cold void in front of her. A second later they heard it hit the water.

John blew inside the body of the flashlight, laid the batteries and the screw base carefully on the ground, and then folded his body around them so that they could not be misplaced.

There was no doubt about it, he told himself grimly, without the flashlight things looked bad. But even with the light, what could they do? Privately he was not nearly as confident about their chances as his words to Dybbuk and Philippa had implied; it was cold in the well shaft, too cold to foresee an early return of enough body heat to generate djinn power. Cold and dark — so dark that he couldn't see his own finger when it was less than half an inch in front of his eyes. As tight spots go, this one looked very tight indeed. The more he thought about it, the more John was of the opinion that the only way they were going to get out of the well was if Groanin came and rescued them. Their best hope now was that whatever had happened to Groanin was only temporary.

Guru Masamjhasara — in Hindi, *masamjhasara* means "I under stand you all" — climbed down from his dentist's chair and walked slowly up to Groanin, fixing him with his best juju eyeball.

Groanin, pinioned between two of the larger *sadhaks*, endured the holy man's scrutiny without a word, not even complaining when the guru placed his evil-smelling hands on Groanin's head and closed his eyes, as if he was trying to read his mind.

"Have we met before?" asked the guru, keeping perfectly still.

"Not before today," said Groanin. "I mean, yesterday. I'm sure I'd remember someone as distinguished as you, Your Holiness."

Behind the guru's eyelids, his eyes revolved slowly as if he were watching the world spinning around. Then he repeated the question, as if he hadn't been listening to a word Groanin had said, or simply didn't believe him — it was impossible to tell which.

"No," said Groanin. *And yet.* And yet, close up, Groanin recognized that there was something very vaguely familiar about the guru. It was almost as if they *had* met many years ago. It was the guru's bad breath that seemed most familiar to Groanin. This was like a fish that had died in a plastic bag on a very hot day, with only a tub of yogurt for company. Also, behind the bushy, Karl Marx–sized beard was a face Groanin thought he just might have seen before. But the beard distracted him. Or rather the things that were in the beard, for now that he was close up to Guru Masamjhasara, Groanin could see all the pieces of food sticking in the hair, which had dropped from his mouth or his fork during several weeks' worth of previous meals. A piece of sweet corn. A grain or two of pilau rice. A pasta shell. An orange seed. A length of spaghetti. Not to mention a bit of old chewing gum and some snot.

"You see, I've got a built-in early warning system about people," declared the guru, in his reedy little English-accented voice, and spread his greasy fingers on Groanin's head like the tentacles of an octopus. "And you, my friend. You worry me."

"I can't think why," said Groanin. "I'm nobody."

"Oh, no," giggled the guru. "I tell everyone who comes to

the ashram. I say, 'You're unique.' Everyone. And they are. Everybody is somebody." He spoke as if his head had just come down from a cloud. "Most especially the people who claim to be nobody." He opened his eyes slowly.

"Perhaps you're confusing me with someone else, sir. Someone that I resemble perhaps."

"I don't think so," said the guru. "You are a most distinguished man, Mr. Gupta. In my life I have met very few men with only one arm. Indeed, if I am honest with myself, I can think of only one other one-armed man that I have ever met."

Groanin smiled. "Oh, well, if that's all it is, then I can understand why I might seem familiar to you," he said coolly. "Yes, I think you're right. Having just the one arm isn't common. I haven't met many one-armed people myself." By now Groanin had decided that it would definitely be in his best interests to persuade the guru he had made a mistake, which was why he chose this particular moment to pull his new arm out of the body of his loose-fitting kurta. "But as you can see, sir, I have two arms."

"That's very odd." The guru frowned. "That's very odd, indeed. I could have sworn you had just the one arm," he said. "But why do you keep one of your arms hidden in this way?" He took hold of Groanin's two hands and squeezed them, as if checking that neither of them was false. "Your yoga teacher, Miss Crabbe, thought so, too."

"Sir, I confess I thought I might escape having to do yoga with just the one arm. That is why I concealed it. It was wrong of me. And I apologize."

"And yet you hid it very well."

"The fact is, sir, I used to be a magician," said Groanin, thinking it best that his story was consistent with the one the children had already told Jagannatha. "And I often used to pose as a one-armed man so that it might help me to pull off some of my conjuring tricks, sir." Groanin squeezed the guru's hands back. "I apologize for the subterfuge, sir. But as you can now see, you have mistaken me for someone else. Most certainly." Groanin smiled and allowed himself a little joke. "After all, I could hardly have grown a new limb since yesterday, now could I?"

Guru Masamjhasara let go of Groanin's hands and, taking hold of his own beard, twisted it, as if he was trying to wring a thought or idea out of its gray bushiness. Instead this merely dislodged the piece of sweet corn, which fell into the gray hair that covered his chest like so many old bedsprings. "No indeed you could not, Mr. Gupta. If indeed that is your name. I agree. You couldn't grow an extra limb. But you might have one added on. By a djinn."

"A *djinn?*" Groanin pretended to conceal a smile. "Well, yes, sir. If you believe those sorts of things *do* exist, then, yes, I suppose a djinn could have done it."

"Oh, they certainly *do* exist," said Guru Masamjhasara. "I know. I've met one. As have you, perhaps."

"Me, sir?" Groanin smiled. "Oh, no, sir. I'm an ordinary man, sir, and I know nothing of such things. My mother taught me that only the high Brahmins and saints can see djinn."

"Unless . . ." The guru wasn't listening to Groanin. "Unless you're a djinn yourself, of course. It might explain your little trick on the rope elevator, this afternoon." He giggled. "Oh, yes. I heard about that. My followers tell me everything."

"That was just plain foolishness, sir," said Groanin. "The Indian rope trick is something I like to do whenever I get the chance. To keep my hand in it — as it were. Look, sir, I'm not a djinn. I'm just an ordinary man."

"Then you won't mind sitting down in my dentist's chair, so that I can examine your mouth," said the guru, and gestured to the two *sadhaks* to bring Groanin to the chair in the middle of the shrine.

Groanin disliked dentists at the best of times. Disliked everything about them: their squeaky fingers, their stupid small talk, their annoyingly wholesome smiles, and their hideous little instruments of torture. But most of all he disliked the smell of a tooth being drilled, which, to Groanin's sharp nostrils, was evocative of all sorts of unpleasant memories of his Manchester childhood.

"What are you going to do?" he yelled as he found himself lifted into the chair.

The guru picked his nose absently for a moment, ate the slimy green result, and then collected a dental pick from an instrument tray before advancing on the butler. "Relax," he said. "I merely wish to ascertain if you have all of your teeth."

"Teeth?" said Groanin. "What have my teeth got to do with anything?" Of course, he knew very well what Guru

Masamjhasara was hoping to determine, but he thought it best to maintain a show of ignorance about the character and ways of the djinn — especially because none of them have wisdom teeth. Even so, he was hardly happy about the idea of the guru putting his dirty-looking fingers inside his mouth, especially the finger that had just made a green and sticky exit from the guru's nose.

"Most people imagine I have this chair just for my own comfort," murmured the guru, peering inside Groanin's mouth. "But of course, it serves a dual purpose, as you yourself are about to discover."

And because he did not think that the guru actually meant to torture him, which was just as well as he had no doubt he would have told the guru whatever he wanted to know, Groanin reluctantly allowed his mouth to be examined.

"Goodness me," said the guru, his nose wrinkled with disgust. "What did you have for supper?"

Groanin tried to answer. He endeavored to say, "That's rich coming from you, Mr. Breath-as-bad-as-a-skunk's-backside," but this was impossible with the guru's dirty fingers and dental pick occupying his mouth.

When the dental examination was complete the guru stood back, wiped his hands on his beard, and let out a loud sigh of disappointment. "No," he said. "You are not a djinn. Of course, there's no telling what you might have tried to do to me, if you had been. I say 'tried' because naturally, I'm prepared for all possibilities." He showed Groanin a medallion around his neck that was much like the one Nimrod had received in his djinnternal mail. "This is my amulet. It was made by my father, the fakir, to render him immune to the power of the djinn. He was a very great man. And a very great fakir." The guru giggled. "I certainly wouldn't have attempted an examination of your teeth without this little amulet of mine. If you had been a djinn you might have —"

Guru Masamjhasara's eyes narrowed and went all juju again.

"But wait a minute," said the guru, looking at the *sadhaks*. "Didn't he come here with three children?"

"Yes, Holiness," said one of the *sadhaks*.

"I wonder," said the guru. "No. They couldn't be. That would be too lucky."

"You leave them kids alone," said Groanin in a way he hoped made him seem properly paternal.

"The children. I wonder. . . ." The guru stroked his long beard, flicked a piece of pilau rice onto the floor, and inclined his head in a way that gave him the look of someone listening to a silent voice. "One and one and one is three," he said quietly. And then, more loudly to the *sadhaks*. "Find them. Find those children."

CHAPTER 15

THE NINTH COBRA

In the darkness of the well shaft, the children continued their blind excavations.

"These stones feel kind of strange," said Philippa, as she chucked another rock into the darkness and heard it splash into the water at the bottom of the shaft. "They're kind of lighter than the ones we were moving in the beginning."

"I was thinking the same thing," admitted Dybbuk. "Maybe it's volcanic rock. Like that stuff you rub your feet with."

"Pumice stone? Yeah. It could be."

They had been excavating for almost an hour and a cavity big enough to sit in comfortably had become a ten- or twelve-foot-long tunnel that offered some hope of a way out of the well shaft. Their clothes were still damp and their bodies too cold to have recovered their djinn powers but, even in the dark, it was plain that their situation had improved a little. And the farther into the wall of the well shaft they dug, the more optimistic they became. Covered with dust and rubble,

Philippa went at her invisible work with enthusiasm, whistling to keep up her spirits.

"How's that flashlight?" Dybbuk asked John.

"The parts seem dry enough," said John. "I think I might try to put it back together now." He dropped the two batteries inside the long metallic tube. "Fingers crossed," he added, and screwed on the spring-loaded base. He took a deep breath and pressed the ON/OFF button.

The flashlight switched on, illuminating the little tunnel they had made. But no one breathed a sigh of relief. Far from it. Instead all three children let out a scream of horror as they suddenly understood exactly where they were. Surrounding them were dozens of human skeletons, for they were in a kind of crypt or tomb, and the rock resting on Philippa's lap was not a rock at all but the skull of a human. Overcome with revulsion, she hurled it out of the tomb and into the well shaft. Similarly, Dybbuk discovered that the stick with which he had been digging through the back wall of the cave was not a stick but a human thigh bone. With this unpleasant discovery came the realization of what had happened to all the poor Indian mutineers whose bodies had been recovered by the British after throwing them down the well. They had been reburied here, one on top of the other like so many cigars, in a crypt in the wall of the well, where they had remained undisturbed for more than one hundred and fifty years.

The skeletons were so numerous that it was impossible to get away from them. In disgust, Philippa turned away from one grinning skull to find herself nose to nose-aperture with another. And, scrambling farther along the crypt, Dybbuk succeeded only in bringing several more skeletons down on top of himself. So that not only were their eyes grimed with the dust of death and human decay, but it also filled their mouths and their lungs.

John recovered his nerve first, shining the flashlight beyond Dybbuk as he struggled to push the skeletons off himself, and then scrambled into the deepest depths of that subterranean charnel house. The back wall of the crypt was made of bricks but the mortar was rotten, and Dybbuk had already succeeded in creating a hole that was big enough to wriggle through. Crawling on his belly, John squeezed past Dybbuk to investigate, pushing his head and shoulders through the hole in the wall. The other two followed him because John had the flashlight and neither Philippa nor Dybbuk had any desire to be left in the dark again with all those dead men.

Seeing a large space ahead of him, with no sign of any skeletons, John launched himself through the hole and, crawling a few yards farther on, soon found himself able to stand up. Breathing a sigh of relief that was not filled with the dust of old human bones, he turned to face his two companions who had come after him. John was smiling.

"It looks like there's a way out of here after all," he said and shone the flashlight at a series of ancient stone steps that rose in front of them.

"Thank goodness for that," said Philippa.

"That's the good news."

"What's the bad news?" asked Dybbuk.

"Haven't you noticed? It's freezing in here. Look." John breathed out over the beam of the flashlight. "You can see your breath."

"It still feels better than that water," muttered Dybbuk.

"Yes," said John, "but don't you see? So long as it's this cold we'll be unable to use djinn power."

Dybbuk shrugged. "The steps must go up to the surface. And that's where the heat is. So I vote we go up. The sooner I get some rays on me the better. I feel like a snake in an icebox."

"Hey," said John. "What with all those skeletons and the flashlight not working and everything, I almost forgot."

He tugged the leather bag out from under his belt and, handing the flashlight to Dybbuk, opened it carefully. Inside was an object about six or seven inches in length and wrapped in several layers of waterproof paper. John unwrapped the paper and gasped as Dybbuk turned the full beam of light onto the object that now lay on the palm of his hand.

It was the figure of a king cobra rearing up on its coils. The snake's body was made of solid gold but the head and the hood had been fashioned to include an enormous emerald. The tail — which was inaccurate in the opinion of Dybbuk, who said it looked more like the tail of a rattlesnake than a cobra — was made from four yellow wisdom teeth, set in gold. It was this last detail — that, and the many deaths the talisman had caused — rather than the size of the Koh-E-Qaf emerald adorning the Cobra King, that gave them all a long and silent pause for thought.

"Hard to believe, isn't it?" John said eventually. "How those four teeth should once have belonged to old Rakshasas."

"It makes you realize just how old he really is," said Dybbuk. Then he shrugged. "Still, it's easy to see why Hermann Goering would have wanted it. That emerald's bigger than a hen's egg. And it must be worth a fortune."

"Yes, but the monetary value is nothing beside the power it would have given someone over Rakshasas," said John. "Imagine it. A djinn of your own to command. I wonder if Goering knew about that. About just how rich and powerful having this talisman *could* have made him."

"If you ask me," said Philippa, "it's evil. It's evil and I think that we should destroy it. Break it into pieces and throw the bits into the well along with all the skulls and bones where nobody can get them. Including the emerald."

"Are you kidding?" said Dybbuk. "After all the trouble we've gone through to find this thing?" He shook his head. "No way. Besides, in case you've forgotten, I've sacrificed a little more than you in getting here. Two friends of mine are dead."

"That's all the more reason why you should agree with me," insisted Philippa. "Have you considered the risk we're taking just by hanging on to it? John, what do you think?"

John heaved a sigh. His cold breath looked like a small cumulus cloud. It was hard to believe they were still in a hot country like India. He disliked agreeing with Dybbuk instead of his twin sister, but the talisman looked much too valuable just to throw it away as Philippa wanted. "I think that before we do anything with the Cobra King we should find Mr. Rakshasas and listen to what he says. It ought to be his call about what to do with it. After all, those are his wisdom teeth and the talisman gives the bearer power over him."

"Whatever that's worth," said Dybbuk. "I can't imagine what good it is having a talisman that gives the holder power over a djinn who's ready for the great lamp in the sky."

"Dybbuk, really," scolded Philippa. "Sometimes you say the most appalling things. Mr. Rakshasas is our friend."

"What did I say?" protested Dybbuk. "You can't deny that he's old. His powers are nearly gone. These days it's all he can do to get in and out of his lamp," He shook his head. "I still don't know why this cobra cult would want to hold him in their power."

"It's not that he doesn't have power," said John. "It's just that being old, he's choosing to conserve it. He doesn't use his power unless he absolutely has to. Either way, there's no guaranteeing that breaking up the Cobra King and chucking the pieces in the well would frustrate anyone determined to find it. For example, they might go to the trouble of getting a scuba diver to go down there. Or a midget submarine." John pointed at the hole in the wall. "Besides, I don't much care for the idea of going back through all those skeletons. They scared me half to death the first time I was in there. So, I'm sorry, Phil, but I agree with Buck. We hang on to it for now."

Dybbuk nodded as if the matter was now decided beyond any further argument.

"All right," said Philippa. "If that's what you both think we should do, then we'll do it. Just don't say I didn't warn you." She stared uncomfortably at the Cobra King. "No good will come from us having it, believe me."

Dybbuk held up his hand as if to silence Philippa and she was about to feel irritated with him, until she realized that he was listening to something else.

"What is it?" she said.

"Can't you hear it?" he said. "A sort of murmuring."

"My ears are still full of water," she said and tapped the side of her skull with the heel of her hand. "Frozen water."

"It's coming from up those steps," said Dybbuk and, still holding the flashlight, led the way forward.

Wrapping the Cobra King in the waterproof paper, John returned it to the leather bag, tucked it under his belt, and followed. Now he could hear the sound, too.

"It might be best to switch off the flashlight," advised Philippa. "Or at least to dim it down a little. Until we know what it is. Just in case someone doesn't want us being here."

"So what if they don't?" said Dybbuk. "We're members of the ashram, right? The whole point of us joining was so that we could come and go without suspicion."

"You're forgetting about Groanin," said Philippa. "I don't believe he would have abandoned us in that horrible well unless something pretty serious had happened to him."

"Phil's right," said John. "We ought to be careful until we know what's happened to him."

"All right," agreed Dybbuk, mounting the stairs. "But we still need a little bit of light, otherwise we could break our necks on these stairs. I know it sounds crazy but they're covered in ice."

John put his fingertips on the step in front of him. "He's right," he said. "How on earth do you get ice down here?"

"I don't know," said Dybbuk. "But I think we're about to find out." He put his hand over the front of the flashlight, turning his hand red, and allowing just enough light to escape so that they could see where they were going.

The murmuring sound grew louder and they soon recognized it as chanting.

"Maybe that's the transcendental meditation class," said John.

Dybbuk glanced at the luminous dial of his watch. "At three o'clock in the morning?" He stopped and listened again. "Besides, when did they ever chant like that in meditation? Listen."

"NA-GA, NA-GA, NA-GA . . ."

"Naga," whispered Dybbuk. "That's what they're chanting. Naga."

All three children shivered a little, not from the cold, but with fear, as it gradually dawned on them that the word being chanted hypnotically, over and over again, was the Sanskrit word for a *serpent*.

Recognizing the Sanskrit word for snake had made all three children fall silent.

"I've got a bad feeling about this," said Philippa.

"You said that already," said Dybbuk.

"In point of fact, I didn't. I said that no good would come of us keeping the Cobra King. I just hope that it isn't connected with the bad feeling I'm having now. Because this would be one time when I'd really hate to be proved right."

"Yeah, I'll bet," said Dybbuk.

Farther up the steps, a dim light was discernible, and Dybbuk turned the flashlight off. At the top of the steep stone stairs, they came upon a narrow tunnel that ended in a metal ladder that ascended fifteen or twenty feet inside a hollow cylinder made of bronze. The cylinder was about four or five feet wide and at the top was an aperture several feet in diameter through which came a bright, flickering light and the monotonous sound of human chanting.

"NA-GA, NA-GA, NA-GA, NA-GA, NA-GA . . ."

The three children mounted the ladder in silence, their fingers half sticking to the frozen metal, and peered carefully over the edge of the hole. An astonishing sight met their tired and dusty eyes.

It was a temple built out of a cavern with a ceiling fifty or sixty feet high and lit, somewhat incongruously, by several strings of electric lightbulbs. A strange mist floated across the floor, like something from a magic show in a theater, enveloping the rubber-booted feet of three or four hundred men and women who stood facing a spot underneath the vantage point occupied by the children, their arms raised in worship. They wore anoraks and fleeces over their orange-colored robes and their faces were smeared with yellow paint. As if hypnotized they continued to chant. "NA-GA, NA-GA, NA-GA, NA-GA . . ."

"It's the cobra cult," whispered Philippa. "The Aasth Naag." The meaning of the last part of Colonel Killiecrankie's message — *Look for the third snake. But beware the eighth* — was now plain to her. "They must be using the ashram as a cover for their activities."

The three young djinn fell silent as they reflected upon the irony of what had happened to them: The cult from which they had hoped to hide the talisman was all around them, and somehow they had landed in the very midst of the people they had most wished to avoid.

By now the true character of the bronze cylinder they were hiding in was clear. A few feet in front of the ladder where the children were standing, a forked tongue extended between two long thin fangs: They were inside the mouth of a huge statue — the statue of a rearing king cobra. This was not an object of worship or veneration, however. That was reserved for the man who now stood immediately beneath their hidden vantage point. It was Guru Masamjhasara, but he was dressed very differently from before. Instead of his white robes he wore a thick fur coat against the curiously intense cold that pervaded the cavern temple, and his previously bare feet were now shod in fashionable, sheepskin boots.

It was John whose keen eyes suddenly perceived the source

of the inexplicably low temperature: In a corner of the temple two *sadhaks* wearing thick leather gloves were handling large blocks of dry ice and moving cylinders of liquid nitrogen. "Now why on earth would they need those?" he said.

"I dunno," said Dybbuk. "Air-conditioning maybe. It is very hot up on the surface. I mean, who knows how hot it might get in here without that stuff?"

"I don't buy that for a minute," said John. "Now that I've lain on one of those beds in the dormitory, I'm sure the guru doesn't give two hoots about the comfort of his followers. This is something else. It has to be. But what?"

The guru shrugged off his fur coat to reveal a bare chest that was covered in the same yellow daub as his cheeks and forehead. Then he raised his hands in the air like a Baptist preacher, and his followers fell silent.

"I give you the substance of things hoped for," the guru said in a loud, creepy voice. "And the evidence of things not seen. Any man or woman who follows me and obeys my commands will receive the gift of miracles and the power over life and death. Tonight, my friends, you will see the truth of that power demonstrated. A power stronger than logic. A power stronger than argument. Yes, my children, a power to which you shall all bear witness."

The guru clapped his hands and two of his followers brought forward a glass tank that was full of writhing snakes. And it was clear that the guru now meant to handle them.

"That must be why they keep the room cold," whispered

Dybbuk. "Snakes are ectothermic. Their body temperature is dependent on the air temperature. When a snake's body gets too cold it becomes sleepy and lethargic. Makes them easier to handle, probably."

"But not those snakes," observed John. "Look. There's an infrared heater in that tank. Those snakes are warm."

Even as he spoke, one of the *sadhaks* took a long stick and poked several times at the snakes in the tank, as if he intended to make them angry, and in this he was successful. One snake, a huge king cobra, bit the stick and it was quickly obvious to the three djinn children hiding in the statue that Guru Masamjhasara wasn't at all interested in handling cold, lethargic, well-behaved snakes. It was angry, aggressive snakes that he wanted to handle.

With great ceremony he approached the tank and picked up a king cobra and straightaway the snake bit his hand, drawing blood, which ran down his arm and silenced Dybbuk's next suggestion — that the snakes had had their fangs removed.

Seeing himself bitten, the guru grinned with delight and picked up another cobra that proceeded to bite him not once but several times. A third cobra sank its fangs so deep into the guru's forearm it could not get them out, and the snake just hung there until the weight of its writhing brown body caused the fangs to break off, and the snake fell to the ground. The guru picked it up and draped it around his neck like a silk scarf. By the time he had picked up the seventh snake, he had been bitten more than twice as many times, none of which seemed to bother him in the slightest.

"I don't understand it," said Dybbuk. "He should be dead by now. Or at the very least lying on the ground in a coma."

John looked at Philippa. "Are you thinking what I'm thinking?" he asked her, remembering what the Yeti — the Baron von Reinnerassig — had told them on Annapurna: that djinn were immune to snake venom. "That he might be one of us?"

"A djinn?" Philippa shook her head. "No. If he was a djinn he'd hardly keep the temperature in this temple cavern so artificially cold. He'd run the risk of losing djinn power in front of his followers. I dunno. Maybe he's just dosed himself up with a lot of antivenom." But this hardly rang true. The snakes were big, powerful cobras, each capable of injecting vast amounts of venom. "Only it would have to be an awful lot of antivenom."

"See the signs," said the guru, now garlanded with so many snakes, he looked like a Christmas tree. "And believe in my power, which is great, for I tell you the time is coming when we shall rule the world."

The guru snatched up two more snakes and, still being bitten, held them up for all to see. "Eight was the number of cobras my predecessor, Aasth Naga, would allow to bite him at any one time. But I am more powerful, for I have the power to resist the poison of nine cobras. I give you the nine cobras."

The guru's audience began to chant again. "NA-GA, NA-GA, NA-GA . . ."

"This is really giving me the creeps," whispered Dybbuk. "These people are nuts."

"That's putting it mildly," said Philippa. "They're murderers, that's what they are."

"But wait, my friends," shouted the guru, silencing his followers once again. "Sometimes, to show power over death we must see death itself. We must stop to admire its power. For my signs do not follow unbelievers. And it is not in an ordinary man to do as I do. As you will now behold! You will see what many times I have survived. You will see death. Bring forth the prisoner!"

The audience parted as, from the rear of the temple, the *sadhaks* brought forward a man, his hands tied behind him and looking quite pale with fear.

The children gasped, for the man marked for death by Guru Masamjhasara was none other than Mr. Groanin.

CHAPTER 16

IN COLD BLOOD

We have to do something," said John. "We can't let Groanin be bitten by one cobra, let alone nine of them. New arm or not, he'll die for sure."

"In case you've forgotten," said Dybbuk, "we're powerless."

"Not entirely," said John.

"I'm not sure I understand," said Dybbuk. "What exactly are you suggesting?"

"That we take Groanin's place, of course," said John. "After all, we're immune to cobra venom. The baron said so."

"Good idea," said Philippa, who was of the same mind as her twin brother.

"Good idea?" Dybbuk sounded doubtful. "Look, maybe there's a difference between being immune to the venom of one cobra and being immune to nine of them. Have you thought of that? And suppose one of those cobras is a djinn.

Have you thought about that? And suppose that baron was just wrong. Or maybe he was lying."

"I thought you knew about this," said John. "When the baron mentioned the fact that we were immune, you seemed to know all about it."

"All right, I lied. I don't know any more about it than you do."

"Why would the baron lie?" said Philippa. "He seemed very nice, to me."

"He was a loony," insisted Dybbuk. "Only a loony would live half his life as the Abominable Snowman. But even if he didn't lie, he didn't say how that immunity works. For instance, what if we're only immune if our powers are working? Suppose we're not immune if it's cold. Which it is. There's a chance we could get killed down there."

"That's better than no chance at all," said John. "Which is what Groanin will have unless we do something about it."

"John's right," hissed Philippa.

"Then what happens?" demanded Dybbuk. "Suppose we do get bitten and we don't die. How will that look?"

John shook his head impatiently. "We don't have all the answers. That's true, Buck, but there's no time to argue about this. Besides, there's no need for all of us to go. Here." He took the flashlight from Dybbuk and then handed it and the leather bag containing the Cobra King to Philippa. "Take the Cobra King and hide it. And look for another way out of here."

Philippa hesitated for a moment and then did as her brother had ordered. There seemed no point in them both being caught. Especially while possessing the Cobra King. "Be careful, John," she said, sliding down the ladder and heading back through the tunnel. Dybbuk followed her.

John climbed onto the top rung of the ladder and, taking hold of the snake's forked tongue, started to lower himself into the cavern temple.

"Wait!" he yelled to the guru beneath him. "Stop! Leave him alone!"

Voices were raised and strong hands grabbed John as he swung above the guru's head on the cobra's tongue for a moment.

"I've heard of snakes regurgitating their food," said the guru. "But this is ridiculous."

He dropped the snakes he was holding back in their tank and then faced John, giggling as usual. "Do you know something?" he said, taking John by the arm. "I had no idea that statue was hollow. Almost ten years I've owned this place and I didn't know. Can you imagine it? What were you doing up there, anyway?"

"Spying on you," said John. He caught Groanin's eye and nodded.

"But where are your two little friends?" the guru asked him.

"Last time I saw them, they were back in the dormitory, asleep," said John.

The guru smiled patiently. "That is not true. We already looked for you there when we arrested your father." He glanced up at the statue, his eyes narrowing with curiosity. "You know, I'll bet they're still in there."

He spoke to his men and two of them quickly stripped down to loincloths. Then one climbed onto the other's shoulders and pulled himself into the statue's mouth. He was gone for several minutes.

"Really," said Guru Masamjhasara. "Why did you and your father come here? To the ashram."

"I told you," insisted John. "To spy on you."

"On purpose? Or by accident?" The guru looked first at John and then at Groanin, and hearing no answer, twisted John's arm painfully.

Hearing John yell with pain, Groanin struggled to escape his two captors, but he had yet to discover the full strength that was in his new arm. "Leave the lad alone," said Groanin.

"We came to prove that *you're a fraud*," said John as an idea suddenly presented itself to him. A way that he might undermine the guru's reputation in front of his followers. He broke free of the guru's bloodstained grip and ran to the snake tank. There were forty or fifty snakes inside it and all of them deadly. But John hardly hesitated. He plunged both his hands into the hissing mass of serpents, picked up a big black cobra, and held it aloft. The audience in the temple murmured loudly at John's apparent foolhardiness. "You see?" said John. "There's nothing to fear. These snakes are harmless. You're all being tricked."

The guru did not try to stop John. Instead, like everyone else in the underground temple, he watched with fascination to see what the outcome of John's actions would be. For a moment, the huge cobra in John's hands seemed equally fascinated. Almost docile, it fixed John with two beady black eyes, its tongue tasting the air in front of its head. The next second the snake hissed loudly, the sound of a half-empty kettle being boiled. A quarter second later the cobra struck, biting John first on his wrist — so deeply that it had to wiggle its head to pull out its fangs — and then squarely on the chest, just above his heart. The audience gasped out loud for, especially with a child, a bite from a big cobra that close to the heart is always fatal.

John was hardly surprised that the cobra bit him, only that it hurt so much. It was like receiving two painful hypodermic shots at the same time from a heavy-handed doctor. He touched his chest and his fingers came away with blood on them. The snake bit him a third time on the hand that was still holding it around the thick middle. John yelped and dropped the snake back in the tank.

Instinctively John pressed his hand to his mouth and sucked at the bite. By now he had no doubts at all that the snakes were venomous. He could actually taste the venom on his lips, which were already turning numb. Had he made a dreadful mistake? Was Dybbuk right? Was immunity from snake venom dependent on heat, like djinn power? John shivered. Suddenly he felt very cold indeed. Cold and sick.

"It hurts, does it not?" Guru Masamjhasara said, and giggled. "Even without the venom you would certainly know you had been bitten, wouldn't you?"

John felt his skin turn hot and cold, and wondered if he was going to throw up.

"I'm told that a boa constrictor has the most painful bite of any snake. But while very deadly, the boa is not a venomous snake. It's the venom that makes the difference. Especially with a snake like the king cobra. Drop for drop, it's actually less lethal than the common cobra's venom. However, the king usually injects as much as seven milliliters of venom per bite. An enormous amount. That's enough to kill an elephant. Or as many as forty twelve-year-old boys." He smiled thinly and nodded as if he was weighing something up. "I'm just guessing your age, boy. But the fact remains that even by now your whole respiratory system ought to be failing rapidly." The guru came close to John and, picking up his wrist, took his pulse. But this was curiosity rather than concern. "Of course we have antivenom in our clinic here and an artificial respirator. However, I can already tell you're not going to need them."

He looked up as above their heads, the *sadhak* who had clambered inside the statue reappeared behind Philippa and Dybbuk and forced them to climb out. More followers of the guru helped them down.

"And is it just you or do your little friends have immunity, too? And if so, why? Why are you immune?"

"I'm not immune," John yelled at the guru's followers. "The snakes are harmless. And he's a fraud. Do you hear? Your guru is a fraud."

The guru grinned patiently. "If that were so," he said,

"then you would hardly have hurried down here to save your father, would you? Which leads me to suppose that he is very different from you. Or perhaps that the three of you are very different from everyone. Is that it?" He released John's wrist, scrutinized the bite on his chest for a moment as if to check that John really had been bitten, and, seeing the two bleeding puncture marks, nodded. "Remarkable. Quite remarkable. You should be dead by now, young man."

The *sadhak* who had forced Philippa and Dybbuk down from the statue handed the guru the leather bag that contained the Cobra King. John glanced at Philippa, who nodded, uncomfortably.

Guru Masamjhasara held the bag as if he hardly dared to think what it might be. "No," he said. "It couldn't be. That would be too fortunate, even for someone as lucky as me. And yet, it would also explain *everything*."

He opened the leather bag, took out the object, tore off the wrapping, and then stared in awe at the priceless talisman he held in his hand. A loud gasp escaped the guru's slackening mouth. "After ten long years of searching," he breathed. "Finally, I have it." It was now that something seemed to dawn on him. A realization. "It was here all along, wasn't it? For ten years I thought it was lost and all that time it was right under my very nose."

The three children said nothing and, grabbing John by the ear, the guru twisted it painfully. "It was here, wasn't it?"

"Aargh! Yes. Leggo!"

"Where was it?" he asked, twisting John's ear some more.

"Leave the lad alone," yelled Groanin. "Or I'll thump you one."

"In the well. *We found it in the well.*" John could see little point in denying the guru this information. Especially as his ear was still between the guru's wiry fingers. "Colonel Killiecrankie left a secret message on an East India Company picture," he said. "The picture was in Field Marshal Hermann Goering's possession. We found the picture, decoded the message, and came here to look for it."

"I knew we should have destroyed it," said Philippa.

"Destroy it? Why do you say that, my dear?"

"Because you wanted it badly enough to kill for it. I can't think of a better reason than that."

"Oh, I think you can," said Guru Masamjhasara. "What do you take me for, child? An idiot? I wanted the Cobra King to have power over a djinn. A very old djinn called Rakshasas." He grinned unpleasantly. "But now that I have you he no longer seems quite as important."

"We don't have any idea what you're talking about," said Dybbuk.

"No?" The guru wagged a finger in Dybbuk's face and the boy djinn could not help but notice the dirt under his fingernails. "I could always give you a proper dental examination. But it would be quicker if you just told me." He leaned over the snake tank and, taking hold of a cobra, held it close to Groanin's face. The snake struck at Groanin but, just in time, the guru jerked it back so that the snake's fangs missed the English butler's nose by only a few inches.

Philippa screamed.

"Next time he might not be so lucky," said Guru Masamjhasara, ignoring a bite to his own hand. "You're djinn, aren't you?" he said to John. "Only a djinn could take a bite like you did just now and live to tell the tale."

"All right. We're djinn," said Dybbuk.

"The three of you?"

"Yes, the three of us. Now leave him alone. He's a human being. And if he's bitten, he'll die."

The guru giggled and tossed the snake back into the tank. "Djinn, eh? So go ahead. Turn me into a rat."

"I wish we could," said Dybbuk. "And then I'd feed you to one of those snakes. Except that they'd probably die because you're so dirty."

"Give me three wishes and I'll let you go." He laughed. "No. I thought not. You don't have any power, do you? Not in here where it's too cold for your hot djinn blood."

"When he gets here," said Philippa, "Mr. Rakshasas is going to turn you into the skunk you are."

Guru Masamjhasara clapped his hands. "The audience is over," he told his followers. Then, glancing at Mr. Bhuttote, he added, "Bring them along. There's something I want to show our special guests."

They left the underground temple, and went through a pair of sliding glass doors into what looked like some scientific laboratories. The white walls looked like the ceiling, which looked like the floor, and there was a strong smell of chemicals.

It was even colder in here than in the cavern temple, and just inside the sliding door was a clothes rack on which was hanging a selection of expensive fur coats. The guru was already wearing his own fur again and these others were now worn by the thugs from the guru's bodyguard.

Dybbuk reached for a coat himself but was prevented from wearing one by the guru himself. "No," he said. "I think I prefer you the way you are now. Which is to say, half frozen." He pointed at Groanin and giggled. "But he can wear one. We have nothing to fear from his getting hot under the collar."

Gratefully Groanin put on one of the fur coats as the guru waved a hand at the modern-looking corridor ahead of them. "Everything here is kept just below freezing. This state-of-the-art medical facility is the most important part of the ashram. And you're about to discover why." He led the way through another set of sliding glass doors, using a numerical keypad to unlock it. "Security is very tight, of course," he said. "As it has to be, considering the great treasure I keep in here." He was still holding the Cobra King of Kathmandu, which he proceeded to brandish triumphantly. "As great a treasure as this. Perhaps more so."

They entered what looked like a small ward in an expensive hospital. There were several empty beds and lots of medical equipment. One medical orderly wearing a thermal suit sat at a desk monitoring several computers, while another was moving a cylinder of liquid nitrogen on a pushcart.

"It's just as well my followers are so generous with their money." He chuckled. "Our bill for liquid nitrogen and dry ice is enormous. We have it flown in by helicopter once a week. Of course, here on our rock, we're not the easiest place to deliver to. It's the price we pay for our privacy, you could say. It costs millions of rupees to keep this place going. So you can't say that we don't look after our special guests."

The guru moved aside a white curtain to reveal two more beds on which were lying two figures, both men wearing orange pajamas. Pipes and wires were attached to their chests and heads to monitor their vital signs, and the two men appeared to be unconscious, asleep, or in a coma — it was hard for the children to say which.

Philippa gasped. John clenched his fists and gritted his teeth. Dybbuk groaned.

"You recognize them, of course," said Guru Masamjha-sara. He smiled at Groanin and pointed to one of the sleeping men. "I think you are probably this man's servant." Then, glancing at the children, he added, "And I think two of you, although I am not altogether sure which two, are his nephew and niece, John and Philippa. Whichever of you is unrelated to the other two is, I suspect, the child who eluded my men in Palm Springs and on Bannerman's Island."

Nimrod and Mr. Rakshasas lay peacefully on their beds, quite oblivious to all that was happening around them. Both of them looked smaller than the last time Groanin and the twins had seen them. Almost shrunken. Shrunken and thinner and somehow older, too. Especially Nimrod.

Deep in his frozen sleep, the twins' djinn uncle swallowed reflexively. The very sight of it made Philippa swallow, too.

"Are they all right?" she asked and wiped away a tear from the corner of her eye.

"You animal," said John. "What have you done to them?"

"Don't worry," said the guru. "They're quite all right, I can assure you. They're much too valuable to let anything happen to them. Of the two, Nimrod requires less maintenance and observation. He is younger and stronger than Mr. Rakshasas, who requires more careful attention. Which is to be expected given his great age." The guru looked from Mr. Rakshasas to the Cobra King and back again. "It's hard to believe that he can be as old as he is. That's how this whole cult of ours got started."

"You swine," said Groanin.

"How very British of you, Mr. *Groanin*. That *is* your name, I think. Oh, I'm not fooled by the color of your skin, sir. It was clever of you children, to think of that. To become Indians." He shook his head. "But a man with one arm is harder to conceal. You did have one arm when you came here, I think. With Nimrod as my guest, the sudden appearance of a man with one arm — even one who appeared to be Indian — was too much of a coincidence."

"Swine," repeated Groanin.

The guru giggled. "Do you know something? I have always wanted someone — an Englishman — to say that to me. To call me a swine. Ever since I was a boy. It makes me feel pleasingly patriotic. Like a true Indian. Yes indeed, it does look like all my wishes are coming true today. After all, I have Mr. Rakshasas and the talisman that gives me complete and absolute power over him. So at last I can risk unfreezing him. Not that I will risk it. Not now, I think. Not now that things have changed so radically."

"I don't get it," said Philippa. "You say you've spent ten years trying to find the talisman. You've even committed murder to get your hands on it. And all so that you can have power over Mr. Rakshasas. And now you say that you're not going to bother?"

"He's old." The guru shrugged. "And not nearly as powerful as he used to be. Of course, I should have been very happy to have used him for my purpose. Only now I have something much better than him. I have the three of you. An unlooked-for bonus. Ironic, isn't it? I spend years, not to mention several million dollars, trying to capture a living djinn. And then, what do you know? I get five all at once. It's just like waiting for a bus."

"It was you who tried to steal our wisdom teeth, wasn't it?" said Philippa.

"Yes. That was my men. For several years now I've had spies stealing dental records in an effort to find children who have precociously early wisdom teeth. In the hope that I might be able to kidnap them. You see, I'd all but given up hope of ever finding this talisman. And I had begun to believe that my time and money would be better spent trying to find some djinn's teeth to make a new one. By the way. My men. What exactly happened to them?"

The children said nothing, so the guru pointed at Groanin and said, "I do advise you to cooperate with me, children. Unless you want me to find a pet for your friend here. A pet cobra, perhaps."

"Our mother turned them into two bottles of wine," said John.

"Really? How very novel. I approve, I think."

"Our teeth are back home in New York," said Philippa. "Protected by djinn power."

"That's right," said John. "Nobody can get them. So what do you want from us?"

"I don't want your teeth, boy djinn," said the guru. "Not now that I have you. No, I want something else. *I want your blood.*

"Because they're more powerful, fully grown adult djinn have to be kept deep-frozen or they could use their powers," explained Guru Masamjhasara. "And then where would I be? My amulet only protects me personally. It wouldn't stop a djinn from making his escape from here. All of which left me with something of a problem. You see, it's impossible to remove blood from the body of a deep-frozen djinn. It simply cannot be done. The blood moves much too slowly. Or hardly moves at all. It's like molasses that has become set. Which is why I needed the Cobra King. Or so I thought.

"For it seems that djunior djinn, such as yourselves, children, lose your powers at much higher temperatures than mature djinn such as Nimrod and Mr. Rakshasas. And this means that your blood can be removed while you're still fully conscious." He grinned. "Oh, don't look so worried. I don't want all of it. Just a pint or two, now and again."

"What are you going to do with it?" Philippa asked politely.

"A very good question," said the guru. "Perhaps I'd better start at the beginning and tell you how all of this got started." He ushered them to three empty beds. "Please make yourselves comfortable, and then I'll begin."

When the children remained standing, the guru added, "Really, I insist," and his burly henchmen took hold of them and strapped each one onto a bed. Seeing the children manhandled in this way was too much for Groanin, who tried to intervene, at least until he found one of the *sadhaks* pointing a gun at his stomach.

"Lock him up," said the guru, and Groanin was hustled away.

The guru watched the children struggling on their beds for a moment and then sat down between John and Philippa wearing a supercilious smile. "There's no point in trying to escape," he said, absently cleaning his ear with the fingernail on his pinkie, and then wiping the yellow-brown wax on his chest hair. "You'll be much more comfortable if you just lie still. Now then, where was I?"

"Being smug," said Dybbuk. "Smug and horrible. You know, it sure beats me why anyone would want to belong to a cult that had you in charge."

"Quiet, Dybbuk," said Philippa. "I want to hear his story. He was going to tell us how this whole thing got started."

"Buck," muttered Dybbuk, through clenched teeth. "Just Buck, okay?"

"So it's true," said the guru. "Female djinn are more intelligent than their male counterparts. I always did wonder if that was true.

"Well then, let's see. Twelve years ago, I was a young doctor in London with a thriving practice in Harley Street. As well as conventional medicine I was offering a number of complementary and alternative therapies. For example, homeopathy, electronic-gem, thought-field, and vortex therapies. I was very successful and making lots of money. One of these alternative therapies had attracted the attention of the Prime Minister's wife, who became my patient and I her trusted confidant.

"One morning in April she telephoned me in a state of panic and asked me urgently to attend her husband at number 10 Downing Street. I arrived to find the Prime Minister behaving most oddly and speaking in the voice of a young girl. His own doctors were strongly of the opinion that the Prime Minister was undergoing some kind of nervous breakdown after working very hard on his reelection, and they were all for having him carted off to the local loony bin until he could make some kind of recovery. But having examined him, I, on the other hand, quickly formed the opinion that the poor man was possessed. Possessed not with some kind of demon or evil spirit but by a djinn. A young djinn much like yourselves, perhaps." He shrugged. "To this day, I have no idea who she was. Only that she appeared to be an American and about twelve or thirteen years of age. I daresay your uncle Nimrod probably has a shrewd idea, for it was he I brought in to help. Nimrod and I had never met. But he had been a friend of my father's, the Fakir Murugan."

Now that the guru had started telling them his story there was something about it that Dybbuk found strangely fascinating. Even compelling. Much more so than John.

"Is that the guy in the picture?" asked John. "The one sitting on the pole with all the knives sticking in his back?"

"Yes. Among the Hindus it is a sign of great faith and shows yogic mastery over the body."

"You mean he put those knives there himself?" said John. The guru nodded. "And here I was thinking the knives were put there by his friends and family."

The guru smiled thinly and ignored John's insult.

"Anyway, Nimrod confirmed my diagnosis and agreed to perform a djinn exorcism. To be perfectly honest, I had my doubts that your uncle could help. But help he did. Nimrod was masterful. Omnipotent. Awe inspiring. You must remember that I had no real knowledge of the power of the djinn back then. I only knew what my father, the fakir, had told me. I had never seen such things for myself, as he had. Things that were quite, quite remarkable. Matter was conjured out of thin air. A bed rose up several feet off the floor. Finally the djinn was driven out of the Prime Minister. From then on, I was in absolute awe of your uncle and all djinnkind."

"Aw," said John. "That's nice."

"Shut up, John," muttered Dybbuk. He swallowed a great lump of emotion in his throat and tried to blink away a tear from the corner of his eye.

"After that, I read every book written about the djinn in the library of a notorious English magus named Virgil Macreeby. At first out of interest. But then to see if there might be a way to take advantage of something that was now in my possession. You see, before summoning Nimrod to Downing Street I had conducted an examination of the Prime Minister during which I drew a sample of the Prime Minister's blood in a hypodermic syringe. After the exorcism was over and the djinn expelled from the Prime Minister's body, I began to ask myself how much, if any, of the young djinn that had possessed him remained in the Prime Minister's sample. And since his blood type was the same as mine it occurred to me to investigate what might happen if I was to transfuse the blood sample taken during his djinn possession into my own body." The guru shrugged. "So I went ahead and did it. And can you imagine what happened? *Nothing at all.* Or so I thought.

"A few days after the transfusion I was obliged to return to India to visit my mother, who had been ill. Within the week she died and I had to help collect the wood for her funeral pyre, which is the custom in this part of the world. While collecting wood, I was bitten, several times, by a cobra. A big one. We were very far from the nearest hospital and I was not expected to live. And yet the curious thing was that in spite of my bite, I felt no ill effects whatsoever. Several people from my mother's village had witnessed me being bitten by the cobra and, seeing me unaffected by the bite, they became afraid of me. Questioning one of the village elders as to why this should be so, I was told that they feared I might be a djinn for, as you know, the djinn are immune to all snakebites except that of the sea snake. At least, so I am informed.

"My not succumbing to the snake's venom was, as you can imagine, a great relief to me. And a source of great fascination. And having obtained a supply of antivenom, just in case my theory proved incorrect, I set out to get bitten again. This time I was bitten by a krait, another Indian snake whose venom is sixteen times as powerful as that of a cobra. Again nothing happened to me and I was led to the conclusion that my apparent immunity was the result of my djinn-tainted blood transfusion. It also prompted me to ask the question: What would be the result if I replaced all of my blood with that of a djinn? Would I not become a djinn myself? With the power to grant wishes and to live for two hundred years?

"I set out to make this possible and I soon discovered a way of combining my immunity to snake venom with what was now my life's ambition. I had heard of the old cobra cults and, in particular, the Aasth Naag and its lost talisman, the Cobra King of Kathmandu. I realized that if I could find the Cobra King it would give me power over Mr. Rakshasas who, coincidentally, was Nimrod's friend. Enough power to remove his blood and use it to replace my own. And so I resurrected the cult. With one difference: Today we are Nine Cobras instead of Eight. Nine has always been a most propitious number for me. I was born at the ninth hour on the ninth day of the ninth month, in the year 1959, at number nine, Nine Elms Road, Calcutta. And I weighed precisely nine pounds.

"Everyone who joins the cult is promised the same thing: the chance to receive some djinn blood, even perhaps, if enough blood is available, the chance to become djinn themselves."

"You're crazy," said John.

"Only with excitement, little djinn," the guru said, giggling. "For, thanks to you, my plans have advanced much more rapidly than I could ever have hoped. Not only do I have the Cobra King, Mr. Rakshasas, and Nimrod, but I also have three healthy young djinn from whom I will get at least a dozen pints of djinn blood per week. This will make me a djinn in no time at all. And when I am a djinn myself, it will be a relatively simple matter to trap yet more djinn and steal their blood, too."

Dybbuk started to wrestle with the straps that were holding him to the hospital bed, but it was useless. "We won't let you," he said through clenched teeth.

"But you have no choice," said the guru. "You are my prisoners. And you will stay here and let me milk your blood whenever I need, like little cows."

"A vampire," said Philippa. "That's what you are, you disgusting man."

"Yes, in a way you are right, of course," admitted the guru. "But don't alarm yourselves too much. You will be well fed and cared for. And djinn bodies are quite remarkable. Perhaps more remarkable than even you yourselves are aware of. Unlike human beings, it seems that you are able to replace lost blood in a matter of days. Much quicker than a human being ever could."

Guru Masamjhasara stood up, peeled on some rubber gloves — which was the first time the children had ever seen him pay any attention to personal hygiene — and then set about preparing the transfusion equipment. Helpless to prevent him, John and Philippa watched as he rolled up Dybbuk's shirtsleeve, sterilized the skin on his forearm with a swab, and then inserted a needle into a vein. A few seconds later, Dybbuk's blood was gently dripping into a blood bag at the side of the bed.

"There now," said the guru. "That wasn't so bad, was it? Really there's nothing to it. Giving blood is as easy as falling off a log."

"I wish you'd fall off a log," snarled Dybbuk. "Or better still, that a log would fall on you. A great big one with a sharp end on it."

Ignoring him, the guru came around the bed to John and quickly attached an empty blood bag to his arm.

"You're a sick person," said John. "Do you know that? If ever I get out of here I'm going to turn you into a toilet."

"But you won't ever get out of here," said the guru. "Not for many years, anyway. The walls around this underground facility are fifty feet thick. It's too cold for djinn power to work. And there's no one here who's going to help you. Not if that means losing out on the possibility of living for two hundred years with djinn powers. You djinn really did come in first in the lottery of life, didn't you? In all sorts of wonderful ways."

"Not so as you'd notice," said Philippa. "Not right now, anyway."

"You have a point," said the guru, feeding a needle into her arm. Giggling his infuriating giggle, he added, "Quite literally, as it happens."

He stood back to admire his handiwork: three plastic bags slowly filling up with valuable djinn blood. Then he peeled off his rubber gloves, put his hands together, and bowed to his three young prisoners. "Be happy in your new home," he said. "It is a place of calm and relaxation. A place of effortless living. And of non-doing. Truly, you have fulfilled your destinies."

CHAPTER 17

SPONTANEOUS ENLIGHTENMENT

In their cell beneath the guru's laboratories the three djinn children sat shivering, eating lunch. They were pale from cold and loss of blood because, being made of fire, djinn do not thrive in cold and require heat to replace blood as quickly as normally they are able. *The fact was the children were dying and neither they nor Guru Masamjhasara had yet realized this.* Despite the guru's assurances that the children would be well looked after, he was in too much of a hurry to become a djinn himself to notice that his precious prisoners were actually becoming quite ill.

"Steak again," said Dybbuk, tucking in eagerly. "We won't starve, at any rate."

"Yes," agreed John. "There is that."

"You idiots," said Philippa, ignoring her own food. Wrapping her arms around herself like a shawl, she shook her head.

"You two idiots just don't get it, do you? They're not giving us steak because they like us, but because red meat is full of iron. Iron is necessary for the replacement of blood cells."

"But it's not just steak," said Dybbuk. "We've got garlic, onions, broccoli, asparagus, avocado, followed by coconut . . ."

"Duh. Those foods are rich in sulfur," said Philippa. "Djinn blood needs high levels of sulfur. By eating well, you're just helping the guru to achieve his ambition."

"What, are you saying we should starve ourselves?" demanded Dybbuk. "Look, he's going to take our blood, anyway, so what difference does it make? It's quite bad enough being freezing cold all the time without feeling hungry as well. Besides, I don't feel quite so cold and tired after I've eaten."

"You're tired because you've been losing blood," said Philippa. "Each of us has given two pints in three days. The next time he takes some he'll have enough djinn blood to completely replace his own mundane blood with ours. After that, who knows what's going to happen?"

The two boys were silent for a moment. "What do you think, Phil?" asked John. "Can he really turn himself into a djinn? I mean, there must be more to it than that, surely."

"I don't know," she said. "But the immunity to cobra venom he's developed since the first transfusion would seem to indicate that he's onto something."

"I'm surprised a mundane hasn't thought of it before," said Dybbuk. "It's kind of obvious when you think about it."

"I think you have to remember that blood transfusions — successful blood transfusions — have existed for fewer than a hundred years," said Philippa. "That's only half of a normal djinn's lifetime."

"Speaking of which," said Dybbuk. "I wonder how long he plans to keep us here?"

"We won't be here for long," said Philippa.

"How do you work that out?"

"For the simple reason that the two Elsewheres the angel Afriel made to take the place of John and me are only supposed to last for an aeon."

"How long is that?" said Dybbuk.

"One million seconds," said John. "Or 11.5740740740 7407407407407407407 days. Phil's right. When they disappear, Mom will realize something's up and come looking for us."

"I hope you're right," said Dybbuk. "Really I do. But think about it: My mother knows I'm missing already. And she's not exactly had much luck in finding me." He shrugged. "If that wasn't enough, we're not so easy to find right now. Not inside fifty feet of solid rock."

"He's got a point," John told Philippa. "Mom's not going to find it easy to track us down in this place. If only there was some way of getting a message to her." He paused for a moment. "Wait a minute. Of course there's a way. The djinnternal mail. Maybe we could get Nimrod to swallow a message for her."

"Yes, that *is* an idea," said Philippa.

"I've heard of putting a message in a bottle," said Dybbuk, "but this is ridiculous. In case you'd forgotten, Nimrod's deep-frozen."

"He might be frozen," said John. "But he can still swallow. I saw him."

"Have you got a better idea?" asked Philippa.

"No, I haven't," admitted Dybbuk.

"All right, then that's our plan," said John, starting to write a message. "Even if it takes us six months, that's what we'll have to do. We have to put a message for Mom in Nimrod's mouth."

This was a good plan. Indeed, it was the best plan available to them. And it would certainly have worked. The trouble was that their mother was no longer in New York but in Babylon or, to be more accurate, Iravotum, which is the secret kingdom of the Blue Djinn of Babylon, whose functions and powers were now held by Layla Gaunt. And it is unlikely that she would have rescued her children. For Mrs. Gaunt's heart had already hardened quite a bit, which is a characteristic of all djinn who are obliged to stay in Iravotum. Anything arriving in her djinnternal mail would probably have been treated with complete indifference. The fact of the matter was that Layla Gaunt was already lost to her children for, being the Blue Djinn of Babylon and the supreme arbiter of djinn justice, she could no longer behave according to her emotions but only according to Logic, which is, of course, transcendental. Logic is the hardest mistress of all and always looks after itself. Mrs. Gaunt's children didn't know it yet but the wonderful, glamorous, loving woman who had nursed and nurtured them was no more, and their only true parent, Edward Gaunt, now stayed miserably at home, inconsolable, neglecting his appearance and his work, staring into space and lamenting the departure of the woman who had given his life its meaning and interest. The two Elsewheres, John 2 and Philippa 2, tried to console Mr. Gaunt but the truth was that they were not much help at all, for even the real twins would have only been able to put a scratch on the black limousine carrying their father's grief.

Sometimes ignorance is bliss. Which is a short way of saying that it was just as well none of this was known to the three children in their cell underneath Guru Masamjhasara's pink fort, otherwise they might have given up all hope, which, added to the regular loss of blood they were suffering, would have been doubly injurious to their health.

Nothing is impossible, of course. Not in this universe. Especially when you are a djinn. As a very great poet once said, "There's nothing you can do that can't be done." And "No one you can save that can't be saved."

The day after John had thought of the plan to use Nimrod's djinnternal mail to send a message to his mother, the three children found themselves summoned for a third time to the laboratories so that each of them could donate a pint of his or her precious blood. This time Jagannatha was on duty in the laboratory. He was wearing the same kind of thermal suit as the other orderly, and Philippa recalled how he'd said he'd been a male nurse before coming to the ashram. Everything was beginning to make sense now.

Meanwhile, Nimrod and Mr. Rakshasas continued to sleep their deep-frozen, cryogenic sleep. But on this particular occasion, Guru Masamjhasara seemed more excited than usual and quickly explained why.

"Today you will have the honor of welcoming me among you as a fellow djinn," he said. "For when we have had a pint from each of you, I intend to use that and the blood you have already donated to replace my entire blood supply."

"The only place I'd welcome you," said Dybbuk, "is under the wheels of a truck."

"I've been waiting for this moment for more than ten years," said the guru, "and nothing is going to spoil my day. Not even you, my young djinn friend."

"You do realize that there's a lot more to being a djinn than just having the power to make things happen," said Philippa, as Jagannatha fitted the needle into Philippa's arm. She felt her heart give a leap when she saw him wink at her.

"Just keep talking to the guru for a moment," he murmured. "Nice and normal. But listen closely to what I'm about to say."

Philippa could hear his voice, but his lips were not moving; then she remembered Jagannatha saying something about how he used to do ventriloquism.

"Yes, there's a lot more to being a djinn than you might think," she said, continuing to speak to the guru. "For example, in the beginning, there are checks on djinn power."

"Are you guys really genies?" Jagannatha asked Philippa. "The whole Aladdin thing? With three wishes and the magic lamp and stuff?"

When Philippa nodded, Jagannatha grinned. "Hot dog," he said. "Okay, kid, I'll help the three of you to escape. You and your father — Mr. Gupta, or whatever his name is. The rope-trick guy. But on one condition."

"If you are referring to wisdom teeth, Philippa," said the guru, "I've already had mine extracted. While I was still at medical school."

"There's more to being a djinn than that," Philippa told the guru.

"Here's the deal," whispered Jagannatha. "If I help you kids get out of here, I want three wishes of my own. After you guys have warmed up a little. Okay? Three wishes just like in the *Arabian Nights*. Deal?"

Philippa nodded. "Deal," she said.

"Did you say something, Jagannatha?" the guru asked him.

"I was just asking her if the needle felt comfortable, sir," said Jagannatha. He attached her line to a blood bag and went to attend to John.

"I'm sorry, Philippa," said the guru. "What were you saying?"

"Just this. That djinn power must be channeled and controlled," Philippa told the guru. "It has to be focused using
your own nominated word of power. Like a magnifying glass
can focus the power of the sun onto a very small spot in the
middle of a sheet of paper so that it burns. A focus word
works in the same way."

"*You* shall teach me, Philippa," said Guru Masamjhasara.
Lying down on a hospital bed and rolling up the sleeve of his
coyote fur coat, he attached his own arm to a pipe in prepa-
ration for the replacement of his entire blood supply. "Yes,
indeed, you shall be my guru." Then he giggled his very irri-
tating giggle.

"Me?" said Philippa. "I don't think so."

"You would prefer that your uncle Nimrod met with an
accident in his sleep perhaps? Or that Mr. Groanin had a
flying lesson from the rooftop of the fort? Without the benefit of a plane? No, Philippa, you will be the guru on my own
journey to enlightenment. The enlightenment of becoming
a djinn. For power is true enlightenment, is it not?"

"No," Philippa said firmly. "Enlightenment is knowing
when not to use djinn power."

"We shall see," said the guru.

He was silent as Jagannatha removed three pints of blood
from the children and added these three to the six that
were already prepared for transfusion into the guru's corpu-
lent body.

Philippa watched Jagannatha in the hope that the

American might catch her eye again and give her some indication of how he proposed to help.

"I hope it poisons you," said John, as the process of replacing the guru's blood supply finally got underway.

"Have you not heard?" said the guru. "We djinn are immune to poison."

John did not contradict him. He hoped that there might be a time when the guru found out the hard way that djinn were not immune to the venom of a spider or a scorpion. More important, he was hoping for some kind of opportunity to get close to Nimrod and place the message he had written in his uncle's mouth.

"That was rude of me," he said humbly. "I'm sorry."

"Please. Don't mention it."

"I was wondering," John said humbly. "I'd like to see my uncle for a moment."

"You can see him from there, can you not?"

"I meant close enough to hold his hand," said John. "I just need to know that he's still alive."

"You won't learn that from holding his hand," said the guru. "Nimrod's hand is as cold as ice. Only his vital signs on the screen above his head can tell you that he's still alive."

"Please?" said John. "It would mean a lot to me."

"What's this? A djinn trick?" The guru began to scratch his behind.

"No, it's no trick. Anyway, what could I do? I've no power and nor has he."

"Nevertheless you would do well to learn some manners,

young djinn. You ask me a favor only a few seconds after you have wished that this transfusion might poison me."

"Yes, you're right," said John. "I did apologize for that. But I apologize again."

The guru finished scratching his behind and lifted the finger to his nostrils in order to smell it. "Then I accept your apology. And you shall hold his hand for a moment. The minute that the transfusion is complete, and I have felt the power of the djinn running through my veins." The guru's giggle was quickly turning into a cackle. "Actually I do believe that this is already happening. I feel fantastic. Such a feeling of inner strength and well-being as I never before experienced. A kind of warmth and feeling of exhilaration spreading through my whole body. Is this how it feels to be a djinn?"

"I suppose so," said John, but at the same time he was thinking that this wasn't how it felt at all. Most of the time — at least when he wasn't freezing-cold and having his blood stolen by a crazy man — it felt kind of ordinary to be a djinn. Normal. The way he imagined anyone else would feel about being themselves. "I mean, I guess it is."

When, after more than an hour, the procedure was complete and the final pint of djinn blood had been transfused into his flabby arm, Guru Masamjhasara sat up, swung his legs over the side of his hospital bed, and took a deep breath, sounding like a man awakening from a long and refreshing sleep.

"I'm starving," he said, scratching his head furiously and grinning broadly at Jagannatha. "I want some food. No, wait. My mouth's dry. Give me some water."

"How do you feel, sir?" asked Jagannatha, handing the guru a large glass of water.

"Never better. Like a million dollars."

"Yeah," muttered Dybbuk. "Green and crinkled. We get the picture."

Ignoring Dybbuk, the guru added, "But different. Very different." He rubbed his hairy chest and stomach. "Inside myself. Like something got switched on inside my head. Something that had been switched off before."

He gulped down the water and, when he had finished it, allowed Jagannatha to place a thermometer under his tongue and then listen to his heart through a stethoscope. The guru handed the empty water glass to a second medical orderly and, still with the thermometer in his mouth, asked for another.

"I don't know why I should feel so thirsty, but I do." The guru waited until Jagannatha had removed the thermometer from his mouth and then gulped down the second glass of water, hardly caring that he spilled some, which dripped off his long bushy beard. "You know, after people donate blood in England they are rewarded with a cup of tea." He laughed. "A cup of tea! How quaint they are. But the curious thing is that it's just what I'd most like now. A good strong cup of Darjeeling." He nodded at the second orderly, who went off to get it.

"Your temperature is rather high," said Jagannatha. "101.6."

"Really?"

Jagannatha looked at the thermometer and then glanced at the children. "That's hardly normal for a human. But is it normal for a djinn?"

The children, who were all aware that 101.6 was a djinn's normal temperature, stayed silent for a moment as the possibility that the guru was now a full-fledged djinn sank into their minds. And it was Philippa who answered first. "No, that doesn't sound right at all."

"Take her temperature," the guru ordered Jagannatha. "Just to make sure that she's not lying."

Jagannatha walked toward Philippa with the thermometer.

"I'm not having that in my mouth," she said. "Not until you've cleaned it."

"Sorry," Jagannatha said and, producing another thermometer, placed it under Philippa's tongue. "98.7," he said after a minute. "Normal."

While this was quite normal for a mundane it was, of course, very low for a djinn. Philippa wasn't well at all. She knew it and the boys knew it, but they said nothing in the hope of lending some confusion to the guru's plans.

"Your temperature should be lower," Jagannatha told Guru Masamjhasara. "Especially given the fact that it's so cold in here."

"Maybe so, but I feel fine." He shrugged off his fur coat.

"Are you sure it's still freezing in here? I wouldn't want any of our guests feeling warm enough to perform some tricks for us."

The second orderly came back with the guru's tea. He took the tea and then waved at a sophisticated-looking temperature gauge on the laboratory wall. "Check the temperature, will you?"

The orderly glanced at the gauge, tapped it experimentally, and then shrugged. "All temperatures are normal, Your Holiness."

"What does that mean?" The guru sounded irritable. "The temperature in here is kept artificially low. There's nothing normal about it."

"Relax, Your Holiness," said Jagannatha. "It's freezing in here. Everything's just fine, sir."

"That's a matter of opinion," said the guru. "You'd better check that gauge. Make sure it's working properly." He stood up, stretched a bit, and then approached Philippa's bedside. "All right, Guru Philippa. Where do we start?"

"It's too cold in here," said Philippa. "We need to go outside in the sun. Djinn are a little like lizards. They need heat to have power."

The guru chuckled. "Do you think I'm stupid? The minute you warm up, I'll be toast. No, no, here's what we will do. You will give me a few useful pointers on the use of djinn power, and then I'll go outside and put them into practice. Although I don't honestly think that will be necessary. I'm not feeling a chill at all. In fact, quite the opposite. This new blood of yours is really fizzing inside of me. Like a bottle of champagne that someone has been shaking. I'm full of vigor. Quite marvelous."

"All right," said Philippa. "Then you'll need to think of a focus word. A word, one word, that you will only use in association with the exercise of your djinn power."

"I get it. Like a mantra. Or a magic word."

"No. It's not as simple as that. Djinn are made of fire. You need to use the word to focus the power. The way I explained earlier. Like a magnifying glass concentrating the heat of the sun onto a sheet of paper. Except that the sound exists inside of you. All your thoughts and concentration have to be gathered onto one spot with your own will."

"Yes, yes, yes," snapped the guru. "I understand all of that. You're describing something with which I'm already familiar through transcendental meditation."

"And it ought to be a really long word," insisted Philippa. "So that you can't utter it by accident. Like when you're asleep. Or forget it."

The guru thought for a second. "A word. Like a code-word. I get it. Yes." He paused again. "All right. I've got one. Now what?"

Philippa shifted uncomfortably on her bed. It was difficult because of the straps binding her down. "It might be easier to see what you were doing and help you if these straps weren't quite so tight."

"In a minute," said the guru. "Perhaps."

"You should start by trying to make something disap-pear," sighed Philippa. "Or at least reduce it in size."

"The teacup," suggested the guru, and placed his cup and saucer on her bedside table.

"Yes, if you like. But, if you don't mind, please move it away from my head. Sometimes, in the beginning, djinn power can be a little unpredictable. Even explosive."

The guru moved the cup and saucer onto a cart and stared at it intently.

"Think how a picture of the cup and saucer's absence is attached to reality," said Philippa, who was just quoting what Nimrod had told her and John when they had first started using djinn power. "When you have anticipated that Logic deals with every possibility, then you utter your focus word. That's what you have to concentrate on."

"So," said the guru, "if I want to make it disappear all I have to remember is to get a good idea of it not being there. And then say my word. Is that it?"

"What is thinkable is possible, too," said Philippa.

The guru smiled. "You're beginning to sound like me," he said.

"Yeah," said Dybbuk. "Stupid."

"Don't spoil my concentration," said the guru. "Or I'll have you deep-frozen like your two friends over there."

He pointed at Nimrod and Mr. Rakshasas, who remained lying on their beds in a state of cryogenic suspension, like figures in some ancient mausoleum. A cold mist swirled around them and it was almost possible to imagine that they had just transubstantiated from inside a lamp or a bottle.

Frowning deeply, the guru focused hard on the cup and saucer for almost a minute before uttering his word. To the children it sounded like FENNIMOREWAXPLUMPER-TON. (Perhaps there is a real word that sounds like FENNIMOREWAXPLUMPERTON, but if so then it does not appear in the *Oxford English Dictionary*, nor, for that matter, the *Oxford Hindustani Dictionary*.) To everyone's surprise, except perhaps the children's, the cup and saucer shattered into several pieces.

The guru laughed with delight and seemed quite unaware of the fact that the effort of focusing his will on the cup and saucer had made him very red in the face, not to mention that there was now tea all over the floor. He was perspiring heavily, too, and looked like a man who had been running in a marathon.

"Did you see that?" he yelled at Jagannatha, who continued to look astonished. "Did you see it? I did that. I destroyed it with my powers."

"It was a good first effort," said Philippa. "You certainly speeded up the molecular structure of the cup and saucer. That much was obvious. Only it seems to me that if you want to make something disappear, you need to get a clearer idea of nothing in your head."

"Phew! This feels like hard work." The guru wiped his brow.

"In the beginning, yes it is," said Philippa. "But it's like physical fitness. You learn to develop the part of your brain where djinn powers are focused. That part we djinn call the Neshamah. It's the source of djinn power. The subtle fire that burns inside us like a flame in an oil lamp." Philippa shook her head. "But I don't know whether you have a Neshamah or not. You're not like the rest of us."

"You mean, not as good as the rest of you," said the guru. "Well, I'll show you subtle fire, young lady." He pointed at his coat, which now lay on the laboratory floor. "Just keep your eyes on that coat."

The guru bent his head toward the coat, which was made of coyote fur, and stared at it fiercely with wide eyes and a brow as furrowed as a plowed field. Trembling visibly and breathing loudly through his nostrils, he looked like a bull that was about to charge a matador's cape. Sweat dripped off his nose, earlobes, and beard and a heat haze surrounded him, like a mirage shimmering over a desert.

"This time, you're going to see something disappear in front of your very eyes," he whispered. "Just you wait and see."

The guru's look of concentration was awful. Almost a minute passed, and it seemed to Philippa that he was now so intent on making something disappear that he was quite oblivious to anything else happening around him. She looked at Jagannatha and caught his eye. It was clear to them both that if he was ever going to help them, now would be a good time.

Perhaps he would have helped them, but just then, the guru's coat moved several inches across the floor, toward Jagannatha's foot. "That's a very impressive demonstration of telekinesis," he remarked coolly. "Or whatever you call it when you move a fur coat with only the power of your mind."

Instinctively he backed away as the coat moved again, but this time it kept on moving and, what was even more unsettling, it started growling, too. Jagannatha grinned nervously and edged toward the laboratory door, as the fur coat took on a distinctly doglike, not to say coyotelike, shape. It was a wise precaution, for a moment later, a large and extremely fierce-looking coyote leaped at Jagannatha, barking loudly and snapping his jaws viciously. The American took to his heels, as did the other medical orderly, and, much to the relief of the children who remained strapped onto their beds, the coyote chased after them.

Meanwhile, Guru Masamjhasara had turned a peculiar shade of dark red, which, even as they watched him, took on a purplish hue, then gray, and finally black. This was alarming enough but much worse was to follow. Smoke started to emerge from his ears, nostrils, and even from underneath his dirty-looking fingernails. The next moment, the guru opened his mouth and let out a bloodcurdling roar, not to mention a large cloud of smoke, and kicked over the cart carrying the Cobra King and the water jug that, conceivably, might have cooled him down and thereby saved him. Then he staggered to the far end of the laboratory and dropped down on a chair between Nimrod and Mr. Rakshasas. And there he sat, his body jerking convulsively, with yet more smoke emerging from his large bottom.

"He's gone crazy," yelled Dybbuk, twisting around under the restraining straps to get a better view of the guru as he went into spasms.

"I don't think so," said John. Even as he spoke, a very thin blue flame enveloped the guru's body and he began to burn, like the wick on a very large candle.

"To me it looks like a case of spontaneous combustion. I read about it in a magazine. Sometimes people just catch fire, for no good reason."

An unpleasant burning odor filled the air and it was a second or two before the children realized that they were smelling the guru's bushy, dirty beard as it was singed by the flame. And even as they watched with horrified fascination, a large, slightly scorched bluebottle fly buzzed noisily out of the burning beard, as if reluctantly vacating a place where it had lived in comfortable squalor for many years.

"There was nothing spontaneous about it," said Philippa. "I think he just found out that djinn are made of fire. The hard way. That, or maybe he just focused too hard on the idea of the Neshamah. The fire that burns inside us."

"Either way, he's toast," said Dybbuk.

And since Guru Masamjhasara did not move, nor ever again make a sound other than a crackling or spitting noise like hot fat on a frying pan, the children soon formed the impression that Dybbuk was right: The guru was dead.

John flexed his arms and shoulders against the restraining straps. But they were made of leather and impossible to shift. "Now what are we going to do?" he asked.

"I think we have to hope that Jagannatha will come back and release us," said Philippa.

They spent the next few minutes shouting for help.

In vain.

The blue flame enveloping the guru's body lengthened to a yellow point a few inches above his head. It was curious, but the guru's face, which was still quite visible through the mask of flame, looked as if he had attained a kind of enlightenment at last. Which in a way, he had.

"I guess we'll just have to lie here awhile and watch." Dybbuk laughed cruelly as he noticed Philippa had turned her head away from the unpleasant spectacle that confronted them. And, never one to shy away from making a tasteless remark when one seemed obvious, he added, "I'll say one thing for him. He makes a nice fire."

CHAPTER 18

ESCAPE FROM CONFINEMENT

For several hours Guru Masamjhasara's body remained perfectly still on the chair between Nimrod and Mr. Rakshasas, burning slowly with a clear blue flame. Unable to unbuckle the restraining straps that kept them bound to their beds, the three children had little choice but to watch and wait for Jagannatha or one of the other medical orderlies to return and release them. But as time went by, it became clear that with the coyote still at large — the children could hear him howling somewhere in the distance — there was little chance of anyone being brave enough to reenter the laboratory. This realization might have left the children feeling very depressed had it not been for the simultaneous discovery that the heat from the guru's spontaneous combustion was causing the two cryogenically frozen bodies of Nimrod and Mr. Rakshasas to *thaw*.

Large pools of water began to collect underneath their

respective beds and soon the entire laboratory floor was wet.
Realizing that a defrosted Nimrod or Mr. Rakshasas might
soon equal a conscious Nimrod or Mr. Rakshasas, the children started to shout at them in the hope that the noise might
offer yet another stimulus to wake up — as if being next to a
burning corpse wasn't enough. And gradually the two older
djinn began to breathe more noticeably until, finally, Nimrod
took a deep, deep breath, let out a loud groan, moved his jaws
several times, yawned, and then opened his eyes.

"Nimrod," said John, who was nearest to his uncle.
"You're awake. Thank goodness."

Nimrod yawned again, blinked blearily, and then sat up
slowly, holding his head as if he was nursing a terrible
migraine. "Bottle me, but I feel awful," he said. "As if I've
been asleep for a hundred years. Where in the name of
Solomon am I? And —"

Seeing the burning man seated next to him, Nimrod
rolled quickly off his bed. "What on earth happened to him?"

"Never mind that now," said John. "Get these straps off
us. We've been stuck here for hours."

"Yes, yes, of course," said Nimrod, stepping carefully
around the guru's burning body. "Forgive me, John, but I
didn't recognize you, or your sister. Or Dybbuk. Is it Dybbuk?
Yes, Dybbuk. You've all changed color since last I saw you.
I took the three of you for citizens of the Indian subcontinent."

John wobbled his head in a very Indian way and answered
in Hindustani. "If you mean Indians," he said, "we are Indian,

for now." And while Nimrod set about unstrapping the three children they told him the whole story, right up to the moment when Guru Masamjhasara had caught fire.

"Silly fellow," said Nimrod. "I could have told him what would happen. If he'd thought to ask." Nimrod went to take a closer look at Mr. Rakshasas, who, being much older, had not yet recovered consciousness. "It wouldn't be the first time this kind of thing happened," he continued. "Mundanes have tried injecting themselves with djinn blood before. There was a Polish knight called Polonus Vorstius in 1654. And the Countess of Cesena in 1731. Both of them caught fire, too, of course. It was their cases that started the whole idea of spontaneous combustion. Which is complete nonsense. Nobody catches fire for no good reason. They caught fire because of the combination of djinn blood and the amount of bacteria that is present on human bodies. You see when bacteria reproduce they cause heat. Lots of heat. And the fact is, mundanes have much more bacteria on their bodies than we do. Especially two hundred years ago, when people took fewer baths than they do now. Bacteria make the human skin highly combustible. Djinn blood acts like a match and simply sets it alight."

"Bacteria, huh?" said Philippa. "That must have been especially true of the guru. His feet and fingernails were filthy. Goodness only knows how much bacteria was lurking on his skin."

"Don't forget his beard," said John. "His beard looked like an old bird's nest."

"Well, there you are then," murmured Nimrod. Seeing something shiny on the floor underneath the bed on which Mr. Rakshasas was lying, Nimrod stooped stiffly to pick it up. It was the Cobra King, which had fallen there when Guru Masamjhasara had knocked over the cart.

Philippa placed a concerned hand on the shoulder of Mr. Rakshasas. "Is he going to be all right, Uncle Nimrod?" she asked, more than a little worried that her turbaned friend's recovery was taking so long.

"Mr. Rakshasas is old. Very old. To be deep-frozen at his age is most unfortunate. But I think this will probably help." Nimrod held the Cobra King gingerly for a moment before lifting Mr. Rakshasas's old hand and wrapping the bony fingers around the priceless talisman. "To be reunited with his own wisdom teeth will certainly speed his recovery."

Even as Nimrod spoke, Mr. Rakshasas opened his eyes. "To be sure, a man can't depend on his own eyes if it's his imagination that's out of focus," he said, staring at the three children who were grouped anxiously around his bed. "But it seems to me that you three *balbachhe*[2] are very like some American children I know."

"It's us, Mr. Rakshasas," said Philippa. "Philippa and John. And Dybbuk."

"You mean you're not *bhikhari*[3]? Because I have no money to give you."

---

[2] *Balbachhe* is the Hindi word for children.
[3] *Bhikhari* is the Hindi word for beggar.

"No. We became Indians so that we might blend in with the local people."

"That was wise of you," said Mr. Rakshasas. "Sure, even a tiger goes out of his way not to get himself noticed." He glanced sideways at Guru Masamjhasara. "Sadly I can't see this fellow blending in anywhere."

"Except perhaps a forest fire or a barbecue," said Dybbuk.

"What's this I'm holding?" Mr. Rakshasas sat up and, finding the Cobra King in his hand, let out a long sigh and wiped a tear from his eye. "'Tis true what they say. The last fish of the day that you catch tastes just as fresh as the first."

"Whatever that means," murmured Dybbuk.

"Finally, after all these years, I have it." Mr. Rakshasas shook his head and smiled at Dybbuk. "I never thought I would. And it feels wonderful."

"You can thank the children for that," said Nimrod. "But only after we've managed to get out of here." His eyes were fixed on a large crack that had opened up inside a blackened scorch mark on the ceiling, immediately above the guru's still-burning body. "Which ought to be sooner than later, I think. I don't like the look of that ceiling."

"Wait," said John. "We can't leave yet. Not without Mr. Groanin. They've got him locked up somewhere down here."

"Groanin?" said Nimrod. "What's he doing here? He hates India."

"Looking after us," Dybbuk said drily.

Nimrod grinned, and then said his focus word "QWERTYUIOP!" But nothing happened. "It's no good," he said. "I'm still half frozen. We'll have to look for him the mundane way. Mr. Rakshasas? Are you able to walk?"

"Yes." Rakshasas moved stiffly off the bed. "But old age is a very high price to pay for wisdom and learning," he added, finding his feet. The twins helped to support him. With the bones in his back clicking audibly, he straightened up and added, "Sure, it's at times like this I wish I'd died young. John, Philippa. Let me put my hands on your shoulders for a while. One step at a time is still good walking and make no mistake."

As soon as the two elder djinn were dressed in their clothes again, they walked to the sliding glass doors of the laboratory with hardly a backward glance as, finally, the burning corpse fell onto the floor, where it and the chair continued to burn in the guru's large amount of body fat.

By now it was certain that Nimrod's concern about the fire had not been misplaced: As well as thawing the cryogenically frozen bodies of himself and Mr. Rakshasas, the heat from the guru's burning body had set fire to the floor of the room immediately above the laboratory, and now the whole under-ground facility was filled with choking smoke.

"How are we ever going to find Groanin in this?" said Dybbuk.

"Simple," said Nimrod and shouted the butler's name at the top of his voice.

The children took up the chorus and, then hushed into silence by Nimrod, they strained to hear an answer. Dybbuk,

327

whose ears were the sharpest of anyone's, pointed down the corridor.

"This way," he said firmly. "I'm sure I heard something down here."

Nimrod grabbed an oxygen mask and a small cylinder of air from the laboratory's medical supply before heading after Dybbuk, for it was obvious to him that unlike the five djinn, Groanin would experience some difficulty breathing.

"In here," said Dybbuk, turning the key in the door to what was clearly the laundry room.

The butler staggered out, coughing and spluttering. "Thank heavens for that," he said. "I say, thank heavens for that. For a moment there I thought I was going to be kippered. Something smoked at any rate." He started to cough again and did not stop until Nimrod had helped him to tie the oxygen mask to his face.

"Sir," he said, astonished to see Nimrod and Mr. Rakshasas. "What happened to you?"

"The guru kidnapped Mr. Rakshasas and me from our hotel in Calcutta," said Nimrod. "Except for you and the children, we might have been kept here for a very long time."

"Where is he?" asked Groanin. "The mad guru, I mean."

"I'm afraid he's on fire," said Nimrod. "We'll all be on fire unless we find a way out of here soon."

Groanin tucked the oxygen cylinder under his new arm and pointed back along the corridor. "It's this way out, I think. I heard lots of people running this way about an hour ago."

"Groanin," said Nimrod. "I can't help noticing that you have two arms."

"Aye, well, *defendit numerus*," said Groanin, winking at the children over the top of his oxygen mask. "Safety in numbers, eh?"

They walked quickly — at least as quickly as Mr. Rakshasas was capable of walking — back down the smoke-filled corridor and through several sets of doors until they came to an elevator. Unlike the one operated by the donkey on the outside of the ashram, this one was electric but appeared not to be working. Several times Dybbuk pressed the button to summon the car but nothing happened and, stepping back to look up at the floor display readout, he fell over something in the smoke. Something furry that was lying on the ground. It was the coyote, overcome with smoke. Dybbuk picked him up and cradled him in his arms.

"We can't leave him here to die," he said by way of explanation. The coyote, seeming to recognize a friend, revived a little and, his previous ferocity quite gone now, licked the djinn boy's face with gratitude.

"Unless we can get these elevator doors open . . ." murmured Nimrod. He didn't finish his sentence but it was plain to everyone exactly what he was thinking. Even djinn couldn't continue breathing smoke indefinitely. And, what was more, at some point the oxygen in Groanin's oxygen tank would run out. "QWERTYUIOP!" Nimrod said loudly now and with greater urgency.

Once again, nothing happened. Nimrod glanced at

Mr. Rakshasas with a question in his eyes but the old djinn shook his head as if to confirm what Nimrod already instinctively knew: that he, too, was still without those few powers he possessed.

"John? Philippa? Dybbuk?" he said. "Does anyone have any djinn power yet?"

The three children shook their heads. The corridor might have been filled with smoke but it was still very cold down there.

"Fat lot of good you lot are," said Groanin and handed Nimrod the oxygen tank to which the mask on his face remained attached. "Here, hold this a minute, while I have a go at this door. Ever since those kids gave me a new arm I've had the notion that both of my arms are really strong now. When the guru's henchmen locked me up I felt certain I could have picked them up and bashed their heads together."

"*We* did that," Dybbuk said proudly. "Made your arms stronger than normal when we gave you the new one. Which reminds me. Why *didn't* you bash their heads together?"

"Because one of them had a gun pointed at me, you daft young pup," said Groanin. "Strong arms are one thing. Being bulletproof is something altogether different."

Groanin forced his fingers into the space between the two elevator doors and, looking more than a little like Samson in the temple of the Philistines, began to apply his whole strength to pulling them apart.

A metallic creaking sound grated through the smoky air like a ship pulling against an anchor. For a moment the elevator doors resisted Groanin's assault and then they suddenly gave way like the two flaps of a cardboard box, bending a little as the butler put his shoulders and then his back into his self-appointed task.

The twins were a little awestruck at the butler's newfound strength and, for a moment, didn't notice that there was no sign of the elevator car. "That's a pity," said Groanin. But up the side of the elevator shaft, extending all the way to the top, was a maintenance ladder. Smoke was already venting upward in a way that promised fresh air, freedom, and for the five djinn, all important power-giving sunshine.

"We can climb up this ladder, sir," Groanin told Nimrod, who was still standing beside him and holding the oxygen tank. "I won't be needing that now, sir," he said, plucking the oxygen mask off his face, and, taking hold of the ladder, began to climb. "I'd best go up first. In case there's anyone up there who needs a punch on the nose." Privately Groanin was hoping he would find one of the *sadhaks* or medical orderlies so that he could give him a good hiding, for he had no doubt that the cowards had left the three children and himself behind to die.

"Yes, you do that, Groanin," said Nimrod. He looked at the children and made a face. "I'll never hear the end of it," he complained. "Him, a mundane, saving our lives like this."

"Only because we saved his first," said Dybbuk.

"Yes, there is that," admitted Nimrod. "I think you'll have to leave the coyote behind," Nimrod told him. "You'll need both hands for the ladder, won't you?"

"Who said anything about carrying him?" said Dybbuk and, lifting the coyote up over his head, draped him around his shoulders like a fur stole. "I'm going to wear him. He should be used to that. Yesterday he was a fur coat. Weren't you, boy?" The coyote licked his face again and curled himself snugly around Dybbuk's neck. He started up the ladder, behind Philippa and John.

Anxiously Nimrod looked around at Mr. Rakshasas. "What do you think, Mr. Rakshasas? Can you manage the ladder?"

Mr. Rakshasas glanced up the side of the shaft and nodded. "It seems to be the only available way to live a long life," he said. "But you go first, Nimrod. I would only slow you down."

Nimrod took hold of the ladder and placed his foot on the first rung. "Would you like me to hold the Cobra King for you?" Nimrod asked him. "It might make it easier for you to climb up."

"No, thank you," said Mr. Rakshasas and tucked the talisman underneath his turban. "This thing will never leave my possession again."

The elevator car blocked the top of the shaft but, fortunately for the six people and the coyote that were climbing up it, there was a floor below this level. Groanin stepped off the ladder and onto a short ledge where he started pulling open the doors to this level with his extra-strong arms. This was trickier than it had been at the bottom of the shaft; Groanin had to be careful not to step back or lose his balance as there was no question that a fall down the shaft would prove fatal. But eventually he succeeded and stepped out into a small corridor immediately below the shrine that led to what looked like a security guard's office. On a desk stood a television monitor that was still broadcasting pictures of the smoke-filled underground laboratories. Anyone watching this would have been afforded an excellent view first of the guru catching fire, and then of the revival of the two senior djinn. It seemed obvious to Groanin that everyone in the ashram had run away in fear of what several irate djinn might do to their human captors.

He walked through the pink fort as far as the tower that housed the rope elevator and found the donkey eating oats in a stable. The rope had been cut. The elevator was gone and, for a moment, Groanin wondered how they were all going to get down off the rock. This was only until he remembered that his master was a powerful djinn and, after warming himself in the hot Indian sun, would doubtless conjure another whirlwind that would quickly transport all of them back to London.

Flexing the muscles in his arms, Groanin walked back to the shrine and the elevator shaft where Mr. Rakshasas was the last to step off the ladder and into the reviving hot sunshine. Groanin rubbed his hands, which was something he hadn't done in many years, and said, "Well then, sir. Back to London is it?"

"Not quite," said Nimrod, stepping into the security

office. "We have to make a small detour via Calcutta. I'm afraid we left a thermos back at our hotel with two rather dangerous djinn inside of it."

"Of course," said Mr. Rakshasas. "The twin tigers of Sunderbans. I'd quite forgotten about them. Yes, you're quite right, Nimrod. It wouldn't do at all to leave those two behind."

"Tigers?" Groanin gulped audibly, and paled. "Did you say, tigers?" He had good reason to fear tigers since it had been a tiger that had bitten off his original left arm, and eaten it. As tigers do.

"Oh, you needn't worry, Groanin," said Nimrod. "I'm sure there's nothing for you to worry about. All the same I'd better check that nothing has happened to that thermos." He picked up the telephone on the desk and called the Grand Hotel. But after he settled the outstanding hotel bill, it was soon clear that no thermos had been found.

"It seems we're already too late," said Nimrod. "Someone has stolen our tiger twins." He stretched like a cat in the sunshine and felt the djinn power surging through his body again. From their smiles it was plain that the three children and Mr. Rakshasas were much recovered, too. And it was only Groanin who was not smiling.

He hugged his new arm fondly. "Look here, sir," he said. "If it's all the same to you, I'd rather not come to Calcutta on some kind of tiger hunt. I'd hate to lose this arm again. To lose one arm to a tiger is unfortunate, but to lose two looks like nothing short of nonchalance."

"I doubt there would be much point in going back to Calcutta to look for that thermos, Groanin," Nimrod told him. "I expect that whoever took it is long gone." He chuckled. "I just wish I could see the thief's face when he opens that thermos. If he doesn't take the proper precautions he's in for a very nasty surprise. Wouldn't you say so, Mr. Rakshasas?"

"Every crime has its punishment, right enough," said Mr. Rakshasas. "But there can be few crimes that actually contain their own punishments. Guru Masamjhasara's crime was one. This looks like another. 'Tis grievous to be caught, for sure. But 'tis doubly grievous to be caught and eaten."

CHAPTER 19

CAVEAT EMPTOR

Three wishes beyond the scope of normal human avarice."
Oleaginus, the mundane slave of Iblis the Ifrit, repeated
the phrase to himself and would have rubbed his clammy
hands if he hadn't been carrying the thermos he had stolen
from Nimrod's hotel room safe in Calcutta. Surely his three
wishes were in the bag, he told himself. Iblis was going to
be so pleased when he handed him the thermos containing
the twins. "Three wishes beyond the scope of normal human
avarice." His first wish was going to be for a billion dollars.
Or perhaps two billion. Two billion was better than one.

Oleaginus had just arrived in Las Vegas from New York,
which was where he'd gone after returning from Calcutta,
just to check up on the twins that Iblis's people had under
surveillance at the Gaunt family home on East 77th Street.
As Oleaginus had suspected, these were not the real twins
but a pair of Elsewheres. Detecting the existence of an
Elsewhere was a relatively simple matter, provided that you

were prepared to act decisively and ruthlessly. Elsewheres did not have a soul, which meant they could not be killed, and, to prove that he must be right and Iblis's people in New York just had to be wrong, Oleaginus had adopted the straightforward solution of stealing a yellow cab and then running down the two fake children.

This hit-and-run accident had looked and felt real enough. A female witness to the accident, which took place on Madison Avenue, had fainted. And there was even a dent on the front fender of the taxi, where the fake twins had hit the car. But even while Oleaginus had been inspecting their squashed-up, mangled, strawberry-jam remains, the two Elsewheres had disappeared without a trace. Returning to the Gaunt home on East 77th Street a few minutes later, Oleaginus had hardly been surprised to spy the two fake djinn children through a window on the second floor. Which seemed to put the matter beyond any doubt in his mind. He had the real twins in the thermos.

Oleaginus walked into the Croesus Hotel and, ignoring the hundreds of gamblers who were already working the slot machines in search of a jackpot, he went straight to the elevator and up to the penthouse, rehearsing his story of how he had caught up with John and Philippa in India, and used the djinn binding provided by Iblis to trap them inside the first container that came to hand.

Nothing much had changed in the huge penthouse. The spectacular view of Las Vegas was still the same. And Iblis was wearing the same pair of black silk pajamas that he had been wearing when Oleaginus had last seen him. But his fingernails and beard were longer, and the rats were bigger and more vicious, squealing with aggression when Oleaginus entered his master's bedroom.

"Welly, welly, welly, welly, welly, welly, well," said Iblis. "Look what the cat dragged in. If it isn't Oleaginus, the human sponge. From the expression on your disgusting face I should say that either you have reconciled yourself to being ugly for the rest of your life, or you have some good news for me. Let's hope it's the latter, for your sake."

Oleaginus smiled nervously and tried to ignore the turmoil he was feeling in his stomach. Being this close to Iblis and his pet rats always made him so nervous that he wanted to go straight to the bathroom and pee for several minutes. Even when you were doing a good job, there was no telling what Iblis might do. The djinn was capable of anything. "I've got them, sir," he said triumphantly. "The twins." He held up the thermos labeled TWINS as if it had been a most-coveted trophy. "They're in here, sir."

"Oleaginus, that's impossible," said Iblis. "The twins are in New York. My men have them under twenty-four-hour surveillance."

"No, sir. Those are two Elsewheres. I ran them over in a stolen cab, just to make sure. Squashed them both like a couple of bugs. They looked as dead as dodos, the pair of them." He shrugged. "But a few minutes later they were alive again at home. Hopping around like nothing at all had happened. I saw them myself."

"That is interesting." Iblis was still full of suspicion. "You used the djinn binding like I told you?"

"Yes, sir," Oleaginus lied.

Iblis smiled a slow, cruel smile that Oleaginus found almost as unnerving as his scowl.

"Oleaginus," he said. "You almost make me believe that there's some purpose to your meaningless existence." Iblis waved him closer. "Bring it here. Your thermos."

Oleaginus approached the bed but as he leaned toward his master to hand him the flask, one of the rats who was fondest of Iblis became jealous and leaped at his throat and, springing back, Oleaginus fumbled the thermos.

"No!" yelled Iblis in an unnaturally loud voice while at the same time, a sort of fire flashed out of the djinn's body, incinerating every one of the rats, and stopped only an inch or two short of Oleaginus himself. The rat that had been leaping at Oleaginus's throat, one millisecond earlier, dropped, still smoking, onto the floor with a dull thud, like a stale bread roll. In the same split millisecond, Iblis swept the rest of the burned rats off his person and, leaping to his feet, came around the bed and caught the fumbled thermos just as Oleaginus failed to catch it himself.

"I see you're not the sporting type, Oleaginus," remarked Iblis.

"Sorry, sir," said Oleaginus. "But the rat. It almost bit me."

"There's no accounting for taste, I suppose," said Iblis, staring at the thermos with excited eyes. He walked across the marble floor of the room to a thermal-imaging device that stood on top of a liquor cabinet and, placing the thermos underneath the heat-sensitive lens, stared through the view-finder at the two dark red shapes that were moving up and down in the glass interior.

Iblis let out a low moan of sadistic pleasure as he observed the contents of the thermos. "Joy," he muttered. "Joy, plea-sure, gladness, exaltation, ecstasy, euphoria, unalloyed delight, to think that . . ." He patted the thermos almost affection-ately and then said, "O brave little flask! That has such terrible children in it!"

Then he looked up from the viewfinder and fixed Oleaginus with his most penetrating stare.

"You've done well," he said in a surprised sort of voice. "For a mundane, that is. Normally I wouldn't dream of bothering to keep a promise I had made to a specimen of life as lowly as yourself, Oleaginus. But then it's not every day I get a chance to do the most hideous and unbelievably cruel things to a couple of children whom I loathe and detest. So what's it to be? Your reward. An IQ that registers three fig-ures? Or just an obscene amount of money?"

Oleaginus shifted uncomfortably under his master's unwavering stare. "Er, you mentioned three wishes, sir?" he said. "In fact, sir, the precise words you used were 'three wishes beyond the scope of normal human avarice.'"

"I do believe you're right," said Iblis. "So you're going for the money, eh? Why am I not surprised? It always amazes me that mundanes who actually get three wishes don't wish to be more intelligent. Or to be more charismatic. That's something much more useful than money. Money's nothing, Oleaginus. Nothing at all. Take my word for it. Numbers, that's all it is."

"Money's only my first wish, sir," said Oleaginus.

"You'd better make it then, hadn't you? Your first wish." Iblis glanced at his watch. He hated giving three wishes to any mundane. It was such a dreadful bore.

"I wish I was dead rich, sir."

For a delicious moment Iblis toyed with the idea of making Oleaginus dead before making him rich, but then rejected it for selfish reasons. It was possible that Oleaginus might still remain useful to him. "Hadn't you better put a figure on that?" he said patiently. "Just in case it's not clear how much you had in mind."

"I wish I had five billion dollars," said Oleaginus.

Iblis waited for Oleaginus to specify the currency but when none came, he snapped his fingers quickly. "There," he said. "That's all fixed. Five billion dollars." He handed Oleaginus a sheet of paper he had unfolded from out of the thin air in front of his servant's bemused face. "This is a statement from an offshore bank in Jamaica where the sum of five billion dollars now awaits you." Iblis might also have added that these were Jamaican dollars, which are hardly as valuable as U.S. dollars. (In fact, a Jamaican dollar is worth exactly one-sixtieth of what a U.S. dollar is worth, which meant that Oleaginus's five billion dollars was only worth about eighty-three million U.S. dollars. Five billion Jamaican dollars is not bad, but it's not five billion U.S. dollars.) It wasn't that Iblis didn't have the power to give Oleaginus five billion U.S. dollars, it was just that he couldn't resist the pleasure of cheating him. Him or any other human, for that matter. This is, after all, why the Ifrit run casinos: to cheat human beings.

"Thank you, sir," said Oleaginus, surveying the numbers on his new bank statement.

"And your second wish is?"

"I'd like to be more attractive, sir."

"You're really trying my patience, Oleaginus, do you know that?" he asked with a long-suffering sigh. For a brief moment Iblis debated turning Oleaginus into a magnet and watching pieces of metal fly across the apartment to stick to his body. Instead he continued to take pity on him. "Be precise, man. Be careful what you wish for. Or I won't be responsible for what happens to you. Did you mean attractive like a magnet?"

"No, sir. To women, sir."

"Then *do* say so."

"I wish I was more attractive to women, sir."

Iblis snapped his fingers a second time. "There. It's done," he said.

Oleaginus turned and looked in a mirror on the wall. "But I look exactly the same," he said, somewhat disappointed.

"Believe me," said Iblis. "With five billion dollars in the bank, you'll be attractive to women, there's no question of that. And your third wish?"

Oleaginus frowned, suspecting he'd been tricked but hardly daring to argue with someone like Iblis who was clearly becoming bored with the whole business of rewarding his servant's success. "I'd like to have a talent, sir," he said. "Some kind of accomplishment."

"Bravo," said Iblis. "You surprise me, Oleaginus. A talent. Since you have neither talents nor accomplishments, I imagine you would be spoiled for choice, however, I must hurry you. I have an appointment with these two children and a bottle of sulfuric acid."

"Acid?"

"To pour inside the flask, of course." Iblis smiled. "One drop at a time."

"Ah."

"So, a talent. What talent do you wish to possess? A talent to amuse? That would be too much to hope for. A talent for mischief? No, perhaps you already have that. A talent for conversation. I might welcome that in a mundane."

"I wish I was a really brilliant pianist, sir," said Oleaginus. "I always wanted to play the piano."

"An excellent choice. Now that is something worth wishing for. And you don't know how fortunate you are. If you had said the guitar I should have killed you immediately since, more than any other kind of human life-form, I hate mundanes who are dumb enough to play the guitar. I've destroyed whole planeloads of people before now, just because the passenger manifest included some scrofulous youth with a guitar."

Iblis snapped his fingers a third time. A concert grand piano appeared in the corner of the room, and Iblis beckoned to Oleaginus to sit down and play.

"What shall I play, sir?"

"You can play anything, so play anything you like," said Iblis and willed him to play an *Impromptu* by Schubert.

"I know, sir. I'll play an *Impromptu* by Schubert."

"Oh, *good* choice," said Iblis. He was already looking forward to the moment when he would point out that Oleaginus would have done better to have used his third wish to escape from Iblis's employment, and that all the money in Jamaica could hardly do him much good if he was still obliged to get and carry for Iblis. Fetch, carry, and play the piano. But that revelation was a future pleasure, something to be enjoyed after he had amused himself with the slow acid dissolution of the Gaunt twins. Which was something he needed to savor. Right away. Picking up the thermos, he spoke loudly at the metallic exterior.

"So," he said. "John and Philippa. I can't begin to tell you what a pleasure it is to meet you both again. Only this time your uncle Nimrod isn't here to save you. And this time I'm not going to be nearly as nice to you as I was the last time." Hearing nothing, he added, "What, Marid? No words of defiance? You disappoint me." Iblis laughed. "But you will be begging me for mercy by the time I have finished with you."

Still hearing nothing, Iblis frowned. There was little pleasure to be gained from tormenting his enemies if his enemies didn't sound as if they were in torment. And grinning horribly, Iblis shook the flask up and down furiously, for several seconds, like a Grand Prix racing driver with a bottle of champagne.

"There," he said. "That should soften you up a bit." Iblis pressed his ear to the flask. "Cat got your tongues, eh? Very well. You force me to be more unpleasant." And uttering their names and his focus word, which was TETRA-GRAMMATONITIS, to bind the two djinn children to his will, he opened the thermos and placed it on the floor. To his considerable surprise, nothing happened. No smoke. No transubstantiation. Nothing.

Iblis glanced accusingly at Oleaginus, who was playing the Schubert piano piece with aplomb. He was about to accuse Oleaginus of making a mistake, that the thermos was empty, when he remembered that he had already seen the two djinn moving around inside the flask, on the thermal imager. "I know you're in there," he said sharply. "You have five seconds to get out here before I start filling the thermos with sulfuric acid."

Almost immediately smoke started to pour out of the thermos — rather a lot of smoke for two children, it might have seemed to Iblis if he hadn't been feeling so pleased with himself. The smoke was much darker than it ought to have been, too. Smoke from a Marid transubstantiation tends to be white, but this cloud of smoke, which quickly separated into two clouds of smoke, was almost black.

"That's more like it," said Iblis. Still he did not suspect that anything was wrong. Even acting together, two

345

immature djinn like John and Philippa would never have been equal to the task of overcoming a djinn as powerful as Iblis. He knew that, which was why he was behaving a little complacently. "And if you're good, then maybe, just maybe I won't dissolve you in acid or bury you alive in the desert."

Released from the thermos in which they had been imprisoned, the two djinn tigers waited until the last possible moment before adopting their tiger shapes. Badly hungover, thirsty, and very, very hungry — not to mention all shook up and angry — they were in the mood to exact a terrible revenge. But they had sensed a powerful djinn presence and knew that surprise was their best tactic, for it was now clear to them that this djinn had mistaken them for someone else.

"You're trying my patience," said Iblis as the two clouds of smoke continued to refuse to adopt their final shape. "Very well. But don't say I didn't warn —"

His sentence remained unfinished as the two black tigers, each of them as big as a small horse and weighing five or six hundred pounds, sprang at once. One of them sank its teeth into Iblis's arm while the other took hold of his head. And because they had the advantage of surprise, there was no time for Iblis to focus his mind long enough to use djinn power. Roaring loudly, the two tigers mauled Iblis horribly and might have succeeded in killing him, too, except that Oleaginus, seeing his master attacked, ran straight for the elevator door. This act of understandable cowardice and disloyalty was enough to save Iblis for, seeing Oleaginus, the first djinn tiger quit chewing the Ifrit's arm and sprang at his mundane servant.

"Don't chew me, I'm only the piano player," yelled Oleaginus as the tiger took hold of his leg. And then his neck.

With only one tiger on him now, Iblis had a second to draw breath, which was just enough time to utter his focus word and abandon his now hopelessly mauled body to the tiger's embrace. Iblis took his spirit quickly out of the penthouse, down the emergency stairs, and into the Croesus Hotel casino where hundreds of men and women sat playing the slot machines.

Gathering himself together after the shock of what had happened, Iblis set about selecting a new body.

CHAPTER 20

LAST REFLECTIONS

It was time to leave the pink fort and the now-deserted ash-ram and fly home.

But which way were they to fly? East or west? If you fly east rather than west, Lucknow is a little nearer to Palm Springs than New York. But if you fly west from Lucknow, London is on the way to New York. The deciding factor to this dilemma turned out to be Dybbuk's mother, Dr. Sachertorte. Nimrod was horrified to discover that she still had no idea of where her son was or even if he was still alive. So it was agreed that Nimrod, Mr. Rakshasas, and Groanin would go west back to London, and the three children would make a separate whirlwind and then fly east to Palm Springs, for Dybbuk's sake.

"Your mother will be worried sick about you, Dybbuk," Nimrod said sternly. "The poor woman. And after all she's been through. What John and Philippa did was bad enough, but at least their mother has had some peace of mind while they've been away. Thanks to those two Elsewheres."

"Yeah, well, there aren't many angels hanging around Palm Springs," said Dybbuk. "Not so as you'd notice, anyway. And none I know who'd whip up a fake me." He smiled bitterly. "Assuming there's a real me. I'm not sure of anything anymore. Not on that account. Besides, that poor woman, as you call her, probably deserves it. For what she did."

Nimrod's expression turned more thoughtful. "Oh, I see," he said, sounding awkward. *"That."* He uttered the word "that" in a way that made the twins think *that* — whatever *that* was — was something he knew all about. And left them feeling more than a little intrigued as to what *that* might be. "You blame *her*, do you?"

"I don't think I'm the first," said Dybbuk. "To blame her. Do you?"

"Perhaps, Dybbuk, we should talk about this in private for a moment," said Nimrod and led Dybbuk, who was accompanied by the coyote, back inside the security office, closing the door behind him.

"I wonder what *that*'s all about," said Philippa.

"You know Dybbuk," said John and shrugged.

"Well, actually no," said Philippa. "I don't think I do, despite all that we've been through. There's something not quite right about Dybbuk. Something I can't quite put my finger on."

"You're exaggerating," said John. But in his heart he

knew Philippa was right. There *was* something about Dybbuk he sensed wasn't as straightforward as it had seemed.

"Am I? Then what's the big secret between him and Nimrod?"

When the two emerged from the office after almost fifteen minutes, no explanations were forthcoming and none were sought. Whatever had been said was private and, despite their intense curiosity, the twins tried to respect their friend's privacy. If Dybbuk did want to talk about it, there would be several hours to talk when they were aboard an eastbound whirlwind.

As soon as Nimrod had sent a water elemental down into the underground laboratories to ensure that the fire was properly extinguished, they went to the highest point in the fort, the tower that housed the rope-elevator equipment, to set their respective whirlwinds into motion.

"What's going to happen to him?" said Philippa. She was talking about the donkey that had turned the capstan that previously had pulled the basket up the side of the rock. Now that the rope had been cut by escaping ashram members, he stood quietly in his stall, eating hay and enjoying a period of rest and relaxation. "Now that everyone has run off, there will be no one to feed and water him."

"Philippa's right," said Dybbuk, who was now inseparable from the coyote and clearly intended taking him aboard the whirlwind to Palm Springs. "We can't just leave him here."

"Sure, there's that donkey sanctuary in Cork," said Mr.

Rakshasas. "You could do worse than sending him there. We could take him with us, and then send him on."

"A donkey," said Nimrod. "Arriving on a whirlwind."

"There's a first time for everything," said Mr. Rakshasas. "Even in Cork. An Irish Pegasus. That's what they'll call it, if anyone notices."

"Oh, very well," said Nimrod. "An Irish Pegasus it is."

They said their good-byes and Philippa, who was to pilot the first leg of the flight, was about to set her whirlwind in motion when Groanin stopped her.

"Aren't *you* forgetting something?" he said. "You three kids are Indians. And, more important, so am I. I'd like my original color back, thank you, miss. I don't mind admitting, me and my stomach have enjoyed being Indian. It's been an experience I shan't forget and has given me a whole new insight into being Johnny Foreigner. Perhaps it was one that was overdue at that. But I am what I am, and that's a fat, balding, pink-skinned boy from Moss Side."

"I thought you were from Manchester, Mr. Groanin," said John.

"Moss Side *is* Manchester, son. You remember that."

So the three children joined hands and, uttering their various focus words, returned Groanin and themselves to their normal color again. But because knowledge cannot be undone, even by djinn power, their ability to speak Hindi remained, which was very *kam ka* (useful) given that more than a billion people speak this language.

Looking like themselves again, the three children repeated their good-byes and then Philippa began to spin them a whirlwind.

"Remember not to fly too fast," shouted Nimrod. "Especially over Oklahoma." But the wind carried his words away before they could be heard by the children and within less than a minute they were flying east, and waving a last farewell to the three figures in the tower.

"I shall miss those kids," said Groanin.

Mr. Rakshasas unwrapped his turban and, removing the Cobra King placed there for safekeeping, he stared at it thoughtfully. "I owe them everything," he said quietly.

"What are you going to do with that?" asked Nimrod.

Sunlight caught the emerald head of the talisman as Mr. Rakshasas brandished it gratefully and then handed it to Groanin. "Here," he said. "You're strong. Break off the emerald, and the tail, will you?"

"Are you sure about that?" asked Groanin.

"Positive."

Groanin did as he was asked and, breaking the Cobra King into three pieces — gold body, emerald head, and wisdom-teeth tail — handed them all back to Mr. Rakshasas.

"There are many poor people in India," said Mr. Rakshasas. He tossed the emerald in his hand like an egg and dropped it into his pocket. "The emerald will be recut into several smaller stones. These and the gold will be sold to help them. As for my teeth." He shook his head. "We'd best drop them off somewhere on the way back home. The

Mediterranean Sea might be a good place. Or the English Channel. No one's ever going to own these again. Not ever."

Philippa flew them as far as Hakone, a hot spring resort near Mount Fuji, which is Japan's highest mountain. They would have stayed longer in Japan, which was somewhere the three children had always wanted to visit, but the twins were anxious to get home and see their parents again. From Japan, John flew them on the second stage of their journey, to the Hawaiian island of Maui, which is about halfway across the Pacific Ocean. Here, Dybbuk took over the flying for the third stage of the journey, to the West Coast of the United States, and on to Palm Springs.

"It feels kind of strange coming back here," he said. "Kind of an anticlimax."

Philippa nodded with what she hoped looked like sympathy. She hadn't forgotten that Dybbuk's best friend, Brad, and Brad's father had been murdered in Palm Springs.

"What about the police?" asked John.

"I can handle the police," Dybbuk said coolly. "I'm a djinn, aren't I?" He laughed. "If they ask too many awkward questions I'll make them disappear."

Philippa and John exchanged a look. Sometimes it was hard to know if Dybbuk was joking or not.

"Your mother will be so happy to see you," said Philippa, who was dying to find out more about Dybbuk's earlier conversation with Nimrod.

"Yeah." Dybbuk hardly sounded convinced of that and only smiled when the coyote licked his hand affectionately. "I'm going to call him Colin," he said. "And keep him as a pet." He patted the animal on the head and folded his ears playfully. "Poor boy. All those years as a coat. You must be starved." But this was hardly true; since bringing the animal out of the pink fort's elevator shaft, Dybbuk had fed Colin at least three large juicy steaks he'd rustled up with djinn power.

A coyote was hardly a conventional pet, and Philippa wondered how Dybbuk's mother would react to Colin and if Dybbuk might be bringing the animal home to spite her in some way. Philippa always thought Dr. Sachertorte was a very nice woman. What could she have done that Dybbuk felt so angry about? When eventually they landed, on a golf course that was behind Dybbuk's home, Philippa could restrain herself no longer and asked him straight out.

"Don't you ever get mad at your parents?" he asked by way of an answer. They were walking across a green, and Dybbuk kicked away a golf ball that was lying there, and then another.

"Sure," said Philippa. "But there's mad and there's getting even, which is what you implied when you were talking to Nimrod. For something she'd done to you."

"Look, Phil," said Dybbuk as they walked across the fairway. "The three of us have been through a lot together. We're friends, right?"

The twins nodded.

"So let's not spoil that friendship by you asking about things I'm not ready to talk about. Back at the ashram I made an important discovery about something. A connection. Something that happened a long time ago that's personal to me and my family. I'll tell you about it sometime, I promise. But not right now, okay?"

"Okay," said the twins and followed Dybbuk into the house, which was built in the style of a Mexican hacienda.

As soon as Dr. Sachertorte saw Dybbuk she whooped with delight and hugged him tightly. "Where on earth have you been?" she asked with tears rolling down her face. "I thought I'd lost you, Dybbuk. I've been worried sick about you."

Dybbuk tolerated her hugging him for a few seconds before he gently pushed her away and explained — with the aid of a few helpful interjections from John and Philippa exactly what had happened. While he spoke, Dr. Sachertorte eyed the coyote and the twins uncomfortably. And when Dybbuk had finished his explanation there was no mention from Dr. Sachertorte of punishing her son. Instead she seemed more concerned with the situation the twins had left in New York.

"So all this time, it's been two Elsewheres who've been in your place at home in New York?" she said.

"I'm afraid so," said Philippa.

"Well, that explains a lot," muttered Dr. Sachertorte.

"Like what?" asked John, sensing for the first time that perhaps something was wrong.

"Nothing. Only I think it's time you two kids went home.

Don't you? I mean if I remember correctly, Elsewheres don't last longer than an aeon. Which is what? Eleven days?"

"To be precise, 11.574074074074074074074074074074074074074 days," said John and glanced at his watch. "According to my watch, we still have a day left."

"You won't be mad at Buck, will you, Dr. Sachertorte?" said Philippa. "I mean, he wouldn't have gone to London or India if it hadn't been for John and me."

"No, dear." Dr. Sachertorte shook her very glamorous head. "I won't be mad at him. I'm just glad to have him home again. Which is where you should be. Okay?" And she smiled a sad sort of smile that left the twins feeling as if there was something she wasn't telling them — not about herself or Dybbuk, but about John and Philippa themselves.

"She's right," John told Philippa. "We ought to be going." He turned to say good-bye to Dybbuk. But there was no sign of him. "Where'd he go?"

"He's probably up in his room," said Dr. Sachertorte, nodding at the stairs.

They found Dybbuk staring at the back of his soul mirror. And the twins had never before seen him looking so sad and disappointed.

"What is it?" asked John.

Seeing the twins in the doorway of his room, Dybbuk hurriedly pulled a sheet over the mirror and shook his head. "Nothing," said Dybbuk and, gently pushing them out of his room, he closed the door behind them. "You're going then," he said, and fixing a smile on his face, he shook John's hand and kissed Philippa lightly on the cheek.

"Yes," said John.

"Thanks," said Dybbuk. "Thanks for everything. It was fun, wasn't it? In spite of everything."

"Yes," said Philippa, who was now very anxious to be gone. "It was fun."

They flew east, across Arizona, New Mexico, and Texas. But somewhere over Oklahoma, Philippa started to fly too fast and, before they knew it, their whirlwind had created a tornado. In this particular part of the United States, tornadoes are not uncommon, although at that time of year, mercifully, they are rarer. The temperatures in the Midwest had been unseasonably high, however, and there was a lot of humidity in the Oklahoman air, so that Philippa's whirlwind created an updraft. Within fifteen minutes of entering the air space above the state, the twins found themselves sitting on top of a full-size twister, a great black cone of wind that ripped through a couple of cornfields and tore up a whole barn before they managed to bring it under control.

"That's what comes of being in too much of a hurry," said John.

"I couldn't help it," admitted Philippa. "I'm worried about what we're going to find at home. I'm certain there's something that Dr. Sachertorte wasn't telling us."

"She *was* acting kind of weird," said John. "But then again you'd probably have to be a bit weird to have Dybbuk as a son. The way he was staring into his soul mirror, it was like he'd seen a ghost or something."

"Maybe he was just thinking about his friend Brad," said Philippa. "Dybbuk doesn't have many friends. He's going to miss him. That's probably what was troubling him." She shrugged. "What else could it be?"

But even Philippa wasn't convinced by her own reasoning and stayed silent until they reached New York, where, under the cover of darkness, she landed the whirlwind in Central Park, right next to the statue of Alice in Wonderland. From there it was a short walk across Park and Madison avenues and home to 77th Street.

John found his door key and they let themselves in, quietly, just in case their parents or Mrs. Trump was with the two Elsewheres. The house seemed unnaturally still, with just the ticking of the grandfather clock in the hall to break the strange silence. They crept upstairs. Reaching the seventh-floor landing, they stopped for a moment, crouching behind the banister as, through the open doors of their two bedrooms, they caught sight of their doubles. John 2 was sitting in John's favorite chair, reading a book, while Philippa 2 was quietly absorbed in writing a poem. Both of them looked spotlessly clean and neat, as if they were straight out of a box. Fascinated, the twins watched themselves for several minutes until John grew bored of watching himself behaving so well and walked into his bedroom.

"Hi," he said.

John 2 looked up from the book he was reading. To John's horror he saw that John 2 was reading the Bible. "Tell me that you haven't been reading that since I left," he said.

"Only in the evening," said John 2.

John let out an exasperated sort of sigh. "But I never do that," he said. "Not that there's anything wrong with reading the Bible, of course. It's just that, well, I'm not that good."

Equally appalled, Philippa looked at her watch. "Me, too," she told Philippa 2. "Right now, I'd be watching TV, instead of writing whatever it is you're writing."

"It's a poem," said Philippa 2. "Or more precisely a haiku. A Japanese poem." She handed the poem to Philippa. "Exactly seventeen syllables. Five, seven, and five. What do you think?"

Philippa read the haiku out loud. "'A fish met a djinn. The fish had just the one wish. The wish was a fish.'" She shrugged. "It's nice," she said politely. "But John's right. We're not usually so well-behaved as you guys seem to be. I'm surprised our mother hasn't called Jenny Sachertorte, our djinn doctor."

"Your mother isn't here," said Philippa 2. "She's gone."

"Gone? What do you mean 'gone'?" Philippa asked her double. "Gone where?"

"Left home."

"That's impossible," said John. "She wouldn't ever leave without telling us."

"She told *us*," said John 2.

"So I guess she thought she'd told *you*," added Philippa 2.

"Ah, I thought I heard voices," said a voice they recognized and, looking around, the twins saw their uncle Nimrod coming up the stairs. "I'm afraid your Elsewhere is right, Philippa. Your mother *did* think she had told you."

"Told us what?" said John. "What's going on, Nimrod?"

"I'm afraid I didn't find out myself, until I got to London," he said quietly. "And as soon as I heard I rushed straight here on another whirlwind. Ayesha, the Blue Djinn of Babylon, is dead and your mother has gone to take her place."

The twins were silent. Suddenly a great deal of what had happened in Iraq a few months before now made sense. How Philippa had been able to leave Iravotum so easily.

Nimrod nodded. "I can see you've already guessed that it's the only possible explanation. Your mother agreed to take your place, Philippa. To become the next Blue Djinn. That's why she's gone. As far as I've been able to discover, she's already there. In Iravotum."

"We'll go after her," said Philippa. "We'll go after her and bring her back."

"No," said Nimrod.

"Why not? John came after me. He proved it could be done. And there's still time, too. You see, I know all about it. Thirty days. That's how long it takes to become hardhearted enough to be the Blue Djinn." Philippa looked at John. "We can do it, John? Can't we?"

John, who knew how hard the journey had been, sat down and nodded somberly. "It'll be tough," he said. "Incredibly tough. But I'm sure we can do it, yes. We can bring her back."

"I'm afraid not," said Nimrod. "Not this time. She's a clever woman, your mother. Very clever."

"What do you mean? What's she done?"

"She made sure that you can't leave New York," said Nimrod. "Not for thirty days." He sighed. "By which time, of course, it will be too late."

"She can't stop us," insisted Philippa. "Not if we really want to go."

"Come with me," said Nimrod, retreating downstairs. "But I think you ought to prepare yourselves for another shock."

Nimrod pushed open the door to Mr. Gaunt's study and went inside, followed closely by John and Philippa. A strange sight met their eyes. In the leather armchair by the desk sat an old man wearing a silk dressing gown. John thought he must have been about eighty years old, but Philippa estimated him as much older. Neither child recognized the old man, although he seemed to recognize them, and it was a minute or two before the truth finally dawned on them.

"Dad?" gasped Philippa.

The old man smiled feebly but said nothing, as if the power of speech had been lost to him. Horrified, the twins crept toward his side. Close up, there could be no doubt about it. The old man was their father, Edward Gaunt.

"What happened to you, Dad?" John asked and, with tears welling up in his eyes, he took hold of his father's bony, liver-spotted hand.

Edward Gaunt grunted and drooled absently.

"Before she left, your mother placed a Methusaleh binding on him," explained Nimrod. "Something that speeds up his metabolism and causes him to age at an increased rate. At the same time she explained to your two doubles that for every day you were not here to check the effect with your own powers, he would age twenty years. Of course, she didn't know that it was two Elsewheres she was speaking to, instead of her own children. Which is why your father has aged so."

"Can't you do something?" asked Philippa.

"I'm afraid not. This is Layla's binding and I can't interfere with it."

"What are we going to do?" wailed Philippa.

"This is all our fault," said John. "If we hadn't gone to India then Dad would still be like he was before we left."

"Listen to me," Nimrod said severely. "If you hadn't gone to India, Mr. Rakshasas and I would still be deep-frozen. Very likely we'd have remained there for a very long time indeed. Certainly for as long as it would have taken Guru Masamjhasara to find the Cobra King of Kathmandu."

Nimrod patted Edward Gaunt's skeletal hand affectionately.

"However, it is my considered opinion that this process of accelerated decrepitude is reversible. In other words, your father will get younger again and return to being his normal self. Eventually. *Just as long as neither of you leaves home in search of your mother.* You'll just have to be patient." Nimrod was silent for a moment as if something had upset him.

Philippa guessed what it was. "I'm sorry, Uncle Nimrod," she said. "You must think we are very selfish children indeed. We're forgetting our manners. Ayesha was your mother."

"I'm sorry, too," said John.

"Thank you, Philippa," he said. "John." From his coat pocket Nimrod took out an enormous cigar and lit it. "So," he sighed, emitting a large cloud of smoke. "As you can see. There can be no question of your both following Layla to Iravotum. Not this time. You must both stay here for thirty days and look after your father and stop him from getting any older."

"What will happen to her, Uncle Nimrod?" John asked miserably. He was missing his mother already. The house had ceased to feel like a home without her there.

"She will fulfill her destiny, John. That's what will happen. I expect all of us will."

Philippa shook her head. "I can't bear to think of her there. In that creepy house. All alone."

"She's only there for thirty days," said Nimrod. "After that she'll be in Berlin. At her official residence there. You'll be able to see her, although I warn you now, she won't be the same. Besides, she's not alone. She has a companion."

"Miss Glumjob?"

"I believe Miss Glumjob has returned to the United States. North Carolina, to be precise. No, I was referring to someone else."

"Who?" chorused the twins.

"Do you remember the French Guianan boy, the garbage

picker whom Iblis put a diminuendo binding on after he was released from that scent bottle in which we had imprisoned him?"

"Yes," said John. "His name was Galibi Magana and the binding turned him into a sort of living doll."

"Mother kept him in a box in the top of her closet," said Philippa. "From time to time she got him out and looked at him and promised to return him to normal one day. Are you saying she took him with her?"

"According to the two Elsewheres," said Nimrod, jerking his head at the stairs, "that's exactly what happened. I've a strong hunch she means to use the power of the Blue Djinn to remove that diminuendo and restore him to proper boyhood."

"Can she do that?" asked John. "Overcome Iblis's power?"

"She's the Blue Djinn. She can do pretty much anything she wants."

"And Galibi will become her companion?" asked Philippa. "Like Miss Glumjob?" If Philippa sounded a little angry at the idea of it, that's because she was. Shaking her head with exasperation, she added, "What was wrong with me? I would have been her companion."

"Me, too," said John.

Nimrod was shaking his head. "You wouldn't have enjoyed it. And she certainly wouldn't have wanted that for you. But it will be a better life for Galibi. Certainly a better one than living in the top of a closet. Or being a garbage picker. This way he'll get an education and some real prospects. And when he's older I daresay she'll find something for him. A job, perhaps. Three wishes. Who knows?"

"This has ruined my life," said Philippa, taking hold of her father's hand. "I don't mind telling you, Nimrod. This really sucks." She wiped the tears from her cheeks and stared out of the window.

"Things could be worse," said Nimrod. "I think that's what you have to tell yourself in order to get through this."

"Worse than your mother leaving home?" sniffed John. "I don't see how anything could be worse than that."

Nimrod left them alone for a while. John was right. There was nothing worse than your mother leaving home. He could still remember his own mother, Ayesha, leaving home, and the pain that he and Layla had felt for months afterward. Even the sadness he now felt at Ayesha's death was nothing compared with that earlier pain. Loss was one thing, but rejection — for that was how he and Layla had perceived it — was quite another. He decided to stay the night.

In the morning the two Elsewheres had disappeared.

"I'm glad they're gone," admitted John. "They were beginning to give me the creeps."

"You could have asked them to leave before now," said Nimrod. "I believe that's all that's required."

"We didn't want to," said Philippa. "Have you ever asked yourself to clear off?"

"Er, no," admitted Nimrod.

"It's not that easy," said John.

"How long were they here, anyway?" asked Nimrod.

"An aeon," said John. "11.57407 —"

"It's all right," said Nimrod, interrupting John's decimal places. "I know how long an aeon is."

"That's how long Afriel said they would last."

"Angels generally mean what they say," said Nimrod. "Which is why it's always a good idea to listen to them when they turn up in our lives. It's true, some of them can be a little earnest. A bit too goody-goody. But it's wise to pay attention to them when they're around. They know things we djinn can never know. Secret things. Mysteries of the universe. Which reminds me. How did Dybbuk seem, when you last saw him?"

"Weird," said Philippa. "Like always."

"No," said John. "That's not true. He was weirder than usual. We left him staring into his soul mirror. And looking like he didn't want anyone else to see it."

"Did you see anything?" asked Nimrod. "I mean, did you catch a glimpse of anything in the boy's soul mirror?"

The twins shook their heads.

"He covered it up again," said John. "Before we could see anything."

"This is quite important. Did he tell you what he saw?"

"No," said John. "But whatever it was, I don't think it made him feel very happy. In fact, he could hardly bear to look at it."

"I wonder," muttered Philippa.

"What?" asked Nimrod.

"I was wondering why Dybbuk could hardly bear to look at his own soul," she said. "He's mischievous. Willful. Capricious. Even a little cruel sometimes. But he's still only a boy. I mean, surely there's nothing really bad about him. Nothing that might appear in his soul."

"I once told you that there were six tribes of djinn," said Nimrod. "But strictly speaking there are seven for, occasionally, a djinn is born who is neither Marid nor Ifrit, Jinn nor Ghul, Jann nor Shaitan. But a hybrid of two tribes. In this case, Marid and Ifrit."

"I don't understand," said Philippa. "Mr. Sachertorte is Marid surely. And so is Dr. Sachertorte."

"Yes, that's perfectly true," said Nimrod. "But here's the thing. A difficult thing. Especially for Dybbuk. Mr. Sachertorte is not Dybbuk's father. He himself discovered this only comparatively recently. That is why he and Dr. Sachertorte no longer live together."

"Are you saying that Dybbuk is half Marid, half Ifrit?" asked John.

Nimrod nodded. "I'm afraid so, John. There is good in Dybbuk. But there is also evil. That is what he sees when he looks into his synopados. Behind the light and the beauty there is something dark and loathsome. And there is a struggle going on inside Dybbuk for which one of these — good or evil — will dominate his soul. Which is why I'm pleased you made friends with him. Because with your help, children, I'm sure the good will win out."

"Poor Dybbuk," said Philippa. "But how did it happen? Jenny Sachertorte seems such a nice person."

"Because Iblis put a binding on Mr. Sachertorte and pretended to be him."

"You don't mean that Iblis is Dybbuk's father?" said John.

"I'm afraid so."

"And Dybbuk knows this?"

"Yes, of course," said Nimrod. "It's a deep, dark secret. Absolutely nobody knows about it except the family. Actually I'm not even sure that Iblis knows about it."

"So how do you know about it?" asked Philippa. "If it's such a big secret."

"Do you remember the exorcism that inspired Guru Masamjhasara to think that he might become a djinn himself?"

"Yes," said John. "You exorcised the prime minister. He said the prime minister had been possessed by a djinn. A girl about twelve years old, he said."

"That girl was Faustina," said Nimrod. "Dybbuk's sister."

"The one who disappeared?" said Philippa.

"You know about that?" said Nimrod.

"Sort of," said Philippa. "We saw her portrait, at Dybbuk's aunt's home. On Bannerman's Island."

"So you've been there, have you?"

"It's where Dybbuk went to hide," explained John, "when the guru's followers were looking for him. Apparently he was very attached to Max, his aunt's gorilla butler."

"Yes, so was . . ." Nimrod paused, and looked thoughtful for a moment, as if remembering something.

"You were telling us about Faustina," said Philippa, prompting him.

"Yes," said Nimrod. "Faustina was considered a very gifted child. A golden child. For example, she was an even better Djinnversoctoannular player than you, Philippa. And very highly thought of by djinn everywhere. Clever. Logical. It was Faustina who told me Iblis was Dybbuk's father, during the exorcism. At the time, the Sachertortes were living in London and her mother, Jenny, who had just given birth to Dybbuk, was an admirer of the Prime Minister. Albeit from a distance. They never actually met, you understand. When Faustina found out about Iblis she set out to do something about it. And having listened to her mother for many months saying how wonderful the Prime Minister was, Faustina decided that the Prime Minister was the only person powerful enough to have Iblis arrested. Which was why she took possession of him in the first place. She was a very willful child. Very like Dybbuk in that respect, at least.

"Of course it all went wrong. She hadn't done a possession before. It was amazing that she managed to do it for as long as she did. But she made the mistake of keeping her own voice, which gave the game away immediately. And then it all got out of hand. The sensation of power became rather intoxicating. And, having realized that the Prime Minister couldn't really help her at all, she became angry with him.

And with her mother. Which is when I turned up and, quite unaware that it was Faustina, exorcised her from his body.

"After the exorcism I learned who it was that had possessed the prime minister, and went looking for Faustina's body. Eventually I found it hidden in Madame Tussaud's Wax Museum. I waited and waited but Faustina's spirit never turned up to get her body back. At least that was what I thought. And then I remembered, rather too late, the blood samples that Dr. Warnakulasuriya — that was what Guru Masamjhasara called himself in those days — had taken from the Prime Minister during his examination and before the exorcism. Which is terribly dangerous for any djinn during an out-of-body experience. You see, children, a tiny part of her soul had been lost forever. Which meant she couldn't gather herself together to get back into her own body. Not one hundred percent." Nimrod puffed on his cigar. "That's what Dybbuk discovered when you were in India. He put two and two together and guessed that it was his own sister that Guru Masamjhasara had been talking about. The sister he's never met."

"Poor Dybbuk," said John.

"Poor *Faustina*," insisted Philippa. "What happened to her?"

"She's still in Madame Tussaud's Wax Museum," said Nimrod. "There she remains — like any other waxwork — to this day. As for her spirit . . ." He shrugged. "Oh, I've made many inquiries all over London. So did Jenny Sachertorte. But we never found anything. Finding a ghost isn't easy. Not even for us djinn. It wasn't like she was properly attached anywhere. Like a house or a building. She's probably still floating around, somewhere."

"How horrible," said Philippa.

"Yes, isn't it?" murmured Nimrod. He was silent for a moment. And then his heart leaped in his chest like a monkey in a cage. Why hadn't he considered Faustina before? Of course! Faustina! She might just be the answer to everything. He would have to consult Mr. Rakshasas, of course. And then make some inquiries at the wax works in London where Faustina's unconscious body was still located. But if he could just track down her lost spirit, there existed just the smallest, quietest, thinnest, most-remote bat-squeak of an improbable hope that someday, somehow, against all the odds, he could still bring about a situation whereby his sister, Layla, might possibly return to her lovely home and beloved family. He didn't want to get the children's hopes up. Not yet. That would be too unfair. Too cruel. Suppose he didn't succeed? It was best to say nothing, he told himself. For the moment at least. Until then John and Philippa would have to bear it, and develop some character.

"Curious, isn't it?" said Nimrod. "The way things connect. How one thing leads to another that leads somewhere else that leads you right back to the beginning. Well, almost. Nothing really exists on its own."

The twins remained silent. Nimrod assumed they were still thinking of poor Faustina and Dybbuk. But they were actually thinking of their mother, robbed of her children, her husband, and her friends, and the dreadful isolation that had been imposed on her, and the fact that, whatever Nimrod said, she now existed on her own, like some sort of ghost. The sheer injustice of it all seemed unbearable.

As yet more minutes passed they began to think of how one day they would change things and bring her back to them forever. Or as long as forever might last. And without moving their lips the children of the lamp swore an oath, a telepathic oath of the kind that only twins could swear, to make things right again. *Whatever the cost to djinnkind and the world.*

"I suppose I shall have to live with you now," said Nimrod. "At least until things get back to normal." He shrugged sheepishly as, meeting their bitter eyes, he realized the impossibility of that ever happening. "Well, almost back to normal." The twins remained silent. "Not normal, no," he continued. "It couldn't be that, could it? No, I'll just stay here for a while. And help you through this difficult period. Groanin, too, if you like. And Mr. Rakshasas, if you want. We're all here for you, children. Whatever you wish, really."

It was Philippa who spoke first.

"Funny, isn't it," she said. "Two djinn who can't wish for what they really want. Who would think that such a thing was even possible?"

"I want to tell you something that Mr. Rakshasas once told me, children," he said. "Years ago. I've always found this to be quite useful, really. And I think it's true whoever or whatever you are. Djinn or mundane. And it's this: Never make a wishbone where your backbone ought to be. Sometimes we must leave things as we find them. And we should recognize that a fact is only a fact because all our wishing cannot make it otherwise. For if we tried to change everything in the world according to our own wills, we would be little better than children."

"But we *are* children," insisted John.

Nimrod smiled and stroked John's head and then Philippa's with affection. "Not anymore, John," he said quietly. "Not anymore."

You can contact P. B. Kerr on his
Web site at www.pbkerr.com